6 2∞

Berkley Books by Brian W. Aldiss

HELLICONIA SPRING
HELLICONIA SUMMER
THE MALACIA TAPESTRY

BRIAN W. ALDISS

HELLICONIA SUMMER

BERKLEY BOOKS, NEW YORK

HELLICONIA SUMMER

A Berkley Book / published by arrangement with
Atheneum Publishers

PRINTING HISTORY
Atheneum edition published 1983
Berkley trade paperback edition / October 1984
Berkley mass market edition / February 1986

ISBN: 0-425-08650-X

A BERKLEY BOOK ® TM 757,375
Berkley Books are published by The Berkley Publishing Group,
200 Madison Avenue, New York, New York 10016.
The name "BERKLEY" and the stylized "B" with design
are trademarks belonging to Berkley Publishing Corporation.

PRINTED IN THE UNITED STATES OF AMERICA

Man is all symmetry,
Full of proportions, one limb to another,
    And all to all the world besides;
    Each part may call the farthest, brother;
For head with foot hath private amity,
    And both with moons and tides.

    More servants wait on Man
Than he'll take notice of: in every path
    He treads down that which doth befriend him
    When sickness makes him pale and wan.
Ah, mighty love! Man is one world and hath
    Another to attend him.

George Herbert: MAN

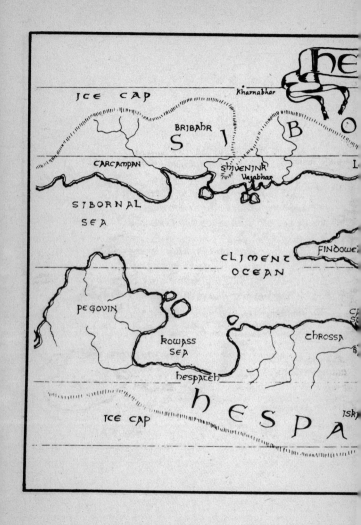

ICE CAP   Kharnabhar   he
                                                              B
                        BRIBAHR
                          S I   B   O

CARCAMPAN   SHIVENJNR
                        Vajabhar   L

SIBORNAL
   SEA

                           CLIMENT   FINDOWE
                            OCEAN

PEGOVIN
                                                     CHROSSA

          KOWASS
            SEA
              hespateh

                              h E S P A
   ICE CAP   ISK

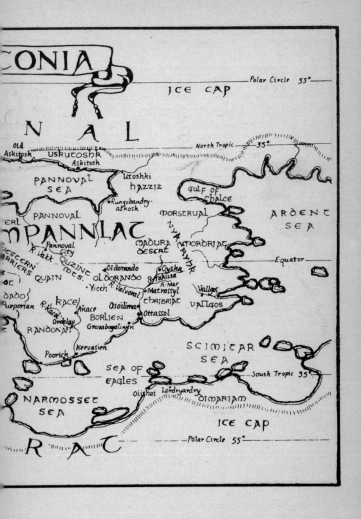

CONTENTS

I

THE SEACOAST OF BORLIEN

Waves climbed the slope of the beach, fell back, and came again. A short way out to sea, the procession of incoming surges was broken by a rocky mass crowned with vegetation. It marked a division between the deeps and the shallows. Once the rock had formed part of a mountain far inland, until volcanic convulsions hurled it into the bay.

The rock was now domesticated by a name. It was known as the Linien Rock. The bay and the place were named Grava-bagalinien after the rock. Beyond it lay the shimmering blues of the Sea of Eagles. The waves splashing against the shore were clouded with sand picked up before they scattered into flurries of white foam. The foam raced up the slope, only to sink voluptuously into the beach.

After surging round the bastion of Linien Rock, the waves met at different angles on the beach, bursting up with re-doubled vigour so as to swirl about the feet of a golden throne which was being lowered to the sand by four phagors. Into the flood were dipped the ten roseate toes of the Queen of Borlien.

1

The dehorned ancipitals stood motionless. With nothing more than the flick of an ear, they allowed the milky flood to boil about their feet, greatly though they feared water. Although they had carried their royal load half a mile from the Gravabagalinien palace, they showed no fatigue. Although the heat was intense, they showed no sign of discomfort. Nor did they display interest as the queen walked naked from her throne to the sea.

Behind the phagors, on dry sand, the majordomo of the palace supervised two human slaves in the erection of a tent, which he filled with bright Madi carpets.

The wavelets fawned about the ankles of Queen Myrdem-Inggala. "The queen of queens" was what the Borlienese peasantry called her. With her went her daughter by the king, Princess Tatro, and some of the queen's constant companions.

The princess screamed with excitement and jumped up and down. At the age of two years and three tenners, she regarded the sea as an enormous, mindless friend.

"Oh, look at this wave coming, Moth! The biggest wave yet! And the next one . . . here it comes . . . ooh! A monster, high as the sky! Oh, they're getting ever so big! Ever so bigger, Moth, Moth, *look*! Just look at this one now, look, it's going to burst and—ooh, here comes another, even huger! Look, look, Moth!"

The queen nodded gravely at her daughter's delight in the placid little waves, and raised her eyes to the distance. Slatey clouds piled up on the southern horizon, heralds of the approaching monsoon season. The deep waters had a resonance for which "blue" was no adequate description. The queen saw azure, aquamarine, turquoise, and viridian there. On her finger she wore a ring sold her by a merchant in Oldorando with a stone—unique and of unknown provenance—which matched the colours of the morning's sea. She felt her life and the life of her child to be to existence as the stone was to the ocean.

From that reservoir of life came the waves which delighted Tatro. For the child, every wave was a separate event, experienced without relation to what had been and what was to

come. Each wave was the only wave. Tatro still lingered in the eternal present of childhood.

For the queen, the waves represented a continuous operation, not merely of the ocean but of the world process. That process included her husband's rejection of her, and the armies on the march over the horizon, and the increasing heat, and the sail she hoped every day to see on the horizon. From none of these things could she escape. Past or future, they were contained in her dangerous present.

Calling good-bye to Tatro, she ran forward and dived into the water. She separated herself from the little figure hesitant in the shallows, to espouse the ocean. The ring flashed on her finger as her hands sliced the surface and she swam out.

The waters were elegant against her limbs, cooling them luxuriously. She felt the energies of the ocean. A line of white breakers ahead marked the division between the waters of the bay and the sea proper, where the great westbound current flowed, dividing the continents of torrid Campannlat and chilly Hespagorat, and sweeping round the world. Myrdem-Inggala never swam further than that line unless her familiars were with her.

Her familiars were arriving now, lured by the strong taint of her femininity. They swam near. She dived with them as they talked in their orchestral language to which she was still a stranger. They warned her that something—an unpleasantness—was about to happen. It would emerge from the sea, her domain.

The queen's exile had brought her to this forsaken spot in the extreme south of Borlien, Gravabagalinien, Ancient Gravabagalinien, haunted by the ghosts of an army which had perished here long ago. It was all her shrunken domain. Yet she had discovered another domain, in the sea. Its discovery was accidental, and dated from the day when she had entered the sea during the period of her menses. Her scent in the water had brought the familiars to her. They had become her everyday companions, solace for all that was lost and all that threatened her.

Fringed by the creatures, MyrdemInggala floated on her back, her tender parts exposed to the heat of Batalix overhead.

The water droned in her ears. Her breasts were small and
cinnamon tipped, her hips broad, her waist narrow. The
sun sparkled on her skin. Her human companions sported
nearby. Some swam close to the Linien Rock, others skipped
along the beach; all unconsciously used the queen as reference point. Their cries rang in competition with the clash of
waves.

Away up the beach, beyond the seawrack, beyond the cliffs,
stood the white and gold palace of Gravabagalinien, the home
to which the queen was now exiled, awaiting her divorce—or
her murder. To the swimmers, it looked like a painted toy.

The phagors stood immobile on the beach. Out to sea, a sail
hung immobile. The southern clouds appeared not to move.
Everything waited.

But time moved. The dimday wore on—no person of standing would venture into the open in these latitudes when both
suns were in the sky. And, as dimday passed, the clouds
became more threatening, the sail slanted eastwards, moving
towards the port of Ottassol.

In due time the waves brought a human corpse with them.
This was the unpleasantness of which the familiars had
warned. They squealed in disgust.

The body came swinging about the shoulder of Linien Rock
as if it still possessed life and will, to be washed up in a shallow
pool. There it lay, carelessly, face down. A sea bird lit on its
shoulder.

MyrdemInggala caught the flash of white and swam over to
inspect. One of the ladies of her court was there already, gazing down in horror at the sight of the strange fish. Its thick
black hair was spikey with brine. An arm was wrapped
brokenly round the neck. The sun was already drying its
puckered flesh when the queen's shadow fell over it.

The body was swollen with putrefaction. Tiny shrimps in
the pool scudded to feed off one broken knee. The court lady
put out her foot and tipped the carcass over. It sprawled on its
back, stinking.

A mass of writhing scupperfish hung from the face, busily
devouring mouth and eye sockets. Even under the glare of
Batalix, they did not cease their guzzling.

The queen turned nimbly about as she heard the patter of

small feet approaching. She seized Tatro and swung the child up above her head, kissing her, smiling warmly at her in reassurance, and then scampering up the beach with her. As she went, she called to her majordomo.

"ScufBar! Get this thing off our beach. Have it buried as soon as possible. Outside the old ramparts."

The servant rose from the shade of the tent, brushing sand from his charfrul.

"At once, ma'am," he said.

Later in the day, the queen, driven by her anxieties, thought of a better way of disposing of the corpse.

"Take it to a certain man I know in Ottassol," she instructed her little majordomo, fixing him earnestly with her gaze. "He's a man who buys bodies. I shall also give you a letter, though not for the anatomist. You are not to tell the anatomist where you come from, you understand?"

"Who is this man, ma'am?" ScufBar looked the picture of unwillingness.

"His name is CaraBansity. You are not to mention my name to him. He has a reputation for craftiness."

She strove to hide her troubled mind from the servants, little thinking that the time would unfold when her honour rested in CaraBansity's hands.

Beneath the creaking wooden palace lay a honeycomb of cool cellars. Some of the cellars were filled with pile on pile of ice blocks, which had been hewn from a glacier in distant Hespagorat. When both suns had set, Majordomo ScufBar descended among the ice blocks, carrying a whale-oil lantern above his head. A small slave boy followed him, clutching the hem of his charfrul for safety. By way of self-defence in a lifetime of drudgery, ScufBar had become hollow-chested, round-shouldered, and pot-bellied, so as to proclaim his insignificance and escape further duties. The defence had not worked. The queen had an errand for him.

He put on leather gloves and a leather apron. Pulling aside the matting from one of the piles of ice, he gave the lantern to the boy and picked up an ice-axe. With two blows, he severed one of the blocks from its neighbour.

Carrying the block, and grunting to convince the boy of its weight, he made his way slowly up the stairs and saw to it that the boy locked the door behind him. He was greeted by hounds of monstrous size, which prowled the dark corridors. Knowing ScufBar, they did not bark.

He made his way with the ice through a back door and into the open. He listened to hear the slave boy bolt it securely from the inside. Only then did he make his way across the courtyard.

Stars gleamed overhead, and an occasional violet flicker of aurora, which lit his way under a wooden arch to the stables. He smelt the tang of hoxney manure.

A stablehand waited in the gloom, shivering. Everyone was nervous after dark in Gravabagalinien, for then the soldiers of the dead army were said to march in search of friendly land-octaves. A line of brown hoxneys shuffled in the gloom.

"Is my hoxney ready, lad?"

"Aye."

The stablehand had equipped a pack hoxney ready for Scuf-Bar's journey. Over the animal's back had been secured a long wicker casket used for transporting goods requiring ice to keep them fresh. With a final grunt, ScufBar slid the block of ice into the casket, onto a bedding of sawdust.

"Now help me with the body, lad, and don't be squeamish."

The body which had been washed into the bay lay in a corner of the stable, in a puddle of sea water. The two men dragged it over, heaved it up, and arranged it on top of the ice. With some relief, they strapped the padded casket lid down.

"What a beastly cold thing it is," said the stablehand, wiping his hands on his charfrul.

"Few people think well of a human corpse," said ScufBar, pulling off his gloves and apron. "It's fortunate that the deuteroscopist in Ottassol does."

He led the hoxney from the stable and past the palace guard, whose whiskery faces peered nervously from a hut near the ramparts. The king had given his rejected queen only the old or untrustworthy to defend herself with. ScufBar himself was nervous, and never ceased to peer about him. Even the distant boom of the sea made him nervous. Once outside the

palace grounds, he paused, took breath, and looked back.

The mass of the palace stood out against the star shingle in fretted outline. In one place only did a light punctuate its darkness. There a woman's figure could be discerned, standing on her balcony and gazing inland. ScufBar nodded to himself, turned towards the coast road, and pulled the hoxney's head eastwards, in the direction of Ottassol.

Queen MyrdemInggala had summoned her majordomo to her earlier. Although she was a religious woman, superstition lingered with her, and the discovery of the body in the water disturbed her. She was inclined to take it as an omen of her own threatened death.

She kissed the Princess TatromanAdala good night and retired to pray. This evening, Akhanaba had no comfort to offer, although she had conceived a simple plan whereby the corpse might be used to good effect.

She feared what the king might do—to her and to her daughter. She had no protection from his anger, and clearly understood that as long as she lived her popularity made her a threat to him. There was one who would protect her, a young general; to him she had sent a letter, but he was fighting in the Western Wars and had not replied.

Now she sent another letter, in ScufBar's care. In Ottassol, a hundred miles distant, one of the envoys of the Holy Pannovalan Empire was due to arrive shortly—with her husband. His name was Alam Esomberr, and he would be bringing with him a bill of divorcement for her to sign. Thought of the occasion made her tremble.

Her letter was going to Alam Esomberr, asking for protection from her husband. Whereas a messenger on his own would be stopped by one of the king's patrols, a grubby little man with a pack animal would pass unremarked. No one inspecting the corpse would think to look for a letter.

The letter was addressed not to Envoy Esomberr but to the Holy C'Sarr himself. The C'Sarr had reason to dislike her king, and would surely give protection to a pious queen in distress.

She stood barefoot on her balcony, looking into the night. She laughed at herself, placing faith in a letter, when the whole world might be about to burn. Her gaze went to the northern

horizon. There, YarapRombry's Comet burned: to some a symbol of destruction, to others of salvation. A nightbird called. The queen listened to the cry even after it had died, as one watches a knife irretrievably falling through clear water.

When she was sure that the majordomo was on his way, she returned to her couch and drew the silk curtains round it. She lay there open-eyed.

Through the gloom, the dust of the coast road showed white. ScufBar plodded beside his load, looking anxiously about. Still he was startled when a figure materialized out of the dark and called to him to halt.

The man was armed and of military bearing. It was one of King JandolAnganol's men, paid to keep an eye on all who came or went on the queen's business. He sniffed at the casket. ScufBar explained that he was going to sell the corpse.

"Is the queen that poor, then?" asked the guard, and sent ScufBar on his way.

ScufBar continued steadily, alert for sounds beyond the creak of the casket. There were smugglers along the coast, and worse than smugglers. Borlien was involved in the Western Wars against Randonan and Kace, and its countryside was often plagued by bands of soldiers, raiders, or deserters.

When he had been walking for two hours, ScufBar led the hoxney under a tree which spread its branches over the track. The track rose steeply ahead, to join the southern highroad which ran from Ottassol all the way westwards to the frontier with Randonan.

It would take the full twenty-five hours of the day to reach Ottassol, but there were easier ways of making the journey than plodding beside a loaded hoxney.

After tying the animal to the tree, ScufBar climbed into a low branch and waited. He dozed.

When the rumble of an oncoming cart roused him, he slipped to the ground and waited crouching by the highway. The aurora flickering overhead helped him to make out the traveller. He whistled, an answering whistle came, and the cart drew to a leisurely stop.

The man who owned the cart was an old friend from the same part of Borlien as ScufBar, by name FloerCrow. Every week in the summer of the small year, he drove produce from local farms to market. FloerCrow was not an outgoing man, but he was prepared to give ScufBar a lift to Ottassol for the convenience of having an extra animal to take a turn between the shafts.

The cart stopped long enough for the pack hoxney to be secured to a rear rail, and for ScufBar to scramble aboard. FloerCrow cracked the whip, and the cart lumbered forward. It was drawn by a patient drab brown hoxney.

Despite the warmth of the night, FloerCrow wore a wide-brimmed hat and thick cloak. A sword stood in an iron socket by his side. His load comprised four black piglets, persimmons, gwing-gwings, and a pile of vegetables. The piglets dangled helplessly in nets on the outside of the cart. ScufBar wedged his body against the slatted backrest, and slept with his cap over his eyes.

He roused when the wheels were making heavy weather over dried ruts. Dawn was bleaching the stars as Freyr prepared to rise. A breeze blew and brought the aromas of human habitation.

Although darkness clung to the land, peasants were already about, making for the fields. They moved shadowy and silent, the implements they carried giving an occasional clank. Their steady pace, the downward inclination of their heads, recalled the weariness that had attended their way home on the previous evening.

Male, female, young, old, the peasants progressed on various levels, some above the level of the road, some below. The landscape, as it slowly revealed itself, was composed of wedges, inclines, and walls, all of a dull brown colour, like the hoxneys. The peasants belonged to the great loess plain, which formed the central southern part of the tropical continent of Campannlat. It ran to the north, almost to the borders with Oldorando, and east to the River Takissa, where Ottassol stood. The loamy soil had been dug over by countless workers for countless years. Banks and cliffs and dams had been constructed, to be continually destroyed or rebuilt by succeeding

generations. Even in times of drought like the present, the loess had to be worked by those whose destiny it was to make crops grow from dirt.

"Whoa," said FloerCrow, as the cart rumbled into a village by the roadside.

Thick loess walls guarded the aggregation of dwellings against robbers. The gateway had broken and crumbled during last year's monsoon and had not been repaired. Although the gloom was still intense, no lights showed from any window. Hens and geese scavenged beneath the patched mud walls, on which apotropaic religious symbols were painted.

One item of cheer was provided by a stove burning by the gate. The old vendor who tended the stove had no need to cry his wares: the wares gave out a smell which was their own advertisement. He was a waffle seller. A steady stream of peasants bought waffles from him to eat on their way to work.

FloerCrow dug ScufBar in the ribs and pointed with his whip to the vendor. ScufBar took the hint. Climbing stiffly down, he went to buy their breakfast. The waffles came straight from the glowing jaws of the waffle iron into the hands of the customers. FloerCrow ate his greedily and climbed into the back of the cart to sleep. ScufBar changed hoxneys, took the reins, and got the cart moving again.

The day wore on. Other vehicles jostled on the road. The landscape changed. For a while, the highway ran so far below the level of the ground that nothing could be seen but the brown walls of fields. At other times, the way ran along the top of an embankment, and then a wide prospect of cultivation was visible.

The plain stretched in all directions, as flat as a board, dotted with bent figures. Straight lines prevailed. Fields and terraces were square. Trees grew in avenues. Rivers had been deflected into canals; even the sails of boats on the canals were rectangular.

Whatever the view, whatever the heat—today's temperature was in the hundreds—the peasants worked while there was light in the sky. Vegetables, fruits, and veronika, the chief cash crop, had to be tended. Their backs remained bent, whether one sun or two prevailed.

Freyr was pitilessly bright in contrast to the dull red face of

Batalix. No one doubted which of the two was master of the
heavens. Travellers faring from Oldorando, nearer the
equator, told of forests bursting into flame at Freyr's command. Many believed Freyr would shortly devour the world;
yet still rows had to be hoed and water trickled on delicate
growths.

The farm cart neared Ottassol. The villages were no longer
visible to the eye. Only fields could be seen, stretching to a
horizon which dissolved in unstable mirages.

The road sloped down into a groove, bounded on either
side by earth walls thirty feet high. The village was called
Mordec. The men climbed down and tethered the hoxney,
which drooped between the shafts until water was brought for
it. Both of their little dun-coloured animals showed signs of
tiredness.

Narrow tunnels led into the soil on either side of the road.
Sunlight showed through them, chopped neatly into rectangular shape. The men emerged from a tunnel into an open
court, well below ground level.

On one side of the court was the Ripe Flagon, an inn carved
out of the soil. Its interior, comfortingly cool, was lit only by
reflections of the light striking down into the courtyard. Opposite the inn were small dwellings, also carved into the loess.
Their ochre facades were brightened by flowers in pots.

Through a maze of subterranean passageways the village
stretched, opening intermittently into courts, many of them
with staircases which led up to the surface, where most of the
inhabitants of Mordec were labouring. The roofs of the
houses were fields.

As they ate a snack and drank wine at the inn, FloerCrow
said, "He stinks a bit."

"He's been dead a while. Queen found him on the shore,
washed up. I'd say he was murdered in Ottassol, most like,
and flung in the sea off a quay. The current would carry him
down to Gravabagalinien."

As they went back to the cart, FloerCrow said, "It's a bad
omen for the queen of queens, no mistake."

The long casket lay in the back of the cart with the
vegetables. Water trickled from the melting ice and dripped to
the ground, where a pool marbled itself with a slow-moving

spiral of dust. Flies buzzed round the cart.

They climbed in and started on the last few miles to Ottassol.

"If King JandolAnganol wants to have someone done away with, he'll do it. . ."

ScufBar was shocked. "The queen's too well loved. Friends everywhere." He felt the letter in his inner pocket and nodded to himself. Influential friends.

"And him going to marry an eleven-year-old slip of a girl instead."

"Eleven and five tenners."

"Whatever. It's disgusting."

"Oh, it's disgusting, right enough," agreed ScufBar. "Eleven and a half, fancy!" He smacked his lips and whistled.

They looked at each other and grinned.

The cart creaked towards Ottassol, and the bluebottles followed.

Ottassol was the great invisible city. In colder times, the plain had supported its buildings, now they supported the plain. Ottassol was an underground labyrinth, in which men and phagors lived. All that remained on the scorched surface were roads and fields, counterpointed by rectangular holes in the ground. Down in the rectangles were the courts, surrounded by facades of houses which otherwise had no external configuration.

Ottassol was earth and its converse, hollowed earth, the negative and positive of soil, as if it had been bitten out by geometrical worms.

The city housed 695,000 people. Its extent could not be seen and was rarely appreciated even by its inhabitants. Favourable soil, climate, and geographical situation had caused the port to grow larger than Borlien's capital, Matrassyl. So the warrens expanded, often on different levels, until they were halted by the River Takissa.

Paved lanes ran underground, some wide enough for two carts to pass. ScufBar walked along one of these lanes, leading the hoxney with the casket. He had parted with FloerCrow at

a market on the outskirts of town. As he went, pedestrians turned to stare, screwing up their noses at the smell which had floated behind him. The ice block at the bottom of the casket had all but melted away.

"The anatomist and deuteroscopist?" he asked of a passerby. "Bardol CaraBansity?"

"Ward Court."

Beggars of all descriptions called for alms outside the frequent churches, wounded soldiers back from the wars, cripples, men and women with horrific skin cancers. ScufBar ignored them. Pecubeas sang from their cages at every corner and court. The songs of different strains of pecubea were sufficiently distinct for the blind to distinguish and be guided by them.

ScufBar made his way through the maze, negotiated a few broad steps down into Ward Court, and came to the door which bore a sign with the name Bardol CaraBansity on it. He rang the bell.

A bolt was shot back, the door opened. A phagor appeared, dressed in a rough hempen gown. It supplemented its blank cerise stare with a question.

"What you want?"

"I want the anatomist."

Tying the hoxney to a hitching post, ScufBar entered and found himself in a small domed room. It contained a counter, behind which a second phagor stood.

The first phagor walked down a corridor, both walls of which it brushed with its broad shoulders. It pushed through a curtain into a living room in which a couch stood in one corner. The anatomist was enjoying congress with his wife on the couch. He rested as he listened to what the ahuman servant had to say, and then sighed.

"Scerm you, I'll be there." He climbed to his feet and leaned against the wall to pull his pants up under his charfrul, which he adjusted with slow deliberation.

His wife hurled a cushion at him. "You dolt, why do you never concentrate? Finish what you're doing. Tell these fools to go away."

He shook his head and his heavy cheeks trembled. "It's the

unremitting clockwork of the world, my beauty. Keep it warm till I return. I don't order the comings and goings of men. . . ."

He moved down the corridor and paused at the threshold of his shop so as to inspect the new arrival. Bardol CaraBansity was a solid man, less than weighty, with a ponderous way of speech and a heavy skull shaped not unlike a phagor's. He wore a thick leather belt over his charfrul, and a knife in the belt. Although he looked like a common butcher, CaraBansity had a well-earned reputation as a crafty man.

With his hollow chest and protruding stomach, ScufBar was not an impressive sight, and CaraBansity made it plain he was not impressed.

"I've got a body for sale, sir. A human body."

Without speaking, CaraBansity motioned to the phagors. They went and brought the body in between them, dropping it down on the counter. Sawdust and ice fragments adhered to it.

The anatomist and deuteroscopist took a step nearer.

"It's a bit high. Where did you acquire it, man?"

"From a river, sir. When I was fishing."

The body was so distended by internal gasses that it bulged out of its clothes. CaraBansity pulled it onto its back and tugged a dead fish from inside its shirt. He threw it at Scuf-Bar's feet.

"That's a so-called scupperfish. To those of us who have a care for truth, it's not a fish at all but the marine young of a Wutra's worm. Marine. Sea, not freshwater. Why are you lying? Did you murder this poor fellow? You look like a criminal. The phrenology suggests it."

"Very well, sir, if you prefer, I did find him in the sea. Since I am a servant of the unfortunate queen, I did not want the fact widely known."

CaraBansity looked at him more closely. "You serve Myr-demInggala, queen of queens, do you, you rogue? She deserves good lackeys and good fortune, does that lady."

He indicated a cheap print of the queen's face, which hung in a corner of the shop.

"I serve her well enough. Tell me what you will pay me for this body."

"You have come all this way for ten roon, not more. In

these wicked times, I can get bodies to cut up every day of the week. Fresher than this one, too."

"I was informed that you would pay me fifty, sir. Fifty roon, sir." ScufBar looked shifty, and rubbed his hands together.

"How does it happen that you turn up here with your malodorous friend when the king himself and an envoy from the Holy C'Sarr are due to arrive in Ottassol? Are you an instrument of the king's?"

ScufBar spread his hands and shrank a little. "I have connections only with the hoxney outside. Pay me just twenty-five, sir, and I'll go back to the queen immediately."

"You scerm are all greedy. No wonder the world's going to pot."

"If that is the case, sir, then I'll accept twenty. Twenty roon."

Turning to one of the phagors standing by, flicking its pale milt up its slotlike nostrils, CaraBansity said, "Pay the man and get him out of here."

"How muzzh I pay?"

"Ten roon."

ScufBar let out a howl of anguish.

"All right. Fifteen. And you, my man, present Bardol CaraBansity's compliments to your queen."

The phagor fumbled in its hempen gown and produced a thin purse. It proffered three gold coins, lying in the gnarled palm of its three-fingered hand. ScufBar grabbed them and made for the door, looking sullen.

Briskly CaraBansity ordered one of his ahuman assistants to shoulder the corpse—an order obeyed without observable reluctance—and followed him along the dim corridor, where strange odours drifted. CaraBansity knew as much about the stars as about the intestines, and his house—itself shaped rather like an intestine—extended far into the loess, with entrances to chambers devoted to all his interests on several lanes.

They entered a workshop. Light slanted down through two small square windows set in fortress-thick earth walls. Where

the phagor trod, points of light glinted under his splayed feet. They looked like diamonds. They were beads of glass, scattered when the deuteroscopist was making lenses.

The room was crammed with learned litter. The ten houses of the zodiac were painted on the wall. Against another wall hung three carcasses in various stages of dissection—a giant fish, a hoxney, and a phagor. The hoxney had been opened up like a book, its soft parts removed to display ribs and backbone. On a desk nearby lay sheets of paper on which CaraBansity had drawn detailed representations of the dead animal, with various parts depicted in coloured ink.

The phagor swung the Gravabagalinien corpse from his shoulder and hung it upside down from a rail. Two hooks pierced the flesh between the Achilles tendon and the calcaneum. The broken arms dangled, the puffy hands rested like shelled crabs on the floor. At a blow from CaraBansity, his assistant departed. CaraBansity hated having the ancipitals about, but they were cheaper than servants or even human slaves.

After a judicial contemplation of the corpse, CaraBansity pulled out his knife and cut the dead man's clothes away. He ignored the stench of decay.

The body was that of a young man, twelve years old, twelve and a half, possibly twelve years and nine tenners, not more. His clothes were of coarse and foreign quality, his hair was cut in a manner generally used by sailors.

"You, my fine fellow, are probably not of Borlien," said CaraBansity to the corpse. "Your clothes are Hespagorat style—probably from Dimariam."

The belly was so distended that it had folded over and concealed a leather body belt. CaraBansity worked it free. As the flesh sank back, a wound was revealed. CaraBansity slipped on a glove and thrust his fist into the wound. His fingers met with an obstruction. After some tugging, he extracted a curved grey ancipital horn, which had punctured the spleen and sunk deep into the body. He regarded the object with interest. Its two sharp edges made it a useful weapon. It had once possessed a handle, which was missing, possibly lost in the sea.

He regarded the body with fresh curiosity. A mystery always pleased him.

Setting the horn down, he examined the belt. It was of superior workmanship, but the sort of standard thing sold anywhere—at Osoilima, for example, where pilgrims provided a ready market for such goods. On the inner side was a button-down pocket, which he flipped open. From the pocket, he withdrew an incomprehensible object.

Frowning, he laid the object in his grubby palm and walked across to the light with it. It was like nothing he had ever seen before. He could not even identify the metal of which it was chiefly made. A shiver of superstitious fear crossed his pragmatic mind.

As he was washing it under the pump, removing traces of sand and blood, his wife, Bindla, entered the workshop.

"Bardol? What are you doing now? I thought you were coming back to bed. You know what I was keeping warm for you?"

"I love it, but I have something else to do." He flashed her one of his solemn smiles. She was of middle age—at twenty-eight and one tenner almost two years younger than he—and her rich russet hair was losing some of its colour; but he admired the way she was still aware of her ripe charms. At present, she was overacting her resentment at the smells in the room.

"You're not even writing your treatise on religion, your usual excuse."

He grunted. "I prefer my stinks."

"You perverse man. Religion is eternal, stinks aren't."

"On the contrary, my leggiandrous beauty, religions change all the time. It's stinks which go on unchanged for ever."

"You rejoice in that?"

He was drying the wonderful object on a cloth and did not answer.

"Look at this."

She came and rested a hand on his shoulder.

"By the boulder!" he exclaimed in awe. He passed it to Bindla, and she gasped.

A strap of cunningly interwoven metal, much like a brace-let, supported a transparent panel in which three sets of numbers glowed.

They read the numbers aloud as he pointed to them with a blunt finger.

06:16:55   12:37:76   19:20:14

The numbers writhed and changed as they watched. The CaraBansitys looked at each other in mute astonishment. They watched again.

"I never saw such a talisman before," Bindla said in awe.

They had to look again, fascinated. The figures were black on a yellow background. He read them aloud.

06:20:25   13:00:00   19:23:44

As CaraBansity put the mechanism to his ear to see if it made any noise, the pendulum clock on the wall behind began to chime thirteen. This clock was an elaborate one, built by CaraBansity himself in his younger days. It showed in pictorial form the rising and setting times of the two suns, Batalix and Freyr, as well as the divisions of the year, the 100 seconds in a minute, the forty minutes in an hour, the twenty-five hours in a day, the eight days in a week, the six weeks in a tenner, and the ten tenners in a year of four hundred and eighty days. There was also an indicator to show the 1825 small years in a Great Year; that pointer now stood at 381, the present date by the Borlien-Oldorando calendar.

Bindla listened to the mechanism, and heard nothing. "Is it a clock of some kind?"

"Must be. Middle numbers make it thirteen o'clock, Borlien time . . ."

She always knew when he was at a loss. He chewed his knuckle like a child.

There was a row of studs along the top of the bracelet. She pressed one.

A different series of numbers appeared in the three apertures.

6877   828   3269
(1177)

"The middle one's the year, by some ancient calendar or other. How can that work?"

He pressed the stud and the previous series appeared. He set the bracelet down on the bench and stared at it, but Bindla picked it up and slipped it over her hand. The bracelet immediately adjusted itself, fitting snugly to her plump wrist. She shrieked.

CaraBansity went across to a shelf of worn reference books. He passed over an ancient folio copy of *The Testament of RayniLayan,* and pulled out a calf-bound *Seer's and Deuteroscopist's Calendrical Tables.* After fluttering through several pages, he settled on one and ran his finger down a column.

Although the year by the Borlien-Oldorando calendar was 381, this reckoning was not universally accepted. Other nations used other reckonings, which were listed in the Tables; 828 was listed. He found it under the ancient, discarded "Denniss Calendar," now associated with withcraft and the occult. Denniss was the name of a legendary king supposed to have ruled all Campannlat.

"The central panel of the bracelet refers to local time . . ." He tested out his knuckle again. "And it has survived inundation in the sea. Where are there craftsmen now who could manufacture such a jewel? Somehow it must have survived from the time of Denniss . . ."

He held his wife's wrist and they watched the numbers busy with their changes. They had found a timepiece of unparalleled sophistication, probably of unparalleled value, certainly of unparalleled mystery.

Wherever the craftsmen were who had made the bracelet, they must be secure from the desperate state to which King JandolAnganol had brought Borlien. Things still held together in Ottassol because it was a port, trading with other lands. Conditions elsewhere were worse, with drought, famine, and lawlessness. Wars and skirmishes wasted the country's lifeblood. A better statesman than the king, advised by a less corrupt scritina, or parliament, would make peace with Borlien's enemies and see to the welfare of the population at home.

Yet it was not possible to hate JandolAnganol—though

CaraBansity regularly tried to do so—because he was prepared to give up his beautiful wife, the queen of queens, to marry a stupid child, a half-Madi. Why should the Eagle do that, if not to cement the alliance between Borlien and its old enemy, Oldorando, for his country's sake? JandolAnganol was a dangerous man, all agreed—but as much under the cudgel of circumstance as the lowest peasant.

The worsening climate could be much blamed. The madness of the heat, increasing generation by generation, till the very trees caught fire . . .

"Don't stand dreaming," Bindla called. "Come and get your ridiculous contraption off my wrist."

II

SOME ARRIVALS AT THE PALACE

The event that the queen feared was already in process. King JandolAnganol was on his way to Gravabagalinien to divorce her. From the Borlienese capital of Matrassyl he would sail down the River Takissa to Ottassol, there to take a coastal ship westward to Gravabagalinien's narrow bay. Jandol-Anganol would present his queen with the Holy C'Sarr's bill of divorcement in front of witnesses. Then they would part, perhaps forever.

This was the king's plan, and very stormy he looked about it.

Accompanied by a brave sound of trumpets, escorted by members of his Household in finest array, King Jandol-Anganol was driven in his state coach down the hill from the palace, through Matrassyl's crooked streets, to the quayside. In the coach with him was a solitary companion: Yuli, his pet phagor. Yuli was no more than a runt, with the brown hairs of his infancy still showing through his white coat. He had been

21

dehorned and sat against his master, shuffling in nervous anticipation of the river journey.

As JandolAnganol stepped out of the vehicle, the captain of the waiting ship came forward and saluted smartly.

"We'll get under way as soon as you are ready," JandolAnganol said. His queen had sailed into exile from this very quay some five tenners earlier. Groups of citizens stood along the riverbank, eager to observe the king who had such a mixed reputation. The mayor had come to bid his monarch farewell. The cheering was nothing like the roar that had sped Queen MyrdemInggala on her way.

The king went aboard. A wooden clapper sounded, crisp as hoof on cobble. Rowers began to row. The sails were unfurled.

As the boat slid out from its mooring, JandolAnganol turned sharply to stare at the mayor of Matrassyl, who stood with his attendants drawn stiffly up on the dock in farewell. Catching the king's glance, the mayor bowed his head submissively, but JandolAnganol knew how angry the man was. The mayor resented his monarch's leaving the capital when the city was under external threat. Taking advantage of Borlien's war with Randonan in the west, the savage nations of Mordriat to the northeast were on the move.

As that surly face fell behind the stern of the ship, the king turned his head to the south. He admitted to himself that there was some justice in the mayor's attitude. From the high, restless grasslands of Mordriat came news that the warlord Unndreid the Hammer was active again. The Borlienese Northern Army, to improve its morale, should have had appointed as its general the king's son, RobaydayAnganol. But RobaydayAnganol had disappeared on the day he heard of his father's plan to divorce his mother.

"A son to trust in . . ." said JandolAngonal to the wind, with a bitter expression. He blamed his son for this journey on which he was embarked.

So the king set his profile southwards, looking for loyal demonstration. On the timbers of the deck, the shadows of the rigging lay in elaborate patterns. The shadows doubled themselves when Freyr rose in splendour. Then the Eagle retired to sleep.

A canopy of silk provided shelter in the poop of the ship. There the king remained for most of the three-day journey, with companions by his side. A few feet below his coign of vantage, almost naked human slaves, Randonanese for the most part, sat at their oars, ready to assist the canvas when the wind failed. The scent of them drifted up occasionally, to mingle with the smells of tar, timber, and bilges.

"We will make a stop at Osoilima," the king announced. At Osoilima, a place of pilgrimage on the river, he would go to the shrine and be scourged. He was a religious man, and needed the goodwill of Akhanaba, the All-Powerful, in the test that was to come.

JandolAnganol was of distinguished and morose bearing. At twenty-five years and a tenner or two, he was still a young man, but lines marked his powerful face, giving him an appearance of wisdom his enemies claimed he did not possess.

Like one of his hawks, he had a commanding way of holding his head. It was to this head that most attention turned, as if the head of the nation were embodied in his skull. There was an eaglelike look to JandolAnganol, emphasised by the sharp bladed nose, the fierce black eyebrows, and the trim beard and moustache, which latter partly concealed a sensuous mouth. His eyes were dark and intense; the darting glance from those eyes, missing nothing, had brought him his nickname in the bazaars, the Eagle of Borlien.

Those who were close to him and had a gift for understanding character claimed that the eagle was always caged, and that the queen of queens still held the lock of the cage. JandolAnganol had the curse of khmir, best described as an impersonal lust, well understood in these hot seasons.

Often the quick head movements, in marked contrast to the concentrated stillness of the body, were the nervous habits of a man who hoped to see where he could turn next.

The ceremony under the high rock of Osoilima was soon over. The king, with blood seeping through his tunic, stepped back on board ship, and the second half of the journey began. Hating the stench of the boat, the king slept on deck at night, lying on a swansdown mattress. His phagor runt Yuli slept by him, guarding his feet.

Behind the king's ship, keeping a discreet distance, was a

second ship, a converted cattle boat. In it sailed the king's most faithful troops, the First Phagorian Guard. It drew protectively closer to the king's ship as they approached Ottassol's inner harbour, on the afternoon of the third day of the voyage.

Flags dropped from masts in the muggy Ottassol heat. A crowd gathered at the quayside. Among the banners and other tokens of patriotism were grimmer signs, saying THE FIRE IS COMING: THE OCEANS WILL BURN, and LIVE WITH AKHA OR DIE FOR EVER WITH FREYR. The Church was taking advantage of a time of general alarm, and trying to bring sinners to heel.

A band marched importantly forward between two warehouses and began to play a regal theme. The plaudits for his majesty as he stepped down the gangplank were restrained.

Greeting him were members of the city scritina and notable citizens. Knowing the Eagle's reputation, they kept their speeches brief, and the king was brief in his reply.

"We are always happy to visit Ottassol, our chief port, and to find it flourishing. I cannot remain here long. You know how great events move forward.

"My unbending intention is to divorce myself from Queen MyrdemInggala by a bill of divorcement issued by the Great C'Sarr Kilandar IX, Head of the Holy Pannovalan Empire and Father Supreme of the Church of Akhanaba, whose servants we are.

"After I have served that bill upon the present queen, in the presence of witnesses accredited by the Holy C'Sarr, as in law I must, then, when the Holy C'Sarr receives the bill, I shall be free to take, and will take, as my lawful spouse Simoda Tal, Daughter of Oldorando. Thus shall I affirm by bonds of matrimony the alliance between our country and Oldorando, an ancient linkage, and confirm our common partnership in the Holy Empire.

"United, our common enemies will be defeated, and we shall grow to greatness as in the days of our grandfathers."

There was some cheering and clapping. Most of the audience rushed to see the phagorian soldiery disembark.

The king had discarded his usual keedrant. He was dressed in a tunic of yellow and black, sleeveless, so that his sinewy arms were well displayed. His trousers were of yellow silk,

clinging close to his limbs. His turn-over boots were of dull leather. He wore a short sword at his belt. His dark hair was woven about the golden circle of Akhanaba, by whose grace he ruled the kingdom. He stood staring at his welcoming committee.

Possibly they expected something more practical from him. The truth was that Queen MyrdemInggala commanded almost as much affection in Ottassol as in Matrassyl.

With a curt gesture to his retinue, JandolAnganol turned and stalked off.

Ahead lay the shabby low cliffs of loess. A length of yellow cloth had been laid across the quayside for the king to walk on. He avoided it, crossed to his waiting coach, and climbed in. The footman closed the door, and the vehicle moved off at once. It entered an archway and was immediately within the labyrinth of Ottassol. The phagorian guard followed.

JandolAnganol, who hated many things, hated his Ottassol palace. His mood was not softened by being welcomed at the gate by his Royal Vicar, the chill, wench-faced Abstrog-Athenat.

"Great Akhanaba bless you, sire, we rejoice to see your majesty's face, and to have your presence among us, just when bad tidings arrive from the Second Army in Randonan."

"I'll hear of military matters from military men," said the king, and paced forward into the reception hall. The palace was cool, and remained cool as the seasons grew hotter, but its subterranean nature depressed him. It reminded him of the two priestly years he had spent in Pannoval as a boy.

His father, VarpalAnganol, had greatly extended the palace. Seeking his son's praise, he had asked him how he liked it. "Cold, copious, ill considered," had been Prince JandolAnganol's answer.

It was typical of VarpalAnganol, never an artist at warfare, not to appreciate that the subterranean palace could never be defended effectively.

JandolAnganol remembered the day the palace was invaded. He was three years and a tenner old. He had been playing with a wooden sword in an underground court. One of the smooth loess walls shattered. From it burst a dozen armed rebels. They had tunnelled through the earth unnoticed. It still

vexed JandolAnganol to recall that he had yelled in terror before charging at them with his toy sword.

There happened to be a change of guard assembling in the court, with weapons ready. After a furious skirmish, the invaders were killed. The illegal tunnel was later incorporated into the design of the palace. That had been during one of the rebellions which VarpalAnganol had failed to put down with sufficient harshness.

The old man was now imprisoned in the fortress at Matrassyl, and the courts and passages of the Ottassol palace were guarded by human and ancipital sentries. JandolAnganol's eyes darted to the silent men as he passed them in the winding corridors; if one so much as moved, he was ready to kill him.

News of the king's black mood spread among the palace staff. Festivities had been arranged to divert him. But first he had to receive the report from the western battlefields.

A company of the Second Army, advancing across the Chwart Heights intending to attack the Randonanese port of Poorich, had been ambushed by a superior force of the enemy. They had fought till dusk, when survivors had escaped to warn the main force. A wounded man had been despatched to report the news back along the Southern Highway semaphore system to Ottassol.

"What of General TolramKetinet?"

"He fights on, sire," said the messenger.

JandolAnganol received the report almost without comment and then descended to his private chapel to pray and be scourged. It was exquisite punishment to be beaten by the lickerish AbstrogAthenat.

The court cared little what happened to armies almost three thousand miles away: it was more important that the evening's festivities should not be spoilt by the king's bile. The Eagle's chastisement was good for everyone.

A winding stair led down to the private chapel. This oppressive place, designed in the Pannovalan fashion, was carved from the clay which lay beneath the loess, and lined with lead to waist level, with stone above. Moisture stood in beads, or

ran in miniature waterfalls. Lights burned behind stained glass shades. The beams from these lanterns projected rectangles of colour into the dank air.

Sombre music played as the Royal Vicar took up his tentailed whip from beside the altar. On the altar stood the Wheel of Akhanaba, two sinuous spokes connecting inner rim with outer. Behind the altar hung a tapestry, gold and red, depicting Great Akhanaba in the glory of his contradictions: the Two-in-One, man and god, child and beast, temporal and eternal, spirit and stone.

The king stood and gazed at the animal face of his god. His reverence was wholehearted. Throughout his life, since his adolescent years in a Pannovalan monastery, religion had ruled him. Equally, he ruled through religion. Religion held most of the court and his people in thrall.

It was the common worship of Akhanaba which united Borlien, Oldorando, and Pannoval into an uneasy alliance. Without Akhanaba there would be only chaos, and the enemies of civilisation would prevail.

AbstrogAthenat motioned to his royal penitent to kneel, and read a short prayer over him.

"We come before Thee, Great Akhanaba, to ask forgiveness for failure and to display the blood of guilt. Through the wickedness of all men, Thou, the Great Healer, art wounded, and Thou, the All-Powerful, art made weak. Therefore Thou has set our steps among Fire and Ice, in order that we may experience in our material beings, here on Helliconia, what Thou dost experience elsewhere in our name, the perpetual torment of Heat and Frost. Accept this suffering, O Great Lord, as we endeavour to accept Thine."

The whip came up over the royal shoulders. Abstrog-Athenat was an effeminate young man, but strong in the arm and assiduous in working Akhanaba's will.

After penitence, the ceremonial of the bath; after the bath, the king ascended to the revelry.

Whips here gave way to the flicking of skirts in the dance. The music was brisk, the musicians fat and smiling. The king

put on a smile too, and wore it like armour, as he remembered
that this chamber had previously been lit by the presence of
Queen MyrdemInggala.

The walls were decorated with the flowers of dimday, with
idront and scented vispard. There were mounds of fruit and
sparkling jugs of black wine. The peasants might starve, but
not the palace.

JandolAnganol condescended to refresh himself with black
wine, to which he added fruit juice and Lordryardry ice. He
sat staring without much attending to the scene before him.
His courtiers kept at a discrete distance. Women were sent to
charm him and sent away again.

He had dismissed his old chancellor before leaving Matrassyl. A new chancellor, on probation, fussed at his side. Made
at once fawning and anxious by his advancement, he came to
discuss arrangements for the forthcoming expedition to
Gravabagalinien. He also was sent away.

The king intended to remain in Ottassol for as short a time
as possible. He would meet with the C'Sarr's envoy and then
continue on with him to Gravabagalinien. After the ceremony
with the queen, he would make a forced march to Oldorando;
there he would marry Princess Simoda Tal and get that whole
business over with. He would then defeat his enemies, with
assistance from Oldorando and Pannoval, and impose peace
within his own borders. Certainly, the child princess, Simoda
Tal, would have to live in the palace at Matrassyl, but there
was no reason why he should have to see her. This scheme he
would accomplish. It ran constantly through his mind.

He looked about for the C'Sarr's envoy, the elegant Alam
Esomberr. He had met Esomberr during his two-year stay in
the Pannovalan monastery, and they had remained friendly
ever since. It was necessary for JandolAnganol to have this
powerful dignitary, sent by Kilandar IX himself, to witness his
and the queen's signature to the document of divorcement,
and to return it to the C'Sarr himself before the marriage was
legally void. Esomberr should be at his side by now.

But Envoy Esomberr had been delayed as he was about to
leave his suite. A scruffy little man with a pot belly, mangy
hair, and travel-stained clothes had talked his way into the envoy's powdered presence.

"I take it you're not from my tailor?"

The scruffy little man denied the charge and produced a letter from an inner pocket. He handed it to the envoy. He stood and wriggled while Esomberr tore open the letter with an elegant gesture.

"It is, sir, intended—intended for onward delivery. For the eyes of the C'Sarr alone, begging your pardon."

"I am the C'Sarr's representative in Borlien, thank you," said Esomberr.

He read the letter, nodded, and produced a silver coin for the bearer.

Muttering, the latter retreated. He left the underground palace, went to where his hoxney was tethered, and began making his way back to Gravabagalinien to report his success to the queen.

The envoy stood smiling to himself and scratching the end of his nose. He was a willowy, personable man of twenty-four and a half years, dressed in a rich trailing keedrant. He dangled the letter. He sent a minion for a likeness of Queen MyrdemInggala, which he studied. From any new situation, personal as well as political advantages were to be gained. He would enjoy his trip to Gravabagalinien, if that were possible. Esomberr promised himself that he would not be too religious for his own enjoyment at Gravabagalinien.

As soon as the royal boat had docked, men and women had crowded into the forecourt of the palace to seek a word with the king. By law, all supplications had to go through the scritina, but the ancient tradition of making a plea direct to the king died hard. The king preferred work to idleness. Tired of waiting and of watching his courtiers gyrate themselves into states of breathlessness, he agreed to hold audience in a nearby room. His runt sat alertly by the small throne, and the king patted him now and again.

After the first two supplicants had come and gone, Bardol CaraBansity appeared before the king. He had thrown an embroidered waistcoat over his charfrul. JandolAnganol recognised the man's strutting walk and frowned as a florid bow was sketched in his direction.

"This man is Bardol CaraBansity, sire," said the chancellor-on-trial, standing at the king's right hand. "You have

some of his anatomical designs in the royal library.''

The king said, ''I remember you. You are a friend of my ex-chancellor, SartoriIrvrash.''

CaraBansity blinked his blood-shot eyes. ''I trust that Sar-toriIrvrash is well, sire, despite being an ex-chancellor.''

''He has fled to Sibornal, if that can be called being well. What do you want of me?''

''Firstly, a chair, sire, since my legs pain me to stand.''

They contemplated each other. Then the king motioned a page to move a chair below the dais on which he sat.

Taking his time about getting himself settled, CaraBansity said, ''I have an object to set before you—priceless, I believe—knowing your majesty to be a man of learning.''

''I am an ignorant man, and stupid enough to dislike flattery. A king of Borlien concerns himself with politics merely, to keep his country intact.''

''We do whatever we do the better for being better informed. I can break a man's arm better if I know how his joints work.''

The king laughed. It was a harsh sound, not often heard from his mouth. He leaned forward. ''What is learning against the increasing rage of Freyr? Even the All-Powerful Akha-naba seems to have no power against Freyr.''

CaraBansity let his gaze rest on the floor. ''I know nothing of the All-Powerful, Majesty. He does not communicate with me. Some public benefactor scribbled the word 'Atheist' on my door last week, so that is my label now.''

''Then take care for your soul.'' The king spoke less challengingly now, and lowered his voice. ''As a deuteroscopist, what do you make of the encroaching heat? Has humankind sinned so gravely that we must all perish in Freyr's fire? Is not the comet in the northern sky a sign of coming destruction, as the common people claim?''

''Majesty, that comet, YarapRombry's Comet, is a sign of hope. I could explain at length, but I fear to vex you with astronomical reckoning. The comet is named after the sage—cartographer and astronomer—YarapRombry of Kevassien. He made the first map of the globe, setting Ottaassaal, as this city was then called, in the centre of the map, and he named the comet. That was 1825 years ago—one great year. The

return of the comet is proof that we circle about Freyr like the comet, and will pass it by with no more than a slight singe!"

The king thought. "You give me a scientific answer, just as SartoriIrvrash did. There must also be a religious answer to my question."

CaraBansity chewed his knuckle. "What does the Holy Pannovalan Empire say on the subject of Freyr? For Akha's sake, it dreads any manifestation in the sky, and therefore uses the comet only to increase the fear of the people. It declares one more holy drumble to eliminate the phagors from our midst. The Church's argument is that if those creatures without souls are eliminated, the climate will immediately cool. Yet we are given to understand that, in the years of ice, the Church then claimed it was the ungodly phagors which brought the cold. So their thinking lacks logic—like all religious thinking."

"Don't vex me. I am the Church in Borlien."

"Majesty, apologies. I merely speak true. If it offends you, send me away, as you sent SartoriIrvrash away."

"That fellow you mention was all for wiping out the ancipitals."

"Sire, so am I, though I depend on them myself. If I may again speak truth, your favouring of them alarms me. But I would not kill them for some silly religious reason. I would kill them because they are the traditional enemy of mankind."

The Eagle of Borlien banged his hand down on the arm of his chair. The chancellor-on-trial jumped.

"I'll hear no more. You argue out of place, you impertinent hrattock!"

CaraBansity bowed. "Very well, sire. Power makes men deaf and they will not hear. It was you, not I, sire, who called yourself ignorant. Because you can threaten with a look, you cannot learn. That is your misfortune."

The king stood. The chancellor-on-trial shrank away. CaraBansity stood immobile, his face a patchy white. He knew he had gone too far.

But JandolAnganol pointed at the cringing chancellor.

"I tire of people who cower before me, like this man. Advise me as my advisor cannot and you shall be chancellor—no doubt to prove as vexing as your friend and predecessor.

"When I remarry, and take for wife the daughter of King Sayren Stund of Oldorando, this kingdom will be linked more firmly to the Holy Pannovalan Empire, and from that we shall derive strength. But I shall come under much pressure from the C'Sarr to obliterate the ancipital race, as is being done in Pannoval. Borlien is short of soldiers and needs phagors. Can I refute the C'Sarr's edict through your science?"

"Hm." CaraBansity pulled at a heavy cheek. "Pannoval and Oldorando have always hated fuggies as Borlien never did. We are not on ancipital migratory routes, as is Oldorando. The priests have found a new pretext to wage an old war. . . .

"There is a scientific line you might take, sire. Science that would banish the Church's ignorance, if you'll forgive me."

"Speak, then, and my pretty runt and I will listen."

"Sire, you will understand. Your runt will not. You must know by repute the historical treatise entitled *The Testament of RayniLayan*. In that volume, we read of a saintly lady, VryDen, wife of the sage RayniLayan. VryDen unravelled some of the secrets of the heavens where, she believed, as I do, that truth, not evil, lives. VryDen perished in the great fire which consumed Oldorando in the year 26. That is three hundred and fifty-five years ago—fifteen generations, though we live longer than they did in those times. I am convinced that VryDen was a real person—not an invention of an Ice Age tale, as the Holy Church would have us believe."

"What's your point?" asked the king. He began to pace sharply about, and Yuli skipped after him. He remembered that his queen set great store by the book of RayniLayan, and read parts of it to Tatro.

"Why, my point is a sharp one. This same VryDen lady was an atheist, and therefore saw the world as it is, unobscured by imagined deities. Before her day, it was believed that Freyr and Batalix were two living sentinels who guarded our world against a war in heaven. With the aid of geometry, this same excellent lady was able to predict a series of eclipses which brought her era to a close.

"Knowledge can build only on knowledge, and one never knows where the next step will lead. But it leads somewhere,

whereas Church dogma leads only in a circle. The Church's very emblem is that circle.''

"Which I prefer to your fumbling steps into darkness.''

"I found a way to see through the darkness into light. With the aid of our mutual acquaintance, SartoriIrvrash, I ground some lenses of glass like the lens in the eye.'' He described how they had constructed a telescope. Through this instrument, they studied the phases of Ipocrene and the other planets in the sky. This intelligence they kept to themselves, since the sky was not a popular subject in those nations under the religious sway of Pannoval.

"One by one, these wanderers revealed their phases to us. Soon we could predict their changes exactly. There's deuteroscopy! From there, SartoriIrvrash and I backed our observations by calculation. Thus we came on the laws of heavenly geometry, which we think must have been known to YarapRombry—but he suffered martyrdom at the hands of the Church. These laws state that the orbits of the worlds lie about the sun Batalix, and the orbit of Batalix lies about Freyr. And the radius vector of the solar movements covers equal areas of space in equal times.

"We discovered also that the fast planet, called by VryDen Kaidaw, has its orbit not about Batalix but about Helliconia, and is therefore a satellite body or moon.''

The king stopped pacing to ask sharply, "Could people like us live on this Kaidaw?''

The question was so at variance with his previous reluctant interest that CaraBansity was surprised. "It is merely a silver eye, sire, not a true world, like Helliconia or Ipocrene.''

The king clapped his hands. "Enough. Explain no more. You could end as did YarapRombry. I understand nothing.''

"If we could make these explanations clear to Pannoval, then we might change their out-of-date thinking. If the C'Sarr could be coaxed to understand celestial geometry, then he might come to appreciate a human geometry enough to allow humankind and ancipitals to revolve about each other as Batalix and Freyr do, instead of promulgating his holy drumbles, which upset orderly life.''

He was about to launch into further explanation, when the

king made one of his impatient gestures.

"Another day. I can't listen to much heresy at a time, though I appreciate the cunning of your thought. You incline to go with circumstances, even as I do. Is this what you came here for?"

For a while, CaraBansity faced the sharp gaze of the king. Then he said, "No, Your Majesty, I came, like many of your faithful subjects, hoping to sell you something."

He brought from his belt the bracelet with the three sets of numbers which he had discovered on the corpse, and presented it to his majesty.

"Did you ever see a jewel like this before, Your Majesty?"

His majesty regarded it with surprise, turning it over in his hand.

"Yes," he said. "Yes, I've seen this very bracelet before, in Matrassyl. It is indeed strange, and it came from a strange man, who claimed to have come from another world. From your Kaidaw." He closed his mouth after this mysterious speech, as if sorry to have spoken.

He watched the numbers in the piece of jewellery writhing and changing for a while, and said, "You can tell me at a more leisurely time how this arrived in your possession. Now this audience is closed. I have other matters to attend to."

He closed his hand over the bracelet.

CaraBansity broke into pained protest. The king's demeanour changed. Rage burned from his eyes, from every line of his face. He leaned forward like a predatory bird.

"You atheists will never comprehend that Borlien lives or dies by its religion. Are we not threatened on every side by barbarians, by unbelievers? The empire cannot exist without belief. This bracelet threatens the empire, threatens belief itself. Its wriggling numbers come from a system that would destroy us. . . ." In a less intense voice, he added, "Such is my conviction, and we must live or die by our convictions."

The deuteroscopist bit his knuckle and said nothing.

JandolAnganol contemplated him, then spoke again.

"If you decide to become my chancellor, return here tomorrow. We will then speak more. Meanwhile, I will keep this atheistic bauble. What will your answer be, do you think? Will you become my chief advisor?"

Seeing the king place the bracelet within his clothes, Cara-Bansity was overcome.

"I thank your majesty. On that question, I must consult my own chief advisor, my wife. . . ."

He bowed low as the king passed him and swept out of the room.

In a nearby corridor of the palace, the C'Sarr's envoy was preparing to attend the king.

The portrait of Queen MyrdemInggala was painted on an oval piece of ivory cut from the tusk of a sea beast. It showed that unmatched face with a brow of flawless beauty, and her hair piled high above it. The queen's deep blue eyes were shielded by full lids, while the neat chin lent a delicate aspect to an otherwise rather commanding mien. These features Alam Esomberr recognised from earlier portraits he had examined in Pannoval—for the queen's beauty was known far and wide.

As he gazed upon this image, the official envoy of the Holy C'Sarr allowed his mind to dwell upon lascivious thoughts. He reflected that in a short space of time he would be face to face with the original masterpiece.

Two agents of Pannoval who spied for the C'Sarr stood before Esomberr. As he stared at the picture, they reported the gossip of Ottassol. They discussed back and forward between themselves the danger the queen of queens would be in once the divorcement between her and JandolAnganol was complete. He would wish to have her removed entirely from the scene. Entirely.

On the other hand, the general multitude preferred the queen to the king. Had not the king imprisoned his own father and bankrupted his country? The multitude might rise up, kill the king, and place MyrdemInggala on the throne. Justifiably.

Esomberr looked mildly upon them.

"You worms," he said. "You hrattocks. You tit-tattlers. Do not all kings bankrupt their countries? Would not everyone lock up his father, given the power? Are not queens always in danger? Do not multitudes always dream of rising up and overthrowing someone or other? You chatter merely of

traditional role-playing in the great but on the whole somewhat typecast theatre of life. You tell me nothing of substance. Agents of Oldorando would be flogged if they turned
in such a report.''

The men bowed their heads. ''We also have to report that
agents of Oldorando are busy here.''

''Let's hope they don't spend all their time rumboing the
port wenches, as you two evidently do. The next time I sum-
mon you, I shall expect news from you, not gossip.''

The agents bowed more deeply and left the room, smiling
excessively, as if they had been overpaid.

Alam Esomberr sighed, practised looking severe, and
glanced again at the miniature of the queen.

''No doubt she's stupid, or has some other defect to coun-
terbalance such beauty,'' he said aloud. He tucked the ivory
into a safe pocket.

The envoy to C'Sarr Kilandar IX was a noble of the deeply
religious Taker family with connections in the deep-dwelling
Holy City itself. His austere father, a member of the Grand
Judiciary, had seen to it that promotion of his son, who
despised him, had come early. Esomberr regarded this journey
to bear witness to his friend's divorcement as a holiday. On
holiday, one was entitled to a little fun. He began to hope that
Queen MyrdemInggala might provide it.

He was prepared to meet JandolAnganol. He summoned a
footman. The footman took him into the presence of the king,
and the two men embraced each other.

Esomberr saw that the king was more nervous in his manner
than previously. Covertly, he assessed that lean bearded profile as the king escorted him into the chambers where revels
were still in progress. The runt Yuli followed behind. Esomberr threw him a look of aversion, but said nothing.

''So, Jan, we have both managed to arrive in Ottassol
safely. No invaders of your realm intercepted either of us on
our way.''

They were friends as friendship went in those circles. The
king remembered well Esomberr's cynical airs and his habit of
holding his head slightly to one side, as if questioning the
world.

''As yet we are free of the depredations of Unndreid the

Hammer. You will have heard of my encounter with Darvlish the Skull.''

"I'm sure the rogues you name are frightful rogues indeed. Would they have been somewhat nicer, one wonders, if they had been given less uncouth names?''

"I trust your suite is comfortable?''

"To speak true, Jan, I abominate your underground palace. What happens when your River Takissa floods?''

"The peasants dam it with their bodies. If the timetable suits you, we shall sail for Gravabagalinien tomorrow. There's been delay enough, and the monsoon approaches. The sooner the divorcement is over the better.''

"I look forward to a sea voyage, as along as it is short and the coast remains within earshot.''

Wine was served them, and crushed ice added.

"Something worries you, cousin.''

"Many things worry me, Alam. It's no matter. These days, even my faith worries me.'' He hesitated, looked back over his shoulder. "When I am insecure, Borlien is insecure. Your master, the C'Sarr, our Holy Emperor, surely would understand that. We must live by our faith. For my faith, I renounce MyrdemInggala.''

"Cousin, in private we can admit that faith has a certain lack of substance, eh? Whereas your fair queen . . .''

In his pocket, the king fingered the bracelet he had taken from CaraBansity. That had substance. That was the work of an insidious enemy who, intuition told him, could bring disaster to the state. He clenched his fist round the metal.

Esomberr gestured. His gestures, unlike the king's, were languid, lacking spontaneity.

"The world's going to pot, cousin, if not to Freyr. Though I must say religion never caused me to lose a wink of sleep. Indeed, religion's often been the cause of sleep in me. All nations have their troubles. Randonan and the dreaded Hammer are your preoccupations. Oldorando now has a crisis with Kace. In Pannoval, we are once more being attacked by the Sibornalese. South through Chalce they come, unable to tolerate their ghastly homeland for another instant. A strong Pannoval-Oldorando-Borlien axis will improve the stability of all Campannlat. The other nations are mere barbarians.''

"Alam, you are requested to cheer me, not depress me, on the eve of my divorcement from MyrdemInggala."

The envoy drained his glass. "One woman's much like another. I'm sure you'll be blissfully happy with little Simoda Tal."

He saw the pain on the king's face. JandolAnganol said, looking away towards the dancers, "My son should be marrying Simoda Tal, but I get no sense from him. MyrdemInggala understands that I take this step in the interests of Borlien."

"By the boulder, does she indeed?" Esomberr felt inside his silk jacket and produced a letter. "You had better read this, which has just come to my hand."

Seeing MyrdemInggala's bold handwriting, JandolAnganol took the sheet tremblingly, and read.

To the Holy Emperor, C'Sarr Kilandar IX, Head of the Holy Pannovalan Empire, in the City of Pannoval, in the country of that name.

Revered Sire—Whose faith is followed devoutly by the undersigned—

Look favourably upon this supplication from one of thy most unlucky daughters.

I, Queen MyrdemInggala, have been punished where no crime was committed. I was unjustly accused of conspiring against Sibornal by my husband the king, and by his father, and stand in grave danger.

Revered sire, my lord King JandolAnganol has treated me with cruel injustice, banishing me from his side to this forlorn seaside place. Here I must stay until the king disposes of me as he will, a victim of his khmir.

I have been a faithful wife to him for thirteen years, and have borne him a son and a daughter. The daughter is yet little, and remains with me. My son has become wild since this division, and I know not where he is.

Since my lord the king usurped his father's throne, ill things have befallen our kingdom. He has made enemies on all sides. To break from a circle of retribution, he plans a dynastic marriage with Simoda Tal, daughter of King Sayren Stund of Oldorando. As I understand, this arrangement has obtained

your approval. To your judgment I must bow. But it will not be enough for JandolAnganol to reject me by a manipulation of the law; he will also require me finally removed from the earthly scene.

Therefore I beseech my revered Emperor to despatch as soon as possible a letter forbidding the king to harm me or my children in any fashion, on pain of excommunication. At least the king professes religious faith; such a threat would have effect upon him.

> *Your distraught daughter-in-religion,*
> *ConegUndunory MyrdemInggala*

This letter will reach you via your envoy in Ottassol, and I pray he will mercifully deliver it to thy cherished hand by the fastest means.

"Well, then we shall have to deal with this," said the king, with a look of pain, clutching the letter.

"*I* will have to deal with this," corrected Esomberr, retrieving the letter.

The following day, the party set sail westwards along the coast of Borlien. With the king went his new chancellor, Bardol CaraBansity.

The king had developed a nervous habit at this time of looking over his shoulder, as if he felt himself watched by Akhanaba, the great god of the Holy Pannoval Empire.

There were those who watched him—or who would watch him—but they were more remote in space and time than JandolAnganol could imagine. They were to be numbered in their millions. At this time, the planet Helliconia held ninety-six million human beings, and possibly a third of that number of phagors. The distant watchers were still more numerous.

The inhabitants of the planet Earth had once watched the affairs of Helliconia with considerable detachment. The transmissions from Helliconia, beamed to Earth by the Earth Observation Station, had begun as little more than a source of entertainment. Over the centuries, as Great Spring on Helli-

conia turned to Summer, matters were changing. Observation
was developing into commitment. The watchers were being
changed by what they watched; despite the fact that Present
and Past on the two planets could never coincide, an emphatic
link was now being forged.

Schemes were in hand to make that link more positive.

The increasing maturity, the increasing understanding of
what it was to be an organic entity, was a debt which the
peoples of Earth owed to Helliconia. They now saw the em-
barkation of the king from Ottassol, not as Tatro saw the
wave on the beach, as a separate event, but rather as a strand
in an inescapable web of cosmology, culture, and history.
That the king possessed free will was never in dispute among
the observers; but whichever way JandolAnganol turned to
exert his will—a ferocious one—the infinite linkages of the
continuum closed behind him again, to leave little more trace
than the keel of his ship upon the Sea of Eagles.

Although the terrestrials viewed the divorce with compassion, they saw it less as an individual act than as a cruel
example of a division in human nature between mistakenly ro-
mantic readings of love and duty. This they were able to do
because something of Earth's long crucifixion was over. The
upheaval of JandolAnganol's divorce from MyrdemInggala
took place in the year 381, by the local Borlien-Oldorando
calendar. As the mysterious timepiece had indicated, on Earth
the year was 6877 years after the birth of Christ; but this suggested a false synchronicity, and the events of the divorce
would become real to the peoples of Earth only when a further
thousand years elapsed.

Dominating such local dates was a cosmic one with more
meaning. Astronomical time in the Helliconian system was at
full flood. The planet and its sister planets were approaching
periastron, the nearest point in the orbit to the brilliant star
known as Freyr.

It took Helliconia 2592 Earth years to complete one Great
Year in its orbit about Freyr, during which time the planet endured extremes of heat and cold. Spring was over. Summer,
the enervating summer of the Great Year, had arrived.

Summer's duration would extend over two and a third
Earth centuries. To those who lived on Helliconia at this time,

winter and its desolations were but legends, although powerful ones. So they would remain yet a while, waiting in the human mind to become fact.

Above Helliconia shone its own local sun, Batalix. Dominating Batalix was its giant binary companion, Freyr, shining at present with an apparent brightness thirty percent greater than Batalix, although it was 236 times more distant.

Despite their involvements in their own history, the observers on Earth watched Helliconian events closely. They saw that strands of the web—the religious strand not the least—had been woven long ago which now entangled the King of Borlien.

III

A PREMATURE DIVORCE

The Borlienese were not a nation of seamen, despite their long seacoast. It followed that they were not great shipbuilders like the Sibornalese, or even some nations of Hespagorat. The ship that took the king to Gravabagalinien and divorce was a small brig with round bows. It kept the coast in sight most of the time and navigated by traverse board, on which the mean course made good during each watch was calculated from the positions of pegs inserted on the board.

An even more tublike brig followed the first, bearing the ancipitals of the First Phagorian Guard.

The king broke from his companions as soon as the ship sailed and went to stand by the rails, staring rigidly ahead, as if anxious to be the first to see the queen. Yuli became miserable at the motion of the sea and sprawled by the capstan. For once the king showed his pet no sympathy.

Its cordage creaking, the brig laboured through calm seas.

The king fell suddenly to the deck. His courtiers ran to him and lifted him. JandolAnganol was carried to his cabin and

placed in his bunk. He was deathly pale and rolled about as if in pain, hiding his face.

A medical man examined him and ordered everyone to leave the cabin except CaraBansity. "Stay by his majesty. He has a touch of seasickness but nothing more. As soon as we get ashore he will be well again."

"I understood that a characteristic of seasickness was vomiting."

"Hrrrm, well, in some cases. Commoners. Royal personages respond in a different fashion." The doctor bowed himself out.

After a while, the king's muttered complaints became articulate. "The dreadful thing I must do. Pray Akhanaba it will soon be over . . ."

"Majesty, let us discuss a sensible, important topic, to calm your mind. That rare bracelet of mine which you hold—"

The king raised his head and said, with his inflexible look, "Get out of here, you cretin. I'll have you flung overboard to the fish. Nothing is important, nothing—nothing on this earth."

"May your majesty soon recover himself," said CaraBansity, backing his awkward bulk out of the cabin.

The ship made fair progress westwards, and sailed into the little bay at Gravabagalinien on the morning of the second day at sea. JandolAnganol, suddenly himself again, walked down the gangplank and into the surf—there was no jetty at Gravabagalinien—with Alam Esomberr close behind him, holding up his cloak tails.

With the latter travelled an escort of ten dignitaries of high ecclesiastical office, referred to by Esomberr as his rabble of vicars. The king's retinue contained captains and armourers.

The queen's palace waited inland, without a sign of life. Its narrow windows were shuttered. A black flag flew at half-mast from a turret. The king's face, turned towards it, was itself as blank as a shuttered window. No man dared look long at it, lest he catch the Eagle's eye.

The second brig was coming in, making awkward progress. Despite Esomberr's impatience, JandolAnganol insisted on

waiting until it was drawn in and a walkway extended from ship to shore, so that his ahuman troops could reach land without having to set foot in the water.

He then made much of forming them up, drilling them, and addressing them in Native. At last he was ready to walk the half mile to the palace. Yuli ran ahead, frisking in the sand, kicking it up, delighted to be on firm ground again.

They were greeted by an ancient woman in a black keedrant and white apron. White hairs trailed from a mole on her cheek. She walked with a stick. Two unarmed guards stood some way behind her.

Close at hand, the white and gold building revealed its shabbiness. Gaps showed where slates on its roofs, planks from its verandahs, uprights in its railings, had fallen away and not been replaced. Nothing moved, except a herd of deer cropping grass on a distant hillside. The sea boomed endlessly against the shore.

The king's costume took up the general sombre note. He wore an undecorated tunic and breeches of a deep blue close to black. Esomberr, by contrast, strolled along in his jauntiest powder blues, offset by a pink short cloak. He was perfumed this morning, to camouflage the stinks of the ship.

An infantry captain blew a bugle to announce their arrival.

The palace door remained closed. The old woman wrung her hands and muttered to the breeze.

Wrenching himself into action, JandolAnganol went up to the door and beat on its wooden panels with the hilt of his sword. The noise echoed within, setting hounds barking.

A key was applied to a lock. The door swung open, propelled by another aged hag, who gave a stiff curtsey to the king and stood there blinking.

All was gloom inside. The hounds that had set up such a din when the door was locked now slunk away into shadowy recesses.

"Perhaps Akhanaba in his somewhat temperamental mercy has sent the plague here," suggested Esomberr. "Thus releasing the occupants from earthly sorrow and rendering ours an unnecessary journey."

The king gave a shout of greeting.

A light showed at the top of the stairs, where all was other-

wise dark. They looked up to see a woman carrying a taper. She bore it above her head, so that her features were in shadow. As she descended the stairs, every step creaked. As she neared those waiting below, the light from outside began to illumine her features. Even before that, something in her carriage declared who she was. The glow strengthened, the face of Queen MyrdemInggala was revealed. She stopped a few paces in front of JandolAnganol and Esomberr and curtseyed first to the one, then the other.

Her beauty was ashen, her lips almost colourless, her eyes dark in her pallid face. Her hair floated in dark abundance about her head. She wore a pale grey gown to the floor which buttoned at the throat to conceal her breasts.

The queen spoke a word to the crone, who went to the doors and closed them, leaving Esomberr and JandolAnganol in the dark, with the intrusive phagor runt behind them. That dark revealed itself as seamed with threads of light. The palace was flimsily built of planking. When the sun shone on it, a skeletal aspect was revealed. As the queen led them to a side room, slivers of light disclosed her presence.

She stood awaiting them in the middle of a room defined by thin geometrics of illumination, where daylight slit round shuttered windows.

"Nobody is in the palace at present," MyrdemInggala said, "except for me and the Princess TatromanAdala. You may kill us now, and there will be no witnesses except the All-Powerful."

"We do not intend to hurt you, madam," said Esomberr. He walked over to one of the windows and opened the shutters. Turning in the dusty light, he saw the husband and wife standing close in the almost empty room.

MyrdemInggala pursed her lips and blew out her taper.

JandolAnganol said, "Cune, as I've said, this divorce is a question of state policy." His manner was abnormally subdued.

"You may force me to accept it. You can never make me understand it."

Esomberr opened the window and called for his retinue and for AbstrogAthenat.

"The ceremony will not detain you long, madam," he said.

He paraded into the center of the room and bowed to her. "My name is Esomberr of the Esomberrs. I am the Envoy and Representative in Borlien of the Great C'Sarr Kilandar IX, the Father Supreme of the Church of Akhanaba and Emperor of Holy Pannoval. My function is to act as witness on behalf of the Father Supreme, in a brief ceremony. That is my public duty. My private duty is to declare that you are more beautiful than any representation of you could ever be."

To JandolAnganol she said faintly, "After all we have been to each other . . ."

Continuing without altering the tone of his voice, Esomberr said, "The ceremony will absolve King JandolAnganol from any further marital ties. Under this special bill of divorcement granted by the Father Supreme himself, you two will cease to be husband and wife, your vows will be rescinded, and you will renounce the title of Queen."

"Upon what grounds am I to be divorced, sir? What is the pretext? How has the revered C'Sarr been told I have offended, to be treated like this?"

The king stood as in a trance, staring rigidly at the air, while Alam Esomberr pulled a document from his pocket, flapped it open, and read.

"Madam, we have witnesses to prove that while you have been taking your holidays here in Gravabagalinien"—he sketched a sensuous gesture—"you have entered the sea in a state of nudity. That you have there consorted carnally with dolphins. That this unnatural act, forbidden by the Church, has been frequently repeated, often within sight of your child."

She said, "You know this is a complete fabrication." She spoke without fire in her voice. Turning to JandolAnganol, she said, "Can the state survive only by dragging down my name, by disgracing me—and by making you lower than a slave?"

"Here comes the Royal Vicar, madam, who will perform our ceremony," said Esomberr. "You need only stand silent. No further embarrassment will be caused you."

AbstrogAthenat entered, radiating the chill of his personality in the space of the chamber. He raised a hand and pro-

nounced a blessing. Two small boys playing the pipes stood behind him.

The queen said coldly, "If this holy farce must take place, I insist that Yuli be removed from the room."

JandolAnganol broke from his reverie to order his runt outside. After a small fuss, it left.

AbstrogAthenat came forward with a paper on which the words of the wedding ceremony were inscribed. He took the hands of the king and queen, making each hold a side of the paper, which they did as if hypnotised. He then read the bill out in a high, clear voice. Esomberr looked from one to the other of the royal pair. They looked at the floor. The vicar lifted a ceremonial sword high. With a muttered prayer, he brought it down.

The paper bond they held was sliced in two. The queen let her half float to the wooden tiles.

The vicar produced a document which JandolAnganol signed, Esomberr signing as witness. The vicar signed it himself, then handed it to Esomberr for its onward transmission. The vicar bowed to the king. He left the room, followed by his two piping boys.

"The deed is done," said Esomberr. Nobody moved.

Heavy rain began to fall. Sailors and soldiers from the ships had crowded to the one open window to catch a glimpse of a ceremony of which they could boast for the rest of their lives. Now they ran for shelter, and officers bellowed at them. The downpour increased. Lightning flashed and presently thunder broke overhead. The monsoons were approaching.

"Ah, well, we must make ourselves comfortable," said Esomberr, striving for his usual lightness of tone. "Perhaps the queen—the ex-queen, excuse me—will have some ladies bring us refreshment." He called to one of his men. "Look down in the cellars. The serving maids will be hiding down there or, failing them, the wine will be."

Rain poured in the open window and the unsecured shutter banged.

"These storms blow in from nowhere and are soon over," JangolAnganol said.

"That's the way to take it, Jan—with a metaphor," said

Esomberr genially. He clapped the king on the shoulder.

Without a word, the queen set down her extinguished taper on a shelf, then turned and left the room.

Esomberr collected two chairs with tapestry seats and set them together, opening up a shutter nearby so that they could watch the fury of the elements. They bot^h sat down, and the king put his head between his hands.

"After your marriage to Simoda Tal, I promise you things will take a turn for the better, Jan. In Pannoval, we are somewhat committed on our northern front against the Sibornalese. The fighting is particularly bitter because of traditional religious differences, you know.

"Oldorando is different. After your forthcoming marriage, you should find that Oldorando will commit themselves to your side. They have difficulties themselves. Or—and this is quite likely—Kace may sue for peace after the marriage. Kace, after all, has blood ties with Oldorando. Right through Oldorando and Kace runs the east-west migratory route of the phagors and of the subhuman races, like the Madis.

"Rrrhm, as you know, dear Simoda Tal's mother, the queen, is herself a sub—well, a protognostic, let's say. That little term, 'subhuman,' is prejudicial. And the Kaci . . . well, it's a wild place. So if they make peace with Borlien, we might even, who knows, induce them to attack Randonan. That would leave you free to deal with the Mordriat trouble, and the fellows with the amusing names."

"Which would suit Pannoval well," said JandolAnganol.

Esomberr nodded. "It would suit everyone well. I'm all for being pleased, aren't you?"

His man returned, accompanied by peals of thunder and five anxious ladies who bore wine jars and were goaded forward by phagors.

The entrance of these ladies put a different aspect on affairs, even to the king who got up and began to walk about the room as if just learning to use his legs. The ladies, finding no harm was immediately being offered, began to smile, and fell readily into their accustomed roles of pleasing male guests and getting them as drunk as possible as soon as possible. The Royal Armourer and various captains put in an appearance and joined in the drinking.

As the storm continued, lamps were lit. Other pretty captives were brought in and music was played. Soldiers under canvas canopies brought a banquet from the brig.

The king drank persimmon wine and ate silver carp with saffron rice.

The roof leaked.

"I'll speak to MyrdemInggala and see my little daughter, Tatro," he said, a while later.

"No. That would be inadvisable. Women can humiliate men. You're the king, she's nobody. We'll take the daughter away with us when we leave. When the sea is calm. I'm for spending the night in this hospitable sieve of yours."

After a while, to overcome the king's silence, Esomberr said, "I have a gift for you. This is a good time to present it, before we are too drunk to focus our eyes." He wiped his hands on his velvet suit and felt in a pocket from which he produced a delicate thin box with an embroidered cover.

"This is a gift from Bathkaarnet-she, Queen of Oldorando, whose daughter's hand you are to take in marriage. The queen executed the embroidery herself."

JandolAnganol opened the box. Inside lay a miniature portrait of Simoda Tal, painted on her eleventh birthday. She wore a ribbon in her hair, and her face was half-turned away, as if in bashfulness or possibly coquetry. Her hair curled richly, but the artist had not disguised her parrot looks. The prominent nose and eyes of a Madi showed clear.

JandolAnganol held the portrait at arm's length, trying to read what might be read. Simoda Tal carried a model of a castle in one hand, the castle on the Valvoral which was part of her dowry.

"She's a pretty girl and no mistake," said Esomberr enthusiastically. "Eleven and a half is the most lascivious age, whatever people pretend. Frankly, Jan, I envy you. Though her younger sister, Milua Tal, is even prettier."

"Is she learned?"

"Is anyone learned in Oldorando? Not if they follow the example of their king."

They both laughed and drank a toast to future pleasure in persimmon wine.

*   *   *

By Batalix-fall, the storm had blown away. The wooden palace vibrated with noise and creaked like a ship before coming to anchor in calm. The royal soldiery had found its way into the cellars, among the ice blocks and the wine. They, and even the phagors, were subsiding into drunken sleep.

No watch was kept. The palace seemed too far from any possible trouble, while Gravabagalinien's macabre reputation deterred intruders. As evening wore on, the noise died. There was vomiting, laughter, and cursing, then nothing more. JandolAnganol slept with his head on a maidservant's lap. Soon she detached herself and left him lying in a corner like a common soldier.

The queen of queens kept watch upstairs over the passing hours. She feared for her small daughter; but the site of her exile had been well chosen. There was nowhere to escape to. Eventually, she sent her ladies-in-waiting away. Though reassured by the silence below, she remained alert, sitting in an anteroom to the chamber where Princess Tatro slept.

A knock came at her door. She rose and went to it.

"Who's there?"

"The Royal Vicar, ma'am, begging entrance."

She hesitated, sighing. She slid back the bolt. Alam Esomberr entered the room, grinning.

"Well, not quite the vicar, ma'am, but a near neighbour, and offering more comfort than is perhaps within our poor vicar's power."

"Please leave. I do not wish to talk with you. I am unwell. I shall call the guard." She was pale. Her hand trembled as she rested it against the wall. She mistrusted the smile on his face.

"Everyone's drunk. Even I—even I, model of excellence that I am, son of my worthy father as I am, am just slightly squiffed."

He kicked the door shut behind him and grasped her arm, pushing her before him until she was forced to sit down on the couch.

"Now—don't be so inhospitable, ma'am. Make me welcome, because I am on your side. I have come to warn you that your ex-husband means to kill you. Your circumstances are difficult, and you and your daughter need protection. I can give you that protection, if you behave kindly to me."

"I was not being unkind. I am merely frightened, sir—but I am not to be frightened into anything I would regret later."

He took her into his arms, despite her struggles. "Later! There's the difference between our sexes, ma'am—that for women there's always a *later*. The prevalence of pregnancy among you must account for all the laters. Let me into your fragrant nest tonight and I swear you shall not regret any laters. Meanwhile, I will have my nows."

MyrdemInggala hit him across the face. He sucked his lips.

"Listen to me. You wrote a letter to the C'Sarr in my care, did you not, my lovely ex-queen? In it, you said that King Jan intended to kill you. Your delivery boy betrayed you. He sold the letter to your ex-husband, who has read every mischievous word you wrote."

"ScufBar betrayed me? No, he's always been in my service."

Esomberr took her by the arms.

"In your new position, you have no one you can depend on. No one except me. I will be your protector if you behave."

She broke into weeping. "Jan loves me still, I know it. I understand him."

"He hates you, and lusts for the embrace of Simoda Tal."

He unfastened his clothes. At that moment the door opened and Bardol CaraBansity lumbered in and marched to the center of the room. He stood with his hands on his hips, fingers of his right hand over the hilt of his knife.

Esomberr jumped up, clutching his trousers, and ordered the deuteroscopist out. CaraBansity stood his ground. His face was heavy and flushed. He looked like a man accustomed to butchery.

"I must ask you to cease consoling this poor lady immediately, sir. I venture to trouble you because there is no guard on the palace and an army approaches from the north."

"Find someone else."

"This is an emergency. We are about to be slaughtered. Come."

He led along the corridor. Esomberr looked back at MyrdemInggala, who stood rigid, staring at him with defiant gaze. He cursed and hurried after CaraBansity.

At the end of the corridor was a balcony which overlooked

the rear of the palace. He followed CaraBansity onto it and stared out into the night.

The air was warm and heavy, and seemed to hug the sea noise to itself. The horizon lay under the weight of the enormous sky.

Near at hand were small moving tongues of flame, winking in and out of existence—Esomberr stared at them uncomprehendingly, still half drunk.

"Men approaching through trees," CaraBansity said, at his elbow. "Perhaps only two of them by my count. In my alarm I must have overestimated their numbers."

"What do they want?"

"A searching question, sire. I will go down and discover its answer, if you will be all right here, sire. Stay and I shall return with intelligence." He gave the escort a crafty sidelong glance.

Esomberr, leaning on the balcony rail, staggered as he looked down and leant back against the wall for safety. He heard CaraBansity's shout and a reply from the newcomers. He closed his eyes, listening to their voices. There were many other voices, some angry, calling to him in accusing manner, though he could not grasp what they were saying. The world swayed.

He roused to hear CaraBansity calling him from below.

"What's that you say?"

"It's bad news, sire, not to be shouted aloud. Please come down."

"What is it?" But CaraBansity gave no answer, speaking in a low voice to the newcomers. Esomberr got himself moving, went into the corridor, and nearly fell down the stairs.

"You're drunker than I thought, you fool," he said aloud.

Making his way out through an open door, he almost barged into CaraBansity and a haggard man, covered in dust, who carried a flambeau. Behind him, another man, equally dust-covered, looked about into the dark as if in fear of pursuit.

"Who are these men?"

The haggard man, eyeing Esomberr with distrust, said, "We're from Oldorando, Your Highness, from the court of His Majesty King Sayren Stund, and a hard journey we've had

of it, with the unrest in the countryside. I have a message for King JandolAnganol and none other."

"The king's asleep. What do you want with him?"

"It's bad news, sir, which I was entrusted to give to him direct."

Esomberr, growing angry, announced who he was. The messenger eyed him stonily. "If you're who you say you are, sir, then you'll have the authority to lead me to the king."

"I could escort him, sire," suggested CaraBansity.

They all went into the palace, dowsing their flambeaux on the ground before entering. CaraBansity led the way into the main chamber, where sleeping figures lay in confusion on the floor. He went over to where the king slept, and shook his arm without ceremony.

JandolAnganol roused and jumped immediately to his feet, hand on sword

The haggard man bowed. "I am sorry to awaken you, sire, and I regret coming late. Your soldiers killed two of my escort, and I barely escaped with my life." He produced documents to prove his identity. He had begun to shake violently, knowing the fate of messengers who bring bad tidings.

The king barely glanced at the documents.

"Tell me your news, man."

"It's the Madis, Your Majesty."

"What of them?"

The messenger shuffled his feet and put a hand to his face to stop his jaw rattling. "The Princes Simoda Tal is dead, sire. The Madis killed her."

There was a silence. Then Alam Esomberr began to laugh.

IV

AN INNOVATION IN THE COSGATT

Alam Esomberr's bitter laughter eventually reached the ears of those who lived on Earth. Despite the enormous gulf between Helliconia and Earth, that response to the labourings of fate met with immediate comprehension.

Between Earth and Helliconia a kind of relay was interposed, the Earth Observation Station called Avernus. The Avernus had its orbit about Helliconia as Helliconia had its orbit about Batalix, and as Batalix had its orbit about Freyr. Avernus was the lens through which terrestrial observers experienced events on Helliconia.

The human beings who worked on the Avernus dedicated their lives to a study of all aspects of Helliconia. That dedication was not of their choosing. They had no alternative.

Beneath that dominating injustice, a general justice prevailed. There was no poverty on the Avernus, no one starving physically. But it was a narrow domain. The spherical station had a diameter of only one thousand metres, most of its in-

habitants living on the inside of the outer shell, and within that compass a kind of inanition prevailed, sapping life of its joy. Looking down does not exalt the spirit.

Billy Xiao Pin was a typical representative of Avernian society. Outwardly, he subscribed to all the norms; he worked without industry; he was engaged to an attractive girl; he took regular prescribed exercise; he had an Advisor who preached to him the higher virtues of acceptance. Yet inwardly Billy craved only one thing. He longed to be down on the Helliconian surface, 1500 kilometres below, to see Queen Myrdem-Inggala, to touch her, speak with her, and make love to her. In his dreams, the queen invited him into her arms.

The distant observers on Earth had other concerns. They followed continuities of which Billy and his kind were unaware. As they watched, suffering, the divorce at Gravabaga-linien, they were able to trace the genesis of that division back to a battle which had taken place to the east of Matrassyl, in a region known as the Cosgatt. JandolAnganol's experiences in the Cosgatt influenced his later actions and led—so it appeared by hindsight—inexorably to divorce.

What became known as the Battle of the Cosgatt took place five tenners—240 days, or half a small year—before the day that the king and MyrdemInggala severed their marriage bonds by the sea.

In the region of the Cosgatt, the king received a physical wound which was to lead to the spiritual severance.

Both the king's life and his reputation suffered in the battle. And they were threatened, ironically, by nothing more than a rabble, the raggle-taggle tribes of Driats.

Or, as the more historically minded of terrestrial observers said, by an innovation. An innovation which changed not only the life of the king and queen but of all their people. A gun.

What was most humiliating for the king was that he held the Driats in contempt, as did every follower of Akhanaba in Borlien and Oldorando. For the Driats, it was conceded, were human—but only just.

The threshold between non-human and human is shadowy.

On one side of it lies a world full of illusory freedoms, on the other a world of illusory captivity. The Others remained animal, and stayed in the jungles. The Madis—tied to a migratory way of life—had reached the threshold of sapience, but remained protognostic. The Driats had just crossed the threshold, and there abided throughout recorded time, like a bird frozen on the wing.

The adverse conditions of the planet, the aridity of their share of it, contributed to the Driats' permanent backwardness. For the Driat tribes occupied the dry grasslands of Thribriat, a country to the southeast of Borlien, across the wide Takissa. The Driats lived among herds of yelk and biyelk which pastured in those high regions during the summer of the great year.

Customs regarded as offensive by the outside world furthered the survival of the Driats. The practised a form of ritual murder, by which the useless members of a family were killed after failing certain tests. In times of near famine, the slaughter of the ancients was often the salvation of the innocents. This custom had given the Driats a bad name among those whose existence was cast in easier pastures. But they were in reality a peaceful people—or too stupid to be warlike in an effective way.

The eruption of various nations southwards along the ranges of the Nktryhk—particularly those warrior nations temporarily banded together behind Unndreid the Hammer—had changed that. Under pressure, the Driats bestirred their bivouacs and went marauding into the lower valleys of Thribriat, which lie in the rain shadow of the massive Lower Nktryhk.

A cunning warlord, known as Darvlish the Skull, had brought order to their ragged ranks. Finding that the simple Driat mind responded to discipline, he formed them into three regiments and led them into the region known as the Cosgatt. His intention was to attack JandolAnganol's capital, Matrassyl.

Borlien already had the unpopular Western Wars on its hands. No ruler of Borlien, not even the Eagle, could hope really to win against either Randonan or Kace, since those

mountainous countries could not be occupied or governed even if conquered.

Now the Fifth Army was recalled from Kace and sent into the Cosgatt. The campaign against Darvlish was not dignified with the title of war. Yet it ate up as much manpower as a war, cost as much, was fought as passionately. Thribriat and the wilderness of the Cosgatt were nearer to Matrassyl than the Western Wars.

Darvlish had a personal animus against JandolAnganol and his line. His father had been a baron in Borlien. He had fought by his father's side when JandolAnganol's father, VarpalAnganol, had appropriated his land. Darvlish had seen his father cut down by a youthful JandolAnganol.

When a leader died in battle, that was the end of fighting. No man would continue. Darvlish's father's army turned and ran. Darvlish retreated to the east with a handful of men. VarpalAnganol and his son pursued them, hunting them like lizards among the stoney mazes of the Cosgatt—until the Borlienese forces refused to go further because no more loot was forthcoming.

After almost eleven years in the wilderness, Darvlish had another chance, and took it: "The vultures shall praise my name!" became his war cry.

Half a small year before the king divorced his queen—before the idea even invaded his mind—JandolAnganol was forced to muster new troops and march at the head of them. Men were in short supply and required pay or the loot the Cosgatt would not yield. He used phagors. The phagor auxiliaries were promised freedom and land in return for service. They were formed into the First and Second Regiments of the Royal Phagorian Guard of the Fifth Army. Phagors were ideal in one respect: both the male and female fought, and their young went into battle with them.

JandolAnganol's father before him had also rewarded ancipital troops with land. It was as a result of this policy —forced on the kings by manpower shortage—that phagors lived more comfortably in Borlien than in Oldorando, and were less subject to persecution.

The Fifth Army marched eastwards, through jungles of

stone. The invaders melted away before it. Most skirmishes were confined to dimday—neither side would fight either during darkness or when both suns were high. But the Fifth Army, under KolobEktofer, was forced to travel during full day.

It travelled through earthquake country, where ravines ran obliquely across its path. Habitation was scanty. The ravines were a tangle of vegetation, but there, if anywhere, water was to be found—as well as snakes, lions, and other creatures. The rest of the land was pocked with umbrella cactus and scrub. Progress across it was slow.

Living off the land was hard. Two kinds of creature dominated the plain, numberless ants and the ground-sloths which lived off the ants. The Fifth caught the sloths and roasted them, but the flesh was bitter in flavour.

Still the cunning Darvlish withdrew his forces, luring the king away from his base. Sometimes he left behind smouldering campfires or dummy forts on elevated sites. Then a day would be wasted as the army investigated them.

Colour-Major KolobEktofer had seen a great explorer in his youth and knew the wilds of Thribriat, and the mountains above Thribriat, where the air finished.

"They will stand, they will stand soon," he told the king one evening when a frustrated Eagle was cursing their difficulties. "The Skull must soon fight, or the tribes will turn against him. He understands that well. Once he knows we're enough from Matrassyl to be without our supply trains, he'll make his stand. And we must be ready for his tricks."

"What kind of tricks?"

KolobEktofer shook his head. "The Skull is cunning, but not clever. He'll try one of his father's old tricks, and much good they did him. We'll be ready."

The next day, Darvlish struck.

As the Fifth Army approached a deep ravine, forward scouts sighted the Driat host drawn up in battle lines on the far bank. The ravine ran from northeast to southwest, and was choked with jungle. It was more than four times a javelin's throw across from one bank to the other.

Using hand signals, the king mustered his army to face the

enemy across the ravine. The Phagorian guards were stationed in front because the ranks of motionless beasts would bring anxiety into the dim minds of the tribesmen.

The tribesmen were of spectral aspect. It was just after dawn: twenty minutes past six. Freyr had risen behind cloud. When the sun broke free of the cloud, it became apparent that the enemy and part of the ravine would be in shadow for the next two or more hours; the Fifth Army would be exposed to Freyr's heat.

Crumbling cliff slopes backed the Driat array, with higher country above. On the royal left flank was a spur of high ground, its angles jutting towards the ravine. A rounded mesa stood between the spur and the cliffs, as if it had been set there by geological forces to guard the Skull's flank. On top of the mesa, the walls of a crude fort could be seen; its walls were of mud, and behind the ramparts an occasional pennant was visible.

The Eagle of Borlien and the colour-major studied the situation together. Behind the colour-major stood his faithful sergeant-at-arms, a taciturn man known as Bull.

"We must find out how many men are in that fort," JandolAnganol said.

"It's one of the tricks he learnt from his father. He hopes we'll waste our time attacking that position. I'll wager no Driats are up there. The pennants we see moving are tied to goats or asokins."

They stood in silence. From the enemy's side of the ravine, under the cliffs, smoke rose in the shadowed air, and an aroma of cooking drifted across to remind them of their own hungry state.

Bull took his officer to one side and muttered in his ear.

"Let's hear what you have to say, sergeant," the king said.

"It's nothing, sire."

The king looked angry. "Let's hear this nothing, then."

The sergeant regarded him with one eyelid drooping. "All I was saying, sire, is that our men will be disappointed. It's the only way a common man—by which I mean myself—can advance himself, sire, to join the army and hope to grab what is going. But these Driats aren't worth looting. What's more

they don't appear to have females—by which I mean women, sire—so that the incentive to attack is . . . well, sire, on the low side."

The king stood confronting him face to face, until Bull backed away a step.

"We'll worry about women when we have routed Darvlish, Bull. He may have hidden his women in a neighbouring valley."

KolobEktofer cleared his throat. "Unless you have a plan, sire, I'd say we have a nigh-on impossible task here. They outnumber us two to one, and although our mounts are faster than theirs, in close combat our hoxneys will be flimsy compared with their yelk and biyelk."

"There can be no question of retreat now that we have caught up with them at last."

"We could disengage, sire, and seek for a more advantageous position from which to attack. If we were on the cliffs above them, for instance—"

"Or could capture them in an ambush, sire, by which I mean—"

JandolAnganol flew into a rage. "Are you officers, or she-goats? Here we are, there stands our country's enemy. What more do you want? Why falter now, when by Freyr-set we can all be heroes?"

KolobEktofer drew himself up. "It is my duty to point out to you the weakness of our position, sire. The smell of some women as booty would have encouraged the men's fighting spirits."

In a passion, JandolAnganol said, "They must not fear a subhuman rabble—with our cross-bowmen we shall rout them in an hour."

"Very good, sire. Perhaps if you would address Darvlish as filth it would increase our men's fighting spirit."

"I shall address him."

A dark look was exchanged between KolobEktofer and Bull, but no more was said, and the former gave orders for the disposition of the army.

The main body of men was dispersed along the ragged lip of the ravine. The left flank was strengthened by the Second Phagorian Guard. The hoxneys, numbering fifty in all, were

in poor condition after their journey. They had been used mainly as pack animals. Now they were unloaded so as to serve as cavalry animals, to impress Darvlish's men. Their loads were piled inside a shallow cave in the spur, and guards put on them, human and phagor. If the day was not carried, those supplies would provide booty for the Driats.

While these dispositions went forward, the wing of shadow suspended from the shoulders of the opposite cliffs was retracting, like a giant sundial set to remind every man of his mortality.

The Skull's forces were revealed as no less imposing than they had seemed when shrouded in blue shade. The ur-human tribes wore a tatterdemalion collection of hides and blankets thrown on their bodies with the same negligence as they threw themselves on their yelks. Some wore bright-striped blankets rolled about their shoulders, to give themselves extra bulk. Some wore knee-high boots, many were barefoot. Their headgear inclined to massive biyelk-fur headpieces—often horned or antlered to denote rank. A feature common to many was the penis, painted or embroidered on their breeches in furious erection to denote their rapacious intent.

The Skull was readily visible. His leather and fur headpiece was dyed orange. Antlers thrust forward from it about his moustachioed face. A sword wound sustained in his earlier battles with JandolAnganol had slashed away his left cheek and the flesh of his lower jaw, leaving him with a permanent death-grin, in which bone and teeth played a part. He managed to look fully as ferocious as his allies, whose fur-fringed eyes and prognathous jaws gave them a naturally savage aspect. A mighty biyelk was his steed.

He raised his javelin above his head and shouted, "The vultures shall praise my name!" A ragged cheer came from the throats about him, echoing from the cliffs behind.

JandolAnganol mounted his hoxney and stood in the stirrups. The shout he gave carried clear to the enemy host.

He called in pidgin Olonets, "Darvlish, have you dared to stand before your face rots away?"

A murmur of sounds rose from both confronting armies. The Skull kneed his biyelk to the edge of the precipice and bellowed across to his enemy.

"Do you hear me, Jandol, you woolly-eared dung-beetle? You were farted out of your father's left instep, so why come you here, daring to face real men? Everyone knows your knackers are knocking together in fear. Crawl away, you dropping, crawl away and take those mangey arse-combings of warriors with you."

His voice echoed back and back again from the cliffs. When the silence was complete, JandolAnganol replied in similar vein.

"Yes, I hear your womanish bleatings, Darvlish of the Dunghills. I hear your claim that those clap-ridden three-legged Others beside you are real men. We all know that real men would never associate with the likes of you. Who could bear the stench of your decay but those barbaric monkeys with phagor-scumber for grandmothers?"

The orange head gear shook in the sunshine.

"Phagor-scumber, is it, you dimday hrattock! You know whereof you talk, since a plateful of phagor-scumber is your daily diet, so much do you worship those horned Batalix-buggerers. Kick them into the ravine and dare to fight fair, you crap-crowned cockroach!"

A roar of savage laughter came from the Driat host.

"If you have so little respect for those who are the climax of creation by comparison with your yelk-yobs, then shake the spiders and scabs from your stinking codpiece and attack us, you cowardly little half-faced Driat dildo!"

This address continued for some while. JandolAnganol was revealed as increasingly at a disadvantage, not having the resources of Darvlish's foul mind on which to draw. While the verbal battle was in progress, KolobEktofer sent off Bull with a small column of men to create a diversion of their own.

The heat intensified. Plagues of stinging things visited both armies. The phagors wilted under the gaze of Freyr and would soon break ranks. The insults wound up.

"Epitaph for an ancipital earth-closet!"

"Catamite of a Cosgatt ground-sloth!"

The Borlienese army started to move along the lip of the ravine, shouting and brandishing their weapons, while the Driat horde did the same on the other side.

KolobEktofer said to the king, "How shall we tackle the mesa fort, sire?"

"I'm convinced you are right. The fort is a decoy. Forget all about it. You lead the cavalry, with infantry and the First Phagorian following. I will march the Second Phagorian behind the mesa, so that the Driats lose sight of us. When you engage them, we will charge from cover and attack their right flank, cutting in behind them. It should then be possible to drive Darvlish into the ravine with a pincer movement."

"I shall carry out your orders, sire."

"Akhanaba be with you, major."

The king spurred his hoxney and rode over to the phagorian guard.

The ancipitals were full of complaint and had to be lectured before they would move. Not comprehending death, they claimed that the air-octaves in the valley did not favour their cause; in the event of defeat, they could not find tether here.

The king addressed them in Hurdhu. This back-of-throat language was not the brand of pidgin Olonets in use between races, but a genuine bridge between human and non-human concepts, said to have originated—like so many innovations —from far Sibornal. Thick with nouns, clotted with gerunds, Hurdhu was palatable alike to human brains and the pale harneys of ancipitals.

Native Ancipital was a language with only one tense, the continuous present. It was not a language adapted to abstract thought; even counting, limited to base three, was finite. Ancipital mathematics, however, dedicated itself to the enumeration of sets of years, and boasted a special eotemporal mode. Eotemporal was a sacred speech-form dealing with the concerns of eternity and purporting to be the language of tether.

Natural death being unknown to phagors, theirs was an *umwelt* largely inaccessible to the understanding of human beings. Even phagors did not easily switch from Native to Eotemporal. Hurdhu, devised to solve such problems, used an intraspecific mode of communication. Yet every sentence in Hurdhu bore a weight of difficulty appropriate to its speakers. Humans required its rigid sentence order, corresponding to Olonets. Phagors required a fixed language in which neolo-

gisms were almost as impossible as abstracts. Thus, the
Hurdhu equivalent for "humanity" was "Sons of Freyr."
"Civilisation" was "many of roofs"; "military formation"
was "spears on move by orders," and so on. It therefore took
JandolAnganol time to make his orders clear to the Second
Phagorian.

When they comprehended fully that the foe confronting
them was befouling their pastures and spitting their runts like
sucking pigs, the stalluns and gillots began to march. They
were almost fearless, although the heat had made them visibly
less alert. With them went their runts, squealing to be carried.

As the Second Phagorian moved, KolobEktofer shouted
orders to the rest of the force. It also got under way. Dust
rose. These movements awakened reciprocal movements in the
Driat company. Those ragged ranks turned from line abreast
into file and marched towards confrontation. The two forces
would meet on the expanse at the foot of the cliffs, between
the throat of the ravine and the mesa.

The pace on both sides began brisk, slowing as an encounter
became inevitable. There was no question of a charge; the
chosen battlefield was strewn with broken boulders me-
morials to the chthonic upheavals which still dominated the
land. It was a question of picking a way towards the enemy.

General shouting gave way to personal insult as the opposed
forces drew nearer. Boots tramped without advancing. They
faced each other, reluctant to close the gap of a few feet between them. Driat lords in the rear were bellowing and prodding, without effect. Darvlish galloped back and forth behind
his men, screaming abuse at them for being scab-devouring
cowards; but the tribesmen were unused to this kind of warfare, preferring quick forays and quick retreats.

Javelins were thrown. At last, sword struck against sword
and blade into body. Insults turned to screams. Birds began to
gather in the sky above. Darvlish galloped the harder. JandolAnganol's detachment appeared round the back of the
mesa, and charged at moderate pace towards the right flank of
the Driats, as planned.

Whereupon, there were triumphant screams from the hillsides above the battle. There, protected by the shade afforded
by the cliffs above them, some of the hags of the tribe—camp

followers, harlots, savage dames—had crouched in ambush. They waited only for the enemy to make the anticipated move and skirt the mesa. Leaping to their feet, they rolled boulders down the slope before them, starting a landslide which roared down upon the Second Phagorian. The phagors froze in dismay and were skittled like ninepins. Many of their children died with them.

The faithful Sergeant Bull had been the first to suspect that tribal women must be close at hand. Women were his particular interest. He had moved with a small column of men while the insult address was at its height. Under cover of umbrella cactus, his column climbed down into the ravine, through its thorn entanglements, and up its farther bank, where they managed to skirt the Driat horde and gain the cliffs without being seen.

Scaling the cliffs was a feat. Bull never gave up. He led his men high above the host, where they found a path dotted with fresh human faeces. They smiled grimly at the discovery, which seemed to confirm their suspicions. They scrambled higher still. When they reached another path, life became easier. They crawled along this track on hands and knees, to avoid being seen by either of the armies below. Their reward was the sight of forty or more tribal women, swaddled in blankets and stinking skirts, squatting on the hillside a little way below them. The boulders piled in front of the witches told their own tale.

The climbers had had to leave their spears behind. Their only weapons were short swords. The hill was too rugged to charge down. Their best hope was to fight the hags with their own weapons, and bombard them with stones and boulders.

These had to be amassed in silence, allowing no telltale stones to roll down the slope to give their position away. Bull's column was still gathering ammunition when the Second Phagorian charged round the mesa, and the hags went into action.

"Let them have it, my bullies," the sergeant shouted. They sent a fusillade of stones flying. The women scattered, screaming, but not before their homemade avalanche was in action. Below them, the phagors were obliterated.

With this encouragement, the Driat horde fought the main

Borlienese force in fiercer spirit, long-swords flashing in the front ranks, javelins being thrown from the rear. The confused body of men broke into struggling groups. Dust rose above the scene. Thuds, shouts, screams sounded.

Bull viewed the scrimmage from his vantage point. He wanted to be down in the thick of it. He could see, intermittently, the gigantic figure of his major, running from group to group, encouraging, wielding his bloody sword without cease. He could also see into the mud fort on top of the mesa. The king had been mistaken. Warriors were hiding there among asokins.

The tide of fighting surrounded the base of the mesa, except where the cliff fall covered the bodies of the phagors of the Second. Bull yelled to warn KolobEktofer of his danger, but nothing could be heard above the din of battle.

Bull ordered his men to climb down the cliffside to the northwest and rejoin the struggle. He lowered himself down the cliff, slithering and falling until he fetched up on hands and knees on the path where the tribal hags had waited. A young woman, hit on the knee by a stone, lay close by. She drew a dagger and flung herself on Bull. He twisted her arm until it cracked and dragged her face down on the ground, kicking her weapon over the edge.

"I'll deal with you later, you strumpet," he said.

The women had left javelins behind in their flight. He picked one up and balanced it, looking towards the mesa. From this lower elevation, he could scarcely glimpse the backs of the men who crouched behind its walls. But one of them, watching through a slit, had sighted him. This man rose. He raised a mysterious weapon to his chest, the other end of which another man steadied over his shoulder.

Tensing himself, Bull flung the javelin with all his might. It flew true at first, but dropped harmlessly outside the walls of the fort.

As he watched in disgust, Bull saw a puff of smoke issue from the weapon the two men were aiming at him. Something like a hornet whistled by his ear.

Groping among the pots and stained rags the women had left behind, Bull found other javelins. He selected one and again stood poised.

The two men on the mesa had also been busy, ramming something in one end of their weapon. They took up their positions as formerly, and again Bull, as he launched his javelin, saw a puff of smoke and heard a bang. Next moment, something struck him a blow in the left shoulder, sending him spinning as if he had been brutally punched. He fell back, sprawling on the path.

The wounded woman hauled herself to her feet, grabbed one of the javelins, and braced herself to thrust it into his undefended stomach. He kicked her legs away, locked his right arm about her neck, and together they rolled down the hillside.

Meanwhile, the musketmen on the mesa rose to full view and commenced to discharge their novel weapons at Kolob-Ektofer's men. Darvlish screamed with delight and flung his biyelk into the fray. He saw that success could be his.

Dismayed by what had happened to the King's force, KolobEktofer fought on, but the matchlock fire was having a devastating effect on his men. Some were hit. None liked the cowardly nature of this innovation which could kill at a distance. KolobEktofer knew immediately that the Driats had purchased these hand-artillery weapons from the Sibornalese, or from other tribes who traded with the Sibornalese. The Fifth were wavering. The only way to win the battle was to silence the fort immediately.

Summoning six hardened old campaigners to his side, he allowed them no time to pause; the struggle was going against the remnants of the king's party. Sword drawn, the colour-major led a scramble up the one accessible path to the top of the mesa, where rubble formed a slope.

As KolobEktofer's party reached the fort, an explosion greeted it. One of the Sibornalese matchlocks had blown up, killing a gunner. At the same time, other guns—there were eleven all told—jammed, or their powder ran out. The Driats were not expert at weapon maintenance. Demoralised, the company allowed themselves to be butchered. They expected no mercy and received none from KolobEktofer. This massacre was observed by the Driats, who surrounded the mesa.

The king's force, or what was left of it, finding its best leaders gone, decided to retire while it was reasonably intact.

Some of KolobEktofer's younger lieutenants made attempts to slash their way to the king's side but, their support failing them, they were themselves cut down. The rest of the force turned and ran for safety, pursued by Driats uttering blood-chilling threats.

Although KolobEktofer and his companions put up a brave fight, they were overwhelmed. Their bodies were hacked to pieces and the pieces kicked into the ravine. Mad with victory despite a high casualty list, Darvlish and his cohorts split into groups to hunt down survivors. By nightfall, only vultures and skulking things were still moving on the field of battle. This was the first time that firearms were used against Borlien.

In a notorious house on the outskirts of Matrassyl, a certain ice trader was waking. The whore whose bed he had shared overnight was already padding about, yawning. The ice trader raised himself on one elbow, scratched his chest, and coughed. The time was just before Freyr-break.

"Any pellamountain, Metty?" he asked.

"It's on the boil," she said in a whisper. Since he had known her, Metty always drank pellamountain tea in the early morning.

He sat on the edge of her bed, peering through the thick twilight at her. He covered himself. Now that desire had gone, he was not proud of his thickening body.

He followed her into the little kitchen-cum-washroom which adjoined her cabin. A basin of charcoal had been blown into life with bellows; a kettle sang on it. The glowing charcoal gave the only light in the room, apart from the tatters of dawn filtering through a broken shutter. By this bad light, he observed Metty as she went about the business of making tea as if she were his wife. Yes, she was getting old, he thought, observing her thin, lined face—probably twenty-nine, maybe even thirty. Only five years his junior. No longer pretty, but good in bed. Not a whore any longer. A retired whore. He sighed. She took only old friends nowadays, and then as a favour.

Metty was dressed, neat and conservative, intending to go to church.

"What did you say?"

"I didn't want to wake you, Krillio."

"It's all right." Affection rising in him, he said reluctantly, "I wouldn't want to leave without saying my thanks and farewells."

"You'll be making back to your wife and family now."

She nodded without looking at him, concentrating on arranging a few leaves of the herb in two cups. Her mouth pursed. Her movements were businesslike—like all her movements, he thought.

The ice trader's boat had docked late the previous day. He had come from Lordryardry with his usual cargo, all the way across the Sea of Eagles, to Ottassol, and then up the stubborn Takissa to Matrassyl. On this trip, besides ice, he had brought his son, Div, to acquaint him with the traders on the route. And to introduce Div to Metty's house, to which he had been coming for as long as he had been trading with the royal palace. His lad was backward in all things.

Old Metty had a girl waiting for Div, an orphan of the Western Wars, slender and fair, with an attractive mouth and clean hair. Almost as inexperienced as Div, you'd say, at first glance. He had looked her over, trying with a coin in her kooni to see if she was free of disease. The copper coin had not turned green, and he had been satisfied. Or almost. He wanted the best for his son, fool though the boy was.

"Metty, I thought you had a daughter about Div's age?"

She was not a communicative woman. "Doesn't this girl suit?"

She flashed him a look as if to say, You mind your business and I'll mind mine. Then perhaps relenting because he was always generous with his money and would never come again, she said, "My daughter Abathy, she wants to better herself, wants to move down to Ottassol. I tell her, there's nothing in Ottassol you won't find here, I said. But she wants to see the sea. All you'll see is sailors, I told her."

"So where is Abathy now?"

"Oh, she's doing well for herself. Got a room, curtains, clothes. . . . Earns a little money, she'll be off south. She soon found herself a rich patron, her being so young and pretty."

The ice trader saw the suppressed jealousy in Metty's eye

and nodded to himself. Ever curious, he couldn't resist asking who the patron was.

She shot one of her sharp glances at gawky young Div and the girl, both standing by the bunk impatient for their elders to go. Pulling a face—mistrusting what she was doing—she whispered a name into the trader's mottled ear.

The trader sighed dramatically. "Well!"

But both he and Metty were too old and wicked to be shocked at anything.

"You going, Da?" Div asked his father.

So then he had left, to let Div get on with it as best he could. What fools men were when young, what clapped-out wrecks when old!

Now, as morning crept in, Div would be sleeping, his head against the girl's, in some lower cabin. But all the pleasure the trader had experienced the night before, performing a fatherly duty, had gone. He felt hungry, but knew better than to ask Metty for food. His legs were stiff—whore's beds were never meant for sleeping.

In a reflective mood, the ice trader realised that he had unwittingly performed a ceremony the previous evening. In handing his son over to the young whore, he was in effect relinquishing his old lusts. And what when lust died? Women had reduced him to beggary once; he had built up a prosperous trade—and never had he stopped lusting after women. But if that central interest withered . . . something had to enter the vacuum.

He thought of his own godless continent of Hespagorat. Yes, Hespagorat needed a god, though certainly not the god of this religion-infested Campannlat! He sighed, wondering why what lay between Metty's narrow thighs should seem so much more powerful than god.

"Off to church, then? Waste of time."

She nodded. Never argue with a client.

Taking the cup she offered, he cradled its warmth in his paw and went to the threshold of the doorless room. There he paused, looking back.

Metty had not lingered over her pellamountain, but diluted it with cold water and gulped it down. Now she pulled on

black gloves which came up to her elbow, adjusting the lace round her wrinkling skin.

Catching his glance, she said, "You can go back to bed. No one stirs in this house yet awhile."

"We've always got on well together, you and I, Metty." Determined to win a word of affection from her, he added, "I get on better with you than with my own wife and daughter."

She heard such confessions every day.

"Well, I hope to see Div next trip, then, Krillio. Goodbye." She spoke briskly, moving forward so that he had to get out of her way. He stepped back into her cabin and she swept past, still fiddling with the top of one glove. She made it clear that the notion of there being any affection between them was just his fantasy. Her mind was on something excluding him.

Carrying his cup back to the bed, he sipped the hot tea. He pushed open the shutter for the pleasure or pain or whatever it was of seeing her walk down the silent street. The crowded houses were pale and closed; something in their aspect disquieted him. Darkness still hung in side alleys. Only one person was to be seen—a man who progressed like a sleepwalker, supporting himself with a hand against the walls. Behind him came a small phagor, a runt, whimpering.

Metty emerged from a door beneath the ice trader's window, took a step into the street. She paused when she saw the man approaching. She knew all about drunks, he thought. Booze and loose women went together, on every continent. But this man was no drunk. Blood ran from his leg to the cobbles.

"I'm coming down, Metty," he called. In another minute, still shirtless, he joined her in the ghostly street. She had not moved.

"Leave him, he's injured. I don't want him in my place. He'll cause trouble."

The injured man groaned, stumbling against the wall. He paused, lifted his head and stared at the ice trader.

The latter gasped in astonishment. "Metty, by the beholder! It's the king, no less . . . King JandolAnganol!"

They ran to him and supported him to the shelter of the whorehouse.

* * *

Few of the king's force returned to Matrassyl. The Battle of the Cosgatt, as it came to be called, inflicted a terrible defeat. The vultures praised Darvlish's name that day.

On his recovery—when he had been nursed at the palace by his devoted queen, MyrdemInggala—the king claimed in the scritina that a great force of enemy had been routed. But the ballads the peddlers sold declared otherwise. The death of KolobEktofer was particularly mourned. Bull was remembered with admiration in the lower quarters of Matrassyl. Neither returned home.

In those days when JandolAnganol lay in his chamber, faint from his wounds, he came to the conclusion that if Borlien was to survive he must form a closer alliance with the neighbouring members of the Holy Pannovalan Empire, in particular Oldorando and Pannoval. And he must at all costs acquire that hand artillery which the bandits of the borderland had used so devastatingly.

All this he discussed with his advisors. In their concurrence was laid the seeds of that plan for a divorce and a dynastic marriage which was to bring JandolAnganol to Gravabagalinien half a year later. Which was to estrange him from his beautiful queen. Which was to estrange him from his son. And which, by an even odder fatality, was to confront him with another death, this one attributed to the protognostic race known as the Madis.

V

THE WAY OF THE MADIS

The Madis of the continent of Campannlat were a race apart.
Their customs were separate from those of either mankind or
the ancipital kind. And their tribes were separate from each
other.

One tribe was progressing slowly westwards, through a
region of Hazziz which had become desert, several days' journey north of Matrassyl.

The tribe had been on its travels for longer than anyone
could tell. Neither the protognostics themselves nor any of the
nations which saw them pass could say when or where the
Madis began their journeyings. They were nomads. They gave
birth while on the move, they grew up and married on the
move, they were finally lost to life on the move.

Their word for Life was Ahd, meaning the Journey.

Some humans who took an interest in the Madis—and they
were few—believed that it was Ahd which kept the Madis
apart. Others believed that it was their language. That language was a song, a song where melody seemed to dominate

words. There was about the Madi tongue a complexity and yet
an incompleteness which seemed to bind the tribe to its way,
and which certainly entangled any human who tried to learn it.

A young human was trying to learn it now.

He had made attempts to speak hr'Madi'h when a child.
Now in adolescence, his situation was more serious, and his
lessons correspondingly more earnest.

He waited beside a stone pillar on which was inscribed a god
symbol. It marked one boundary of a land-octave or health-
line, although for that ancient superstition he cared little.

The Madis approached in irregular groups or in file. Their
low melody preceded them. They passed him by without looking at him, though many of the adults stroked in passing the
stone by which he stood. They wore, men and women alike,
sacklike garments loosely tied at the waist. The garments had
high stiff hoods which could be raised against bad weather,
giving their wearers a grotesque appearance. Their wooden
shoes were primitively cut, as if the feet which had to bear
them through Ahd were of no consideration.

The youth could see the trail winding back like a thread
through the semidesert. There was no end to it. Dust hung
over it, veiling it slightly. The Madis moved with a murmur of
protognostic language. At any time, someone was singing to
some others, the notes passing along the line like blood
through an artery. The youth had once assumed this discourse
to be a commentary on the way. Now he inclined to the idea
that it was some kind of narrative; but what the narrative
might concern he had no idea, since for the Madis there was
neither past nor future.

He awaited his moment.

He searched the faces coming towards him as if looking for
someone loved and lost, anticipating a sign. Although the
Madis were human in physical appearance, their countenances
held a tantalising quality, their protognostic innocence, which
reminded those who looked on them of animal faces or the
faces of flowers.

There was one common Madi face. Its eyeballs protruded,
with soft brown irises nestled in thick eyelashes. Its nose was
pronouncedly aquiline, reminiscent of a parrot's beak. The
forehead receded, the lower jaw was somewhat undershot.

The whole effect was startlingly beautiful in the youth's eyes. He was reminded of a lovely mongrel dog he had worshipped as a child, and also of the white-and-brown flowers of the dogthrush bush.

By one distinguishing mark could the male face be told from the female. The male had two bosses high on their temples and two on their jaws. Sometimes these bosses were dappled with hair. Once, the youth had seen a male with short stubs of horn emerging from the bosses.

The youth looked with fondness on the array of faces as it passed. He responded to the Madi simplicity. Yet hatred burned in his harneys. He wished to kill his father, King JandolAnganol of Borlien.

Motion and murmur flowed past him. Suddenly, there was his sign!

"Oh, I thank you!" he exclaimed, and moved forward.

One of the Madis, a female driving arang, had turned her gaze away from the trail, to look directly at him, giving him the Look of Acceptance. It was an anonymous look, gone as soon as it came, a gleam of intelligence not to be sustained. He fell in beside the female, but she paid him no further attention; the Look had been passed.

He had become a part of the Ahd.

With the migrants went their animals, pack animals such as the yelk, trapped in the animals' great summer grazing grounds, as well as the semi-domesticated animals: several kinds of arang, sheep and fhlebiht—all hoofed animals— together with dogs and asokins, which seemed as dedicated to the migratory life as their masters.

The youth, who called himself only Roba and detested the title of prince, remembered with scorn how the bored ladies of his father's court would yawn and wish they were "as free as the wandering Madi." The Madi, with no more consciousness than a clever dog, were enslaved by the pattern of their lives.

Every day, camp was struck before dawn. At sunrise, the tribe would be off, moving to an untidy pattern. Throughout the day, rest periods occurred along the column, but the rests were brief and took no account of whether two suns or one ruled in the sky. Roba became convinced that such matters did not enter their minds; they were eternally bound to the trail.

Some days, there were obstacles on the route, a river to be crossed, a mountainside. Whatever it was, the tribe would accomplish it in their undemonstrative way. Often a child was drowned, an old person killed, a sheep lost. But the Ahd went on, and the harmony of their discourse did not cease.

At Batalix-set, the tribe came to a slow halt.

Then were chanted over and over the two words that meant "water" and "wool." If there was a Madi god, he was composed of water and wool.

The men saw to it that all the animals of their herd had water before they prepared the main meal of the day. The women and girls took down crude looms from their pack animals and on them wove rugs and garments of dyed wool.

Water was their necessity, wool their commodity.

"Water is Ahd, wool is Ahd." The song had no precision, but it recognised truth.

The men sheared the wool from their animals and dyed it, the women from the age of four walked along the trail teasing the wool onto their distaffs. All the articles they made were made from wool. The wool of the long-legged fhlebiht was finest and went to make satara gowns fit for queens.

The woven articles were either stowed on pack animals or else worn by male and female alike under their drab outer garments. Later, they were traded at a town along the route, Distack, Yicch, Oldorando, Akace. . . .

After the evening meal, eaten as dusk thickened, all the tribe slept huddled together, male, female, animal.

The females came on heat rarely. When it was the time of the female Roba travelled with, she turned to him for her satisfaction, and he found delight in that fluttering embrace. Her orgasms were marked by peals of song.

The path the Madis took was as pre-ordained as the pattern of their days. They journeyed to the east or to the west by different trails; those trails sometimes crossed, sometimes wandered a hundred miles apart. A journey in one direction took an entire small year, so that such knowledge of passing time as they had was spoken of in terms of distance—that understanding was Roba's entry point into hr'Madi'h.

That the Journey had been in progress for centuries, and

perhaps for centuries before that, was evidenced by the flora
growing along its way. These flower-faced creatures, who
owned nothing but their animals, nevertheless dropped things
all along their route. Faeces and seeds were scattered. As they
walked, the women were in the habit of plucking herbs and
plants such as afram, henna, purple hellebore, and mantle.
These yielded dyes for their rugs. The seeds of the plants were
shed, along with the seeds of food plants like barley. Burrs
and spores adhered to the coats of the animals.

The Journey temporarily laid waste the grazing along its entire length. Yet it also caused the earth to bloom.

Even in semi-desert, the Madis walked through an avenue of
trees, bushes, herbs which they themselves had accidentally
planted. Even on barren mountainsides, flowers blossomed
which were otherwise seen only in the plains. The eastward
and westward avenues—called ucts by the Madis—ran like rib-
bons, sometimes intertwined, right across the equatorial continent of Helliconia, marking an original trail of scumber.

Endlessly walking, Roba forgot his human connections and
the hatred of his father. The Journey through the ucts was his
life, his Ahd. At times, he could deceive himself and believe
that he understood the murmured narrative that passed
through the daily bloodstream.

Although he preferred migratory life to the scheming life of
the court, it was a struggle to adapt himself to Madi eating
habits. They retained a fear of fire, so their cooking was
primitive, though they made a flat unleavened bread, called a
la'hrap, by spreading a dough over hot stones. This la'hrap
they stored to eat either fresh or stale. With it went blood and
milk drawn from their animals. Occasionally, during feasts,
they ate raw pulverised meat.

Blood was important to them. Roba wrestled with a whole
nexus of words and phrases which had something to do with
journeys, blood, food, and god-in-blood. He often meant to
clarify his thoughts at night, to write down his knowledge
when all was quiet; but directly they had eaten their frugal
meal, everyone fell asleep. Roba also slept.

No power could stop his eyelids closing. He slept without
dreams, as he imagined his travelling companions did. Per-

haps if they ever learnt to dream, he thought, they would turn
that mysterious corner which separated their existence from a
human one.

When the female, having clung to him for her brief ecstasy,
fell away, he wondered in the moment before sleep if she was
happy. There was no way he could ask or she answer. And he?
He had been lovingly brought up by his mother, the queen of
queens, and yet he knew that in all human happiness lies an
unremitting sorrow. Perhaps the Madis escaped that sorrow
by failing to become human.

Mist coiled over the Takissa and over Matrassyl, but above
the city the suns burned. Because the air stifled in the palace,
Queen MyrdemInggala lay in her hammock.

She had spent the morning dealing with supplicants. Many
of her citizens were known to her by name. Now she dreamed
in the shade of a small marble pavilion. Her reveries were of
the king, who had recovered from his wound and then, without a word of explanation, had gone away on a journey—
some said upriver to Oldorando. She had not been invited. Instead, he had taken with him the orphaned phagor runt, a survivor, like the king, of the Battle of the Cosgatt.

Beside the pavilion, MyrdemInggala's chief lady-in-waiting,
Mai TolramKetinet, played with Princess Tatro. She amused
her with a painted wooden bird which flapped its wings. Other
toys and storybooks lay scattered on the tesserae of the
pavilion.

Scarcely aware of her daughter's prattle, the queen allowed
the bird to fly free in her mind. She had it flutter up into the
branches of a gwing-gwing tree, where the ripe fruit hung in
bunches. In the magic of her thought, Freyr became a
harmless gwing-gwing. Its threatening advance towards the
world became nothing more than the fructiferous ripeness.
Under the same magic which drowsed beneath the queen's
lids, she both was and was not the soft gwing-gwing flesh.

Their flesh came down and touched the ground. The globes
of their summery weight were furred. They rolled under the
hedges, sprawled in the velvets of the moss beneath, their
cheeks gentle against the verdure. And the wild boar came.

It was a boar but it was her husband, her master, her king.

The boar pranced upon the fruit, crushed it, devoured it, until juices suppurated at its chin. Even as she filled the garden with her syruped thought, she prayed to Akhanaba to deliver her from the rape—or, rather, to let her enjoy and not to punish her for her excess. Comets flew through the sky, mists boiled above the city, the burn of Freyr fell on them because she allowed herself to dream of the great boar.

The king was upon her now in reverie. His immense bristled back arched over her. There were nights, there were nights in the summer, when he would call her to his bedchamber. She would go barefoot, anointed. Mai trailed beside her with the whale-oil lamp, its flame carried in a bubble of glass like some incandescent wine. She would appear before him knowing that she was the queen of queens. Her eyes would be wide and dark, her nipples already aglow, her thighs alive with an orchard of gwing-gwings ripe for the tusk.

The pair of them would throw themselves into their embraces with a passion which was ever new. He would call her by her pet name, like a child calling in its sleep. Their flesh, their souls, seemed to rise up like steam from two hot streams mingling.

Mai TolramKetinet's duty was to stand beside their couch and throw a light upon their transports. They were not to be denied the sight of each other's naked body.

Sometimes the girl, staid though she was in her daylight nature, would be overcome, and thrust her hand into her own kooni. Then JandolAnganol, ruthless in his khmir, would harvest the girl down beside the queen and take her as if there were nothing to choose between the two women.

Of this, no word was ever spoken by the queen in daylight. But her intuition informed her that Mai told her brother, now the general of the Second Army, what occurred; she knew by the way that young general looked at her. Sometimes in her hammock, daydreaming, she wondered how it would be if Hanra TolramKetinet also joined in those encounters in the king's bedchamber.

The khmir sometimes failed. On occasions, when dusk moths flew and her lamp again waxed incandescent, JandolAnganol came by secret passage to where she lay. No one

else had his footfall. It was, she thought, at once rapid and in-
decisive, the very footprint of his character. He flung himself
upon her. The gwing-gwings were there, but not the tusk. Fury
would seize him at this betrayal of his own body. In a court
where he trusted few, that was the ultimate treason.

Then intellectual khmir would seize him. He would flagel-
late himself with a hatred as intense as his previous passion.
The queen screamed and wept. In the morning, slave women
would go down on their knees, bitter-mouthed and sly-eyed,
to mop his blood from the tiles beside her bed.

To this characteristic of her master's, the queen of queens
never made reference. Not to Mai TolramKetinet, not to the
other ladies of the court. Like his footfall, it was part of him.
He was as impatient with his own desires as he was with those
of his courtiers. He could not be still enough to face himself,
and while his wounds healed he had been alone with his
thoughts.

Summoning more branches of gwing-gwings to soften what
she was saying to herself, she told herself that the vein of
weakness was part of his strength. He would be weaker without it. But she could never tell him she understood. She
screamed instead. And the next night, the humpbacked animal
would be rooting among the hedgerows again.

Sometimes in the day, when it seemed the gwing-gwings
blushed for their devouring, she would plunge naked into her
pool, sinking down into the embrace of the water—and looking upwards would see the bright scattered blast of Freyr
across the surface. One day—oh, she knew it in her eddre—
Freyr would come blasting down into the depths of the pool to
burn her for the intensity of her desires. Good Akhanaba,
spare me. I am the queen of queens, I too have khmir.

And of course she watched him in the day.

Talking with his courtiers, with wise men or fools—or perhaps even with that ambassador from Sibornal who fixed her
with a look she feared—the king would stretch forth a hand
and pluck an apple from a bowl. He would snatch without
looking. It might be one of the cinnabrian apples, brought
upriver from Ottassol. He would bite into it. He would eat
it—not as his courtiers ate apples, who nibbled round the flesh
and left a fat central spindle to be thrown on the floor. The

King of Borlien ate whole-heartedly, yet without apparent enjoyment, and devoured the entire fruit, skin, flesh, core, plump brown pips. All would go, ground down, while he talked. He would then wipe his beard, apparently never giving a thought to the fruit. And secretly MyrdemInggala would think of the boar in the hedges.

Akhanaba punished her for her wanton thoughts. He punished her with the understanding that she would never know Jan, however close they were. By the same token—this was more painful—he would never know her as she desired to be known. As Hanra TolramKetinet mysteriously knew her, without a word being exchanged.

The spell of her reverie was broken by approaching footsteps. Opening one eye, MyrdemInggala saw the chancellor approaching. SartoriIrvrash was the only man in the court allowed into her private garden; it was a right she had granted him on the death of his wife. From her perspective of twenty-four and a half years, SartoriIrvrash was old at thirty-seven years and several tenners. He would not interfere with her women.

Yet she shut her eye again. This was the time of day when he returned from a certain nearby quarry. JandolAnganol had told her, laughing harshly, about the experiments SartoriIrvrash carried out on wretched captives in cages. His wife had been killed by those experiments.

His bald pate shone in the sun as he removed his hat to Tatro and Mai. The child liked him. The queen would not intervene.

SartoriIrvrash bowed to the recumbent form of the queen, and then to her daughter. He spoke to the child as if she were an adult, which possibly explained why Tatro liked him. There were few people in Matrassyl who could claim to be his friend.

This retiring man, of medium height and dishevelled dress, had been a power in Borlien for a long while. Thus when the king lay incapacitated by the wound received in the Cosgatt, SartoriIrvrash had ruled in his stead, directing the affairs of state from his untidy desk. If no one was his friend, all respected him. For SartoriIrvrash was disinterested. He played no favourites.

He was too solitary for favourites. Even the death of his

wife appeared to have made no difference to his regime. He did not hunt or drink. He rarely laughed. He was too cautious to be caught in a mistake.

Nor had he even the customary swarm of relations on whom to bestow patronage. His brothers were dead, his sister lived far away. SartoriIrvrash passed muster as that impossible creature, a man without faults, serving a king who was full of them.

In a religious court, he had only one point of vulnerability. He was an intellectual and an atheist.

Even the insult of his atheism had to be overlooked. He tried to convert nobody to his way of thinking. When not occupied with affairs of state, he worked on his book, filtering truth from lies and legends. But that did not stop him occasionally showing a more human side of his nature and reading fairy tales to the princess.

SartoriIrvrash's enemies in the scritina often wondered how he—so cold-blooded—and King JandolAnganol—so hot-blooded—kept from each other's throat. The fact was, SartoriIrvrash was a self-effacing man; he knew how to swallow insults. And he was too remote from other people to be offended by them—until pressed too far. That time would come, but it was not yet.

"I thought you weren't coming, Rushven," said Tatro.

"Then you must learn to have more faith in me. I always appear when I am needed."

Soon Tatro and SartoriIrvrash were sitting together in the pavilion and the princess was thrusting one of her books at him, demanding a story. He read the one which always made the queen uneasy, the fairy tale of the silver eye.

"Once upon a time, there was a king who ruled over the kingdom of Ponptpandum in the West, where all the suns set. The people and phagors of Ponptpandum feared their king for they thought he had magic powers.

"They longed to be rid of him, and to have a king who would not oppress them, but nobody knew what to do.

"Whenever the citizens thought of a scheme, the king found out. He was such a great magician that he conjured up a huge silver eye. This eye floated in the sky all night, spying on everything that happened in the unhappy kingdom. The eye

opened and shut. It came fully open ten times every year, as everyone knew. Then it saw most.

"When the eye saw a conspiracy, the king knew about it. He would then execute all the conspirators, whether men or phagors, outside the palace gate.

"The queen was sad to see such cruelty, but she could do nothing. The king swore that, whatever else he did, he would never harm his lovely queen. When she begged him to be merciful, he did not strike her, as he would have done anyone else, even his advisors.

"In the lowest dungeon of the castle was a room guarded by seven blind phagor guards. They had no horns, because all phagors when they grew up sawed off their horns at the annual fair in Ponptpandum, so as to try and look more human. The guards let the king enter the cell.

"In the cell lived a gillot, an old female phagor. She was the only horned phagor in the kingdom. She was the source of all the king's magic. By himself, the king was nothing. Every evening, the king would beseech the gillot to send the silver eye up into the sky. Every evening, she did as requested.

"Then the king saw all that was happening in his kingdom. He also asked the old gillot many searching questions about nature, which she answered without fail.

"One night when it was bitterly cold she said to him, 'O King, why do you seek such knowledge?'

" 'Because there is power in knowledge,' replied the king. 'Knowledge sets people free.'

"To this the gillot said nothing. She was a wizard and yet she was his prisoner. At last she said in a terrible voice, 'Then the time has come to set me free.'

"At her words, the king fell into a swoon. The gillot walked from her dungeon, and commenced to climb the stairs. Now the queen had long wondered why her husband went to an underground room every night. On this night, her curiosity had got the better of her. She was descending the stairs to spy on him when she encountered the gillot in the dark.

"The queen screamed in terror. In order that she should not scream again, the phagor struck her a heavy blow and killed her. Roused by the sound of his queen's much-loved voice, the king woke and ran upstairs. Finding what had occurred, he

drew his sword and slew the phagor.

"Even as she fell to the ground, the silver eye in the sky began to spiral away. Farther and farther it went, growing smaller and smaller, until it was lost to view. At last the people knew they were free, and the silver eye was never seen again."

Tatro was silent for a moment.

"Isn't that an awful bit where the gillot gets killed?" she said. "Would you read it again?"

Raising herself on one elbow, the queen said, teasingly, "Why do you read Tatro that silly story, Rushven? It's a pure fairy story."

"I read it because Tatro likes it, ma'am," he said, smoothing his whiskers, as he often did in her presence, and smiling.

"Knowing your opinion of the ancipital race, I cannot imagine you relish the notion that humankind once looked up to phagors for wisdom."

"Madam, what I relish about the story is that kings once looked up to others for wisdom."

MyrdemInggala clapped her hands with pleasure at the answer. "Let us hope that that at least is no fairy story. . . ."

In the course of their Ahd, the Madis came once more to Oldorando, and to the city bearing that name.

A sector of the city called the Port, beyond the South Gate, was set aside for the migrants. There they made one of their rare halts, for a few days. Celebrations of a modest sort took place. Spiced arang were eaten, elaborate zyganke were danced.

Water and wool. In Oldorando, the garments and rugs woven during the Journey were bartered with merchants for a few necessities. One or two human merchants had gained the trust of the Madis. The tribes always needed pans and goat bells; they were not workers of metal.

It also happened that some members of the tribe always arranged to remain in Oldorando, either until the tribe next returned or permanently. Lameness or illness was reason for leaving the Ahd.

Some years earlier, a lame Madi girl had left the Ahd and gained employment as a sweeper in the palace of King Sayren

Stund. Her name was Bathkaarnet-she. Bathkaarnet-she had the traditional Madi face, part flower, part bird, and she would sweep where she was put to sweep without tiring, unlike the lazy Oldorandans. While she swept, small birds would cluster round her without fear, and listen to her song.

This the king saw from his balcony. In those days, Sayren Stund had not surrounded himself with protocol and religious advisors. He had Bathkaarnet-she brought to him. Unlike most Madis, this girl had an active gaze which could focus like a human's. She was very humble, which suited the nervous Sayren Stund.

He decided to have her taught Olonets, and a good master was employed. No progress was made until the king was inspired to sing to the girl. She sang in response. More language came to her, but she could never speak, only sing.

This shortcoming would have maddened many. It pleased the king. He found that her father had been human and had joined the journey when a youth, running away from slavery.

The king, despite contrary advice, married Bathkaarnet-she, converting her to his faith. Soon she bore him a two-headed son, who died. Then she bore two normal daughters who lived. First Simoda Tal, and then the mercurial Milua Tal.

Prince RobaydayAnganol had heard this story when a boy. Now, as Roba, and dressed as a Madi, he made his way from the Port to one of the gates at the rear of the palace. He wrote a note to Bathkaarnet-she, which a servant bore away.

He stood waiting patiently in the heat, where a nocturnal-flowering zaldal climbed and spread. To the prince, Oldorando was a strange city. Not a phagor was to be seen.

His intention was to learn as much about the Madis as he could from the Madi queen before returning to the Journey. He had determined that he would be the first man to sing the Madi tongue fluently. Before leaving his father's court, he had often talked to Chancellor SartoriIrvrash, who had inspired in him a love of learning—another reason for his falling out with his father, the king.

Roba waited by the gate. He had kissed the rough cheek of his female, talced with the dust of the roadside, knowing that he could never find her again even when he rejoined the

Journey. For then the Look of Acceptance might be flashed by someone else—or, if by her again, how was he to recognise her for sure? He felt strongly that the quality of individuality was a precious thing, granted only to humans and, to a lesser degree, to phagors.

After an hour, he saw the servant returning, watched his self-important human strut, so unlike that Madi shamble which carried them safe across a lifetime. The man walked round two sides of the palace square, under shady cloisters, rather than brave the breath of Freyr in the open.

"Very well, the queen will grant you five minutes' audience. Be sure to bow to her, you rogue."

He slipped through the side gate and began to walk across the square, using the Madi shamble, which kept the spine supple. A man was walking towards him with a hesitant kind of arrogance which needed no display. It was his father, King JandolAnganol.

Roba removed his old sack hood and bent down, sweeping the ground with it, using languid but steady strokes, Madi-fashion. JandolAnganol passed him, talking animatedly to another man, and never even gave him a glance. Roba straightened up and continued on his way to the queen.

The lame queen sat in a silver swing. Her toes were brown and ringed. She was rocked by a green-clad lackey. The room in which she greeted Roba was overgrown with vegetation, among which pecubeas flitted and preets sang.

When she discovered who he was, as she soon did, she refused to sing of her earlier life and instead warbled in fulsome terms about JandolAnganol.

This was not to Roba's taste. A kind of madness came over him, and he said to the queen, "I want to sing the song of your birth-tongue. But your song is of my birth-curse. To know that man you praise, you must become his son. There's no room for flesh and blood in that man's heart, only for abstracts. Religion and country. Religion and country, not Tatro and Roba, in his harneys."

"Kings believe in such matters. I know it. I know they are set above us to dream of grand things we cannot," the queen sang. "It's empty where kings live."

"Grandeur's a stone," he said emphatically. "Under that

stone he imprisons his own father. And I, his own son—he would imprison me for two years in a monastery. Two years to teach me grandeur! A vow of silence in a Matrassyl monastery, to introduce me to that stone Akhanaba . . .

"How could I bear it? Am I a rickyback or slug, to crawl beneath a stone? Oh, my father's heart is stone, so I ran, ran like a footless wind, to join the Ahd of your kind, kind queen."

Then Bathkaarnet-she began to sing. "But my kind are the scum of the earth. We have no intelligence, only ucts, and in consequence no guilt feelings. What do you call that? No conscience. We can only walk, walk, walk our lives away—except for me who luckily am lame.

"My dear husband, Sayren, has taught me the value of religions, which is unknown to poor ignorant Madis. Fancy to live for centuries and not know that we exist only by the grace of the All-Powerful! So I respect your father for all his religious feelings. He scourges himself every day he is here."

As the singing voice ceased, Roba asked bitterly, "And what is he doing here? Looking for me, a wandering part of his kingdom?"

"Oh, no, no." There was fluting laughter. "He has been here conferring with Sayren, and with Church dignitaries from distant Pannoval. Yes, I saw them, they spoke to me."

He stood before her, in such a way that the lackey had to swing her more gently. "Who confers and never speaks? Who has—and still seeks?"

"Who can tell what kings confer about?" she sang.

One of the bright birds fluttered into his face, and he beat it down.

"You must know what they are planning, Your Majesty."

"Your father has a wound. I see it in his face," she sang. "He needs his nation to be powerful, to smite his enemies to the dust. For that, he will sacrifice even his queen, your mother."

"How will he sacrifice her?"

"He will sacrifice her to history. Is not a woman's life less than man's destiny? We are nothing but lame things in the hands of men. . . ."

*　　　*　　　*

His ways became dark. He had presentiments of evil. His reason fled. He tried to return to the Madis and forget human treachery. But the Ahd required peace or at least absence of mind. After some days of walking, he left the uct and wandered away into the wilderness, living in forest trees or in dens lions had forsaken. He talked to himself in a language all his own. He lived on fruits and fungi and things that crawled beneath stones.

Among the things that crawled beneath stones was a small crustacean, a rickyback. This little humpbacked creature had a tiny face peering from under its chitin shell, and twenty delicate white legs. Rickybacks congregated under logs and stones in their dozens, all packed snug together.

He lay watching them, playing with them, lying on his side with one arm crooked to support his head, flipping them gently over with a finger. He marvelled at their lack of fear, at their laziness. What was their purpose? How could they exist, doing so little?

But these little creatures had survived through the ages. Whether Helliconia was unbearably hot or unbearably cold—SartoriIrvrash had told him this—the rickybacks remained close to the ground, hiding away, and had probably done nothing more since time began.

They were wonderful to him, even as they lay kicking their dainty limbs in ridiculous attempts to right themselves.

His wonder was replaced by unease. What could they be doing if the All-Powerful had not put them here?

As he lay there, the thought was as powerfully presented to him as if someone spoke the words that he might be mistaken and his father might be right; perhaps there was an All-Powerful directing human affairs. In which case, much that had seemed to him wicked was good, and he was deeply mistaken.

He stood up, trembling, forgetting the insignificant creatures at his feet.

He looked up at the thick clouds in the sky. Had someone spoken?

If there was an Akhanaba, then he must surrender his will to the god. Whatever the All-Powerful decreed must be done. Even murder was justified, if the end was Akhanaba's.

At least he believed in the original beholder, that mother figure who saw to the earth and all its works. That misty figure, identified with the world itself, took precedence over Akhanaba.

The days went by, and the suns travelled across them, scorching him. He was lost to the wilderness, hardly knowing he was lost, speaking to no one, seeing no one. There were nondads about, evasive as thought, but he had no business with them. He was listening to the voice of Akhanaba, or the beholder.

As he wandered, a forest fire overtook him. He plunged in a brook full-length, watching the roaring machine of conflagration rush up one slope of a hill and down the other, exhaling energy. In the furnace of its flames he saw the face of a god; the smoke trailing out behind was the god's beard and hair, grey with cosmic wisdom. Like his father, the vision in its passage left destruction behind it. He lay with half his face in the water and both eyes staring, one under water, one above, seeing two universes lit by the visitant. When the visitant had gone by, he rose, going up the hill as if drawn in the wake of the monster, to stagger among smouldering bushes.

The fire god had left a trail of black. He would see it ahead, still pursuing its course like a whirlwind of vengeance.

Prince RobaydayAnganol began to run, laughing as he went. He was convinced that his father was too powerful to kill. But there were those near him who could be killed, whose deaths would lessen him.

The thought roared into his mind like fire, and he recognised it for the voice of the All-Powerful. No longer did he feel pain; he had become anonymous, like a true Madi.

Caught up in the uct of his own life, RobaydayAnganol saw the stars wheel over his head every night. He saw as he fell asleep YarapRombry's Comet blazing in the north. He saw the fleet star Kaidaw pass overhead.

Robayday's keen eyes picked out the phases of Kaidaw when it was at zenith. But it moved rapidly, traversing the sky from south to north. As he watched it hurl itself towards the horizon, it was no longer possible to distinguish the Kaidaw's

disc; it sank to a pinpoint of bright light and then disappeared.

To its inhabitants, the Kaidaw was known as the Avernus, Earth Observation Station Avernus. During this period, it was home for some six thousand inhabitants, men, women, children, androids. The human beings were divided into six scholarly families or clans. Each clan studied some aspect of the planet below, or of its sister planets. The information they gathered was signalled back to Earth.

The four planets which circled about the G-class star known as Batalix comprised the great discovery of Earth's interstellar age. Interstellar exploration—"conquest," as the peoples of that arrogant age called it—was conducted at enormous expense. The expense became so ruinous that interstellar flight was eventually abandoned.

Yet it yielded a transformation in the human spirit. A more integrated approach to life meant that people no longer sought to exact more than their fair share from a global production system now much better understood and controlled. Indeed, interpersonal relationships took on a kind of sanctity, once it was realised that, of a million planets within reasonable distance from Earth, not one could sustain human life or match the miraculous diversity of Earth itself.

With emptiness the universe was prodigal beyond belief. With organic life, it was niggardly. As much as anything, it was the scale of desolation of the universe which caused mankind to turn with abhorrence from interstellar flight. By then, however, the planets of the Freyr-Batalix system had been discovered.

"God built Earth in seven days. He spent the rest of his life doing nothing. Only in his old age did he stir himself and create Helliconia." So said one terrestrial wag.

So the planets of the Freyr-Batalix system were of prime importance to the spiritual existence of Earth. And of those planets, Helliconia was paramount.

Helliconia was not unlike Earth. Other human beings lived there, breathed air, suffered, enjoyed, and died. The ontological systems of both planets were parallel.

Helliconia was a thousand light-years from Earth. To travel

from one world to the other in the most technologically advanced starship took over fifteen hundred years. Human mortality was too frail to sustain such a journey.

Yet a deep need in the human spirit, a wish to identify with something beyond itself, sought to sustain a bond between Earth and Helliconia. Despite all the difficulties imposed by the enormous gulfs of space and time, a permanent watch post was built in orbit about Helliconia, the Earth Observation Station. Its duty was to study Helliconia and send back its findings to Earth.

So began a long one-sided involvement. That involvement exercised one of mankind's most attractive gifts, the power of empathy. Ordinary terrestrials turned every day—or would turn long hence—to learn how their friends and heroes fared on the surface of the remote planet. They feared phagors. They watched developments at the court of JandolAnganol. They wrote in the Olonets script; many people spoke one or other of the languages. To some extent, Helliconia had unwittingly colonised Earth.

This bond continued long after the end of Earth's great interstellar age.

Indeed, Helliconia, prize of that age, was another cause of its decline. There it was, this world of splendour and terror, as beautiful as any dream—and to step on it was death for any human. Not immediate, but certain death.

Pervading the atmosphere of Helliconia were viruses which, through long processes of adaptation, were harmless to the natives. At least they were harmless throughout most of the Great Year. But to anyone from Earth, those unfilterable viruses formed a barrier like the sword of the angel who—in an ancient Earth myth—guarded the entrance to the Garden of Eden.

And to many people aboard the Avernus, a garden of Eden was what the planet below them resembled, at least when the slow cruel centuries of the winter of the Great Year had passed.

The Avernus had its parks, with streams and lakes, and a thousand ingenious electronic simulations with which to chal-

lenge its young men and women. But it remained an artificial world. Many aboard it felt that their lives remained artificial lives, without the zest of reality.

This sense of artificiality was particularly oppressive in the case of the Pin clan. For the Pin clan was in charge of cross-continuities. Their responsibility was mainly sociological.

The chief task of the Pin clan was to record the unfolding of the lives of one or two families through the generations throughout the 2592 Earth years of the Great Year and beyond. Such data, impossible to collect on Earth, was of great scientific value. It meant also that the Pin family built up an especially close identification with their subjects below.

That proximity was reenforced by the knowledge which shadowed all their days—the knowledge that Earth was irrecoverably far away. To be born on station was to be born into unremitting exile. The first law governing life on the Avernus was that there was no going home.

Computerborgoid ships occasionally arrived from Earth. These linkships, as they were called, always provided emergency accommodation in which humans could travel. Possibly some faint hope existed on Earth that one of the Avernians would be able, as a result of new methods, to return to Earth; more likely, the ships, old-fashioned in design, had never been modernised. The gulf of space and time made the thought of such passage a mockery; even bodies sunk deep in cryogenic sleep fell into decay over one and a half thousand years.

Helliconia lay incomparably nearer than Earth. Yet the viruses kept Helliconia sacrosanct.

Existence on the Avernus was utopian—that is to say, pleasant, equable, and dull. There were no terrors to face, no injustices, no shortages, and few sudden shocks. There was no revelatory religion; religious faith hardly commended itself to a society whose duty it was to watch the upheavals on the world below. The metaphysical agonies and ecstasies of individual egos were ruled incorrect.

Yet to some Avernians of every generation, their world remained a prison, its orbit an uct going nowhere. Certain members of the Pin clan, looking down on poor crazed Roba wandering in the wilderness, were consumed by envy of his freedom.

The intermittent arrival of link-ships merely emphasised their oppression. In earlier days, a link-ship had caused a riot. It had come full of cassettes of news—ancient news of cartels, sports, nations, artifacts, names, all unknown. The leader of the riot had been caught and, in an unprecedented move, sent down to his death on the surface of Helliconia.

Everyone on the Observation Station had watched avidly his extraordinary adventures before he succumbed to the virus. They had lived vicariously on the planet on their doorstep.

From that time on, there had to be a safety valve, a tradition of ritualised sacrifice and escape. So the ironically named Helliconia Holiday Lottery came into being. The lottery was held once every ten years during the centuries of the Helliconian summer. The winner of the lottery was allowed to descend to his certain death, and to choose any place at which to land. Some preferred solitude, some cities, some mountains, some the plains. No winner ever refused to go or turned aside from fame and freedom.

Lottery time came round again 1177 Earth years after apastron—the nadir of the Great Year.

The three previous winners had been women. On this occasion, the prizewinner was Billy Xiao Pin. He made his choice without difficulty. He would go down to Matrassyl, capital city of Borlien. There he would gaze upon the face of the queen of queens before the helico virus overcame him.

Death was to be Billy's prize; a death in which he would mingle richly with the centuries-long orchestration of Helliconia's Great Summer.

VI

DIPLOMATS BEARING GIFTS

King JandolAnganol eventually returned from Oldorando to his queen. Four weeks passed. He ceased to limp. Yet the incident of the Cosgatt was not lost. It was midwinter's day, and diplomats from Pannoval were expected in Matrassyl.

A dead heat lay over the Borlienese capital, enshrouding the palace on the hill which overlooked the city. The outer walls of the palace shimmered, as if they were a mirage that could be walked through. Centuries ago, in the winter of the Great Year, midwinter's day had been celebrated in earnest; now it was otherwise. People were too hot to care.

The native courtiers idled in their chambers. The Sibornalese ambassador added ice to his wine and dreamed of the cool women of his home country. Arriving diplomats, loaded with baggage and bribes, sweated under their ceremonial robes and collapsed on couches once the official welcome was over.

The Chancellor of Borlien, SartoriIrvrash, went to his musty room and smoked a veronikane, concealing his anger from the king.

This occasion would lead to ill things. He had not arranged it. The king had not consulted him.

Being a solitary man, SartoriIrvrash conducted a solitary kind of diplomacy. His inward belief was that Borlien should not be drawn further into the orbit of powerful Pannoval by an alliance with it or with Oldorando. The three countries were already united by a common religion which Sartori-Irvrash, as a scholar, did not share.

There had been centuries when Borlien was dominated by Oldorando. The chancellor did not want to see them return. He understood better than most how backward Borlien was; but falling under Pannoval's power would not cure that backwardness. The king thought otherwise, and his religious advisors encouraged him so to think.

The chancellor had introduced strict laws into Matrassyl to govern the comings and goings of foreigners. Perhaps his solitariness included a touch of xenophobia; for he banned Madis from the city, while no foreign diplomat was allowed to enjoy sexual intercourse with a Matrassylan woman, on pain of death. He would have introduced laws against phagors had not the king flatly intervened.

SartoriIrvrash sighed. He desired only to pursue his studies. He detested the way power had been thrust upon him; in consequence, he became a tyrant in petty ways, hoping to steel himself to be bold when the stakes were high. Uncomfortable wielding the power he had, he wished for total power.

Then they would not be in this present dangerous situation, where fifty or more foreigners could lord it in the palace as they liked. He knew with cold certainty that the king intended to bring in change and that a drama was in store which would affect the reasonable tenor of his life. His wife had called him unfeeling; SartoriIrvrash knew it was true to say that his emotions centred round his work.

He hunched his shoulders in a characteristic way; possibly the habit made him look more formidable than he was. His thirty-seven years—thirty-seven years and five tenners, in the precise way the Campannlatians measured age—had told on him, wrinkling his face round his nose and whiskers to make him resemble an intelligent vole.

"You love your king and your fellow men," he instructed

himself, and left the refuge of his chambers.

Like many similar strongholds, the palace was an accumulation of old and new. There had been forts in the caves under the Matrassyl rock during the last great winter. It grew or shrank, became stronghold or pleasure dome, according to the fortunes of Borlien.

The distinguished personages from Pannoval were disturbed by Matrassyl, where phagors were allowed to walk in the street without molestation—and without causing molestation. In consequence, they found fault with JandolAnganol's palace. They called it provincial.

JandolAnganol, in the years when fortune was less against him and his marriage to MyrdemInggala still new, had brought in the best provincial architects, builders, and artists to patch the ravages of time. Particular care had been lavished on the queen's quarters.

Although the general atmosphere of the palace tended towards the military, there was none of the stifling etiquette which marked the Oldorandan and Pannovalan courts. And in places, some kind of higher culture flourished. The apartments of Chancellor SartoriIrvrash, in particular, provided a rat's nest of arts and learning.

The chancellor moved grudgingly on his way to consult with the king. To his mind came thoughts which were pleasanter than affairs of state. Only the previous day he had solved a problem which had long puzzled him, an antiquarian problem. Truth and lies were more easily distinguished in the past than the present.

The queen approached him, wearing one of her flame-red gowns, accompanied by her brother and the Princess Tatro, who ran and clutched his leg. The chancellor bowed. Despite his absorption he saw by the queen's expression that she too was anxious about the diplomatic visit.

"You will have business with Pannoval today," she said.

"I have to consort with a set of pompous asses, and all the while my history is not getting written." Then he caught himself and laughed sharply. "My pardon, ma'am, I meant to say merely that I do not reckon Prince Taynth Indredd of Pannoval a great friend of Borlien . . ."

She sometimes had a slow way of smiling as if she was reluc-

tant to be amused, which started at her eyes, included her nose, and then worked about the curves of her lips.

"We'd agree on that. Borlien lacks great friends at the present."

"Admit it, Rushven, your history will never be finished," said YeferalOboral, the queen's brother, using an old nickname. "It simply gives you an excuse to sleep all afternoon."

The chancellor sighed; the queen's brother had not his sister's brains. He said severely, "If you stopped kicking your heels about the court, you could set up an expedition and sail round the world. How that would add to our knowledge!"

"I wish that Robayday had done some such thing," said MyrdemInggala. "Who knows where the lad is now?"

SartoriIrvrash was not going to waste sympathy on the queen's son. "I made one new discovery yesterday," he said. "Do you wish to hear of it or not? Will I bore you? Will the mere sound of such botherations of knowledge cause you to jump from the ramparts?"

The queen laughed her silvery laugh and held his hand. "Come, Yef and I are no dolts. What's the discovery? Is the world getting colder?"

Ignoring this facetiousness, SartoriIrvrash asked, frowning, "What colour is a hoxney?"

"I know that," cried the young princess. "They're brown. Everyone knows hoxneys are brown."

Grunting, SartoriIrvrash lifted her up into his arms. "And what colour were hoxneys yesterday?"

"Brown, of course."

"And the day before that?"

"Brown, you silly Rushven."

"Correct, you wise little princess. But if that is the case, then why are hoxneys depicted as being striped in two brilliant colours in the illuminations in ancient chronicles?"

He had to answer his own question. "That is what I asked my friend Bardol CaraBansity down in Ottassol. He flayed a hoxney and examined its skin. And what has he discovered? Why, that a hoxney is not a brown animal as we all believe. It is a brown-striped animal, with brown stripes on a brown background."

Tatro laughed. "You're teasing us. If it's brown and

brown, then it's brown, isn't it?"

"Yes and no. The lie of the coat shows that a hoxney is not a plain brown animal. It consists of brown stripes. What possible point could there be to that?

"Well, I have hit upon the answer, and you will see how clever I am. Hoxneys were once striped in brilliant stripes, just as the chronicles show. When was that? Why, in the spring of the Great Year, when suitable grazing was available again. Then the hoxneys needed to multiply as rapidly as possible. So they put on their most brilliant sexual display. Nowadays, centuries later, hoxneys are well established everywhere. They don't need to breed exponentially, so mating display is out. The stripes are dulled down to neutral brown—until the spring of the next Great Year calls them out again."

The queen made a moue. "If there *is* another Great Year spring, and we don't all tumble into Freyr."

SartoriIrvrash clapped his hands pettishly together. "But don't you see, this—this adaptive geometry of the hoxneian species is a guarantee that we *don't* tumble into Freyr—that it comes near every great summer, and then again recedes?"

"We're not hoxneys," said YeferalOboral, gesturing dismissively.

"Your Majesty," said the chancellor, addressing himself earnestly to the queen, "my discovery also shows that old manuscripts can often be trusted more than we think. You know the king your husband and I are at odds. Intercede for me, I pray. Let a ship be commissioned. Let me be allowed two years away from my duties to sail about the world, collecting manuscripts. Let us make Borlien a centre of learning, as it once was in the days of YarapRombry of Keevasien. Now my wife is dead, there's little to keep me here, except your fair presence."

A shadow passed over her face.

"There is a crisis in the king, I feel it. His wound has healed in his flesh but not in his mind. Leave your thought with me, Rushven, and let it wait until this anxious meeting with the Pannovalans is over. I fear what is in store."

The queen smiled at the old man with considerable warmth. She easily endured his irritability, for she understood its source. He was not entirely good—indeed, she considered

some of his experiments pure wickedness, especially the experiment in which his wife was killed. But who was entirely good? SartoriIrvrash's relationship with the king was a difficult one, and she often tried, as now, to protect him from JandolAnganol's anger.

Endeavouring to deliver him from his own blindness, she added gently, "Since the incident in the Cosgatt, I have to be careful with his majesty."

Tatro tugged SartoriIrvrash's whiskers. "You mustn't go sailing at your age, Rushven."

He set her down on the ground and saluted her. "We may all have to make unexpected journeys before we are finished, my dear little Tatro."

As on most mornings, MyrdemInggala and her brother walked along the western ramparts of the palace and gazed out over the city. This morning, the mists that little winter usually brought were absent. The city lay clear below them.

The ancient stronghold stood on a cliff looming over the town, in a deep curve of the Takissa. Slightly towards the north, the Valvoral gleamed where it joined the greater river. Tatro never tired of looking down at the people in the streets or on the river craft.

The infant princess extended a finger towards the wharfs and cried, "Look, ice coming, Moth!"

A fore- and aft-rigged sloop was moored by the quayside. Its hatches had recently been opened, for steam poured forth into the air. Carts were drawn up alongside the ship, and blocks of finest Lordryardry ice gleamed for a moment in the sun as they were swung from the hold into the waiting vehicles. As ever, the delivery was on time, and the palace with its guests would be awaiting it.

The ice carts would come rumbling up the castle road, winding as the road wound, with four oxen straining at the shafts, to gain the fortress which stood out like a ship of stone from its cliffs.

Tatro wanted to stand and watch the ice carts come all the way up the hill, but the queen was short of patience this morning. She stood slightly apart from her child, looking about her with an abstracted air.

JandolAnganol had come at dawn and embraced her. She

sensed that he was uneasy. Pannoval loomed. To make matters worse, bad news was coming from the Second Army in Randonan. It was always bad news from Randonan.

"You can listen to the day's discussion from the private gallery," he said, "if it won't bore you. Pray for me, Cune."

"I always pray for you. The All-Powerful will be with you."

He shook his head patiently. "Why isn't life simple? Why doesn't the faith make it simple?" His hand went to the long scar on his leg.

"We're safe while we're here together, Jan."

He kissed her. "I should be with my army. Then we'd see some victories. TolramKetinet is useless as a general."

There's nothing between the general and me, she thought —yet he knows there is. . . .

He had left her. As soon as he was gone, she felt gloomy. A chill had fallen over him of late. Her own position was threatened. Without thinking, she linked her arm through her brother's as they stood on the ramparts.

Princess Tatro was calling, pointing to servants she recognised wending their way up the hill to the palace.

Less than twenty years earlier, a covered way had been built up the hillside to the walls. Under its protection, an army had advanced on the besieged fortress. Using gunpowder charges, it blew an entrance into the palace grounds. A bloody battle was fought.

The inhabitants were defeated. All were put to the sword, men and women, phagors and peasants. All except the baron who had held the palace.

The baron disguised himself and—binding his wife, children, and immediate servants—led them to safety through the breached wall. Bellowing to the enemy to get out of his way, he had successfully bluffed a path to freedom with his mock prisoners. Thus his daughter escaped death.

This Baron RantanOborol was the queen's father. His deed became renowned. But the fact was that he could never regain his former power.

The man who won the fortress—which was described, like all fortresses before they fall, as impregnable—was the warlike grandfather of JandolAnganol. This redoubtable old warrior

was then busy unifying eastern Borlien, and making its frontiers safe. RantanOborol was the last warlord of the area to
fall to his armies.

Those armies were largely a thing of the past, and Myrdem-
Inggala, by marrying JandolAnganol and securing some
future for her family, had come to live in her father's old
citadel.

Parts of it were still ruinous. Some sections had been rebuilt
in JandolAnganol's father's reign. Other grand rebuilding
schemes, hastily started, slowly crumbled in the heat. Piles of
stone formed a prominent part of the fortress landscape.
MyrdemInggala loved this extravagant semi-ruin, but the past
hung heavy over its battlements.

She made her way, clutching Tatro's hand, to a rear building with a small colonnade. These were her quarters. A featureless red sandstone wall was surmounted by whimsical
pavilions built in white marble. Behind the wall were her
gardens and a private reservoir, where she liked to swim. In
the middle of the reservoir was an artificial islet, on which
stood a slender temple dedicated to Akhanaba. There the king
and queen had often made love in the early days of their marriage.

After saying good-bye to her brother, the queen walked up
her stairs and along a passage. This passage, open to the
breeze, overlooked the garden where JandolAnganol's father,
VarpalAnganol, had once raced dogs and flown multi-
coloured birds. Some of the birds remained in their cotes—
Roba had fed them every morning before he ran away. Now
Mai TolramKetinet fed them.

MyrdemInggala was conscious of an oppressive fear. The
sight of the birds merely vexed her. She left a maid to play
with Tatro in the passage, and went to a door at the far end
which she unlocked with a key hidden among the folds of her
skirt. A guard saluted her as she passed through. Her footsteps, light as they were, rang on the tiled floor. She came to
an alcove by a window, across which drapes had been drawn,
and seated herself on a divan. Before her was an ornate trellis.
Through this she could watch without being observed from the
other side.

From this vantage point, she could see over a large council

chamber. Sun streamed in through latticed windows. None of the dignitaries had yet arrived. Only the king was there, with his phagor runt, the runt that had been a constant companion ever since the Battle of the Cosgatt.

Yuli stood no higher than the king's chest. Its coat was white and still tipped with the red tassels of its early years. It skipped and pirouetted and opened its ugly mouth as the king held out a hand for it. The king was laughing and snapping his fingers.

"Good boy, good boy," he said.

"Yezz, I good boy," said Yuli.

Laughing, the king embraced it, lifting it off the ground.

The queen shrank back. Fear seized her. As she lay back, the wicker chair beneath her creaked. She hid her eyes. If he knew she was there, he made no attempt to call.

My wild boar, my dear wild boar, she called silently. What has become of you? Her mother had been gifted with strange powers: the queen thought, Something awful is going to overwhelm this court and our lives. . . .

When she dared look again, the visiting dignitaries were entering, chatting among themselves and making themselves comfortable. Cushions and rugs were scattered everywhere. Slaves, female and scantily clad, were busily providing coloured drinks.

JandolAnganol walked among them in his princely way and then flung himself down on a canopied divan. SartoriIrvrash entered, nodding sober greetings, and stationed himself behind the king's divan, lighting a veronikane as he did so. The runt Yuli settled on a cushion, panting and yawning.

"You are strangers in our court," said the queen aloud, peeping through her trellis. "You are strangers in our lives."

Near JandolAnganol sat a group of local dignitaries, including the mayor of Matrassyl, who was also head of the scritina, JandolAnganol's vicar, his Royal Armourer, and one or two army men. One of the military was, by his insignia, a captain of phagors but, out of deference to the visitors, no phagor was present, except for the king's pet.

Among the foreign group, most conspicuous were the Sibornalese. The ambassador to Borlien, Io Pasharatid, was from Uskut. He and his wife sat tall and grey and distant from

each other. Some said that they had quarrelled, some that Sibornalese were simply like that. The fact remained that the two, who had lived at the court for more than nine ten-ners—they were due to complete their first year in another three weeks—rarely smiled or exchanged a glance.

"You I fear, Pasharatid, you ghost," said the queen.

Pannoval had sent a prince. The choice had been carefully made. Pannoval was the most powerful nation among the seventeen countries of Campannlat, its ambitions restrained only by the war it had constantly to wage against Sibornal on its northern front. Its religion dominated the continent. At present, Pannoval courted Borlien, which already paid levies in grain and church taxes; but the courtship was that between an elderly dowager and an upstart lad, and what the lad was sent was a minor prince.

Minor he might be, but Prince Taynth Indredd was a portly personage, making up in bulk what he lacked in significance. He was distantly related to the Oldorandan royal family. Nobody greatly liked Taynth Indredd, but a diplomat in Pannoval had sent with him as chief advisor an ageing priest, Guaddl Ulbobeg, known to be a friend of JandolAnganol since the days when the king had served his priestly term in the monasteries of Pannoval.

"You men with clever tongues," sighed the queen, anxious behind her lattice.

JandolAnganol was speaking now in a modest tone. He remained seated. His voice ran fast, like his gaze. He was in effect giving a report on the state of his kingdom to his visitors.

"All of Borlien is now peaceful within its borders. There are some brigands, but they are not important. Our armies are committed in the Western Wars. They drain our lifeblood. On our eastern borders, too, we are threatened by dangerous invaders, Unndreid the Hammer and the cruel Darvlish the Skull."

He looked about him challengingly. It was his shame that he had received a wound from such an unimportant adversary as Darvlish.

"As Freyr draws nearer, we suffer from drought. Famine is everywhere. You must not expect Borlien to fight elsewhere. We are a country large in extent, poor in produce."

"Come, cousin, you are too modest," said Taynth Indredd. "Everyone knows from childhood that your southern loess plain forms the richest land on the continent."

"Richness lies not in land but in land properly farmed," replied JandolAnganol. "Such is the pressure on our borders that we must press peasants into the armies, and let women and children work the farms."

"Then you certainly need our help, cousin," said Taynth Indredd, looking about for the applause he felt his point merited.

Io Pasharatid said, "If a farmer has a lame hoxney, will a wild kaidaw assist him?"

This remark was ignored. There were those who said that Sibornal should not have been present at this meeting.

In the manner of one making everything clear, Taynth Indredd said, "Cousin, you press us for assistance at a time when every nation is in trouble. The riches our grandfathers enjoyed are gone, while our fields burn and our fruits shrivel. And I must speak frankly and say that there is an unresolved quarrel between us. That we greatly hope to resolve, and must resolve if there is to be unanimity between us."

A silence fell.

Perhaps Taynth Indredd feared to continue.

JandolAnganol jumped to his feet, a look of anger on his dark features.

The little runt, Yuli, scrambled up alertly, as if to do whatever his master might bid.

"I went to Sayren Stund in Oldorando to ask for help only against common enemies. Here you gather like vultures! You confront me in my own court. What is this quarrel you dream up between us? Tell me."

Taynth Indredd and his advisor, Guaddl Ulbobeg, conferred. It was the latter, the friend of the king's, who answered him. He rose, bowed, and pointed to Yuli.

"It's no dream, Your Majesty. Our concern is real, and so is that creature you bring here amongst us. From the most ancient times, human kind and phagor kind have been enemies. No truce is possible between beings so different. The Holy Pannovalan Empire has declared holy crusades and drumbles

against these odious creatures, with a view to ridding the world of them. Yet your majesty gives them shelter within his borders.''

He spoke almost apologetically, his gaze downcast, so as to rob his words of force. His master restored the force by shouting, ''You expect aid from us, coz, when you harbour these vermin by the million? They overran Campannlat once before, and will again, given the opportunity you provide.''

JandolAnganol confronted his visitors, hands on hips.

''I will have no one from outside my borders interfere with my interior policies. I listen to my scritina and my scritina does not complain. Yes, I welcome ancipitals to Borlien. A truce is possible with them. They farm infertile land that our people will not touch. They do humble work that slaves shrink from. They fight for no pay. My treasury is empty—you misers from Pannoval may not understand that, but it means I can afford only an army of phagors.

''They get their reward in marginal land. Moreover, they do not turn and run in the face of danger! You may say that that is because they are too stupid. To which I reply, that I prefer a phagor to a peasant any day. As long as I am King of Borlien, the phagors have my protection.''

''You mean, we believe, Your Majesty, that the phagors have your protection as long as MyrdemInggala is Queen of Borlien.'' These words were spoken by one of Taynth Indredd's vicars, a thin man whose bones were draped in a black woollen charfrul. Again, tension filled the court. Following up his advantage, the vicar continued, ''It was the queen, with her well-known tenderness towards any living thing, and her father, the warlord RantanOborol—whom your majesty's grandfather dispossessed of this very palace not twenty years back—who began this degrading alliance with the ancipitals, which you have maintained.''

Guaddl Ulbobeg rose and bowed to Taynth Undredd. ''Sire, I object to the trend this meeting is taking. We are not here to vilify the Queen of Borlien but to offer aid to the king.''

But JandolAnganol, as if weary, had sat down. The vicar had sought out his vulnerable spot: that his claim to the throne

was recent and his consort the daughter of a minor baron.

With a sympathetic glance at his lord, SartoriIrvrash rose to face the Pannovalan visitors.

"As his majesty's chancellor, I find myself amazed—yet it's an amazement blunted somewhat by custom—to discover such prejudice, I might even say animosity, among members of the same great Holy Pannovalan Empire. I, as you may understand, am an atheist, and therefore observe detachedly the antics of your Church. Where is the charity you preach? Do you aid his majesty by trying to undermine the position of the queen?

"I am grown to the withered end of life, but I tell you, Illustrious Prince Taynth Indredd, that I have as great a hatred of phagors as you. But they are a factor of life we must live with, as you in Pannoval live with your constant hostilities against Sibornal. Would you wipe out all Sibornalese as you would wipe out all phagors? Is it not killing itself that is wrong? Doesn't your Akhanaba preach that?

"Since we are speaking frankly, then I will say that there has long been belief in Borlien that if Pannoval were not engaged in fighting Sibornalese colonists along a wide front to the north, then it would be invading us to the south, as you now attempt to dominate us with your ideologies. For that reason, we are grateful to the Sibornalese."

As the chancellor stooped to confer with JandolAnganol, the Sibornalese ambassador rose and said, "Since the progressive nations of Sibornal so rarely receive anything but condemnation from the Empire, I wish to record my astonished gratitude for that speech."

Taynth Indredd, ignoring this sarcastic interjection, said in the direction of SartoriIrvrash, "You are so much at the withered end that you mistake the reality of the situation. Pannoval serves as a bastion between you and southward incursions of the warlike Sibornalese. As a self-proclaimed student of history, you should know that those same Sibornalese never cease—generation after generation—from trying to quit their loathesome northern continent and take over ours."

Whatever the truth of this last assertion, it was true that the Pannovalans were as offended to find Sibornalese as phagors

in the council room. But even Taynth Indredd knew that the
real bastion between Sibornal and Borlien was geographical:
the sharp spines of the Quzint Mountains and the great corridor between the Quzints and Mordriat called Hazziz which
at this period was a scorching desert.

JandolAnganol and SartoriIrvrash had been conferring.
The chancellor now spoke again.

"Our pleasant guests bring up the subject of the warlike
Sibornalese. Before we enter into further botheration and insults, we should proceed to the heart of the matter. My lord
King JandolAnganol was lately grievously wounded in defending his realm, so much that his life hung by a thread. He
praises Akhanaba for his deliverance, while I praise the herbs
my surgeons applied to the wound. I have here the cause of the
injury."

He called forth the Royal Armourer, a small and savagely
moustached man dressed in leather who stumped into the centre of the room and then produced a leaden ball, which he held
up between thumb and forefinger of a gloved hand. In a formal voice, he announced, "This is a shot. It was dug from out
his majesty's leg with a surgeon's knife. It caused great injury.
It was fired from a piece of hand artillery called a matchlock."

"Thank you," said SartoriIrvrash, dismissing the man.
"We recognise that Sibornal is greatly progressive. The
matchlock is evidence of that progress. We understand that
matchlocks are now being made in Sibornal in great numbers,
and that there is later development, by name a wheel lock,
which will spread greater devastation. I would advise the Holy
Pannovalan Empire to show genuine unity in the face of this
new development. Let me assure you, this innovation is more
to be feared than Unndreid the Hammer himself.

"I must furthermore advise you that our agents report that
the tribes which invaded the Cosgatt were supplied with these
weapons not from Sibornal itself, as might be expected, but
from a Sibornalese source in Matrassyl."

At this statement, all eyes in the court turned to the Sibornalese ambassador. It happened that Io Pasharatid was just
refreshing himself with an iced drink. He paused with the glass
halfway to his mouth, a look of distress on his face.

His wife, Dienu Pasharatid, reclined on cushions nearby. She rose now, a tall and graceful woman, thin, greyish in cast, severe in appearance.

"If you statesmen wonder why in my country you are called the Savage Continent, look no further than this latest lie of magnitude. Who would be to blame for such arms trading? Why should my husband be always mistrusted?"

SartoriIrvrash pulled his whiskers, so that his face was tugged into an involuntary smile. "Why do you mention your husband in connection with this incident, Madame Dienu? No one else did. I didn't."

JandolAnganol rose again. "Two of our agents, posing as Driat tribesmen, went into the lower bazaar and bought one of these new inventions. I propose a demonstration of what this weapon can do, so that you will be in no doubt that we have entered a new era in warfare. Perhaps then you will see my need to retain phagors in my army and my realms."

Addressing himself directly to the Pannovalan prince, he said, "If your refinement will allow you to tolerate the presence of ancipitals in the room . . ."

The diplomats sat up and stared apprehensively at the king.

He clapped his hands. A leather-clad captain from his cortege went to a passage and called an order. Two dehorned phagors marched smartly into the room. They had been standing motionless in the shadows. Their white pelages picked up the light as they passed by the windows. One of them carried a long matchlock before him. A passage was cleared across the middle of the chamber as he set it down and crouched beside it to prepare for firing.

The hand-artillery piece had a six-foot iron barrel and a stock of polished wood. Both barrel and stock were bound at intervals with silver wire. Near the muzzle was a folding tripod of sturdy design with two clawed feet. The phagor packed powder into the mechanism from a horn carried at his belt, and used a ramrod to tamp a round lead ball down the barrel. He settled himself and lit a fuse. The captain of phagors stood over him to see that all was performed properly.

Meanwhile, the second phagor had moved to the other end of the chamber and stood near the wall, looking forward and

twitching an ear. Any humans lolling about on cushions had rapidly cleared a wide space for him.

The first phagor squinted along the barrel, using the tripod to support the muzzle. The fuse spluttered. There was a terrific explosion and a puff of smoke.

The other phagor staggered. A yellow stain appeared high up on its chest, where its intestines were situated. It said something, clutching the spot where the shot had entered its body. Then it fell dead, collapsing with a thud on the floor.

As smoke and smell filled the council hall, the diplomats began to cough. Panic took them. They jumped up, tugging their charfruls, and ran into the open. JandolAnganol and his chancellor were left standing alone.

After the morning's demonstration of fire power, of which the queen had been a secret onlooker, she went and hid herself in her quarters.

She hated the calculations that power entailed. She knew that the Pannoval contingent, led by the odious Prince Taynth Indredd, were not aiming their remarks against Sibornal, for it was taken for granted that Sibornal was a permanent enemy; that relationship, sour though it was, was well understood. JandolAnganol was the target of their talk, for they wished to bind him closer to them. And in consequence she—who had power over him—was also their target.

MyrdemInggala lunched with her ladies. JandolAnganol, by the laws of courtesy, lunched with his guests. Guaddl Ulbobeg earned black looks from his master by pausing at the king's place and saying, in a low voice, "Your demonstration was dramatic, but hardly effective. For our northern armies are having increasingly to fight against Sibornalese forces armed with those very matchlocks. However, the art of their manufacture can be learnt, as you will see tomorrow. Beware, my friend, for the prince will force a hard bargain on you."

After her lunch, scarcely tasted, the queen went alone to her quarters and sat at her favourite window, on the cushioned seat built round its bay. She thought of the odious Prince Taynth Indredd, who resembled a frog. She knew that he was

related to the equally disgusting King of Oldorando, Sayren Stund, whose wife was a Madi. Surely even phagors were preferable to these scheming royalties!

From her window, she looked across her garden to the tiled reservoir where she swam. On the far side of the reservoir, a tall wall rose, hiding her beauty from prying eyes, and in the bottom of the wall, just above water level, was a small iron grille. The grille formed the window to a dungeon. There, JandolAnganol's father, the deposed King VarpalAnganol, was imprisoned, and had been since shortly after the queen's marriage. In the reservoir were gold carp, visible from where she sat. Like her, like Varpal Anganol, they were prisoners here.

A knock came at her door. A servant opened it, to announce that the queen's brother awaited her pleasure.

YeferalOboral was lolling against the rail at her balcony. They both knew that JandolAnganol would long since have killed him, but for the queen.

Her brother was not a handsome man; all the beauty in the line had been bestowed in superabundance on MyrdemInggala. His features were meagre, his expression sour. He was brave, obedient, patient; otherwise his qualities were few. He never carried himself well, as did the king, as if to emphasise that he intended to cut no figure in life. Yet he served JandolAnganol without protest, and was devoted to a sister whose life he held so much more dear than his own. She loved him for his ordinariness.

"You were not at the meeting."

"It wasn't for the likes of me."

"It was horrible."

"I heard so. For some reason, Io Pasharatid is upset. He's generally so cool, like a block of Lordryardry ice. Yet the guards say he has a woman in town—imagine! If so, he runs a great risk."

MyrdemInggala showed her teeth in a smile. "I detest the way he looks at me. If he has a woman, so much the better!"

They laughed. For a short while, they lingered, talking of cheerful things. Their father, the old baron, was in the country now, complaining of the heat and too old to be reckoned a

danger to the state. He had recently taken up fishing, as a cool pursuit.

The courtyard bell rang. They looked down to see Jan-dolAnganol enter the court, closely followed by a guard carry-ing a red silk umbrella over his head. The phagor runt was close to him, as ever. He called to his queen.

"Will you come down, Cune? Our guests must be enter-tained during a lull in our discussions. You will delight them more than ever I could."

She left her brother and went down to join him under the sunshade. He took her arm with formal courtesy. She thought he looked weary, though the fabric of the umbrella reflected a flush like fever on his cheeks.

"Are you coming to a treaty with Pannoval and Oldorando which will ease the pressures of war?" she asked timidly.

"The beholder knows what we're coming to," he said abruptly. "We must keep on terms with the devils, and placate them, otherwise they'll take advantage of our temporary weakness and invade us. They're as full of cunning as they are of fake holiness." He sighed.

"The time will come when you and I will be hunting and en-joying life again, as of old," she said, squeezing his arm. She would not rebuke him for inviting his guests.

Ignoring her pious hope, he burst out angrily, "Sartori-Irvrash spoke unwisely this morning, admitting his atheism. I must get rid of him. Taynth holds it against me that my chancellor is not a member of the Church."

"Prince Taynth also spoke against me. Will you get rid of me because I am not to his liking?" Her eyes flashed angrily as she spoke, though she tried to keep lightness in her tone. But he replied sullenly, "You know, and the scritina knows, that the coffers are empty. We may be driven to much we have no heart for."

She drew her hand sharply from his arm.

The visitors, together with their concubines and servants, were grouped in a green courtyard, under colonnades. Wild beasts were being paraded; a group of jugglers was entertain-ing with its paltry tricks. JandolAnganol steered his queen among the emissaries. She noted how the countenances of the

men lit up as she spoke to them. I must still be of some value to Jan, she thought.

An old Thribriatan tribesman in elaborate braffista headgear was parading two gorilloid Others on chains. The creatures attracted several onlookers. Away from their arboreal habitat, their behaviour was uncouth. They most resembled—so one of the courtiers said—two drunken courtiers.

The froglike Prince Taynth Indredd was standing under a yellow sunshade, being fanned and smoking a veronikane as he watched the Others perform some limited tricks. Beside him, laughing uproariously at the captives, was a stiff girl of some eleven years and six tenners.

"Aren't they funny, Unk?" she said to the prince. "They're quite like people, except for all the fur."

The Thribriatan, hearing this, touched his braffista and said to the prince, "You like see me make Others fight each other?"

The prince humorously produced a silver coin in the palm of his hand.

"This if you'll make them rumbo each other."

Everyone laughed. The girl screamed with humour. "Unkie, how rude you are! Would they really?"

Mournfully polite, the tribesman said, "These beasts have no khmir like humans. Only every tenner make love, do rumbo. Is more easy make fight."

Shaking his head and laughing, the prince retained his coin. It was as he turned away that MyrdemInggala addressed him. His small companion drifted off, suddenly bored. She was dressed as an adult, and her cheeks were rouged.

When the queen decently could, she left JandolAnganol and Taynth Indredd talking, and crossed to the fountain to speak with the girl. The latter was staring moodily into the water.

"Are you looking for fish?"

"No, thank you. We have much bigger fish than that at home in Oldorando." She indicated their size in a childlike way, using her hands.

"I see. I've just been talking to your father, the prince."

The girl looked up at her interrogator for the first time, with an expression of contempt. Her face astonished MyrdemInggala, so strange was it, with huge eyes fringed by abnormally

long lashes, and a nose like the beak of a little parakeet. By the beholder, thought the queen, this is a half-Madi child! What a funny little thing! I must be nice to it.

It was saying, "Zygankes! Taynth my father! He's not my father. Whatever made you think that? He's only a distant cousin by marriage. I wouldn't have him for a father—he's too fat." As if to strike a pleasanter note, the girl said, "In truth, this is the first time I have been allowed to travel away from Oldorando without my father. My women are with me, of course, but it's terribly boring there, isn't it? Do you have to live here?"

She squinted as she peered up at the queen. A characteristic in her face made her look at once pretty and stupid.

"You know what? You look quite attractive, for an old person."

Keeping a serious face, the queen said, "I have a nice cool reservoir, sheltered from view. Would you like a swim? Is that permitted?"

The girl considered. "I can do what I like, of course, but I don't think a swim would be ladylike just now. I am a princess, after all. That always has to be considered."

"Really? Do you mind telling me your name?"

"Zygankes, it is *primitive* in Borlien! I thought everyone knew my name. I am the Princess Simoda Tal, and my father is the King of Oldorando. I suppose you've heard of Oldorando?"

The queen laughed. Feeling sorry for the child, she said, "Well, if you've come all the way from Oldorando I think you deserve a swim."

"I'll swim when I please, thank you," said the young lady.

And when the young lady pleased was next morning at dawn. She found her way to the queen's quarters and woke her. MyrdemInggala was more amused than vexed. She roused Tatro and they went down with Simoda Tal to the reservoir, accompanied only by their maids, who bore towels, and a phagor guard. The child dismissed the phagors, saying that they disgusted her.

A chill light lay across the scene, but the water was more

than tepid. Once, in JandolAnganol's father's time, carts of snow and ice had been brought from the mountains to cool the reservoirs, but considerations of manpower and the stirrings of Mordriat tribes had terminated such luxuries.

Although no windows but her own faced over the reservoir, the queen always swam in a filmy garment which covered her pale body. Simoda Tal had no such reservations. She threw off her garments to reveal a stocky little body prinked with dark hairs, which stood out like pine trees on snowy hillsides.

"Oh, I love you, you're beautiful!" she exclaimed to the queen, rushing up as soon as she was naked and embracing the older woman. MyrdemInggala was unable to respond freely. She felt something inappropriate in the embrace. Tatro screamed.

The young girl swam and surface-dived close to the queen, repeatedly opening her legs as she performed in the water, as if eager to assure MyrdemInggala that she was fully adult where it was most important to be.

At the same time, SartoriIrvrash was being wakened from his couch by an officer of the court. The guards had reported that the Sirbonalese ambassador, Io Pasharatid, had left on hoxneyback, alone, an hour before Freyr-dawn.

"His wife, Dienu?"

"She is still in her quarters, sir. She is reported to be upset."

"Upset? What does that mean? The woman's intelligent. I can't say I like her, but she's intelligent. Botheration. . . . And there are so many fools. . . . Here, help me out of bed, will you?"

He drew a gown round his shoulders and roused the slave woman who had served as his housekeeper since his wife died. He admired the Sibornalese. He had estimated that at this time of the Great Year there were possibly fifty million humans living in the seventeen countries of Campannlat; those countries could not agree with each other. Wars were endemic. Empires rose and fell. There was never peace.

In Sibornal, cold Sibornal, things fell out differently. In the seven countries of Sibornal lived an estimated twenty-five million humans. Those seven nations formed a strong alliance. Campannlat was incomparably richer than the northern continent, yet perpetual squabbles between its nations meant that

little was achieved—except religions which thrived on desperation. This was why SartoriIrvrash hated the job of chancellor.
He had a contempt for most of the men he worked for.

The chancellor had paid bribes, and knew as a result that
Prince Taynth Indredd had brought to the palace a chest of
weapons—the very weapons discussed yesterday. Clearly, they
were designed as bargaining power, but what the bargain
would be remained to be seen.

It was not improbable that the Sibornalese ambassador had
also gained news of the chest of matchlocks. That could account for his hasty departure. He would be heading north,
towards Hazziz and the nearest Sibornalese settlements. He
should be brought back.

SartoriIrvrash sipped a mug of pellamountain tea which the
slave woman brought and turned to the waiting officer.

"I made a fabulous discovery yesterday regarding hoxneys,
which influences the history of the world—a remarkable
discovery! But who took account of it?" He shook his bald
head. "Learning means nothing, intrigue is everything. So I
have to bestir myself at dawn to capture some fool riding
north. . . . What a botheration it is! Now. Who's a good hox-
neyman near at hand? One we can trust, if such exists. I know.
The queen's brother, YeferalOborol. Fetch him, will you? In
his boots."

When YeferalOborol appeared, SartoriIrvrash explained
the situation.

"Fetch this madman Pasharatid back. Ride hard and you'll
catch him up. Tell him—something. Let me think. Yes, tell
him that the king has decided to make no commitment to
Oldorando and Pannoval. Instead, he wishes to sign a treaty
with Sibornal. Sibornal has a fleet of ships. Tell him we will
offer them anchorage in Ottassol."

"What would Sibornalese ships be doing so far from
home?" YeferalOborol asked.

"Leave him to decide that. Just persuade him to return
here."

"Why do you want him back?"

SartoriIrvrash squeezed his hands together. "Guilt. That's
why the scerm has left so suddenly. I mean to find out exactly
what he has done. There's always more than arm up a Sibor-

nalese sleeve. Now please go, and no more questions."

YeferalOborol rode north through the city, through its
streets which were even then crowded with early risers, and
through the fields beyond. He rode steadily, trotting and
walking his hoxney by turns.

He came to a bridge across the Mar, where that river flowed
into the Takissa. A small fort stood, guarding the bridge. He
stopped and changed to a fresh hoxney.

After another hour's riding, when the heat was becoming
intense, he stopped by a stream and drank. There were fresh
hoxney-shoe prints by the water, which he hoped were those of
Pasharatid's mount.

He continued north. The country became less fertile. Habitation was scarce. The thordotter blew, parching throats, drying skins.

Giant boulders were strewn about the landscape. A century
or so ago, this region had been popular with hermits, who
built small churches beside or on top of the boulders. One or
two old men could still be seen, but the intense heat had driven
most of them away. Phagors worked patches of earth under
the boulders; brilliant butterflies fluttered about their legs.

Behind one of the boulders, Io Pasharatid stood waiting for
his pursuer. His mount was exhausted. Pasharatid expected
capture and was surprised when he saw a solitary rider approaching. There was no accounting for the foolishness of the
Campannlatians.

He loaded his matchlock, set it in position, and awaited the
right moment to apply his fire. His pursuer was approaching
at a steady pace, riding among the boulders and taking no particular care.

Pasharatid lit the fuse, tucked the butt into this shoulder,
narrowed his eyes, and aimed the gun. He hated using these
beastly weapons. They were for barbarians.

Not every firing was a success. This one was. There was a
loud explosion, the bullet flew to its mark. YeferalOborol was
blown off his mount with a hole in his chest. He crawled into
the shadow of a boulder and died.

The Sibornalese ambassador caught the hoxney and continued his journey north.

*   *   *

It must be said: there were no riches in King Jandol-Anganol's court to rival the riches of the courts friendly to him in Ordorando and in Pannoval City. In those more favoured centres of civilisation, treasures of all kinds had accumulated; scholars were protected, and the church itself—though this was truer of Pannoval—encouraged learning and the arts to a limited extent. But Pannoval had the advantage of a ruling dynasty which, encouraging a proselytising religion, made for stability.

Almost every week, ships unloaded on to Matrassyl's harbour cargoes of spices, drugs, hides, animals' teeth, lapis lazuli, scented woods, and rare birds. But of these treasures, few reached the palace. For JandolAnganol was an upstart king, in the eyes of the world and possibly in his own eyes. He boasted of his grandfather's enlightened rule, but in truth his grandfather had been little better than a successful warlord—one of many who disputed Borlienese territory—who had had the wit to band phagors into formidable armies under human captaincy and so subdue his enemies.

Not all those enemies had been killed. One of the most striking "reforms" of JandolAnganol's father's reign was to appoint a parliament, or scritina; the scritina represented the people and advised the king. It was based on an Oldorandan model. VarpalAnganol had formed the membership of the scritina from two categories of men, from the leaders of guilds and corps, such as the Ironmakers Corps, who had traditional power in the land, and from defeated warlords or their families, thus giving them the chance to air their grievances and him a way of deflating their wrath. Much of the cargo unloaded at Matrassyl went to paying this disaffected body of men.

When the young JandolAnganol deposed and imprisoned his father, he had sought to abolish the scritina. The scritina had refused to be abolished. It met irregularly and continued to harass the king and to make its own members rich. Its leader, BudadRembitim, was also mayor of Matrassyl.

The scritina called an extraordinary meeting. It would certainly demand a fresh attempt to subdue Randonan and stronger defences against the warlike tribes of Mordriat, who were no more than two or three days gallop from their homes.

The king would have to answer them and commit himself to a definite line of action.

The king presented himself before the scritina that afternoon, when his distinguished visitors were taking a siesta. He left his runt behind and sank into this throne in grim silence.

After the difficulties of the morning, another set of difficulties. His gaze went round the wooden council chamber as if seeking them out.

Several members of the old families rose to speak. Most of them harped on a fresh theme and a stale one. The stale one was the emptiness of the exchequer. The fresh one was the inconvenient report from the Western Wars that the frontier city of Keevasien had been sacked. Randonanese units had crossed the Kacol River and stormed the city.

This led to complaints that General Hanra TolramKetinet was too young, too unskilled, to command the army. Every complaint was a criticism of the king. JandolAnganol listened impatiently, drumming his fingers on the arm of his throne. He recalled again the wretched days of his boyhood, after his mother had died. His father had beaten and neglected him. He had hidden in cellars from his father's servants, and vowed to himself that, when he was grown up, he would let nobody stand in the way of his happiness.

After he was wounded in the Cosgatt, after he had managed to find his way back to the capital, he lay in the state of weakness which recalled to his mind the past he wished to shut away. Again he was powerless. It was then he had observed the handsome young captain, TolramKetinet, smile at MyrdemInggala, and receive an answering smile.

As soon as he had managed to crawl from his bed, he promoted TolramKetinet to general, and sent him off to the Western Wars. There were men in the scritina who believed—with good reason—that their sons were much more deserving of promotion. Every setback in the stubborn jungles to the west reinforced their belief, and their anger with the king. He knew he needed a victory of some kind very soon. For that he found himself forced to turn to Pannoval.

The next morning, before meeting formally again with the diplomats, JandolAnganol went early to see Prince Taynth Indredd in his suite. He left Yuli outside, where the runt settled

down comfortably, sprawling like a dog by the door. This was the king's concession to a man he disliked.

Prince Taynth Indredd was breakfasting off a gout cooked in oatmeal, served with tropical fruits. He listened, nodding assent, to what JandolAnganol had to say.

He remarked, with seeming irrelevance, "I hear that your son has disappeared?"

"Robay loves the desert. The climate suits him. He often departs, and is away for weeks at a time."

"It's not the proper training for a king. Kings must be educated. RobaydayAnganol should attend a monastery, as you did, and as I did. Instead, he's joined the protognostics, so I hear."

"I can look after my own son. I require no advice."

"Monastery is good for you. Teaches you that there are things you have to do, even if you don't like them. Bad things loom in the future. Pannoval has survived the long winters. The long summers are more difficult. . . . My deuteroscopists and astronomers report bad things of the future. Of course, it's their trade, you might say."

He paused and lit a veronikane, making a performance of it, breathing out the smoke luxuriously, sweeping the cloud away with languorous gestures.

"Yes, the old religions of Pannoval spoke truth when they warned that bad things came from the sky. Akhanaba's origins were as a stone. You know that?"

He rose and waddled over to the window, where he climbed up on the sill and looked out. His large behind stuck out in JandolAnganol's direction.

The latter said nothing, waiting for Taynth Indredd to commit himself.

"The deuteroscopists say that Helliconia and our attendant sun, Batalix, are being drawn nearer to Freyr every small year. For the next few generations—eighty-three years, to be precise —we move ever nearer to it. After that, if celestial geometries prove correct, we draw slowly away again. So the next generations are the testing ones. Advantage will go increasingly to the polar continents of Hespagorat and Sibornal. For us in the tropics, conditions will become steadily worse."

"Borlien can survive. It's cooler along the south coast.

Ottassol is a cool city—below ground, much like Pannoval.''

Taynth Indredd turned his froglike face over one shoulder in order to inspect JandolAnganol.

"There's a plan, you see, coz. . . . I know you have little affection for me, but I'd prefer you to hear it from me than have it from your friend, my old holy advisor, Guaddl Ulbobeg. Borlien will be all right at nearpoint, as you say. So will Pannoval, safe in its mountains. Oldorando will suffer most. And both your country and mine need to see Oldorando remain intact, or it will fall to barbarians. Do you suppose you could accommodate the Oldorandan court, Sayren Stund and his like —in Ottassol?"

The question was so startling that JandolAnganol was for once at a loss for words.

"That would be for my successor to say . . ."

The Prince of Pannoval changed his tone of voice, and the subject.

"Coz, take some fresh air at the window with me. See, there below is my charge, Simoda Tal, eleven years and six tenners old, daughter of the Oldorandan line, her ancestry traceable back to the Lords Den ruling Old Embruddock in the chill times.''

The girl, thinking herself unobserved, skipped in the court-yard below, dried her hair in a desultory fashion, and whirled her towel about her head now and again.

"Why does she make the journey with you, Taynth?"

"Because I wished you to see her. A pleasant girl, is she not?"

"Pleasing enough.''

"Young, it's true, but, from certain signs I have had, of a quite lascivious nature.''

JandolAnganol felt a trap was about to spring. He withdrew his head and began to pace the room. Taynth Indredd turned about and settled himself comfortably on the ledge, blowing out smoke.

"Cousin, we wish to see the member states of the Holy Pannoval Empire draw ever closer. We must protect ourselves against bad times—not only now but to come. In Pannoval, we have always had Akhanaba's gift of foresight. That is why

we wish you to marry this pretty young princess, Simoda Tal.''

The blood sank from JandolAnganol's face. Straightening himself, he said, ''You know I am already married—and to whom I am married.''

''Face some unpleasant facts, coz. The present queen is the daughter of a brigand. She is not a fit match for you. The marriage degrades you and your country, which demands a better status. Married to Simoda Tal, though, yours would be a force to be reckoned with.''

''It cannot be done. In any case, the mother of that girl down there is a Madi. Isn't that so?''

Taynth Indredd shrugged. ''Are Madis worse than the phagors you dote on? Listen, coz, we want this new match to go as smoothly as possible. No hostility, only mutual help. In eighty-three more years, Oldorando will be aflame from one end to the other, with temperatures near to one hundred and fifty degrees, according to calculation. Oldorandans will have to move southwards. Form a dynastic marriage now, and they will be in your power then. They will be poor relations begging at your door. All Borlien-Oldorando will be yours—or your grandsons' at least. It is a chance never to be missed. Now let's have some more fruit. The squaanej are excellent.''

''It cannot be done.''

''It can. The Holy C'Sarr is prepared to annul your present marriage by a special bill.''

JandolAnganol raised a hand as if to strike the prince. He retained the hand at the level of his eyes and said, ''My present marriage is my past marriage and my future one. If we need this dynastic marriage, then I will marry off Robayday to your Simoda. It would make an equal match.''

The prince leaned forward and pointed a finger at JandolAnganol. ''Certainly not. Forget the suggestion. That boy is crazy. His grandma was the wild Shannana.''

The Eagle's eyes flashed. ''He's not crazy. A little wild.''

''He should have attended a monastery, as you did and as I did. Your religion must tell you that your son is inadmissible as a suitor. You must make the sacrifice, if you choose to regard it as such. You will be rewarded for any sense of loss by

our considerable aid. When we have your consent, we shall
present you with a chest full of the new weaponry, together
with all necessary priming. More chests will follow. You can
train gunners for use against Darvlish the Skull as well as the
Randonanese tribes. You will gain every advantage."

"And what will Pannoval gain?" JandolAnganol asked
bitterly.

"Stability, coz, stability. Over the next unstable period. The
Sibornalese are not going to grow less powerful as Freyr
nears."

He nibbled at one of the purple squaanej.

JandolAnganol stood rooted where he was, looking away
from the prince.

"I am already married to a woman I love. I will not put
MyrdemInggala aside."

The prince laughed. "Love! Zygankes, as Simoda Tal
would say! Kings cannot afford to think in such terms. You
must put your country first. For Borlien's sake, marry Simoda
Tal, unify, stabilise . . ."

"And if I don't?"

Taking his time, Taynth Indredd selected another squaanej
from the bowl.

"In that case, you will be wiped from the field of play,
won't you?"

JandolAnganol knocked the fruit from his hand. It rolled
across the floor and stopped against the wall.

"I have my religious convictions. It would go against those
convictions to put my queen aside. And there are those in your
Church who would support me."

"You don't mean poor old Ulbobeg?"

Although the prince's hand shook, he bent and selected
another fruit.

"First of all, find some pretext to send her away somewhere. Get her out of the court. Send her to the coast. Then
think about all the advantages which will accrue when you do
as we wish you to do. I must return to Pannoval at the end of
the week—with the news that you will make a dynastic marriage which the Holy C'Sarr himself will bless."

*   *   *

The day continued difficult for JandolAnganol. During the morning's meeting, while Taynth Indredd sat silent on his frog-throne, Guaddl Ulbobeg expounded the plan for the new marriage. This time, it was set out in diplomatic terms. When this action was taken, then those benefits would accrue. Great C'Sarr Kilandar IX, Father Supreme of the Church of Akhanaba, would approve both a bill of divorcement and the second marriage.

Wisely, nothing was said about what might or might not accrue in eighty-three years. Most diplomacy was concerned with getting through the next five years.

The royal household gave a luncheon for the guests, over which Queen MyrdemInggala presided, the king sitting at her side without eating, his little phagor waiting behind him. High-ranking members of the Borlienese scritina were also present.

A wealth of roasted crane, fish, pig, and swan was consumed.

After the banquet, Prince Taynth Indredd made his reply. Pretending to reciprocate for the feast, he had his bodyguard give a demonstration of the capabilities of the new matchlocks. Three mountain lions were brought in chains into one of the inner courtyards and despatched.

While the smoke was still clearing, the weapons were given to JandolAnganol. They were presented almost contemptuously, as if his assent to the Pannovalan demands was taken for granted.

The reason for the demonstration was clear. The scritina would demand that the king get more matchlocks from Pannoval to fight the various wars. And Pannoval would supply them—at a price.

No sooner was this ceremony concluded than two traders entered the palace grounds, bringing with them a body sewn into a sack, lashed to the back of an ancient kaidaw. The sack was opened. YeferalOboral's body rolled out, with part of its chest and shoulder blown away. It was a tormented king who stalked into his chancellor's chambers that evening. Batalix was setting among roll after roll of cloud, on which Freyr's light intermittently shone. The warm western glow lit the dull corners of the room.

SartoriIrvrash rose from the long cluttered table at which he was sitting and bowed to the king. He was wrestling with his "Alphabet of History and Nature." All about lay ancient sources and modern reports, at which the king's quick eye glared dismissively.

"What decision should I give Taynth Indredd?" demanded the king.

"May I speak clearly, Your Majesty?"

"Speak." The king flung himself untidily into a chair, and the runt stood behind it so as to avoid SartoriIrvrash's gaze.

SartoriIrvrash bowed his head so that the king could see only his expressionless bald pate. "Your Majesty, your first duty lies not to yourself but to your country. So says the ancient Law of Kings. The plan of Pannoval to cement our present good relations with Oldorando by a dynastic marriage is workable. It will render your throne more secure, its tenure less open to question. It will guarantee that in future we may turn to Pannoval for aid.

"I think in particular of aid in the form of grain, as well as weapons. They have great fields in their more temperate north, towards the Pannoval Sea. This year, our harvest is poor, and will become yet poorer as the heat increases. Whereas our Royal Armourer can presumably imitate the Sibornalese matchlocks.

"There is, therefore, everything to be said for your making the match with Simoda Tal of Oldorando, despite her scanty ears—everything but one thing. Queen MyrdemInggala. Our present queen is a good and holy woman, and the condition of love prospers between the two of you. If you sever that love, you will suffer harm as a result."

"Perhaps I can come to love Simoda Tal."

"Perhaps you can, Your Majesty." SartoriIrvrash turned to look out of his small window at the sunsets. "But with that love will go the bitter thread of hate. You will never find another woman like the queen; or, if you do, that woman will not bear the name of Simoda Tal."

"Love's not important," said JandolAnganol, beginning to pace the floor. "Survival's more important. So says the prince. Perhaps he's right. In any case, what advice are you

giving me? Are you saying yes or no?''

The chancellor tugged at his whiskers. ''The phagor question is another botheration. Did the prince bring it up this morning?''

''He said nothing on that subject this morning.''

''He will. The people for whom he speaks will. Just as soon as a deal is made.''

''So, your advice, Chancellor? Should I say yes to Pannoval or no?''

The chancellor kept his eye on the litter of papers on his table, and sank down on the bench. His hand fluttered a parchment, causing it to rustle like old leaves.

''You tax me, sire, on a crucial matter, a matter where the needs of the heart run into confrontation with the demands of the state. It's not for me to say yes or no. . . . Is this not a religious matter, best taken to your vicar?''

JandolAnganol struck his fist on the table. ''All matters are religious, but in this particular matter I must turn to my chancellor. That you reverence the present queen is a quality for which I respect you, Rushven. Nevertheless, put that consideration apart and deliver me your judgment. Should I set her aside and make this dynastic marriage, in order to safeguard the future of our country? Answer.''

In the chancellor's mind lay the knowledge that he must not be responsible for the king's decision. Otherwise, he would be made a scapegoat later; he knew the king's volatile disposition, dreaded his rages. He saw many arguments for the coalition between Borlien and Oldorando; to have peace between the two traditionally hostile neighbours would benefit all; in that union, if it was wisely handled—as he could handle it— would be a bulwark against Pannoval as well as against the ever thrusting continent of the north, Sibornal.

On the other hand, he felt as much loyalty to the person of the queen as he did to the king. In his egocentric way, he loved MyrdemInggala like a daughter, especially since his wife had been killed in such horrible circumstances. Her beauty was before him every day to warm his scholarly old heart. He had but to lift a finger, to say vigorously, ''You must stand by the woman you love—that is the greatest alliance you can

make . . . ,'' but, peeping up at the stormy face of his king, his courage failed him. There was his great lifelong project, his book, to be defended.

The question was too large for any but the king himself to answer.

"Your majesty will have a nose bleed if you become overexcited. I pray, drink some wine . . ."

"By the beholder, you are all that is worst in men, a very grave of help!"

The old man hunched his shoulders further into his patterned charfrul and shook his head.

"As your advisor, my duty in such a difficult personal matter is to formulate the problem clearly for you. You it is who must decide what resolution is best, Majesty, for you of all people must live with that decision. There are two ways of looking at the problem you face."

JandolAnganol made towards the door and then stopped. He confronted the older man down the length of the room.

"Why should I have to suffer? Why should not kings be exempt from the common lot? If I did this thing demanded of me, should I be a saint or a devil?"

"That only you will know, sire."

"You care nothing, do you—nothing about me or the kingdom, only for that miserable dead past you work over all day."

The chancellor gripped his trembling hands between his knees.

"We may care, Your Majesty, and yet be unable to do anything. I put it to you that this problem which confronts us is a result of the deteriorating climate. As it happens, I'm studying at present an old chronicle of the time of another king, by name AozroOnden, who was lord of a very different Oldorando almost four centuries ago. The chronicle refers to AozroOnden's slaying of two brothers who had between them ruled the known world."

"I know the legend. What of it? Am I threatening to kill anyone at present?"

"This pleasant story, set in an historical record, is typical of the thinking of those primitive times. Perhaps we are not meant to take the story literally. It is an allegory of man's

responsibility for the death of the two good seasons, represented as two good men, and his causing the cold winters and
burning summers which now afflict us. We all suffer from that
primal guilt. You cannot act without feeling guilt. That is all I
say."

The king let out a growl. "You old bookworm, it's love that
tears me apart, not guilt!"

He went out, banging the door behind him. He was not
going to admit to his chancellor that he did feel guilt. He
loved the queen; yet by some perverse streak in him he longed
to be free, and the realisation tortured him.

She was the queen of queens. All Borlien loved her, as they
did not love him. And a further turn of that particular screw:
he knew she deserved their love. Perhaps she took it too much
for granted that he loved her. . . . Perhaps she had too much
power over him. . . .

And that bastion of her body, ripe as corn sheaves, the soft
seas of her hair, the ointments of her loins, the dazzlement of
her gaze, the wholeness with which she smiled. . . . But what
would it be like to rip into the pubescent body of that preten-
tious semi-Madi princess? A different thing entirely . . .

His tortuous thoughts, winding this way and that, were
penned in among the intricacies of the palace. The palace had
accumulated almost by accident. Courts had been filled in by
buildings and servants' quarters improvised from ruins. The
grand and the sordid lay side by side. The privileged who lived
here above the city suffered almost as many inconveniences as
those in the city.

One token of inconvenience lay in the grotesque arrangements on the skyline, now visible outlined against the darken-
ing cloud overhead. The air in the valley lay stifling upon the
city, like a cat indifferently sprawled upon a dying mouse.
Canvas sails, wooden vanes, and little copper windmills had
been perched high on air stacks in order to drag a breath of
freshness down to those who suffered in chambers below. This
orchestra of semaphoric bids for relief creaked above the
king's head as he walked through his maze. He looked up
once, as if attracted by a chorus of doom.

No one else was about, except sentries. They stood at every
turn, and most of them were phagors. Weapon bearing,

marching, or rigidly on guard, they might have been the sole possessors of the castle and its secrets.

JandolAnganol saluted them absently as he went through the gathering shadows. There was one person to whom he could go for advice. It might be advice of a villainous order, but it would be given. The person who gave it was himself one of the secrets of the castle. His father.

As he drew nearer to an innermost part of the palace where his father was confined, more sentries stiffened at his approach, as if by some potent regal quality he could freeze them with his presence. Bats fluttered from nooks in the stonework, hens scattered underfoot; but the place was strangely silent, dwelling on the king's dilemma.

He made for a rear staircase protected by a thick door. A phagor stood there, his high military caste denoted by the fact that he had retained his horns.

"I will enter."

Without a word, the phagor produced a key and unlocked the door, pushing it wide with his foot. The king descended, walking slowly with a hand on the iron rail. The gloom was thick, and thickened as the stair curved down. At the bottom was an anteroom where another guard stood before another locked door. This also was opened to the king.

He came into the damp set of chambers reserved for his father.

Even in his self-absorption, he felt the chill and the damp. A ghost of remorse moved in his harneys.

VarpalAnganol sat in the end room of three, wrapped in a blanket, gazing into a log fire smouldering in a grate. A grille high in one wall let in the last of daylight. The old man looked up, blinking, and made a slapping noise with his lips, as if moistening his mouth preparatory to speech, but he said nothing.

"Father. It's I. Have you no lamp?"

"I was trying to calculate what year it was."

"It's 381, winter." It was some weeks since he had set eyes on his father. The old man had aged considerably, and would soon be one with the gossies.

He got himself to the standing position, supporting himself with an arm of the chair.

"Do you want to sit down, my boy? There's only the one chair. This place is not very well furnished. It will do me good to stand for a while."

"Sit down, Father. I want to talk to you."

"Have they found your son—what's his name? Roba? Have they found Roba?"

"He's crazy, even the foreigners know it."

"You see, he liked the desert as a child. I took him there, and his mother. The wide sky . . . ."

"Father, I am thinking of divorcing Cune. There are state reasons."

"Oh, well, you could lock her up with me. I like Cune, nice woman. Of course, we'd need another chair. . . ."

"Father, I want some advice. I want to talk to you." The old man sank down on the chair. JandolAnganol crossed in front of him and squatted facing him, back to the feeble fire. "I want to ask you about—love, whatever love is. Are you attending? Everyone is supposed to love. The highest and the lowest. I love the All-Powerful Akhanaba, and perform my worship every day; I am one of his representatives here on earth. I also love MyrdemInggala, above all women who ever breathed. You know that I have killed men I thought looked lustfully upon her."

A pause followed while his father gathered his thoughts.

"You're a good swordsman, that I never denied." The old man tittered.

"Didn't a poet say that Love is like Death? I love Akhanaba and I love Cune, yes. Yet under that love—I often ask myself—under that love, isn't there a vein of hatred? Should there be? Does every man feel as I do?"

The old man said nothing.

"When I was a child, how you beat me! You punished me by locking me out. Once you locked me down here in this very cellar, remember? And yet I loved you, loved you without question. The fatal innocent love of a boy for his father. How is it I can love nobody else without that poison of hate leaking in?"

The old man wriggled in the chair as his son spoke, as if possessed of an incurable itch.

"There's no end to it," he said. "No end at all. . . . We can-

not tell where one emotion ends and the next begins. Your trouble's not hate but guilt. That's what you feel—guilt, Jan. I feel it, all men feel it. It's an inherited misery bred in the bone, for which Akha punishes us with cold and heat. Women don't seem to feel it the way men do. Men control women, but who's to control men? Hate's not bad at all. I like hate, I've always enjoyed hate. It keeps you warm at nights. . . .

"Listen, when I was young, lad, I hated almost everyone. I hated you because you wouldn't do as you were told. But guilt—guilt's a different matter, guilt makes you miserable. Hate cheers you up, makes you forget guilt."

"Love?"

The old man sighed, blowing his bad breath into the dank atmosphere. It was so dark that his son could not see his face, only the gap in it.

"Dogs love their masters, that I do know. I had a dog once, a wonderful dog, white with a brown face, eyes like a Madi. He used to lie beside me on my bed. I loved that dog. What was his name?"

JandolAnganol stood up. "Is that the only love you've ever felt? Love for some scumbering hound?"

"I don't remember loving anyone else. . . . Anyway, you are going to have a divorcement of MyrdenInggala, and you want an excuse so that you don't feel so guilty about it, eh?"

"Is that what I said?"

"When? I don't remember. What time is it, do you reckon? You must announce that she and YeferalOborol, that brother of hers, plotted to murder the Sibornalese ambassador, and that's how her brother was killed. A conspiracy. There's a perfect excuse. And then when you put her away, you will please Sibornal as well as Pannoval and Oldorando."

JandolAnganol clutched his forehead. "Father—how did you learn of YeferalOborol's death? His body was brought back only an hour ago."

"You see, son, if you keep very still, as I have to with my stiff joints, everything comes to you. I have more time. . . . There is another possibility . . ."

"What's that?"

"You can just have her disappear in the darkness one night. Never seen again. Now that the brother's gone, there's no one

interested enough to make a real fuss. Is her old father still alive?"

"No. I couldn't do that. I wouldn't even dream of doing it."

"Of course you would . . . ." He panted a little by way of laughter. "But my conspiracy idea is a good one, eh?"

The king went to stand under the window. Waves of light floated on the domed brick ceiling of the prison. Outside was the queen's reservoir. His sorrow accumulated like water. How treacherous this old man still was. . . .

"Good? Full of guile and taking advantage of circumstances, yes. I see clearly where I had my character from."

He hammered on the door for release.

After the cellars, the evening world appeared bathed in light. He took a side door and emerged by the reservoir, where a flight of steps led down to the water. Once a boat had been moored there; he remembered playing in it as a boy; now it had disintegrated and sunk.

The sky was the hue of stale cheese, flecked with wisps of grey cloud. On the far side of the pool, like a cliff, rose the queen's quarters, its elegant outlines black against the sky. A light burned dimly in one window. Perhaps his beautiful wife was there, preparing for her bed. He could go and beg her forgiveness. He could lose himself in her beauty.

Instead, unpremeditatedly, he jumped forward into the reservoir.

He held his hands together above his head as if he were falling from a building. Air belched out from his clothes. The water grew dark rapidly as he sank.

"Let me never rise," he said.

The water was deep and cold and black. He welcomed terror, trying to embrace the mud at the bottom. Bubbles streamed from his nose.

The processes of life commanded by the All-Powerful would not allow him to escape into the avenues of death. Despite his struggles, he found himself drifting upward again. As he surfaced, gasping, the queen's light went out.

VII

THE QUEEN VISITS
THE LIVING AND THE DEAD

The next day dawned hot and heavy. The queen of queens allowed herself to be bathed by her women. She played with Tatro for a while, and then summoned SartoriIrvrash to meet her in the family vault.

There she paid her last respects to her brother. Soon he would be buried in his correct land-octave. His body lay swathed in yellow cloth on a block of Lordryardry ice. She noted with grief how even death had not transformed his plain features. She wept for all things prosaic and exotic, for all that had happened and failed to happen to her brother in his lifetime. So the chancellor found her.

He wore an ink-smeared smock. There was ink on his fingers. He bowed low, and there was ink on his pate.

"Rushven, I have a farewell to say here, but I wish also to greet my brother now that his soul has passed to the world below. I wish you by me while I go into pauk, to see that nobody disturbs me."

He looked troubled. "Madam. May I recall two items to

your troubled mind. First, that pater-placation—pauk, if you prefer the old-fashioned term—is discouraged by your church. Second, it is not possible to commune with gossies before their mortal bodies are buried in their land-octaves."

"And third, you believe that pauk is a fairy tale anyway." She gave him a wan smile as she resurrected an old argument between them.

He shook his head. "I know well what once I said. However, times change. Now I confess that I myself have learned to go into pater-placation, to console myself by communing with the spirit of my departed wife."

He bit his lips. Reading her expression, he said, "Yes, she has forgiven me."

She touched him. "I'm glad."

Then the academic rose up in him again, and he said, "But you see, Your Majesty, there is a philosophical difficulty in believing that the pater-placation ritual is other than subjective. There *cannot* be gossies and fessups under the ground with whom living people talk."

"We know there are. You and I and millions of peasants talk to our ancestors whenever we wish. Where's the difficulty?"

"Historical records, of which I have plenty, all report that the gossies were once creatures of hatred, bewailing their failed lives, pouring scorn on the living. Over the generations, that has changed; nowadays, all anyone gets is sweetness and consolation. That suggests that the whole experience is wish-fulfilment, a kind of self-hypnosis. Moreover, stellar geometry has outmoded the antique idea that our world rests on an original boulder, towards which fessups descend."

She stamped her foot. "Must I call the vicar? Am I not under grief and strain enough, without having to listen to your preposterous historical lectures at this hour?"

She was immediately sorry for her outburst, and put an arm through his as they ascended to her room.

"It's a comfort, whatever it is," she said. "Praise be, there's a realm of the spirit beyond knowledge."

"My dear queen, though I hate religion, I recognise sanctity when I am in its presence." When she squeezed his arm, he was emboldened to add, "But the Holy Church has never

quite accepted pater-placation as part of its ritual, has it? It does not know what to make of gossies and fessups. In consequence, it would like to ban it, but if it did so, then a million peasants would quit the Church. So it ignores the entire question.''

She looked down at her smooth hands. Already she was preparing herself for the act. "How very sensible of the Church,'' she murmured.

SartoriIrvrash, in his turn, was sensible enough to make no reply.

MyrdemInggala led the way through into her inner chamber. She sank down on her bed, composing herself, controlling her breathing, relaxing her muscles. SartoriIrvrash sat quietly by her bed, circling his forehead with the holy sign, to begin his vigil. He saw that already she was moving into the pauk state.

He kept his eyes tight closed, not daring to gaze upon her defenceless beauty, and listened to her infrequent exhalations.

The soul has no eyes, yet it sees in the world below.

The soul of the queen cast its regard downwards as it began its long descent. Beneath lay space more vast than night skies, more rich, more imposing. It was not space at all: it was the opposite of space, of consciousness even—a peculiar rupellary density without feature.

Just as the land regards an ocean-going ship as a token of freedom, while the sailors confined on that ship regard the land in similar terms, so the realm of oblivion was at once space and non-space.

To consciousness, the realm appeared infinite. In its downward direction, it ceased only where the races of manlike-kind began, in a green and unknown, unknowable womb, the womb of the original beholder. The original beholder—that passive motherly principle—received the souls of the dead who sank back into her. Although she might be no more than a fossil scent entombed in rock, she was not to be resisted.

Above the original beholder were the gossies and fessups, floating, thousands upon thousands upon thousands, as if all

the stars of night had been stacked in order, and arranged in accordance with the ancient idea of land-octaves.

The queen's exploratory soul sank down, floating like a feather towards the fessups. At close quarters, they resembled not stars so much as mummified chickens, with hollow eyes and stomachs, their legs dangling clumsily. Age had eroded them. They were transparent. Their insides circulated like luminescent fish in a bowl. Their mouths were open like fish, as if trying to blow a bubble towards a surface they would never see again. In their upper strata, where the gossies were less ancient, little dusts still escaped from phantom larynxes, the very last apostrophes remaining to the possessive case of life.

To some souls venturing there, the ranks of the departed were terrifying. For the queen they held consolation. She looked down upon them, those mouths pickled in obsidian, and was reassured to believe that at least some wreckage remained from existence, and would ever remain until the planet was consumed by fire. And who knew if even then . . .

For venturing souls, no compass bearings seemed possible. Yet there was direction. The beholder was a lodestone. All here had been collected according to plan, as stones on seashores are graded according to size. The ranks of fessups stretched below the whole earth, leading beyond Borlien and Oldorando to far Sibornal and even to the remote parts of Hespagorat, to semi-legendary Pegovin beyond the Climent Sea, even to the poles.

The soul barque moved to a breeze that did not blow, finally drifting to the gossie of what had once been her mother, the wild Shannana, wife to RatanOborol, ruler of Matrassyl. The maternal gossie resembled a battered birdcage, its ribs and hipbones forming tentative golden patterns against the darkness, like a leaf crushed long ago in a child's book. It spoke.

Gossies and fessups were tormenting things. As negatives of being, they recalled only the incidents in their lives which were pleasant. The good had been interred with them; the evil, the dross, lost along with freedom of action.

"Dear Moth, I come dutifully before you again, to see how you fare." Her ritual salutation.

"My dear daughter, there are no troubles here. All is serene, nothing can go awry. And when you appear, everything is gained. My joyous and beautiful one, how did I squeeze such an offspring from my unworthy loins? Your grandmother is also here, delighted also to be back in your presence."

"It is a comfort to be in your presence, too, Moth." But the words were a formula against entropy.

"Oh, no, but you must not say that, because the delight is all ours, and often I think how in the hurried days of my life I never cherished you enough, certainly not as much as your virtue warranted. There was always so much to be done, and another battle fought, and one may wonder now why energy was spent on those unimportant things, whereas the real joy of life was being close with you and seeing you grow up into—"

"Mother, you were a kind parent, and I not a dutiful enough child. I was always headstrong—"

"Headstrong!" exclaimed the old gossie. "No, no, you did nothing to offend. One sees these things differently in this stage of existence, one sees what the true things are, what's important. A few little peccadillos are nothing, and I'm only sorry if I made a fuss at the time. That was just my stupidity— I knew all along that you were my greatest treasure. Not to pass on life, that's the failure—as those down here without offspring will testify in endless dole."

She continued joyfully in this vein, and the queen let her ramble on, placated by her words, for the fact was that in life she had found her mother self-absorbed and without more than perfunctory kindness. It delighted her to find that this battered cage should remember events of her childhood which she had forgotten. Flesh had died; memory was embalmed here.

At last she interrupted her. "Moth, I came down here half-prepared to meet with YeferalOborol, expecting his soul to have joined you and grandmother."

"Ah . . . then my dear son has come to the end of earthly years? Oh, praise be, that's good news indeed, how glad we shall be to be united with him, since he never mastered pater-placation as you have, you clever girl. How glad you make us."

"Dear Mother, he was shot by a Sibornalese gun."

"Splendid! Splendid! The sooner the better, as far as I'm concerned. That is a treat. . . . And when do we expect him?"

"His mortal remains will be buried within a few hours."

"We shall watch for him, and what a welcome we shall give to him. You'll be here with us one day, too, never fear. . . ."

"I look forward to it, Moth. And I have a request, which you must pass to your fellow fessups. It is a difficult question. There is one on the surface still who loves me, though he has never spoken his love; I have felt it radiating from him. I feel I can trust him as I can trust few men. He has been sent from Matrassyl to fight in a distant land."

"We have no wars down here, sweet child."

"This trusted friend of mine is often in pauk. His father is here in the world below. My friend's name is Hanra Tolram-Ketinet. I want you to pass a message on to his father, to ask Hanra's whereabouts, for it is essential that I get a message to him."

A hissing silence before the shade of Shannana spoke again.

"My sweet child, in your world nobody communicates fully with another. So much is unknown. Here we have completion. There can be no secrets when the flesh is divested."

"I know, Moth," said the soul. It feared that kind of completion. It had heard the statement many times. It explained once more what it required from the revered gossie. After many a diversion, understanding was reached, and the soul's enquiry was passed along the ranks, like a breeze rustling the dead leaves of a forest.

For the soul, there was difficulty in sustaining herself. Phantasms of the upper world seeped in, and a noise like frying. A curtain blew, something rattled with a deadly music. The soul began drifting, despite the cajolings of her mother's gossie.

At last a message returned to her through the obsidian. Her friend was still among the living. The gossies of his family declared that he had spoken with them recently, when his corporeal part was near a village called Ut Pho in the jungles of the Chwart Heights on the eastern margins of the land called Randonan.

"My thanks for what I needed to know," cried the soul. As it poured forth its gratitude, the maternal gossie puffed dust

from its throat and spoke again.

"Here we pity your poor disrupted lives, when physical sight blinds you. We can communicate with a greater voice beyond your knowledge, where many voices are one. Come soon and hear for yourself. Join us!"

But the frail soul knew these claims of old. The dead and the living were opposing armies; pauk was only a truce.

With many cries of affection, it left the spark which had once been Shannana, to sail upwards towards the spectrums of movement and breath.

When MyrdemInggala was strong enough, she dismissed SartoriIrvrash from her suite with suitable courtesies and no mention of what she had learned in pauk.

She summoned Mai TolramKetinet, sister to the friend of whom she had been enquiring in the world below. Mai aided her through the ritual of a post-pauk bath. The queen sluiced down her body with extra care, as if it had been sullied by its journey towards death.

"I wish to go into the city, Mai—in disguise. You will accompany me. The princess will remain here. Prepare two sets of peasant clothes."

When she was alone, MyrdemInggala wrote a letter to General TolramKetinet, apprising him of the threatening events at court. She signed the letter, sealed it with her seal, enclosed it in a leather pouch, and sealed that with a stronger seal.

Dismissing feelings of faintness, she dressed in the peasant clothes Mai brought, and concealed the message pouch in them.

"We shall leave by the side gate."

The side gate attracted less attention. There were always beggars and other importuners at the main gate. There were also heads of criminals on poles at present, which stank.

The guard let them through indifferently, and the women walked down the winding road to the city. At this hour, JandolAnganol was probably asleep. It was his habit, learnt from his father, to rise at dawn and show himself, crowned, on his balcony, for all to see. Not only did this gesture induce a feel-

ing of security in the nation; it impressed everyone with the long hours the king worked—"like a one-legged peasant," as the expression was. But the king generally went back to bed after his appearance.

Heavy cloud rolled overhead. The scorching wind, the thordotter, blew from the southeast, picking at their petticoats, blowing its hot breath in their faces till their eyes dried. It was a relief to gain the narrow alleys at the foot of the hill, despite the dust that whipped at their heels.

"We'll seek a blessing in the church," said MyrdemInggala. There was a church at the end of the street, with steps winding down round its curving wall in the traditional way of Old Borlienese church architecture. Little of the church was above ground except the dome. In this way, the fathers of the church imitated the desire to live underground which possessed the Takers, those holy men of Pannoval who had brought the faith to Borlien, centuries ago.

The two women were not alone in their descent. An old peasant shuffled before them, led by a boy. He held out a hand to them. His story was that he had given up his holding because the heat had killed his crops, and had come to beg in town. The queen gave him a silver coin.

Darkness prevailed inside the church. The congregation knelt in a pool of darkness intended to remind them of their mortal state. Light filtered down from above. The painted image of Akhanaba behind the circular altar was lit by candles. The long bovine face, blue-painted, the eyes kind but inhuman —these were lapped by uncertain shadows.

To these traditional elements was added a more modern embellishment. Near the door, lit by one candle, stood a stylised portrait of a mother, with sad downcast eyes, her hands spread. Many of the women shuffling in kissed the original beholder as they passed her.

No formal service was in progress but, since the church was nevertheless half full, a priest was praying aloud in a high nasal singsong.

"Many come to knock at thy door, O Akhanaba, and many turn away without a knock.

"And to those who turn away and those who stand in all piety knocking,

"Thou sayest, 'Cease to cry "When willst thou open to me, O All-Powerful One?"

" 'For I say that all the while the doors stand open, and never has been shut.' These things are there to be seen but you see them not."

MyrdemInggala thought of what her mother's gossie had said. They communicated with a greater voice. Yet Shannana did not mention Akhanaba. Looking up at the face of the All-Powerful, she thought, it's true, we are surrounded by mystery. Even Rushven can't understand it.

"All about you lies all that you need, if you will accept and not take by force. If you would but lay down your self, you would find what is greater than yourself.

"All things are equal in this world, but also greater."

" 'Ask not therefore if I am man or animal or stone:

" 'All these I am and more that you must learn to perceive.' "

The chanting went on, the choir joining in. The queen reflected how excellently the alto voices chimed with the stone vaulting overhead; here indeed were spirit and stone united.

She put a hand under her clothes and placed it on her breast, trying to still the beating of her heart.

Despite the beauty of the singing, the apprehension in her would not be soothed. There was no time to contemplate eternity under the pressure of dire events.

When the priest had blessed them, she was ready to go on. The two women, shawls about their heads, went out again into the wind and daylight.

The queen led them to the quayside, where the River Takissa looked dark and choppy, like a narrow sea. A boat just in from Oldorando was mooring with some difficulty. Small boats were being loaded, but there was less activity than usual because of the thordotter. Empty carts, barrels, timbers, winches, and other equipment essential to river life stood about. A tarpaulin whipped back and forth in the wind. The queen walked on determinedly until they reached a warehouse over which was a sign reading: LORDRYARDRY ICE TRADING COMPANY.

This was the Matrassyl headquarters of the famous ice captain, Krillio Muntras of Lordryardry.

The warehouse had an assortment of doors on all floors, large and small. MyrdemInggala chose the smallest on the ground floor and walked in. Mai followed.

Inside was a cobbled court, with fat men rolling barrels of their own shape over to a dray.

"I wish to speak with Krillio Muntras," she said to the nearest man.

"He's busy. He won't speak to anyone," the man said, regarding her suspiciously. She had drawn a veil across her face, so as not to be recognised.

"He'll speak to me." She withdrew from a finger of her left hand a ring with the colours of the sea in it. "Take this to him."

The man departed, muttering. By his stature and accent, she knew he was from Dimariam, one of the countries of the southern continent of Hespagorat. She waited impatiently, tapping her foot on the cobbles, but after a moment the man was back, his attitude much changed. "Pray allow me to show you to Captain Muntras."

MyrdemInggala turned to Mai. "You will wait here."

"But, ma'am—"

"And do not obstruct the men in their work."

She was shown into a workshop smelling of glues and fresh-shaved wood, where old men and apprentices were sawing up timbers and making them into chests and iceboxes. The workbenches were bearded with long curly shavings. The men watched the hooded female figure curiously as it passed.

Her guide opened a door hidden behind overalls. They climbed a dusty stair to a floor where a long low room commanded a view of the river. Clerks worked at one end of the room, shoulders bent over ledgers. At the other end was a desk with a chair as solid as a throne, from which a fat brown man had risen, to come forward with a beaming face. He bowed low, dismissed the guide, and led the queen into a private room beyond his desk.

Although his room overlooked a stable yard, it was well furnished, with prints on the wall, with an elegance at variance with the functional appearance of the rest of the building. One of the prints depicted Queen MyrdemInggala.

"Madam Queen, I am proud to receive you." The Ice Cap-

tain beamed again and set his head on one side as far as it would go, the better to regard MyrdemInggala as she removed her veil and headgear. He was himself simply dressed in a charfrul, the full shift with pockets worn by many natives of the equatorial regions.

When he had her comfortably seated and had given her a glass of wine chilled with fresh Lordryardry ice, he thrust out a hand to her. Opening his fist, he revealed her ring, which he now returned ceremoniously, insisting on fitting it on her dainty finger.

"It was the best ring I ever sold."

"You were only a humble pedlar then."

"Worse, I was a beggar, but a beggar with determination." He struck his chest.

"Now you are very rich."

"Now, what are riches, madam? Do they buy happiness? Well, frankly, they at least permit us to be miserable comfortably. My state, I will admit to you, is better than that of most common folk."

His laugh was comfortable. He hitched a plump leg unceremoniously over the edge of the table and lifted his glass to toast her, evaluating her. The queen of queens raised her eyes to his. The Ice Captain lowered his gaze, protecting himself from a tremor of feeling much like awe. He had dealt in girls almost as widely as ice; before the queen's beauty, he felt himself powerless.

MyrdemInggala talked to him about his family. She knew he had a clever daughter and a stupid son, and that the stupid son, Div, was about to take over the ice trade on his father's retirement. That retirement had been postponed. Muntras had made his last trip a tenner and a half ago, at the time of the Battle of the Cosgatt—only it had proved not to be his last trip, since Div needed further instructions.

She knew the Ice Captain was gentle with his silly boy. Yet Muntras's father had been harsh with him, sending him out as a lad to earn money begging and peddling, in order to prove he was capable of taking over a one-ship ice business. She had heard this tale before, but was not bored by it.

"You've had an eventful life," she said.

Perhaps he thought some sort of criticism was implied, for

he looked uncomfortable. To cover his unease, he slapped his leg and said, "I'm not ashamed to say that I have prospered at a time when the majority of citizens are doing the reverse."

She regarded his solid countenance as if wondering if he understood she was also of that majority, but merely said, in her composed way, "You told me once you started in business with one boat. How many have you now, Captain?"

"Yes, Madam Queen, my old father started with but one old hooker, which I inherited. Today, I hand over to my son a fleet of twenty-five ships. Fast seagoing sloops, and ketches, hookers, and doggers, to ply the rivers and coasts, each adapted to the trade. There you see the benefits of dealing in ice. The hotter it gets, the more a block of good Lordryardry ice will fetch in the market. The worse things get for others, the more they improve for me."

"But your ice melts, Captain."

"That's so, and many the jokes people make about it. But Lordryardry ice, being pure off the glacier, melts less rapidly than other ices sold by other traders." He was enjoying himself in her presence, though he had not failed to notice a clouded air about her, so different from her normal disposition.

"I'll put another point to you. You are devout in the religion of your country, Madam Queen, so I do not need to remind you of redemption. Well, my ice is like your redemption. The less there is, the scarcer it becomes, and the scarcer it becomes, the more it costs. My boats now sail all the way from Dimariam, across the Sea of Eagles, up the Takissa and Valvoral rivers to Matrassyl and Oldorando City, as well as along the coast to Keevasien and the ports of the deadly assatassi."

She smiled, perhaps not entirely pleased to hear religion and trade intermingled. "Well, I'm glad someone fares well in a bad age." She had not forgotten the time when she as a young girl on her first visit to Oldorando had met the Dimariamian in the bazaar. He was in rags, but he had a smile; and he had produced from an inner pocket the most beautiful ring she had ever seen. Shannana, her mother, had given her the money. She had returned the next day to buy it, and had worn it ever since.

"You overpaid me for that ring," Krillio Muntras said, "and with the profit I went home and bought a glacier. So I have been in your debt ever since." He laughed, and she joined in. "Now, Madam Queen, you come here not to bargain about ice, since that I supply through the palace majordomo. Can I do you a favour?"

"Captain Muntras, I am in a difficult situation, and I need help."

He looked suddenly cautious. "I do not want to lose the royal favour which permits me, a foreigner, to trade here. Otherwise . . ."

"I appreciate that. All I ask of you is reliability, and of that you will surely avail me. I wish you to deliver a letter for me, secretly. You mention Keevasien, on the border with Randonan. Can you reliably deliver a letter to a certain gentleman fighting in Randonan in our Second Army?"

Muntras's expressive face looked so glum that his cheeks tightened themselves round his mouth. "In war, everything is doubtful. The news is that the Borlienese army fares badly, and Keevasien too. But—but—for you, Madam Queen . . . My boats go up the Kacol River above Keevasien, as far as Ordelay. Yes, I could send a messenger from there. Provided it's not too dangerous. He'd need paying, of course."

"How much?"

He thought. "I have a boy who would do it. When you're young, you don't fear death." He told her how much it would cost. She paid out willingly enough and handed over the pouch with the letter to General TolranKetinet.

Muntras made her another bow. "I'm proud to do it for you. First, I must deliver a freight to Oldorando. That's four days upriver, two days there and two days back. A week in all. Then I'll be back here and straight south for Ottassol."

"Such delay! Do you have to go to Oldorando first?"

"Have to, ma'am. Trade's trade."

"Very well, I'll leave it to you, Captain Muntras. But you understand that this is of vital importance and absolutely secret, between you and me? Carry out this mission faithfully, and I'll see you have your reward."

"I'm grateful for the chance to help, Madam Queen."

When they parted, and the queen had taken another glass of

refreshing wine, she was more cheerful and battled almost gaily back to the palace with her lady-in-waiting, the sister of the general to whom her letter was now despatched. She could hope, whatever the king had decided.

Throughout the palace, doors banged and curtains fluttered in the wind. Pale of face, JandolAnganol talked to his religious advisors. One of them finally said to him, "Your Majesty, this state is holy, and we believe that you have already in your heart come to a decision. You will cement this new alliance for holy reasons, and we shall bless you for it."

The king replied vehemently, "If I make this alliance, it will be because I am wicked, and welcome wickedness."

"Not so, my lord! Your queen and her brother conspired against Sibornal, and must be punished." They were already halfway to believing the lie he had set in circulation; it was his old father's lie, but now it had become common property and possessed them one by one.

In their own chambers, the visiting statesmen, awaiting the king's word, complained about the discomfort of this miserable little palace and of the poverty of the hospitality. The advisors quarrelled amongst themselves, jealous of each other's privileges; but one thing they agreed on. They agreed that if and when the king divorced his queen and married Simoda Tal, the question of the large phagor population of Borlien should be reopened.

Old histories told how ancipital hordes had once descended on Oldorando and burned it to the ground. That hostility had never died. Year by year, the phagor population was being reduced. It was necessary that Borlien should follow the same policy. With Simoda Tal and her ministers at JandolAnganol's side, the issue could be pressed harder.

And with MyrdemInggala gone, with her softhearted ways, it would be convenient to introduce drumbles.

But where was the king, and what was his decision?

The time was a few minutes after fourteen o'clock, and the king stood naked in an upper chamber. A great pendulum of pewter swung solemnly against one wall, clicking out seconds. Against the other wall hung an enormous mirror of silver. In

the shadows stood serving wenches, waiting with vestments to dress JandolAnganol to appear before the diplomats.

Between the pendulum and the mirror JandolAnganol stood or paced. In his indecision, he ran his finger down the scar on his thigh, or pulled the pallid length of his prodo, or regarded the reflection of those bloody devotional stripes which stretched from his shoulderblades down to his thin buttocks. He snarled at the lean whipped thing he saw.

The king could easily send the diplomats packing; his rage, his khmir, were fully equal to such a deed. He could easily snatch up the thing dearest to him—the queen—and brand her mouth with hot kisses, vowing never to allow her from his sight. Or he could do the opposite—be a villain in private and become a saint in the eyes of many, a saint ready to throw everything away for his country.

Some of those who observed him from afar, such as the Pin family on the Avernus, who studied the cross-continuities of the king's family, claimed that the decision was made for the king in a distant past. In their records lay the history of JandolAnganol's family through sixteen generations, back to the time when most of Campannlat lay under snow, back to a distant ancestor of the king's, AozroOn, who had ruled over a village called Oldorando. Along that line, untraced by those who were part of it, lay a story of division between father and son, submerged in some generations but never absent.

That pattern of division lay deep in JandolAnganol's psyche, so deep he did not notice it in himself. Beneath his arrogance was an even older self-contempt. His self-contempt made him turn against his dearest friends and consort with phagors; it was an alienation which early years had fostered. It was buried, but not without voice, and it was about to speak.

He turned abruptly from the mirror, from that shadowy figure who lurked there in silver, and summoned up the maids. He raised his arms and they dressed him.

"And my crown," he said, as they brushed his flowing hair. He would punish the waiting dignitaries by his distance from them.

A few minutes later, the dignitaries found relief from their boredom by rushing to the windows when marching feet were heard outside. They looked down on great rough heads

crowned by gleaming horns, on muscular shoulders and coarse
bodies, on hoofs that echoed and war harness that creaked.
The Royal First Phagorian Guard was parading—a sight that
caused unease in most human spectators, since the ancipitals
were so hinged at knee and elbow that lower leg and lower arm
could turn in all directions. The march was uncanny, with an
impossible forward flexure of the leg at every step.

A sergeant called an order. The platoons halted, going from
movement to the instant immobility characteristic of phagors.

The scorching wind stirred the trailing hairs of the platoon.
The king stepped from between platoons and marched into the
palace. The visiting statesmen regarded each other uneasily,
thoughts of assassination in their heads.

JandolAnganol entered the room. He halted and surveyed
them. One by one, his guests rose. As if he struggled to speak,
the king let the silence lengthen. Then he said, "You have
demanded of me a harsh choice. Yet why should I hesitate?
My first duty is solemnly pledged to my country.

"I am resolved not to let my personal feelings enter the matter. I shall send away my queen, MyrdemInggala. She will
leave this day, and retire to a palace on the seacoast. If the
Holy Pannovalan Church, whose servant I am, grants me a
bill of divorcement, I shall divorce the queen.

"And I shall marry Simoda Tal, of the House of Oldorando."

Clapping and murmurs of congratulation rose. The king's
face was expressionless. As they were approaching, before
they could reach him, he turned on his heel and left the room.

The thordotter slammed the door behind him.

VIII

IN THE PRESENCE OF MYTHOLOGY

Billy Xiao Pin's face was round, as were, in general disposition, his eyes and nose. Even his mouth was a mere rosebud. His skin was smooth and sallow. He had left the Avernus only once previously, when close members of the Pin family had taken him on an Ipocrene fly-past.

Billy was a modest but determined young man, well-mannered like all members of his family, and it was believed that he could be relied upon to face his death with equanimity. He was twenty Earth years old, or just over fourteen by Helliconian reckoning.

Although the Helliconia Holiday Lottery was ruled by chance, it was generally agreed—at least among the thousand-strong Pin family—that Billy was an excellent choice as winner.

When his good fortune was announced, he was sent on a tour of the Avernus by his doting family. With him went his current girl friend, Rose Yi Pin. The moving corridors of the satellite were event-oriented, and those who travelled them

often found themselves caught in technological typhoons, or surrounded by animated computer graphics, sometimes of a malignant kind. The Avernus had been in its orbit for 3269 years; every facility available was mustered to counteract the killing disease which threatened its occupants: lethargy.

Together with a group of friends, Billy took a holiday in a mountain resort. There they slept in a log hut high above the ski slopes. Such synthetic pleasure spots had once been based on real Earth resorts; now they were rejigged to imitate Helliconian locations. Billy and his friends appeared to ski in the High Nktryhk.

Later, they sailed the Ardent Sea to the east of Campannlat. Setting out from the one harbour on a thousand miles of coast, they had as background the eternal cliffs of Mordriat, rising out of the foam straight to heights of almost six thousand feet, their shoulders wreathed in cloud. The Scimitar waterfall fell and paused and fell again in its plunge of over a mile towards the racing sea.

Pleasing though such excitements were, the mind was always aware that every danger, each remote vista, was imprisoned in a mirrored room no more than eighteen feet long by twelve feet wide.

At the conclusion of the holiday, Billy Xiao Pin went alone to his Advisor, to squat before him in the Humility position.

"Silence recapitulates long conversations," said the Advisor. "In seeking life you will find death. Both are illusory."

Billy knew that the Advisor did not wish him to leave the Avernus, for the profound reason that the Advisor feared any dynamism. He was devoured by the deadly illusionism which had become prevalent philosophy. In his youth, he had written a poetic treatise one hundred syllables long entitled, "On the Prolongation of One Helliconian Season Beyond One Human Life-Span."

This treatise was a product of, and a sustaining factor in, the illusionism which gripped the Avernus. Billy had no intellectual way of fighting the philosophy; but now that he was about to leave the ship, he felt a hatred of it which he dared to voice.

"I must stand in a real world and experience real joy, real hurt. If only for a brief while, I must endure real mountains

and walk along stone streets. I must encounter people with real destinies."

"You still overuse that treacherous word 'real.' The evidence of our senses is evidence only to our senses. Wisdom looks elsewhere."

"Yes. Well. I'm going elsewhere."

But morbidity did not know where to stop. The aged man continued to lecture. Billy continued meekly to listen.

The old man knew that sex was at the bottom of it. He saw that Billy had a sensuous nature which needed to be curbed. Billy was giving up Rose to seek out Queen MyrdemInggala—yes, he knew Billy's desires. He wished to see the queen of queens face to face.

That was a sterile idea. Rose was not a sterile idea. The real —to use that word—was to be found not extraneously but within the mystery of personality: in Billy's case, Rose's personality, perchance. And there were other considerations.

"We have a role to fulfil, our role towards Earth the Obligation. Our deepest satisfaction comes from fulfilling that role. On Helliconia, you will lose role and society."

Billy Xiao Pin dared raise his eyes so as to regard his old Advisor. The huddled figure was planted, each of his outbreaths directing his weight down to anchor against the floor, each in-breath lifting his head towards the ceiling. He could not be perturbed, not even by the loss of a favourite pupil.

This scene was being recorded by ever-watching cameras and broadcast to any of the six thousand who might care to flip to this chamber. There was no privacy. Privacy encouraged dissidence.

Watching the wise simian eyes, Billy saw that his Advisor no longer believed in Earth. Earth!—the subject Billy and his contemporaries discussed endlessly, the ever-interesting topic. Earth was not accessible like Helliconia. But Earth for the Advisor and hundreds like him had become a sort of ideal—a projection of the inner lives of those aboard.

As the voice shaped its crisp nothings, Billy thought he saw that the old man did not believe in the objective reality of Helliconia either. For him, ensconced in the sophistry of argument which formed so large a part of the station's intellectual life, Helliconia was merely a projection, an hypothesis.

The great lottery prize was designed to counteract this withering of the senses. The youthful hope of the ship—which in magical ways centred about that great object of study disrobing its seasons below them—died, generation by generation, until the enforced imprisonment became voluntary imprisonment. Billy had to go and die that others might live.

He had to go to where that sloe-eyed queen thrust her body against the breath of the thordotter as she climbed to the castle.

The speech ceased at last. Billy took his chance.

"Thousand thanks for all your care, Master." Bowing. Leaving. Breathing deeper.

His departure from the Avernus was stage-managed as a great event. Everyone felt strongly about his going. This was the actual proof that Hell
iconia existed. The six thousand were becoming less able to live imaginatively beyond the station, in spite of all the instruments which were devised to enable them to do so. The prize was a gesture of supreme worth, even to the losers.

Rose Yi Pin turned her neat small face up to Billy's and wrapped her arms round him for the last time. "I believe you will live for ever down there, Billy. I shall watch you as I grow old and ugly. Just beware of their silly religions. Life here is sane. Down there they are mad in the head with religious notions—even that so beautiful queen of yours."

He kissed her lips. "Live your orderly life. Don't fret."

Suddenly fury burst from her. "Why do you ruin my life? Where's the order, with you gone?"

He shook his head. "That you must discover for yourself."

The automated craft was waiting to take him from purgatory. Billy climbed through the passage into the little shell, and the door hissed shut behind him. Terror gripped him; he strapped himself into the seat and enjoyed the emotion.

The choice as to whether to make the descent with the windows shuttered or not was his. He pressed a button. Up flew the shutters and he was rewarded with a view of a magical whale from whose flank he was not excommunicated. A belt of irregular stars spread into the distance like the curl of a comet's tail. Gasping, he realised that these stars were unproc-

essed rubbish ejected from the Avernus, falling into orbit about the station.

At one moment, the Avernus was an immensity, its eighteen million tons obscuring the field of vision; at the next, it was dwindling, and Billy forgot to look. Helliconia was in view, as familiar as his own face in a mirror, but now seen more nakedly, with cloud drifting across its lit crescent and the peninsula of Pegovin striking like a club into the central sea. The great southern ice cap dazzled.

He looked for the two suns of the binary system as the windows darkened to fend off their light.

Batalix, the nearer sun, was lost behind the planet, only 1.26 astronomical units away.

Freyr, visible as a grey ball behind the opaqued glass, was immensely bright at 240 astronomical units. When at 236 astronomical units distance, Helliconia would reach perihelion, its nearest point to Freyr; that time was only 118 Earth years away. Then once more Batalix and its planets would be carried away on their orbits, not to come so close to the dominant member of the system for another 2592 Earth years.

To Billy Xiao Pin, this set of astronomical figures, which he had learned along with his alphabets at the age of three, made a neat diagram. He was about to land where the diagram became an untidy question of history, of crises and challenges.

His round face elongated at the thought. Although Helliconia had been under constant observation for such a long while, it remained in many ways a mystery.

Billy knew that the planet would survive perihelion, that temperatures at the equator would soar to 150 degrees but nothing worse; that Helliconia had an extraordinary system of homeostasis, at least as powerful as Earth's, which would maintain as steady a state of equilibrium as possible. He did not share the superstitious fears of the peasantry that Freyr was about to devour them—though he understood how such fears might arise.

What he did not know was whether various nations would survive the testing heat. Tropical countries like Borlien and Oldorando were most threatened.

The Avernus had been in existence and observing since before the spring of the previous Great Year. It had once ex-

perienced the slow spread of the Great Winter on the planet below, had witnessed multitudes dying and nations going down. How precisely that pattern would be repeated in the Winter still far distant remained to be seen. The Earth Observation Station would have to function and the six families to exist for another fourteen Earth centuries before that mystery was resolved.

To this awe-inspiring world, Billy had committed his soul.

Trembling took Billy in every limb. He was to embrace this world, he was to be born.

The craft made two orbits of the planet, braking as it did so, and landed on a plateau to the east of Matrassyl.

Billy rose from his seat and stood listening. At last he remembered to breathe. An android had been sent down with him, an alter ego to defend him. The Avernians felt their vulnerability. The product of generations of soft-bred men, Billy was reckoned to need protection. The android was programmed to be aggressive. It carried defensive weapons. It looked human, and indeed its face was moulded to resemble Billy's, which it did in all but mobility; its expressions changed sluggishly, giving it a permanent air of gloom. Billy disliked it. He looked at it as it stood expectantly in a recess shaped to its body.

"Stay where you are," Billy said. "Go back to the Avernus with the craft."

"You need my protection," said the android.

"I will manage as best I can. It's my life now." He pressed a delay switch which would ensure automatic liftoff in an hour's time. Then he activated the door and climbed from the craft.

He stood on the wished-for planet, breathing its scents, letting a thousand strange sounds come to his ears. The unfiltered air bruised his lungs. Dizziness assailed him.

He looked up. All above him stretched a sky of most beautiful resonant blue, without feature. Billy was accustomed to looking at space; paradoxically, the arch of sky appeared vaster. The eye was drawn forever into it. It covered the living world and was its most beautiful expression.

To the west, Batalix in aureoles of gold and tan was preparing to set. Freyr, its disc only thirty percent the size of Batalix's, burned with splendid intensity almost at zenith. All

around it swam the great blue envelope which was the first of Helliconia to be seen from space, and the unmistakable imprimatur of it as a life-bearing planet. The visiting life-form lowered his head and passed a hand over his eyes.

At a short distance stood a group of five trees, overhung with fleshy creepers. Towards them Billy made his way, walking as if gravity had only just been invented. He fell against the nearest trunk, embracing it, to have his hands torn by thorns. Nevertheless, he clung tight, closing his eyes, flinching from every inexplicable sound. He could not move. When the craft lifted for its return to the mother station, he wept.

Here was the real, with a vengeance. It penetrated all his senses.

By clinging to the tree, lying on the ground, hiding beside a fallen trunk, he accustomed himself to the experience of being on an immense planet. Distant objects, clouds, and a line of hills, in particular, terrified him with their implications of size and—yes—reality. Just as alarming were all the small live things with random inclinations of their own, whole phyla absent from existence aboard the Avernus. He looked down in anguish as a small winged creature alighted on his left hand and used it as a highway to his sleeve. What was most alarming was the knowledge that all these things were beyond his control; no touch of a switch could tame them.

There was in particular the problem of the suns, which he had not taken into account. On the Avernus, light and dark were largely matters of temperament; here, one had no choice. As dimday was followed by night, Billy felt for the first time the ancient precariousness of his kind. Long ago, mankind had built huddling places against the dark. Cities had developed, had grown to metropolises, and had taken off into space; now he felt himself back at the beginning of history.

He survived the night. Despite himself, he had fallen asleep, to wake unharmed. Doing his accustomed morning exercises brought him back to a sense of himself. He was enough in control to walk from the shelter of the cluster of trees and to rejoice in the morning. After drinking and eating from his rations, he set off in the direction of Matrassyl.

Walking along a jungle path, bemused by bird calls, he became aware of a footstep behind him. He turned. A phagor

froze to instant immobility, only a few paces away.

Phagors were part of the mythology of the Avernus. Their portraits and models of them were accessible everywhere. This one, however, had the presence and individuality of life. It chewed as it regarded Billy, saliva leaking from its broad lower lip. Over its bulky figure was a one-piece garment, dyed here and there with saffron. Tufts of its long white hair were similarly dyed, giving it an unhealthy appearance. A dead snake was knotted over one shoulder—evidently a recent catch. In its hand it carried a curved knife. This was neither an idealised museum replica nor a child's cuddly toy. As it stepped nearer, it exuded a rancid odor which made Billy giddy.

He faced it squarely and spoke slowly in Hurdhu. "Can you give me directions to Matrassyl?"

The creature went on ruminating. It appeared to be chewing on some kind of scarlet nut; juice of that colour trickled from its mouth. A drop sprayed into Billy Xiao Pin. He reached up and brushed it from his cheek.

"Matrassyl," it said, pronouncing the word leadenly as "Madrazzyl."

"Yes. Which way is Matrassyl?"

"Yes."

The look in its cerise eyes—impossible to determine whether it was meek or murderous. He wrenched his gaze away, to find that more phagors stood near, bushlike among the befoliaged shadow.

"Can you understand what I say?" His sentences came from the phrasebook. He was bewildered by the unreality of the situation.

"A taking to a place is within ability."

From a creature that had the natural force of a boulder, good sense was hardly to be expected, but Billy was left in a little doubt as to its intentions. The creature rolled forward with an easy motion and pushed Billy along the path. Billy moved. The other figures tramped among the undergrowth, keeping pace.

They reached a broken slope. Here the jungle had been cleared—some trees had been hacked down, and scuttling pigs saw to it that further growth would never reach maturity.

Among casual attempts at cultivation were huts or, rather, roofs supported by posts.

In the shade provided by these huts, lumpish figures lay like cattle. Some rose and came towards the foragers, one of whom sounded a small horn to announce their arrival. Billy was surrounded by male and female ancipitals, creaghs and gillots and runts, glaring up at him inquisitively. Some runts ran on all fours.

Billy dropped into the Humility position.

"I'm trying to get to Matrassyl," he said. The absurdity of the sentence made him laugh; he had to check himself before he became hysterical, but the noise had the effect of making everyone stand back.

"The lower kzahhn has proximity for inspection," a gillot said, touching his arm and making a motion of her head. He followed her across a stone-strewn dell, and everyone else followed him. Everything he passed—from tender green shoots to round boulders—was rougher than he could have visualised.

Under an awning set against the dell's low cliff sprawled an elder phagor, arms bent at impossible angles. It sat up in smooth movements and revealed itself as an ancient gillot, with prominent withered dugs and black hairs sprouting from her coat. A necklace of polished gwing-gwing stones hung about her neck. She wore a face bracelet buckled across the prow of her nose as mark of rank. This was evidently the "lower kzahhn."

Remaining seated, she looked up at Billy.

She spoke to him questioningly.

Billy had been a junior in the great sociological clan of Pin, and not a conscientious one at that. He worked in the division which studied the family of Anganols, generation by generation. There were those among his superiors who were conversant with the histories of the present king's predecessors back to the previous spring, some sixteen generations past. Billy Xiao Pin spoke Olonets, the main language of Compannlat and Hespagorat, and several of its variants, including Old Olonets. But he had never attempted the ancipital tongue, Native; nor had he properly mastered the language the lower

kzahhn was speaking, Hurdhu, the bridge language used in these times between man and phagor.

"I don't understand," he said, in Hurdhu, and felt a strange sensation when she understood, as if he had stepped from the real world into some strange fairy story.

"Understanding is to me of you being from a far place," she said, translating her own language, noun-choked, into Hurdhu. "What situation is that far place?"

Perhaps they had seen the space-craft land.

He gestured vaguely, and recited a prepared speech. "I come from a distant town in Morstrual, where I am the kzahhn." Morstrual was even more remote than Mordriat, and safe to name. "Your people will be rewarded if they escort me to King JandolAnganol in Matrassyl."

"King JandolAnganol."

"Yes."

She became immobile, gazing ahead. A stallun squatting nearby passed her a leather bottle from which she drank in slobbering fashion, letting the liquid spill. It smelt pungent and spiritous. Ah, he thought, raffel: a deleterious drink distilled by ancipitals. He had fallen in with a poor tribe of phagors. Here he was, dealing capably with these enigmatic beasts, and on the Avernus everyone would be watching him through the optical system. Even his old Advisor. Even Rose.

The heat and the short walk over rough ground had taxed him. But a more self-conscious motive made him sit down on a flat stone and spread his legs, resting his elbows on his knees, to stare nonchalantly at the creature confronting him. The most incredible occurrences became everyday when there was no alternative.

"Ancipital race carry much spears for his crusade for King JandolAnganol." She paused. Behind her was a cave. In its shade, dim cerise eyes gleamed. Billy guessed that tribal ancestors would be stored there, sinking through tether to pure keratin. At once ancestor and idol, every undead phagor helped direct its successors through the painful centuries when Freyr dominated.

"Sons of Freyr fight other Sons of Freyr each season, and we lend spears."

He recognised the traditional phagorian term for human-kind. The ancipitals, unable to invent new terms, merely adapted old ones.

"Order two of your tribe to escort me to King Jandol-Anganol."

Again her stillness—and all the others, as Billy looked round, conspiring to that same immobility. Only the pigs and curs trundled about, forever searching for titbits in the dirt.

The old gillot then began a long speech which defied Billy's understanding. He had to halt her in the middle of her ramblings, asking her to start again. Hurdhu tasted as pungent as goat's cheese on his tongue. Other phagors came up, closing round him, choking him with their dense smell—but not as unpleasant as anticipated, he thought—all aiding their leader with her explanation. As a result, nothing was explained.

They showed him old wounds, backs bereft of skin and fur, broken legs, shattered arms, all exhibited with calm insistence. He was revolted and fascinated. They produced pennants and a sword from the cave.

Gradually he took their meaning. Most of them had served with King JandolAnganol in his Fifth Army. Some weeks ago, they had marched against Driat tribes. They had suffered a defeat here in the Cosgatt. The tribes had used a new weapon which barked like a giant hound.

These poor folk had survived. But they dared not go back to the king's service in case that giant hound barked again. They lived as they could. They dreamed of returning to the cool regions of the Nktryhk.

It was a long tale. Billy became vexed by it, and by the flies. He took some of their raffel. It was deleterious, just as the textbooks said. Feeling sleepy, he ceased to listen when they tried to describe the Cosgatt battle to him. For them, it might have happened yesterday.

"Will two of you escort me to the king or will you not?"

They fell silent, then grunted to each other in Native Ancipital.

At length, the gillot spoke in Hurdhu to him.

"What gift is from your hand for such escort?"

On his wrist he wore a flat grey watch, its triple set of flicking figures telling the time on Earth, on Central Campannlat,

and on the Avernus. It was standard equipment. The phagors would not be interested in time-telling, for their eotemporal harneys remained set in a temporality which registered only sporadic movement; but they would like the watch as decoration.

The old lower kzahhn's mottled face hung over his arm as he extended it to her gaze. Of her horns, one had been broken halfway and its tip replaced with a wooden peg.

She pulled herself up in a squatting position and called to two of the younger stalluns.

"Do what the thing demands," she said.

The escort stopped when a pair of houses was sighted in the distance. They would go no farther. Billy Xiao Pin removed the watch from his wrist and offered it to them. After contemplating it for a while, they refused to accept it.

He could not understand their explanation. They seemed to have lapsed from Hurdhu into Native. He grasped that numbers were involved. Perhaps they feared the ever changing numbers. Perhaps they feared the unknown metal. Their refusal was made without emotion; they simply would not take it; they wanted nothing. "JandolAnganol," they said. Evidently they still respected the king's name.

As he went forward, Billy looked back at them, partly obscured by a spray of flowering creeper hanging from a tree. They did not move. He feared them; he also felt a kind of marvel, that he had been in their company and was still sane.

Soon he found himself moving from that dream to another just as wonderful, as he walked in the narrow streets of Matrassyl. The winding way took him under the great rock on which the palace stood. He began to recognise where he was. This and this he had seen through the optics of the Avernus. He could have embraced the first Helliconians he saw.

Churches had been built into the rock; the stricter religious orders imitated the preferences of their masters in Pannoval and locked themselves away from the light. Monasteries huddled against the rock, three stories high, the more prosperous ones built in stone, the poorer in wood. Despite himself, Billy lingered, to feel the grain of the timber, running his nails in its

cracks. He came from a world where everything was renewed
—or destroyed and reconstituted—as soon as it aged. This ancient wood with the grain outstanding: how superb the accident of its design!

The world was choked with detail he could never have
imagined.

The monasteries were cheerfully painted red and yellow, or
red and purple, carrying the circle of Akhanaba in those colours. Their doors bore representations of the god, descending
in fire. Black locks of hair escaped from his topknot. His
eyebrows curled upwards. The smile on his half-human face
revealed sharp white teeth. In each hand he carried torches. A
cloth garment wound itself like a serpent about his blue body.

There were representations too, on banners, of saints and
familiars and bogeys: Yuli the Priest, Denniss the King,
Withram and Wutra, and streams of Others, large and black,
small and green with claws for toenails and rings on their toes.
Among these supernatural beings—fat and bald or shaggy—
went humans, generally in supplicatory postures.

Humans were shown small. Where I come from, Billy said
to himself, humans would be shown large. But here they went
in supplicatory postures, only to be mown down by the gods in
one way or another. By flames, by ice, by the sword.

Memories of school lessons came to Billy, fertilised by reality. He had learnt how important religions were on backward
Helliconia. Sometimes nations had been converted to a different religion in a day—it had happened to Oldorando, he
recalled. Other nations, losing their religion as suddenly, had
collapsed and disappeared without trace. Here was the very
bastion of Borlien's creed. As an atheist, Billy was both attracted and repelled by the lurid fates depicted on all sides.

The monks looked not too stricken by the dreadful state of
the world; devastation was merely part of a greater cycle, the
background of their placid existences.

"The colours!" Billy said aloud. The colours of devastation
were like paradise. There is no evil here, he told himself,
bedazzled. Evil is negative. Here everything is robust. Evil was
where I came from, in negativity.

Robust. Yes, it's robust. He laughed.

Mouth open, arms out, he stood in the middle of the street.

Aromas drifting like colours of the air detained him. Every step of his way had been haunted by smells of various kinds—a dimension of life missing on the Avernus. Nearby, under the shadow of the cliff, was a well, with stalls clustering by it. Monks were flocking from their buildings to buy food there.

Billy was teased by the thought that they were performing just for him. Death might come. It would be worth it just to have stood here and caught these savoury smells, and to have seen the monks lift greasy buns to their faces. Above them, from a monastic balcony fluttered a red and yellow banner, on which he could read the legend, ALL THE WORLD'S WISDOM HAS ALWAYS EXISTED. He laughed to himself at this antiscientific legend: wisdom was something that had to be hammered out—otherwise, he would not be here.

Here in the traffic of the street, Billy's understanding grew of how priest-ridden Helliconian society was, and of how the Akhanaban faith influenced action. His antipathy to religion was deep-rooted; now he found himself in a civilisation founded on it.

When he approached the stalls, a stall holder called to him. She was a tall woman, shabbily dressed, with a big red face. She maintained a bright-burning fire in a basin. Waffles were her trade. Billy had on him forged money, as well as other equipment for his visit. Pulling some coins from a pocket, he paid the woman and was rewarded with a savoury-smelling waffle. The waffle irons had imprinted on them the Akhanaban religious symbol, one circle within another, the two connected by oblique lines. He thought for the first time, as he bit into it, that the symbol possibly represented in a crude way the orbit of the lesser sun, Batalix, about the greater.

"It won't bite you back," said the waffle woman, laughing at him.

He moved away, triumphant at having negotiated the transaction. He ate more delicately than the monks, conscious of the eyes of the Avernus. Still munching, he continued along the street, a swagger in his step. Soon he was treading up the slopes that led to Matrassyl palace. It was wonderful. Real food was wonderful. Helliconia was wonderful.

The route became more familiar. Having studied the family

now called royal through three generations, Billy knew the layout of the palace and its surroundings in some detail. More than once he had watched the archival tapes which showed this stronghold being taken by the forces of the grandfather of the present king.

At the main gate, he asked to speak to JandolAnganol, producing forged documents which showed him to be an emissary from the distant land of Morstrual. After an interrogation in the guard house, he was escorted to another building. A long wait ensued until he was taken to a section of the palace he recognised as the chancellor's domain.

Here he kicked his heels, staring at everything—the rugs, the carved furniture, the stove, the curtains at the window, the stains on the ceiling—in a kind of fever. The waffle had given him hiccups. The world was a maze of fascinating detail, and every strand in the carpet on which he stood—he guessed it to be of Madi origin—had a meaning which led back into the history of the planet.

Queen MyrdemInggala, queen of queens, had stood in this very room, had placed her sandalled feet upon this woven carpet, and the beasts and birds figured there had gratefully received her weight as she passed by.

As Billy stood looking down at the carpet, a wave of dizziness overcame him. No, it couldn't be death already. He clutched his stomach. Not death by that waffle? He sank into a chair.

Outside lay the world where everything had two shadows. He felt its heat and power. It was the real world of the queen, not the artificial world of Billy and Rose. But he might not be up to it. . . .

He gave a loud hiccup. He understood now what his Advisor meant when he had said that Billy might find fulfilment with Rose. But that could never have been while the queen of his imagination stood in his way. The real queen was now somewhere close at hand.

The door opened—even that was a wonder, that wooden door. A lean old secretary appeared, who conducted him to the chancellor's suite. There he sat on a chair in an antechamber and waited. To his relief, the hiccups died and he felt less ill.

Chancellor SartoriIrvrash appeared, walking wearily. His shoulders were bent and, despite a show of courtesy, his manner was preoccupied. He listened to Billy without interest and ushered him into a large room where books and documents took up a major part of the space. Billy looked at the chancellor with awe. This was a figure out of history. This was once the hawkish young advisor who had assisted JandolAnganol's grandfather and father to establish the Borlienese state.

The two men seated themselves. The chancellor pulled agitatedly at his whiskers and muttered something under his breath. He seemed not to listen as Billy described himself as coming from a town in Morstrual on the Gulf of Chalce. He hugged his lean body as if comforting himself.

When Billy's words ran out, he sat in puzzlement as silence descended. Did the chancellor not understand his Olonets?

SartoriIrvrash spoke at last. "We'll do whatever we can to be of assistance, sir, although this is not the easiest of times, not by any means."

"I want a conversation with you, if I can, as well as with his majesty and the queen. I have knowledge to offer, as well as questions to ask."

He gave a belated hiccup.

"Apologies."

"Yes, yes. Excuse me. I am what someone once termed a connoisseur of knowledge, but this happens to be a day of deepest—deepest botheration."

He stood, clutching at his stained charfrul, shaking his head as he regarded Billy as if for the first time.

"What is so bad about today?" asked Billy in alarm.

"The queen, sir, Queen MyrdemInggala . . ." The chancellor rapped his knuckles on the table for emphasis. "Our queen is being put away, expelled, sir. This is the day she sails for exile. For Ancient Gravabagalinien."

He put his hands up to his face and began to weep.

IX

SOME BOTHERATION
FOR THE CHANCELLOR

There was an old country saying among the peasants of the land still known locally as Embruddock concerning the continent on which they lived: "Not an acre is properly habitable, and not an acre is uninhabited."

The saying represented at least an approach to the truth. Even now, when millions believed that the world was to die in flames, travellers of all kinds crossed and recrossed Campannlat. From whole tribes, like the migrant Madis and the nomadic nations of Mordriat, down to pilgrims, who counted out their pilgrimage not in miles but in shrines, robber bands, who counted territory in throats and purses; and solitary traders, who travelled leagues to sell a song or a stone for a greater price than it would fetch at home—all these found fulfilment in movement.

Even the fires that consumed the interior of the continent, stopping short only at rivers or deserts, did not deter travellers. Rather, they added to their numbers, contributing refugees in quest for new homes.

One such group arrived in Matrassyl down the Valvoral in time to see Queen MyrdemInggala leave for exile. The royal press gang gave them little time to gape. Its officers descended on the new arrivals in their leaky tub and marched the men away to serve in the Western Wars.

That afternoon, the natives of Matrassyl had temporarily forgotten the wars—or shelved the thought of them in favour of this newer drama. Here was the most dramatic moment of many dull lives: poverty, committing them to mere endurance, forced them to live vicariously through the illustrious. For this reason, they appointed and tolerated the vices of their kings and queens, so that shock or delight might enter their existences.

Smoke drifted over the town, shrouding the crowds mute along the quayside. The queen came in her coach. It moved between lines of people. Flags waved. Also banners, saying REPENT YE! and THE SIGNS ARE IN THE SKY. The queen looked neither to right nor to left.

Her coach stopped by the river. A lackey jumped down and opened the door for her majesty. She put forth a dainty foot and stepped down upon the cobbles. Tatro followed, and the lady-in-waiting.

MyrdemInggala hesitated and looked round. She wore a veil, but the aura of her beauty was about her like a perfume. The lugger that was to take her and her entourage downstream to Ottassol, and thence to Gravabagalinien, awaited her. A minister of the Church in full canonicals stood on deck to greet her. She walked up the gangplank. A sigh escaped the crowd as she left Matrassylan soil.

Her head was low. Once she had gained the deck and accepted the minister's greeting, she pulled back her veil and lifted a hand in farewell, her head high.

At the sight of that peerless face, a murmur rose from the wharves and walks and roofs nearby, a murmur which rumbled into a cheer. This was Matrassyl's inarticulate farewell to its queen of queens.

She gave no further sign, letting the veil drop, turning on her heel and going below, out of sight.

As the ship weighed anchor, a young court gallant ran forward to stand on the edge of the quay and declaim a popular

poem, "And Summer's Self She Is." There was no music, no
more cheering.

No one standing there in silent farewell knew of the events
at the court that afternoon, though news of fearful deeds
would leak out soon enough.

The sails were hoisted. The ship of exile moved slowly from
the quayside and began its journey downstream. The queen's
vicar stood on the deck and prayed. Nobody in the watching
crowd, on the street, on the cliffs, or perched on rooftops,
stirred. The wooden hull began to shrink with distance, its
detail to be lost.

The people went silently away to their homes, taking their
banners with them.

The Matrassyl court swarmed with factions. Some factions
were unique to the court; others had nationwide support. The
best-supported of the latter groups was undoubtedly the Myrdolators. This ironically named clique opposed the king on
most issues and supported the queen of queens on all.

Within the major groupings were minor groupings. Self-
interest saw to it that each man was divided in some way
against his brother. Many reasons could be invented for supporting or opposing a closer union with Oldorando, in the
continual jockeying for position in court.

There were those—haters of women perhaps—who hoped
to see Queen MyrdemInggala disgraced. There were those—
dreaming of possessing her perhaps—who wished to see her
remain. Of those who wished to see her remain, some of the
most fervent Myrdolators believed that she should stay and
the king should go. After all, they argued, to look at the affair
legalistically—and to ignore her physical attractions—the
queen's claim to the throne of Borlien was as valid as the
Eagle's.

Envy saw to it that the enemies of both king and queen were
perpetually active. On the day of departure of the queen many
were ready to take up arms.

On the morning of that day, JandolAnganol had moved
against the malcontents.

By a ruse, the king and SartoriIrvrash had the Myrdolators

meet together in a chamber in the palace. Sixty-one of them foregathered, some of them greybeards who had professed loyalty to MyrdemInggala's parents, RantanOboral and Shannana the Wild. They stormed indignantly in to the meeting. The Household Guard slammed the doors on them and guarded the chamber. While the Myrdolators screamed and fainted in the heat, the Eagle, with malicious glee on his face, went to a final meeting with his lovely queen.

MyrdemInggala was still overwhelmed by the turn in her fortunes. Her cheeks were pale. There was a feverish look in her eyes. She could not eat. She started at small things. When the king came upon her, she was walking with Mai TolramKetinet, discussing prospects for her children. If she was threatened, so were they. Tatro was small, and a girl. It was upon Robayday that the brunt of the king's vengeance might fall. Robayday had disappeared on one of his wild excursions. She perceived that she would not even be able to say good-bye to him. Nor would her brother be here to exert influence over his wilful nephew.

The two women walked in MyrdemInggala's dimday garden. Tatro was playing with Princess Simoda Tal—an irony which could be borne if not contemplated closely.

This garden the queen had created herself, directing her gardeners. Heavy trees and artificial cliffs screened the walks from Freyr's eyes. There was sufficient shade for genetic sports and melanic forms of vegetation to flourish.

Dimday plants flowered beside fullday ones. The jeodfray, a fullday creeper with light pink-and-orange flowers, became the stunted albic, hugging the ground. The albic occasionally put forth grotesque scarlet-and-orange buds along a fleshy stem, to attract the attention of dimday moths. Nearby were olvyl, yarrpel, idront, and spikey brooth, all relishing shade. The ground-loving vispard produced hooded blossoms. It was the adaptation of a nocturnal species, the zadal bush, and had moved towards lighter conditions rather than darker.

Such plants had been brought by her subjects from different parts of the kingdom. She had no great understanding of the astronomy which SartoriIrvrash tried to instil in her, or of the slow protracted manoeuvres of Freyr along the heavens, except through her appreciation of these plants, which repre-

sented an instinctive vegetable response to those confusingly abstract ellipses of which the chancellor loved to talk.

Now she would visit this favoured place no more. The ellipses of her own life were moving against her.

The king and his chancellor appeared at the gate. She sensed their wish for formality even from a distance. She saw the tension in the king's stance. She laid a hand on her lady-in-waiting's wrist in alarm.

SartoriIrvrash approached and bowed formally. Then he took the lady-in-waiting off with him, in order to leave the royal couple alone.

Mai instantly broke into anxious protests.

"The king will murder Cune. He suspects she loves my brother Hanra, but it is not so. I'd swear to it. The queen has done nothing wrong. She is innocent."

"His calculations run otherwise, and he will not murder her," said SartoriIrvrash. He hardly looked the figure to comfort her. He had shrunk inside his charfrul and his face was grey. "He rids himself of the queen for political reasons. It has been done before."

He brushed a butterfly impatiently from his sleeve.

"Why did he have Yeferal murdered, then?"

"That piece of botheration is not to be laid at the king's door but rather at mine. Cease your prattle, woman. Go with Cune into exile and look after her. I hope to be in touch some time, if my own situation continues. Gravabagalinien is no bad place to be."

They entered into an archway and were immediately embraced within the stuffy complexities of the building.

Mai TolramKetinet asked in a more even voice, "What has overcome the king's mind?"

"I know only of his ego, not his mind. It is bright like a diamond. It will cut all other egos. It cannot easily tolerate the queen's gentleness."

When the young woman left him, he stood at the bottom of the stairwell, trying to steady himself. Somewhere above him, he heard the voices of the visiting diplomats. They waited with indifference to hear how the matter worked out and would be departing soon, whatever happened.

"Everything finally goes . . ." he said to himself. In that

moment, he longed for his dead wife.

The queen, meanwhile, stood in her garden, listening to the low, hasty voice of JandolAnganol, trying to thrust his emotions upon her. She recoiled, as from a great wave.

"Cune, our parting is forced on me for the survival of the kingdom. You know my feelings, but you also know that I have duties which must be performed. . . ."

"No, I won't have it. You obey a whim. It is not duty but your khmir speaking."

He shook his head, as if trying to shake away the pain visible in his face.

"What I do I have to do, though it destroys me. I have no wish for anyone at my side but you. Give me a word that you understand that much before we part."

The lines of her face were rigid. "You have traduced the reputation of my dead brother and of me. Who gave the order for the spreading of that lie but you?"

"Understand, please, what I have to do for my kingdom. I have no will that we part."

"Who gave the order for our parting but you? Who commands here but you? If you don't command, then anarchy has come, and the kingdom is not worth saving."

He gave her a sideways look. The eagle was sick. "This is policy I must carry through. I am not imprisoning you but sending you to the beautiful palace of Gravabagalinien, where Freyr does not dominate the sky so greatly. Be content there and don't scheme against me, or your father will answer for it. If the war news improves, who knows but we may be together again."

She rounded on him, by her vehemence making him look into her overflowing face.

"Do you then plan to wed that lascivious child of Oldorando this year and divorce her next, as you do me this? Have you an endless series of matrimonies and divorcements in mind by which to save Borlien? You talk of sending me away. Be warned that when I am sent, I remain forever away from you."

JandolAnganol reached out a hand, but dared not touch her.

"I'm saying that in my heart—if you believe I have one—I

am not sending you away. Will you understand that? You live only by religion and principle. Have some understanding of what it means to be king.''

She plucked a twig of idront and then flung it from her.

''Oh, you've taught me what it is to be a king. To incarcerate your father, to drive off your son, to defame your brother-in-law, to dismiss me to the ends of the kingdom—that's what it is to be a king! I've learnt the lesson from you well.

''So I will answer you, Jan, after your own fashion. I cannot prevent your exiling me, no. But when you put me away, you inherit all the consequences of that act. You must live and die by those consequences. That is religion speaking, not I. Don't expect me to alter what is unalterable.''

''I do expect it.'' He swallowed. He seized her arm tightly and would not let it go, despite her struggles. He walked her along the path, and butterflies rose up. ''I do expect it. I expect you to love me still, and not to stop simply from convenience. I expect you to be above humanity, and to see beyond your suffering to the suffering of others.

''So far, in this pitiless world, your beauty has saved you from suffering. I have guarded you. Admit it, Cune, I have guarded you through these dreadful years. I returned from the Cosgatt only because you were here. By will I returned. . . . Won't your beauty become a curse when I am not by to act as shield? Won't you be hunted like a deer in a forest, by men the likes of whom you have never known? What will your end be without me?

''I swear I will love you still, despite a thousand Simoda Tals, if you will tell me now—just tell me, as we kiss goodbye—that you still hold me dear, despite what I have to do.''

She broke from him and steadied herself against a rock, her face in shadow. Both of them were pale and sweated.

''You mean to frighten me, and so you do. The truth is, you drive me away because you do not understand yourself. Inwardly, you know that I understand you and your weaknesses as does no one else—except possibly your father. And you cannot bear that. You are tortured because I have compassion for you. So yes, damn you, since you wrench it from me, yes, I do love you and will do so until I am merged with the original

beholder. But you can't accept that, can you? It's not what you desire.''

He blazed up. "There! You hate me, really! Your words lie!''

"Oh, oh, oh!" She uttered wild cries and began to run. "Go away! Go away! You're crazed. I declare what you ask and it maddens you! You want my hatred. Hatred is all you know! Go away—I hate you, if that satisfies your soul.''

JandolAnganol did not attempt to pursue her.

"Then the storm will come," he said.

So smoke began to flow down and fill the bowl of Matrassyl. The king was like a man possessed after parting from MyrdemInggala. He ordered straw from the stables and had it piled about the doors of the chamber in which the Myrdolators were still imprisoned. Jars of purified whale oil were brought. JandolAnganol himself snatched a burning brand from a slave and hurled it into the kindling.

With a roar, flames burst upwards.

That afternoon, as the queen sailed, the fire raged. Nobody was allowed to check it. Its fury went unabated.

Only that night, when the king sat with his runt drinking himself insensible, were servants able to come with pumps and quench the blaze.

When pale Batalix rose next morning, the king, as was his custom, rose and presented himself to his people by the dawn light.

A larger crowd than usual awaited him. At his appearance, a low inarticulate growl arose, like the noise a wounded hound might make. In fear of the many-headed beast, he retired to his room and flung himself down on his bed. There he stayed all day, neither eating nor speaking.

On the succeeding day, he appeared to be himself again. He summoned ministers, he gave orders, he bade farewell to Taynth Indredd and Simoda Tal. He even appeared briefly before the scritina.

There was reason for him to act. His agents brought news that Unndreid the Hammer, Scourge of Mordriat, was again

moving southwestwards, and had formed an alliance with
Darvlish, his enemy.

In the scritina, the king explained how Queen MyrdemInggala and her brother, YeferalOboral, had been planning to
assassinate the ambassador from Sibornal, who had made his
escape. It was for this reason that the queen was being sent
into exile; her interference in state affairs could not be
tolerated. Her brother had been killed.

This conspiracy must be an object lesson to all in this time
of peril for the nation. He, the king, was drawing up a plan by
which Borlien would become more closely linked to its traditional friends, the Oldorandans and Pannovalans. These plans
he would disclose fully in good time. His challenging gaze
swept round the scritina.

SartoriIrvrash then rose, to demand that the scritina look
upon new developments in the light of history.

"With the battle of the Cosgatt still fresh in our minds, we
know that there are new artilleries of attack available. Even
the barbarous tribes of Driats have these new—*guns*, as they
are called. With a gun, a man can kill an enemy as soon as he
can see him. Such things are mentioned in old histories, although we cannot always trust what we read in old histories.

"However. We are concerned with guns. You saw them
demonstrated. They are made in the great northern continent
by the nations of Sibornal, who have a pre-eminence in manufacturing arts. They possess deposits of lignite and metal ores
which we do not. It is necessary for us to remain on good
terms with such powerful nations, and so we have put down
firmly this attempt to assassinate the ambassador."

One of the barons at the back of the scritina shouted
angrily, "Tell us the truth. Wasn't Pasharatid corrupt? Didn't
he have a liaison with a Borlienese girl in the lower town, con-
travening our laws and his?"

"Our agents are investigating," said SartoriIrvrash, and
went on hastily. "We shall send a deputation to Askitosh,
capital of the nation Uskutoshk, to open a trade route, hoping
that the Sibornalese will be more friendly than hitherto.

"Meanwhile, our meeting with the distinguished diplomats
from Oldorando and Pannoval was successful. We have
received a few guns from them, as you know. If we can send

sufficient quantities of guns to our gallant General Hanra TolramKetinet, then the war with Randonan will be quickly over.''

Both the king's speech and SartoriIrvrash's were received coldly. Supporters of Baron RantanOboral, MydremInggala's father, were present in the scritina. One of them rose and asked, ''Are we to understand that it is these new weapons which are responsible for the deaths of sixty-one Mydrolators? If so, they are powerful weapons indeed.''

The chancellor's reply was uncertain.

''An unfortunate fire broke out at the castle, started by the ex-queen's supporters, many of whom lost their lives in the blaze they had themselves caused.''

As SartoriIrvrash and the king left the chamber, a storm of noise broke out.

''Give them the wedding,'' said SartoriIrvrash. ''They'll forget their anger as they coo over the prettiness of the child bride. Give them the wedding as soon as possible, Your Majesty. Make the fools forget one swindle with another.''

He looked away to hide his revulsion for his own role.

Tension hung over all who lived in the castle of Matrassyl, except for the phagors, whose nervous systems were immune to expectation. But even the phagors were uneasy, for the stench of burning still clung to everything.

Scowling, the king retired to his suite. A section of the First Phagorian stood duty outside his door, and Yuli remained with them while JandolAnganol prayed in his private chapel with his Royal Vicar. After prostrating himself in prayer, he had himself scourged.

While being bathed by his female servants, he summoned his chancellor back to him. SartoriIrvrash appeared after a third summons, clad in an ink-stained flowered charfrul and rush slippers. The old man looked aggrieved, and stood before the king without speaking, smoothing his beard.

''You're vexed?'' JandolAnganol addressed him from the pool. The runt sat a short distance away, its mouth open.

''I'm an old man, Your Majesty, and have endured deep botheration this day. I was resting.''

"Writing your damned history, more likely."

"Resting and grieving for the murdered sixty-one, if truth be told."

The king struck the water with the flat of his hand. "You're an atheist. You have no conscience to appease. You don't have to be scourged. Leave that to me."

SartoriIrvrash showed a tooth in a display of circumspection.

"How can I serve your majesty now?"

JandolAnganol stood up, and the women swathed him in towels. He stepped from the bath.

"You have done enough in the way of service." He gave SartoriIrvrash one of his darkly brilliant looks. "It's time I put you out to pasture, like the old hoxneys of which you are so fond. I'll find someone more to my way of thought to advise me."

The women huddled by the earthenware pitchers which had brought the royal bathwater, and listened complacently to the drama.

"There are many here who will pretend to think as you wish them to think, Your Majesty. If you care to put trust in such, that is your decision. Perhaps you will say how I have failed to please. Have I not supported all your schemes?"

The king flung away his towels, and paced naked and dangerous about the room. His gaze was as hasty as his walk. Yuli whined in sympathy.

"Look at the trouble about my ears. Bankrupt. No queen. Unpopular. Mistrusted. Challenged in the scritina. Don't tell me I'll be a favourite of the mob when I wed that chit from Oldorando. You advised me to do this, and I have had sufficient of your advice."

SartoriIrvrash had backed against one wall, where he was fairly safe from the king's pacing. He wrung his hands in distress.

"If I may speak . . . I have faithfully served you and your father before you. I have lied for you. I lied today. I have implicated myself in this gruesome Myrdolators' crime for your sake. Unlike other chancellors you might elect, I have no political ambitions— You are good enough to splash me, your majesty!"

"Crime! Your sovereign is a criminal, is he? How else was I to put down a revolt?"

"I have advised you with your good in mind, rather than my advancement, sire. Never less than in this sorry matter of the divorcement. You will recall that I told you you would never find another woman like the queen and—"

The king seized a towel and wrapped it about his narrow waist. A puddle formed round his feet. "You told me that my first duty lay with my country. So I made the sacrifice, made it at your suggestion—"

"No, Your Majesty, no, I distinctly—" He waved his hands distractedly.

" 'I dizztingtly,' " said Yuli, picking up a new sword.

"You merely want a scapegoat on which to vent your rage, sire. You shall not dismiss me like this. It's criminal."

The words echoed about the bath chamber. The women had made as if to escape from the scene, then had frozen in cautionary gestures, lest the king turn upon them.

He turned on his chancellor.

As his face flushed with rage, the colour chased itself down his jaw to his throat. "Criminal again! Am I criminal?" You old rat, you dare give me your orders and insults! I'll settle with you."

He marched over to where his clothes lay spread.

Fearing that he had gone too far, SartoriIrvrash said in a shaking voice, "Your Majesty, forgive me, I see your plan. By dismissing me, you can then be free to blame me before the scritina for what has occurred, and thus show yourself innocent in their eyes. As if truth can be moulded that way. . . . It is a well-tried tactic, well-tried—transparent, too—but surely we can agree on how precisely—"

He faltered and fell silent. A sickly evening light filled the room. Traces of an auroral storm flickered in the cloud mass outside. The king had drawn his sword from its scabbard where it lay on the table. He flourished it.

SartoriIrvrash backed away, knocking over a pitcher of scented water, which rushed to escape in a flood across the tiled floor.

JandolAnganol began a complex pattern of swordplay with an invisible enemy, feinting and lunging, at times appearing

hard pressed, at times pressing hard himself. He moved rapidly about the room. The women huddled against the wall, tittering with nervousness.

"Heigh! Yauh! Ho! Heigh!"

He switched direction, and the naked blade darted at the chancellor.

As it stopped an inch from his collarbone, the king said, "So, where's my son, where's Robayday, then, you old villain? You know he'd have my life?"

"Well I know the history of your family, sire," said SartoriIrvrash, ineffectually covering his chest with his hands.

"I must deal with my son. You have him hidden in the warren of your apartments."

"No, sire, that I do not."

"I am told you do, sire, the phagor guard told me. And he whispered, sire, that you still have some blood in your eddre."

"Sire, you are overtaxed by the ordeals you have undergone. Let me get—"

"Get nothing, sire, but steel in the gullet. So reliable! You have a visitor in your rooms."

"From Morstrual, sire, a boy, no more."

"So, you keep boys now . . ." But the subject seemed to lose its interest. With a shout, the king flung up his sword so that it embedded itself in the beams overhead. When he reached up and grasped its hilt, the towel fell from him.

SartoriIrvrash stooped to retrieve it for his majesty, saying, falteringly, "I understand from whence your madness comes, and allow—"

Instead of seizing the towel, the king seized the old man's charfrul and swung him about by it. The towel went flying. The chancellor uttered a cry of alarm. His feet slipped from under him, and they fell together heavily, in the flood of water.

The king was back on his feet as nimbly as a cat, motioning to the women to help SartoriIrvrash up. The chancellor groaned and clutched his back as two of them assisted him.

"Now go, sire," said the king. "Get packing—before I demonstrate to you just how mad I am. Remember, I know you for an atheist and a Myrdolator!"

*   *   *

In his own chambers, Chancellor SartoriIrvrash had a woman slave anoint his back with ointments, and indulged in some luxurious groans. His personal phagor guard, Lex, looked on impassively.

After a while, he called for some squaanej juice topped with Lordryardry ice, and then laboriously wrote a letter to the king, clutching his spine between sentences.

Honoured Sire,

I have served the House of Anganol faithfully, and deserve well from it. I am prepared still to serve, despite the attack upon my person, for I know how your majesty suffers in his mind at present.

As to my atheism and my learning, to which you so frequently object, may I point out that they are one, and that my eyes are opened to the true nature of our world. I do not seek to woo you from your faith, but to explain to you that it is your faith which puts you in your present difficult situation.

I see our world as a unity. You know of my discovery that a hoxney is a striped animal, appearances to the contrary. This discovery is of vital importance, for it links the seasons of our Great Year, and gives us new understanding of them. Many plants and animals may have similar devices by which to perpetuate their species through the Year's conflicting climates.

Could it be that humanity has, in religion, a similar mode of perpetuation? Differing only as humanity differs from the brute beasts? Religion is a social binding force which can unify in times of extreme cold or, as now, of extreme heat. That social binding force, that cohesion, is valuable, for it leads to our survival in national or tribal entities.

What it must not do is rule our individual lives and thinking. If we sacrifice too much to religion, then we are prisoners of it, as Madis are prisoners of the uct. You must, sire, forgive my pointing this out to you, and I fear that you will not find it palatable, but you yourself have shown such a slavishness to Akhanaba—

He paused. No, as usual he was going too far. The king in his anger would destroy him if he read that sentence. Laboriously, he took a fresh sheet of parchment and wrote a modified version of his first letter. He charged Lex with delivering it.

Then he sat and wept.

He dozed. Later, he awoke to find Lex standing over him, his milt flicking up the slots of his nostrils. He had long grown used to the silence of phagors; though he hated the creatures, they were less bothersome than human slaves about the place.

His table clock told him it was near the twenty-fifth hour of the day. He yawned, stretched, and put on a warmer garment. Outside, the aurora flickered over an empty courtyard. The palace was asleep—except perhaps for the king. . . .

"Lex, we'll go and speak with our prisoner. Have you fed him?"

The phagor, immobile, said, "The prisoner has his food, sir." He spoke in a low voice, buzzingly, so that the honorific came out as "zzorr." His Olonets was limited, but SartoriIrvrash, in his abhorrence, refused to learn Hurdhu.

Among the shelves covering most of a long wall stood a cupboard. Lex swung it away from the wall to reveal an iron door. Clumsily, the ancipital inserted a key in the lock and turned it. He pulled the door open; man and phagor entered a secret cell.

This had once been an independent room. In the days of VarpalAnganol, the chancellor had had its external door plastered over. Now the only means of entry lay through his study. Stout bars had been fixed over the window. From outside, the window was lost in the muddle of the castle facade.

Flies buzzed in the room, or hung as if sleeping in the thick air. They crawled over the table, and over the hands of Billy Xiao Pin.

Billy sat on a chair. He was chained to a strong eye anchored in the floor. His clothes were stained with sweat. The stench in the room was overwhelming.

Producing a sachet of scantiom, pellamountain, and other herbs, SartoriIrvrash pressed it to his nose and gestured towards a cessbucket standing in a corner of the room.

"Empty that." Lex moved to obey.

The chancellor took a chair and placed it beyond the reach
of any lunge his prisoner might make. He sat down carefully,
nursing his back and grunting. He lit a long veronikane before
he spoke.

"Now, BillishOwpin, you have been here for two days. We
shall have another discussion. I am the Chancellor of Borlien,
and, if you lie to me, it is well within my powers to torture
you. You introduced yourself to me as the mayor of a town on
the Gulf of Chalce. Then, when I locked you up, you claimed
that you were a much grander person, who came from a world
above this one. Who are you today? The truth now!"

Billy wiped his face on his sleeve and said, "Sir, believe me,
I knew of this secret room before I arrived here. Yet I am ignorant of many aspects of your manners. My initial mistake
was to pose as someone I am not—which I did because I
doubted if you would believe the truth."

"I may say without vanity that I happen to be one of the
foremost seekers after truth of my generation."

"Sir, I know it. Therefore set me free. Let me follow the
queen. Why lock me up when I mean no harm?"

"I lock you up because I may get some good out of you.
Stand up."

The chancellor surveyed his captive. Certainly, there was
something odd about the fellow. His physiology was not the
attenuated one of a Campannlatian, nor had he the barrel
shape of those freak humans, sometimes displayed at fairs,
whose ancestors (according to medical thought) had escaped
the near-universal bone fever.

His friend CaraBansity in Ottassol would have said that
underlying bone structure accounted for the peculiar rounded
quality of the captive's features. The man's skin texture was
smooth, with a notable pallor, though his button nose was
sunburnt. His hair was fine.

And there were more subtle differences, such as the quality
of the captive's gaze and its duration. He seemed to look away
to listen, and regarded SartoriIrvrash only when he spoke—
although fear could account for that. His eyes were often cast
upward, instead of down. In particular, he spoke Olonets in a
foreign style.

All this the chancellor observed before saying, "Give me an

account of this world above from which you claim to come. I am a rational man, and I shall listen without prejudice to what you have to say." He drew upon his kane and coughed.

Lex returned with an empty bucket and stood motionless against one wall, fixing his cerise glare on an undefined point in the middle distance.

When Billy sat down, his chains rattled. He placed his weighted wrists on the table before him and said, "Merciful sir, I come, as I told you, from a much smaller world than yours. A world perhaps of the size of the great hill upon which Matrassyl Castle stands. That world is called Avernus, though your astronomers have long known it as Kaidaw. It lies some fifteen hundred kilometers above Helliconia, with an orbital period of 7770 seconds, and its—"

"Wait. On what does this hill of yours lie? On air?"

"There is no air about Avernus. In effect, the Avernus is a metal moon. No, you don't have that word in Olonets, sir, since Helliconia possesses no natural moon. Avernus orbits Helliconia continually, as Helliconia orbits Batalix. It travels through space, as Helliconia does, and moves continually, as Helliconia does. Otherwise, it would fall under the pull of gravitation. I think you understand this principle, sir? You know of the true relationships between Helliconia on the one hand and Batalix and Freyr on the other."

"I understand what you say very well." He slapped at a fly crawling over his bald pate. "You are addressing the author of 'The Alphabet of History and Nature,' in which I seek to synthesise all knowledge. It is understood by few men—but I happen to be one of them—that Batalix and Freyr revolve about a common focus, while Copaise, Aganip, and Ipocrene revolve with Helliconia about Batalix. The haste of our sister worlds in their orbits is commensurate with their stature and their distance from the parent body, Batalix. Furthermore, cosmology informs us that these sister worlds sprang from Batalix, as men spring from their mothers, and Batalix sprang from Freyr, which is its mother. In the realm of the heavens, you will find me suitably informed, I flatter myself."

He looked up at the ceiling and blew smoke among the flies.

Billy cleared his throat. "Well, it's not quite like that. Batalix and its planets form a relatively aged solar system

which was captured by a much larger sun, which you call Freyr, some eight million years ago, as we reckon time."

The chancellor moved restlessly, crossing and uncrossing his legs, with a peevish expression on his face. "Among the impediments to knowledge are the persecutions of those who seek power, the difficulties of investigation, and—this in particular—a failure to recognise what should be investigated. I set all this out in my first chapter.

"You clearly have some knowledge, yet you betray it by mingling it with falsehood for your own reasons. Remember that torture is a friend of truth, BillishOwpin. I'm a patient man, but this wild talk of millions angers me. You won't impress me by mere numbers. Anyone can invent figures out of thin air."

"Sir, I do not invent. How many people inhabit all Campannlat?"

The chancellor looked flustered. "Why, some fifty million, according to best estimates."

"Wrong, sir. Sixty-four million people, and thirty-five million phagors. In the time of VryDen, whom you like to quote, the figures were eight million humans and twenty-three million phagors. The biomass relates directly to the amount of energy arriving at the planetary surface. In Sibornal there are—"

SartoriIrvrash waved his hands. "Enough—you try to vex me. . . . Return to the geometry of the suns. Do you dare claim there is no blood relationship between Freyr and Batalix?"

From gazing down at his hands, Billy looked askance at the old man who sat beyond his reach. "If I tell you what really happened, honoured Chancellor, would you believe me?"

"That depends whether your tale is within credence." He puffed out a cloud of smoke.

Billy Xiao Pin said, "I caught only a glimpse of your beautiful queen. So what is the point of my being here, dying here, if I fail to tell you this one great truth?" He thought of Myrdem-Inggala passing, glorious in her floating muslins.

And he began. The phagor stood by the stained wall, the old man sat in his creaking chair. The flies buzzed. No sounds came from the outside world.

"On my way here, I saw a banner saying, in Olonets, 'All the world's wisdom has always existed.' That is not so. It may

be a truth for the religious, but for the scientific it is a lie. Truth resides in facts which must be painfully discovered and hypotheses which must be continually checked—although where I come from, facts have obliterated truth. As you say, there are many impediments to knowledge, and to the meta-structure of knowledge we call *science*.

"Avernus is an artificial world. It is a creation of science and the application of science we call—you have no such word—*technology*. You may be surprised to hear that the race from which I come, which *evolved* on a distant planet called Earth, is younger than you Helliconians. But we suffered fewer natural disadvantages than you."

He paused, almost shocked to hear that charged word, *Earth*, pronounced in these surroundings.

"So I shall not lie to you—though I warn you you may find that what I say does not fit into your world-picture, Chancellor. You may be shocked, even though you are the most enlightened of your race."

The chancellor stubbed out his veronikane on the top of the table and pressed a hand to his head. It ached. The prison room was stifling. He could not follow the young stranger's speech, and his mind wandered to the king, naked, and the sword embedded dangerously in a beam above them. The prisoner talked on.

Where Billy came from, the cosmos was as familiar as a back garden. He spoke in matter-of-fact tones about a yellow G_4-type star which was some five thousand million years old. It was of low luminosity and a temperature of only 5600K. This was the sun now called Batalix. He went on to describe its only inhabited planet, Helliconia, a planet much like distant Earth, but cooler, greyer, older, its life processes slower. On its surface, over many eons, species developed from animal to dominant being.

Eight million years ago by Earth reckoning, Batalix and its system moved into a crowded region of space. Two stars, which he called A and C, were orbiting each other. Batalix was drawn within the massive gravitational field of A. In the series of perturbations which followed, star C was lost, and A acquired a new companion, Batalix.

A was a very different sun from Batalix. Although between

only ten and eleven million years old, it had evolved away
from the main sequence of stars and was entering stellar old
age. Its radius was over seventy times the radius of Batalix, its
temperature twice as great. It was an A-type supergiant.

Try as he might, the chancellor could not listen attentively.
A sense of disaster enveloped him. His vision blurred, his
heart beat with an irregular throb which seemed to fill the
room. He pressed his scantiom sachet to his nose to help his
breathing.

"That's enough," he said, breaking into Billy's discourse.
"Your kind is known in history, talking in strange terms,
mocking the understandings of wise men. Perhaps it is a delu-
sion we suffer from. . . . Small wonder if we do. Only two
days ago—only fifty hours—the queen of queens left Matrassyl, charged with conspiracy, and sixty-one Myrdolators were
cruelly murdered. . . . And you talk to me of suns swooping
here and there as fancy takes them. . . ."

Billy drummed the fingers of one hand on the table and
fanned away flies with the other. Lex stood nearby, motionless as furniture, eyes closed.

"I'm a Myrdolator myself. I'm much to blame for these
crimes. Too used to serving the king . . . as he's too used to
serving religion. Life was so placid. . . . Now who knows what
fresh botherations will happen tomorrow?"

"You are too sunk in your own little affairs," Billy said.
"You're as bad as my Advisor on the Avernus. He doesn't entirely believe in the reality of Helliconia. You don't entirely
believe in the reality of the universe. Your *umwelt* is no larger
than this palace."

"What's an *umwelt?*"

"The region encompassed by your perceptions."

"You pretend to know so much. Is it correct, as I perceive,
that the hoxney is a brown-striped animal which wore coloured stripes in the spring of the Great Year?"

"That is correct. Animals and plants adopt different
strategies to survive the vast changes of a Year. There are
binary biologies and botanies, some following one star, as
previously, some the other."

"Now you return to your perambulating suns. In my belief,
established over thirty-seven years, our two suns are set in our

skies as a constant reminder of our dual nature, spirit and
body, life and death, and of the more general dualities which
govern human life—hot and cold, light and dark, good and
evil."

"You say my kind is known in history, Chancellor. Maybe
those were other visitors from the Avernus, also trying to
reveal the truth, and being ignored."

"Revelations through some crazed geometries? Then they
perished!" SartoriIrvrash rose, resting his fingers on the table,
frowning.

Billy also laboriously rose, rattling his chains. "The truth
would free you, Chancellor. Whatever you think, those
'crazed geometries' rule the universe. You half-know this.
Respect your intellect. Why not go further, break from your
umwelt? The life that teems on Helliconia is a product of those
crazed geometries you scoff at.

"That A-type sun you know as Freyr is a gigantic hydrogen
fusion-reactor, pouring out high-energy emissions. When
Batalix and its planets took up orbits round it, eight million
years ago, they were subjected to bombardments of X rays
and ultraviolet radiation. The effect on the then-sluggish
Helliconian biosphere was profound. There was rapid genetic
change. Dramatic mutations occurred. Some new forms survived. One animal species in particular rose to challenge the
supremacy previously enjoyed by a much older species—"

"No more of this," cried SartoriIrvrash, waving a hand in
dismissal. "What is this about species changing into other
species? Can a dog become an arang, or a hoxney a kaidaw?
Everyone knows at least that every animal has its place, and
humans their place. So the All-Powerful has ordained."

"You're an atheist! You don't believe in the All-Powerful!"

Confused, the chancellor shook his head. "I'd prefer to be
ruled by the All-Powerful than by your crazed geometries. . . .
I had hoped to make a present of you to King JandolAnganol,
but you would drive him madder than he is already."

Wearily, SartoriIrvrash realised that the king could not be
placated at present by rational means. SartoriIrvrash himself
felt far from rational. Listening to Billy, he was reminded of
another young madman—the king's son, Robayday. Once a

charming child, then overtaken by a kind of mad fancy, espousing the desert like a parched mother, expert at killing game, at times hardly making sense . . . the plague of his royal parents.

He wondered at his own long struggle to make sense of the world. How was it that such an omnipresent problem oppressed so few?

Billy might be a figment of his tired imagination, the darker side of rationality, sent to plague him.

He turned to the phagor. "Lex, guard him. I'll think how to dispose of him and his *umwelts* on the morrow."

In his bedchamber, loneliness overwhelmed the chancellor. The king had seized him and flung him to the floor! He felt the bumps of his bruised spine, felt how ugly his body was growing as the years squeezed it dry. The days contained so much shame.

His slave woman came at his call, looking reluctant as he had looked reluctant when summoned before the king.

"Massage my back," he ordered.

She lay against him, running a rough but gentle hand from his skull to his pelvis. He smelt of veronikane, phagors, and piss. She was Randonanese, with tribal marks cut in her cheeks. She smelt of fruit. After a while, he rolled over to face her, his prodo stirring. There was one comfort given to believers and atheists alike, one refuge from abstraction. The chancellor thrust one hand between the dark exiled thighs and reached with the other into her shift, to clasp the slave woman's breasts.

She drew him close.

Petitions were being signed on the Avernus for a party to descend to the Helliconian surface and rescue Billy Xiao Pin. No serious notice was taken of the petitions. Billy's contract clearly stated that, whatever difficulties he found himself in, no help would be forthcoming. Which did not prevent many young ladies of the Pin family from threatening to commit suicide if the government did not act at once.

But the work of the station continued as usual, as it had done for the previous thirty-two centuries. Little the Aver-

*nians knew how Earth's technocrats had programmed them
for obedience. The great families continued to analyse all incoming data, and the automatic systems continued to broadcast signals to distant Earth.*

*Gigantic auditoria shaped like conch shells stood all round
that faraway planet.*

*To the people of Earth, Helliconian events were news. The
signals were received first of all on Charon, on the extreme
fringes of the solar system. There again they were analysed,
classified, stored, transmitted. The most popular transmission
went to Earth via the Eductainment Channel, which carried
various continuous dramas from the binary system. The
events at King JandolAnganol's court were at present the
highest-rating news. And that news was a thousand years old.*

*Those who listened to that news formed part of a global
society undergoing a change as profound as any on Helliconia.
The Decline of the Modern Ages had been hastened by greatly
increased glaciation at the terrestrial poles, leading to the
Great Ice Age. In the ninth century of the sixth millennium
after the birth of Christ, the glaciers were again retreating, and
the peoples of Earth moving northwards in their wake. Old
racial and national antipathies were in abeyance. A mood appropriate to the congenial climate of Earth prevailed, in which
sophisticated sensibilities were directed to exploring the relationship between the biosphere, its living things, and the
gubernatory globe itself.*

*For once, leaders and statesmen arose who were worthy of
their people. They shared a true vision and inspired the
populace. They saw to it that the drama of the distant planet
Helliconia was studied as an object lesson in folly as well as an
endless tapestry of circumstance.*

*To the great conch shells, millions of terrestrials had come
to watch the departure of the queen, the burning of the Myrdolators, the quarrel between the king and his chancellor.
These were contemporary events, in that they influenced the
emotional climate of those who looked up at the gigantic
images. But the events were also fossil events, compressed
with the strata of light on which they had arrived. They
seemed to burst up with renewed heat and life on reaching the
consciousness of terrestrial human beings, as long-buried trees*

of Earth's Carboniferous Age yield the sun's energies when coal burns in a grate.

Those fires did not touch everyone. In some quarters, Helliconia was regarded as the relic of an age long past, a period of troubled history best forgotten, when human affairs had been little better managed on Earth than on Helliconia. The new men turned their faces to a new way of life in which the human and its engines were not to be the ultimate arbiter. Some who worked towards those goals found time still to cheer for crabbed SartoriIrvrash, or to become Myrdolators.

The terrestrial followers of the queen were many, even in the new lands. Day and night, they awaited their fossil news.

X

BILLY CHANGES CUSTODY

Whether Akhanaba or the "crazed geometries" were in charge of events in Matrassyl—whether those events were pre-ordained or the result of blind happenstance—whether free will or determinism determined—the fact was that the next twenty-five hours were miserable ones for Billy Xiao Pin. All the bright colours he had experienced in his early hours on Helliconia had faded. Nightmare took over.

On that winter's day in the Great Summer when Chancellor SartoriIrvrash interrogated Billy and did not listen properly, there was a period of night of almost five hours' duration when neither Freyr nor Batalix was in the sky.

YarapRombry's Comet could be seen low on the northern horizon. Then it was swallowed by a freak fog. The thordotter did not blow, as expected, but sent fog in its stead.

The fog arrived the way the queen left, by river. It made itself felt first as a cold shiver down the naked spines of wharfmen, ferrymen, and others whose livelihood lay along the confluences of the Valvoral and the Takissa.

Some of those watermen, going home, took the insidious element with them into the houses which lined the poor streets behind the docks—and made them the poorer for it. Wives, peering out as they dragged shutters across windows, saw godowns dissolve into a universal sepia puddle.

The puddle rose higher, brimming over the cliffs, as cunning as ill health, and penetrated the castle walls.

There, soldiers in their thin uniforms, shaggy-coated phagors, stirred the infection after them as they patrolled, coughed into it, became devoured by it. The palace itself did not long resist the invasion, but took on the aspects of a ghost of a place. Through the empty rooms where Queen Myrdem-Inggala had lived, the fog went mournfully without a sound.

The marauder also found entry to the world under the hill. It snuffled amid that nest of gongs and exclamations and prayers and prostrations and processions and suppressions where holiness was manufactured; there, its uncanny breath mingled easily with the exhalations of vigils and congregations, and created purple haloes about devotional candles, as if here, and here alone, it found a kindred place where it was welcome. It coiled along floors among bare feet, and found out the secret places of the mountain.

To those secret places, Billy Xiao Pin was being escorted.

He rested his head wearily on his table once SartoriIrvrash had left him, letting tired thoughts run riot through his head. When he tried consciously to check on them, the thoughts were gone like criminals over a wall. Had he once described Helliconia as a "form of argument"? Well, there was no arguing with the reality. He recalled all his glib debates about reality with his Advisor, back on the Avernus. Now he had a dose of reality, and it would kill him.

The criminal thoughts crept into action again, to be checked when the doglike Lex placed a bowl of food before him.

"Do eating," the ancipital commanded, as Billy looked mistily up at him.

The food was a porridge into which highly coloured fruit had been chopped. He took up a silver spoon and began to eat. The taste was insipid. After a few spoonfuls, drowsiness overcame him. He pushed the bowl away, groaning, and lay

his head on the table again. Flies settled on the food, and on his undefended cheek.

Lex went to the wall opposite to the one by which he and the chancellor habitually entered, and tapped on one of the wooden panels. A countertap answered, to which he responded with two wide-spaced answering taps. A section of panelling opened into the room, scattering dust.

A female ancipital entered the cell, moving with the gliding movement of her kind. Without hesitation, she and Lex lifted the paralysed Billy and carried him into the narrow passage now revealed. She closed and bolted the panel door behind them.

The palace contained neglected passages in plenty; this one, in its unfinished state, gave every appearance of having been neglected for centuries. The two great ahumans filled it.

Phagor slaves were as common about Matrassyl Palace as phagor soldiers. When employed as stone masons, for which work they had a rough aptitude, they had walled in a retroversion in the great walls, roofed it over, and utilised it as one of their own convenient ways about the building.

Billy, in a state of paralysis, but still conscious, found himself being carried down stairs that went back and forth as if forever denied an exit. His head dangled over the gillot's shoulder, knocking against her shoulderblade at every step.

At ground level, they paused. Damp hung in the air. Somewhere out of his sight, a torch smouldered. Hinges squeaked. He was being lowered down into the earth through a trapdoor. His terror could escape only in the faintest sigh.

The torch appeared as his head fell back, to be eclipsed by a shaggy head. He was somewhere underground and three-fingered hands were clutching him. Mauve and red pupils glowed in the gloom. Sickly smells and shuffling sounds surrounded him. A trapdoor slammed, its echoes shuttling away into distance.

His viewpoint showed little more than a monstrous back. Another door, more waiting, more stairs, more insane whispers. He passed out—yet remained aware of jolts of descent which continued for uncounted time.

They were making him walk like a drunken man. His feet were dead. Of course—they had drugged his food. Head roll-

ing to one side, he gathered that they were in a large underground chamber, moving along a wooden walk set near the ceiling. Banners hung from the walk. Below, humans in long garments congregated, barefoot. He recalled their name in a moment: monks. They sat at long tables, where phagors in similar garments served them. Memories returned to Billy Xiao Pin; he recollected the monasteries under the hill where he had bought a waffle. He was being taken through the maze of holy ways carved in the rock beneath JandolAnganol's palace.

The walking revived him. Two phagors escorted him, both gillots. Probably Lex had returned to do duty for the chancellor, who would now be asleep. He gave a feeble call to the monks below, but nobody heard him in the babble of voices. They left the lighted space.

More corridors. He tried to protest, but the females hustled him on. By his side, a band of carving braided the stone wall. He tried to grip it; his hand was snatched away.

Down again.

Total darkness, smelling of rivers and things unborn.

"Please let me go." His first words. A gate opened.

He was marched into a different world, an underground ancipital kingdom. The very air was different, its sounds and stinks alien. Water lapped. Proportions were different: archways were wide and low, cavernous. The way was rough and uphill. It was like climbing into a dead mouth.

Nothing in the Avernus had prepared Billy for this adventure. Crowds of phagors were gathering to inspect him, thrusting their cow faces into his. They jostled him before a council of ancipitals, male and female. In niches round the walls were stacked their totems, aged phagors sinking further and further in tether; the oldest totem was like a little black doll, almost entirely composed of keratin. Leading the council was a young kzahhn, Ghht-Yronz Tharl.

Ghht-Yronz Tharl was no more than a creaght. The dense white coat over his shoulders was still red-tipped. His long curving horns were painted with a spiral design, and he kept his head thrust low, with a pugnacious gesture so as not to scrape the tips of those horns on the roof of the chamber.

As for that chamber itself, though its roof was indeed rough

and unfinished, its form was approximately circular. Indeed, the auditorium—if such a term was applicable among such an inhuman audience—was built in the shape of a wheel. Ghht-Yronz Tharl stood stiffly upright, puffing out his chest, at the hub of the wheel.

Stalls for the audience radiated like spokes from the hub. Most of the floor was divided into low stalls. Here members of the council stood motionless, or merely twitching a shoulder or ear. In each stall was a trough and a length of chain stapled into the stonework. Runnels for water or urine were cut in the floor and ran to ditches by the perimeter of the wheel.

The fog seemed to have penetrated here, or else the sickly breath of the ancipital race lent a blue aura to the torches. Taking in what he could of this scene as he was examined by rough hands, Billy saw ramps leading upwards, and others, their entrances unwelcoming, leading even further underground.

A perception came to him: in these caves, at this time, phagors gathered to escape the heat; the time would come when men huddled here, to escape the cold. The phagors would then take over the outside world.

Some kind of order was called, and interrogation began. It was evident that Lex had informed Ghht-Yronz Tharl of the content of Billy's conversation with SartoriIrvrash.

Sitting by the kzahhn was a middle-aged female human, a shapeless woman in a dress of stammel, who translated a series of questions from the kzahhn into Olonets. The questions concentrated on Billy's arrival from Freyr—the phagors would hear nothing of Avernus. If this son of Freyr had arrived from otherwhere, then it followed that he came from Freyr, whence, in ancipital eyes, all evil came.

He could hardly understand their questions. Nor could they understand his answers. He had had difficulties with the Borlienese chancellor; here the cultural difference was much wider—he would have said insuperable except that occasionally he made himself understood. For instance, these nightmarish creatures grasped the point that Helliconia's time of intensifying heat would pass in three or four human lifetimes, to be replaced by a long continued slide towards winter.

At this juncture, the questioning broke off, and the kzahhn

sank into a trance in order to communicate with the ancestors of his component present. A human slave brought Billy flavoured water to drink. He begged to be allowed back to the palace, but in a short while his questioning was resumed.

It was curious that the phagors grasped what SartoriIrvrash could not, that Billy had travelled through space, though the Native Ancipital phrase for "space" was an almost untranslatable conglomerate, meaning "immeasureable pathway of air-turns and great year procedures." More briefly, they sometimes spoke of it as "Aganip pathway."

They examined his watch without touching it. He was pushed from one to another of the audience, along the spokes of the council wheel, so that all could see it. His explanation that the three dials showed time on Earth, Helliconia, and Avernus meant nothing to them. Like the phagors he had met outside Matrassyl, they made no attempt to take the instrument and soon reverted to other topics.

His eyes streamed, his nose ran—he had an allergy to their dense coats against which he had been forced to brush.

Between sneezes, Billy told them all he knew about the situation on Helliconia. His fear drove him to reveal everything. When they heard something they could absorb or that interested them especially, the kzahhn would pass on the information to his keratinous ancestor, either for storage or information, Billy was not sure which—phagors had not come within his discipline on the Avernus.

Did they tell him at some point, when he laboured unnecessarily to explain how seasons came and went, that the monastic caverns in the hills were occupied at some seasons by phagors, at others by Sons of Freyr? Once, in a different existence, he had boasted that Avernus held too little otherness for him; now, in a mist of otherness, the curious line of language weaved between Hurdhu, Native, and Eotemporal, between scientific and figurative.

Like a child finding that animals can talk, Billy listened as they spoke to him. "Possibility for revenge against Sons of Freyr at inharmonious season-of-Great-Year has no being. Surviving alone must have all our duty. Watchfulness fills our harneys. All time exists till Freyr-death. Kzahhn JandolAnganol has protective arm for ancipitals' survival in lands of his

component. Therefore, the order is for our legions to make formation in a reinforcement of Kzahhn JandolAnganol. Such is our present law of inharmonious season. Carefulness is what you Billy must take not to make a further torment for this kzahhn of weakness named JandolAnganol. Hast comprehension?''

With the noun-freighted sentences whirling in his head, he tried to declare his innocence. But questions of guilt, or freedom from it, were outside their *umwelt*. As he spoke, bafflement reinforced the hostility in the air.

Behind their hostility was fear of a kind, an impersonal fear. They saw JandolAnganol as weak, and they feared that when the alliance with Oldorando was sealed by dynastic marriage, their kind might become as subject to persecution in Borlien as in Oldorando. Their hatred of Oldorando was clear and, in particular, their hatred for its capital, which they called by the Eotemporal name of Hrrm-Bhhrd Ydohk.

While ancipital affairs were a mystery—a blank—to mankind, the ancipitals had a good grasp of mankind's affairs. Such was mankind's arrogant contempt of them that phagors were often present, though ignored, at the most delicate discussions of state. Thus the humblest runt could act effectively as a spy.

Confronting their stolid forms, Billy thought they intended to hold him to ransom, to influence the king against his new marriage; feebly he tried to convey that the king did not even know of his existence.

As soon as the words had left him, he saw that he had put himself in another danger. They might keep him here, in a worse prison than his previous one, if they realised that his presence in the palace was a secret. But the shaggy council was pursuing another line of thought, reverting once more to the question of Batalix's capture by Freyr, an event which seemed of obsessive importance to them.

If not from Freyr, then was he from T'Sehn-Hrr? This question he could not understand. By T'Sehn-Hrr, did they mean the Avernus, Kaidaw? Evidently not. They tried to explain, he tried. T'Sehr-Hrr remained a mystery. He was one with the keratinous figures propped against the wall, doomed to say the same thing many times, in an ever decreasing voice. Talk-

ing to phagors was like trying to wrestle with eternity.

The council passed him among them, pressing him here, turning him there. Again they were interested in looking at the three-faced watch on his wrist. Its writhing figures fascinated them. But they made no efforts to remove or even touch it, as if they sensed in it a destructive force.

Billy was still seeking for words when he realised that the kzahhn and his council were departing. Clouds gathered in his head again. He found himself staggering into a familiar chair, let his forehead rest on a familiar table. The gillots had returned him to his cell. A pale shrouded dawn was at hand.

Lex was there, without horns, emasculated and almost faithful.

"Steps are necessity to bed for a sleep-period," he advised.

Billy started to weep. Weeping, he slept.

The fog reached far and wide and took a turn up the River Valvoral to view the jungles embracing either bank. Caring nothing for national frontiers, it penetrated far into Oldorando. There it met, among other river traffic, the *Lordryardry Lady* heading southeastward to Matrassyl and the distant sea.

With the last of its ice cargo sold profitably in Oldorando, the flat-bottomed boat now bore cargoes for the Borlienese capital or Ottassol: salt; silks; carpets of all descriptions; tapestries; blue gout from Lake Dorzin, boxed with smashed ice; carvings; clocks; with tusks, horns, and furs in variety. The small deck cabins were occupied by merchants who travelled with their goods. One merchant had a parrot, another a new mistress.

The best deck cabin was occupied by the boat's owner, Krillio Muntras, famous Ice Captain of Dimariam, and his son, Div. Div, who was slack of jaw and, for all his father's encouragement, would never rival his father's success in life, sat gazing at the hazily sketched scenery. His bottom was planted on the deck. Occasionally, he spat into the passing water. His father sat solidly in a canvas chair and played on a doubleclouth—perhaps with a deliberate sentimentality, for this was his last voyage before retirement. His last last voyage. Muntras matched a pleasant tenor voice to his tune.

The river flows and will not cease, no,
No—not for love or life itself, oh . . .

The passengers roaming the deck included an arang, which
was to provide the sailors with their supper. Except for the
arang, the passengers were markedly respectful to the ice captain.

Fog curled like steam off the surface of the Valvoral. The
water became darker still as they neared the cliffs of Cahchazzerh, whose steep faces overlooked the river. The cliffs, folded
like old linen, rose a few hundred feet to be crowned with
dense foliage which, in its exuberance, appeared to be lowering itself down the overhanging rock by means of creepers and
lianas. Much of the cliff had been colonised by swallows and
mourner birds. The latter launched themselves and came to in-
vestigate the *Lordryardry Lady*, wheeling above it with their
melancholy shrieks as it prepared to moor.

Cahchazzerh was remarkable for nothing but its situation
between cliff and river, and its apparent indifference to the
falls of the one or the rise of the other. At the water's edge, the
town consisted of little but a wharf and a few godowns, one of
which bore a rusty sign saying LORDRYARDRY ICE TRADING CO.
A road led back to scattered houses and some cultivation on
top of the cliffs. The town marked a last stop before Matrassyl
on the downstream journey.

As the vessel moored up, a few dockhands bestirred themselves, while near-naked boys—indispensable adjuncts of such
places—came running. Muntras put down his musical instrument and stood grandly in the bows, accepting the salutations
of the men ashore, every one of whom he knew by name.

The gangplank went down. Everybody aboard disembarked
to walk about and buy fruit. Two merchants whose journeys
terminated here saw to it that the sailors unloaded their
possessions safely. The boys dived for coins in the river.

An incongruous item in this sleepy scene was a table, laid
with a gaudy cloth, which stood outside the Lordryardry warehouse, a white-clad waiter in attendance. Behind the table
were four musicians who, on the instant of the boat's side kissing the wharf, gave forth with a lively rendering of "What a
Man the Master Is!" This reception was the farewell present

of the local staff of the ice company to their boss. There were three staff. They came forward, smiling, although they had been through the performance before, to conduct Captain Krillio and Div to their seats.

One of the three employees was a gangling youth, embarrassed by the whole affair; the other two were white-haired and older than the man they had served so long. The oldsters managed to shed a tear for the occasion, while covertly summing up young Master Div, in order to estimate to what extent their jobs were threatened by the change in command.

Muntras shook each of the trio by the hand and subsided into the waiting chair. He accepted a glass of wine, into which were dropped sparkling fragments of his own ice. He gazed out across the sluggish river. The far bank could scarcely be seen for mist. As a waiter served them little cakes, there was conversation consisting of sentences beginning, "Do you remember when—" and concluding with laughter.

The birds still wheeling overhead masked a sound of shouts and barking. As these noises became more obtrusive, the Ice Captain asked what was happening.

The young man laughed, as the two old men looked uneasy. "It's a drumble up in the village, Captain." He jerked a thumb towards the cliffs. "Killing off fuggies."

"They're great on drumbles in Oldorando," Muntras said. "And often enough the priests use the drumbles as an excuse to kill off so-called heretics as well as phagors. Religion! Fgh!"

The men continued with reminiscences of the time when they had all been engaged in building up the inland ice trade, and of the Ice Captain's dictatorial father.

"You're lucky not to have a father such as he was, Master Div," one of the old men said.

Div nodded as if he was not too sure on that point and left his chair. He ambled to the river's edge and looked up the cliff, whence came distant shouts.

In a minute, he called to his father, "It's the drumble."

The others made no response and went on talking, until the youth called again. "The drumble, Pa. They're just going to heave the fuggies over the cliffside."

He pointed upwards. Some of the other boat travellers were

also pointing, craning their necks to look up the cliff.

A horn gave a tantivy, and the baying of hounds intensified. "They're great on drumbles in Oldorando," the captain repeated, getting heavily to his feet and walking out to where his son stood, open-mouthed, on the bank.

"You see, it's government orders, sir," said one of the old men, following and peering into the Ice Captain's face. "They kill off the phagors and take their land."

"And then don't work it properly," added the Ice Captain. "They should leave the poor damned things alone. They're useful, are phagors."

Hoarse phagor shouting could be heard, but little action could be seen. However, in a short time, human shouts of triumph rang out and the riot of vegetation on the cliffs became disturbed. Broken branches flew, rocks tumbled, as a figure emerged from obscurity and plunged downwards, alternately flying and bouncing, to the enormous inconvenience of the mourner birds. The figure crashed onto the narrow bank under the cliff, made to sit up, and toppled into the water. A three-fingered hand was raised, to sink slowly as its owner was carried away by the flood.

Div broke into empty laughter. "Did you see that?" he exclaimed.

Another phagor, endeavouring to escape its human tormentors, began well by leaping down the cliff. Then it slipped and crashed headlong, bouncing on a spur of rock and cartwheeling into the water. Other figures followed, some small, some large. For a spell, figures were raining down the cliff. At the crest of the cliff, where the underpinning was steeper, two phagors jumped free, clutching each other by the hand. They broke through the outermost branches of an overhanging tree, fell clear of the rock, and dropped into the river. An overadventurous dog followed them down, to crash on the bank.

"Let's be away from here," said Muntras. "I don't care for this. Right, men, gangplank up. All aboard who's getting aboard. Look lively!"

He shook hands with his old staff in a perfunctory way and strode towards the *Lordryardry Lady* to see his orders carried out.

One of the Oldorandan merchants said to him, "I'm glad to

see that even in these benighted parts they're trying to rid us of those shaggy vermin.''

"They do no harm," said Muntras brusquely, his solid figure not pausing in its stride.

"On the contrary, sir, they are mankind's oldest enemy, and during the Ice Age reduced our numbers almost to nothing.''

"That was the dead past. We live in the present. Get aboard, everyone. We're pushing off from this barbarous spot with all haste.''

The crew, like their captain, were men from Hespagorat. Without argument, they got the gangplank up and the boat under way.

As the *Lady* drifted into midstream, her passengers could see ancipital corpses floating in the water, surrounded by clouds of yellow blood. One of the crew called out. Ahead was a live phagor, making wretched attempts to swim.

A pole was quickly brought and thrust over the side. The boat had no sail up, for there was no wind, but the current was carrying it with increasing speed. Nevertheless, the phagor understood what was happening. After thrashing furiously, he grasped the end of the pole with both hands. The river brought him against the bulwarks, where he was hauled up to safety.

"You should have let him drown. Fuggies can't stand the water," said a merchant.

"This is my vessel, and my word is law here," said Muntras, with a dark look. "If you have any objections to what goes on, I can put you off right now."

The stallun lay panting on the deck in a spreading pool of water. Ichor ran from a wound in his head.

"Give him a dram of Exaggerator. He'll survive," said the captain. He turned away when the fierce Dimariamian liquor was brought forward and retired to his cabin.

Over his lifetime, he considered, his fellow human beings had grown nastier, more spiteful, less forgiving. Maybe it was the weather. Maybe the world was going to burn up. Well, at least he was going to retire in his own home town of Lordry-ardry, to a stout building overlooking the sea. Dimariam was always cooler than damned Campannlat. People were decent there.

He would call in on King JandolAnganol when in Matrassyl, on the principle that it was always wise to call on sovereigns of one's acquaintance. The queen was gone, together with the ring he had once sold her; he must see about delivering her letter when he reached Ottassol. Meanwhile he would hear the latest news of the unfortunate queen of queens. Maybe he would also call on Matty; otherwise he would never see her again. He thought affectionately of her well-run whorehouse, better than all the squalid knocking-shops of Ottassol; although Matty herself had put on airs and went to church daily since the king rewarded her for her assistance after the Battle of the Cosgatt.

But what would he do in Dimariam when he was retired? That did need thought; his family was not a great source of comfort. Perhaps he could find some minor profitable mischief to keep him happy. He fell asleep with one hand resting on his music instrument.

The stocky Ice Captain arrived at a city muted by the events recently played out on its stage.

The king's problems were mounting. Reports from Randonan talked of soldiers deserting in companies. Despite constant prayer in the churches, crops were still failing. The Royal Armourer was having little success in manufacturing copies of the Sibornalese matchlocks. And Robayday returned.

JandolAnganol was in the hills with his hoxney Lapwing, walking through a copse beside his mount. Yuli trotted behind his master, delighted to be in the wilds. Two escorts rode behind at a distance. Robayday jumped from a tree and stood before his father.

He bowed deeply. "Why, it is the king himself, my master, walking in the woods with his new bride." Leaves fell from his hair.

"Roba, I need you at Matrassyl. Why do you keep escaping?" The king did not know whether to be pleased or angry at this sudden apparition.

"To keep escaping is never to escape. Though what keeps me prisoner I know not. Difference must be between fresh air and grandfather's dungeon. . . . If I had no parents, then I

might be free." He spoke with a roving eye, unfocussed. His hair, like his speech, was tumbled. He was naked except for a kind of fur kilt over his genitals. His ribs showed, and his body was a tracery of scars and scratches. He carried a javelin.

This weapon he now stuck point first in the ground and ran to Yuli clasping the runt's arms, crying out in affection.

"My dearest queen, how wonderful you look, so well dressed in that white fur with the red tassels! To keep off the sun, to hide your delectable body from all but this lecherous Other, who swings on you, no doubt, as if you were a bough. Or a sow. Or a broken vow."

"You make me hurted," cried the little phagor, struggling to get free.

JandolAnganol reached out to take his son's arm, but Robayday darted to one side. He tugged a flowering creeper which hung from a caspiarn and, with a quick movement, twined it round Yuli's throat. Yuli ran about, calling hoarsely, lips curled back in alarm, as JandolAnganol took tight hold to his son.

"I don't intend to hurt you, but cease this foolery and speak to me with the respect you owe me."

"Oh me, oh me! Speak to me in respect of my poor mother. You have planted horns upon her, you gardener in bogs!" He gave a cry and fell back as his father struck him across the mouth.

"Cease this unkind nonsense at once. Be silent. If you had kept your sanity and had been acceptable to Pannoval, then you might have married Simoda Tal in my place. Then we would have been spared much pain. Do you think only for yourself, boy?"

"Yes, as I make my own scumber!" He spat the words out.

"You owe me something, who made you a prince," said the king with bitterness. "Or have you forgotten you're a prince? We'll lock you up at home until you come back to your right mind."

With his free hand up to his bleeding mouth, Robayday muttered, "There's more comfort in my wrong mind. I'd rather forget my rights."

By this time, the two lieutenants had come up, swords out. The king turned, ordering them to put up their weapons, dis-

mount, and take his son captive. As his attention was distracted, Robayday broke free of his father's grasp and made off, with great leaps and whoops, among the trees.

One of the lieutenants put an arrow to his crossbow, but the king stopped him. Nor did he make any attempt to follow his son.

"I not have liking to Robay," squealed Yuli.

Ignoring him, JandolAnganol mounted Lapwing and rode swiftly back to the palace. With his brows knitted, he resembled more than ever the eagle that gave him his nickname.

Back in the seclusion of his quarters, he submitted himself to pauk, as he rarely did. His soul sank down to the original beholder and he spoke with the gossie of his mother. She offered him full consolation. She reminded him that Robayday's other grandmother was the wild Shannana, and told him not to worry. She said he should not hold himself guilty for the deaths of the Myrdolators, since they had intended treason to the state.

The fragile casket of dust offered JandolAnganol every verbal comfort. Yet his soul returned to his body troubled.

His wicked old father, still alive in the ponderous basements, was more practical. VarpalAnganol never ran out of advice.

"Warm up the Pasharatid scandal. Get our agents to spread rumours. You must implicate Pasharatid's wife, who impudently remains here to carry her husband's office. Any tale against the Sibornalese is readily believed."

"And what am I to do regarding Robayday?"

The old man turned slightly in his chair and closed one eye. "Since you can do nothing about him, do nothing. But anything you could do to speed your divorce and get the marriage over with would be useful."

JandolAnganol paced about the dungeon.

"As to that, I'm in the hands of the C'Sarr now."

The old man coughed. His lungs laboured before he spoke again. "Is it hot outside? Why do people keep saying it's hot? Listen, our friends in Pannoval *want* you to be in the C'Sarr's hands. That suits them but it doesn't suit you. Hurry matters if you can. What news of MyrdemInggala?"

The king took his father's advice. Agents with an armed

escort were dispatched to distant Pannoval City beyond the Quzints, with a long address beseeching the C'Sarr of the Holy Pannovalan Empire to hasten the bill of divorce. With the address went icons and other gifts, including holy relics fabricated for the occasion.

But the Massacre of the Myrdolators, as that affair was now called, continued to exercise the minds of people and scritina. Agents reported rebellious movements in the city, and in other centres such as Ottassol. A scapegoat was needed. It had to be Chancellor SartoriIrvrash.

SartoriIrvrash—the Rushven once beloved of the king's family—would make a popular victim. The world mistrusts intellectuals, and the scritina had particular reason to hate both his high-handed ways and his long speeches.

A search of the chancellor's suite would be certain to reveal something incriminating. There would be the notes of his breeding experiments with the Others, Madis, and humans he kept captive in a distant quarry. And there were the voluminous papers relating to his "Alphabet of History and Nature." These papers would be full of heresies, distortions, lies against the All-Powerful. How both scritina and Church would lick their chops at that prospect! JandolAnganol sent in a guard, led by no less a personage than Archpriest BranzaBaginut of Matrassyl Cathedral.

The search was more successful than anticipated. The secret room was discovered (though not its secret exit). In that secret room was discovered a secret prisoner of curious quality. As he was dragged away, this prisoner screamed in accented Olonets that he came from another world.

Great piles of incriminating documents were taken into the courtyard. The prisoner was taken before the king.

Although it was now twenty past thirteen in the afternoon, the fog had not cleared; rather, it had deepened, taking on a yellowish tinge. The palace drifted in a world of its own, the ventilation devices on its chimneys like the masts of a sinking fleet. Perhaps claustrophobia played a part in the uncertainty of the king's moods as he swung between meekness and anger, between calm and wild excitement. His hair stood dishevelled on his forehead. His nose bled by fits and starts, as if forced into the role of safety valve. About the corridors he went,

followed by a train of unhappy courtiers who infuriated him with placatory smiles.

When SartoriIrvrash was brought forth and confronted by the trembling Billy, JandolAnganol struck the old man. After which he seized up his chancellor like an ancient rag doll, wept, begged forgiveness, and suffered another nose bleed.

It was while JandolAnganol was in a penitent mood that Ice Captain Muntras arrived at the palace to pay his respects.

"I will see the captain later," said the king. "As a traveller, he may bring me news of the queen. Tell him to wait on me. Let the world wait."

He wept and snarled. In a minute, he called back the messenger.

"Bring in the Ice Captain. He shall witness this curiosity of human nature." This was said as he prowled about Billy Xiao Pin.

Billy shifted from foot to foot, half-inclined to blubber, unnerved by the bloody state of the royal nostrils. On the Avernus, such demonstrations of feeling, if they ever occurred, would take place in seclusion. "On the Prolongation of One Helliconian Season Beyond One Human Life-Span" had been firm, if brief, on the subject of feeling. "Sensation: superfluous," it said. The excitable Borlienese believed otherwise. Their king did not look like a sympathetic listener.

"Um—hello," managed Billy, with an anguished smile. He gave a violent sneeze.

Muntras entered the room, bowing. They were in a cramped and ancient part of the palace which smelt of mortar, though it was mortar four hundred years old. The Ice Captain stood on his two flat feet and looked about curiously as he delivered his greetings.

The king barely acknowledged Muntras's courtesies. Pointing to a pile of cushions, he said, "Sit there and don't speak. Observe what we have found rotting in the recesses of this pile. The fruit of treachery!"

Turning abruptly back to Billy, he asked, "How many years have you festered in SartoriIrvrash's clutches, creature?"

Disconcerted by the king's regal brand of Olonets, Billy stammered. "A week—even eight days . . . I forget, Your Majesty."

"Eight days is a week, slanje. Are you the poor results of an experiment?"

The king laughed, and all those present—less from humour than from a care for their lives—echoed him. Nobody wished to seem to be a Myrdolator.

"You smell like an experiment." More laughing.

He summoned up two slaves and told them to wash Billy and change his clothes. As this was done, food and wine appeared. Men came running, bent in the attitude of mobile bows, bearing warmed kid-meat served in orange rice.

While Billy ate, the king marched about the chamber, disdaining food. JandolAnganol occasionally pressed a silken cloth to his nose, or stared at his left wrist where his son, in escaping his grasp, had scratched his flesh. Pacing somewhat awkwardly by his side was the Archpriest BranzaBaginut, an enormous man whose bulk, rigged overall in saffron and scarlet canonicals, caused him to resemble a Sibornalese warship in full sail. His heavy face might have belonged to a village wrestler was it not for a lurking humour in his expression. He was widely respected as a shrewd man and one who supported the king as a benefactor of the Church.

BranzaBaginut loomed over the king, who wore by contrast only breeches, was unbooted, and allowed his dirty white jacket to gape, revealing a boney chest.

The room itself was undecided in its role, being somewhere between a reception chamber and a storeroom. There were plenty of rugs and cushions of a mouldy sort, while old timbers were stacked in one corner. The windows looked out on a narrow passage; men passed that way occasionally, carrying piles of SartoriIrvrash's papers into the courtyard.

"Let me question this person, sire, on religious matters," said BranzaBaginut to the king. Receiving nothing in the way of disagreement, the dignitary sailed in the direction of Billy and asked, "Do you come from a world where Akhanaba the All-Powerful rules?"

Billy wiped his mouth, reluctant to cease eating.

"You know I can easily give you an answer to please you. Since I have no wish to displease you, or his majesty, may I offer it you, knowing it to be untrue?"

"Stand when you address me, creature. You give me your

answer to my question and I tell you soon enough whether or not I am pleased by it."

Billy stood before the massive ecclesiastic, still nervously wiping his mouth.

"Sir, gods are necessary to men at some stages of development . . . I mean, as children, we need, each of us, a loving, firm, just father, to help our growth to manhood. Manhood seems to require a similar image of a father, magnified, to keep it in good check. That image bears the name of God. Only when a part of the human race grows to a spiritual manhood, when it can regulate its own behaviour, does the need for gods disappear—just as we no longer need a father watching over us when we are adults and capable of looking after ourselves."

The archpriest smoothed a large cheek with a hand, appearing struck by this explanation. "And you are from a world where you look after yourselves, without the need of gods. Are you saying that?"

"That is correct, sir." Billy looked fearfully about him. The Ice Captain reclined nearby, filling his face with the royal food, but listening intently.

"This world you come from—Avernus, did I hear?—is it a happy one?"

The priest's innocent-seeming question set Billy in a good deal of confusion. Had the same question been put to him a few weeks ago on the Avernus, and by his Advisor, he would have had no trouble answering. He would have responded that happiness resided in knowledge, not in superstition, in certainty, not in uncertainty, in control, not in chance. He would have believed that knowledge, certainty, and control were the singular benefits derived from and governing the lives of the population of the observation station. He would certainly have laughed—and even his Advisor would have spared a wintery chuckle—at the notion of Akhanaba as bringer of felicity.

On Helliconia, it was different. He could still laugh at the idolatrous superstition of the Akhanaban religion. And yet. And yet. He saw now the depth of meaning in the word "godless." He had escaped from a godless state to a barbaric

one. And he could see, despite his own misfortunes, in which world the hope of life and happiness more strongly lay.

As he was stuttering over his reply, the king spoke. JandolAnganol had been meditating Billy's previous answer. He said challengingly, "What if we have no sound image of a father to guide us to manhood? What then?"

"Then, sir, Akhanaba may indeed be a support to us in our trouble. Or we may reject him completely, as we reject our natural father."

This reply caused the king's nose to bleed again.

Billy seized the moment to bluff his way out of replying to BranzaBaginut's question by saying to him, with more confidence than he felt, "My lord, I am a person of importance, and have received bad treatment from this court. Let me go free. I can work with you. I can tell you details about your world you need to know. I have nothing to gain—"

The Archpriest clapped his large hands together, and said in a gentle voice, "Don't deceive yourself. You are of no importance whatsoever, except when you condemn further Chancellor SartoriIrvrash of conspiring against his royal majesty."

"You have made no attempt to assess my importance. Supposing I tell you that thousands of people are watching us at this moment? They wait to see how you behave towards me, to test you. Their judgement will influence how you are set down in history."

Colour rose to the dignitary's cheeks. "It is the All-Powerful who watches us, no one else. Your dangerous lies of godless worlds would overturn our state. Hold your tongue, or you will find yourself on a bonfire."

In some desperation, Billy approached the king, displaying his watch with its three faces to him. "Your Majesty, I beg you to free me. Look on this artifact I wear. Every person on the Avernus wears a similar one. It tells the time on Helliconia, on Avernus, and on a distant controlling world, Earth. It is a symbol of the tremendous strides we have made in conquering our environment. To a sympathetic audience, I could convey marvels far in advance of anything Borlien could manage."

Interest woke in the king's eyes. He lowered his silk and

asked, "Can you make me a functioning matchlock, the equal of Sibornal's?"

"Why, matchlocks are nothing. I—"

"Wheel locks, then. You could produce a wheel lock?"

"Well, no, I—sir, it's a question of the tensile strengths of the metal. I daresay I could devise— Such things are obsolete where I come from."

"What kind of weapon can you make?"

"Sir, first interest yourself in this watch, which I beg you to accept as a present, in token of my faith." He dangled the watch before the king, who showed no inclination to accept it. "Then let me free. Then let me work from first principles with some of your learned men, such as the Archpriests here. Very soon we might devise a good, accurate pistol, and radio, and an internal combustion engine. . . ."

He saw the expressions on both the king's and the archpriest's face, changed his mind about what he was going to say, and instead held out the watch again in supplicatory fashion.

The little figures wriggled and changed under the king's inspection. His majesty seized the timepiece; he and BranzaBaginut inspected it, whispering. Prophets had spoken of a time when magical machineries would appear and the state would be overthrown and the Empire destroyed.

"Will this jewel tell me how long I have left to reign? Can it inform me of the age of my daughter?"

"Sir, it is science, plain science, not magic. Its case is of platinum trawled from space itself. . . ."

The king brushed it away with a sweep of his hand.

"The jewel is evil. I know it. Kings as well as deuteroscopists are cunning about the future. Why did you come here?" He threw the watch back to Billy.

"Your Majesty, I came to see the queen."

JandolAnganol was disconcerted by this reply and stepped back as if he were confronting a ghost. Said BranzaBaginut, "So you are not only an atheist but a Myrdolator? And you expect to be welcome here? Why should his majesty tolerate any more of your riddling? You are neither lunatic nor jester. Where did you come from? SartoriIrvrash's armpit?"

He advanced threateningly on Billy, who backed against a wall. Other members of the court began to close in, anxious to show their sovereign how they regarded unroasted Myrdolators.

Krillio Muntras rose from his cushions and advanced to where the king stood, looking about sharply in some indecision.

"Your majesty, why not ask your prisoner by what ship he arrived from this other world of his?"

The king looked as if undecided as to whether to become angry. Instead, he said, with his nose still covered, "Well, creature, to please our ice trader—by what vehicle came you here?"

Edging round the perimeters of BranzaBaginut, Billy said, "My ship was of metal, a ship entirely enclosed, carrying its own air. I can make all this comprehensible with the aid of diagrams. Our science is advanced, and could aid Borlien. . . . The ship brought me down to Helliconia safely, then left, to return on its own to my world."

"Has it a mind then, this vessel?"

"That's difficult to answer. Yes, it has a mind. It can calculate—navigate through space, perform a thousand actions by itself."

JandolAnganol bent in a careless way and lifted up a wine jar, elevating it slowly until it was above his head. "Which of us is mad, creature, you or I? This vessel has a mind—yes, yes, it too can navigate all by itself. Look!" He flung it. The jar flew through the air, crashed into a wall and broke, splashing its contents all about. This small violence caused everyone to become as immobile as phagors.

"Your Majesty, I endeavoured to answer your—" He sneezed violently.

"It's guilt and anger only that forces me to try and get reason out of you. But why should I bother? I'm deprived, I have nothing, this place is an empty larder, with rats for courtiers. All has been taken away, yet still more is asked of me. You too ask something of me. . . . I am confronted by demons all the way. . . . I must do penance again, Archpriest, and your hand must not be light upon me. This is SartoriIrvrash's

demon, I do believe. Tomorrow, I will endeavour to address
the scritina and all will be changed. Today I am merely a
father who bleeds a lot . . ."

He said in a lower voice, to himself, "Yes, that's it, simply,
I must change myself."

He lowered his eyes and looked weary. A drip of blood fell
to the floor.

Ice Captain Muntras gave a cough. As a practical man, he
was embarrassed by the king's outburst.

"Sire, I come on you at a bad time, as I see. I am just a
trader, and so had best be on my way. For the past many
years, I have brought you the best Lordryardry ice straight off
the best slice of our glaciers and at the best prices. Now, sire, I
will give you my grateful thanks for your custom and hospitality at
the palace, and take my leave of you for ever. Despite the fog,
it's best I was off back home."

The speech seemed in a measure to revive the king, who put
a hand on the Ice Captain's shoulder. The eyes of the latter
were round in innocence.

"I would I had such men as you about me, talking plain
sense all the time, Captain. Your service has been appreciated.
Nor do I forget your assistance to me when I was wounded
after that fearsome occasion in the Cosgatt—as I am wounded
now. You are a true patriot."

"Sire, I am a true patriot of my own country, of Dimariam.
To which I am about to retire. This is my last trip. My son will
carry on the ice trade with all the devotion I have shown you
and the—hm—the ex-queen. As the weather grows hotter,
your majesty will perhaps be needing additional loads of ice?"

"Captain, you good trader in better climates, you should be
rewarded for your service. Despite my dreadful state of
penury, and the meanness of my scritina, I ask—is there
anything I might present you with as a token of our esteem?"

Muntras shuffled. "Sire, I am unworthy of reward, and do
not seek one, but supposing I said to you that I would make an
exchange? On the journey here from Oldorando, I, being a
compassionate man, rescued a phagor from a drumble. He is
recovered from a watery ordeal, often fatal to his kind, and
must find a living away from Cahchazzerh, where he was
persecuted. I will present this stallun to you as a slave if you

will present me with your prisoner, whether demon or not. Is it a deal?''

"You may have the creature. Take it away, together with its mechanical jewel. You need give me nothing in return, Captain. I am in your debt if you will remove it from my kingdom."

"Then I will take him. And you shall have the phagor, so that my son may call on you in the same civil terms as I have always done. He's a good boy, sir, is Div, though with no more polish than his father."

So Billy Xiao Pin passed into the keeping of the Ice Captain. And on the following day, when the fog was dispersing before a slight breeze, the king's cloudiness also dispersed. He kept his promise to address the scritina.

To that body, who sat coughing in their pews, he presented the appearance of a changed man. Having attested to the wickedness of Chancellor SartoriIrvrash, and to his major role in the reverses recently suffered by the state, JangolAnganol launched into a confession.

"Gentlemen of the scritina, you swore fealty to me when I ascended the throne of Borlien. There have been reverses to our dearly beloved kingdom, that I do not deny. No king, however, powerful, however benevolent, can greatly change the condition of his people—that I now realise. I cannot command droughts or the suns which bring such plagues on our land.

"In my desperation, I have committed crimes. Urged on by the chancellor, I was responsible for the deaths of the Myrdolators. I confess and ask your forgiveness. It was done to set the kingdom right, to stop further dissension. I have given up my queen, and with her all lust, all seeking for self. My marriage to the Princess Simoda Tal of Oldorando will be a dynastic one—chaste, chaste, I swear. I will not touch her except to breed. I will take thought for her years. I shall henceforth devote myself wholeheartedly to my country. Give me your obedience, gentlemen, and you will have mine."

He spoke controlledly, with tears in his eyes. His audience sat in silence, gazing up at him sitting on the gilded throne of

the scritina. Few felt pity for him; most saw only the opportunity to exploit this fresh instance of his weakness.

Despite the absence of a moon, there were tides on Helliconia. As Freyr drew nearer, the planet's watery envelope experienced an increase in tidal strength of some sixty percent above conditions at apastron, when Freyr was more than seven hundred astronomical units distant.

MyrdemInggala, in her new home, liked to walk alone by the shore of the sea. Her troubled thoughts blew away for a while. This was a marginal place, the strip between the kingdoms of the sea and the kingdoms of the land. It reminded her of her dimday garden left behind, placed between night and day. She was only vaguely aware of the constant struggle that went on at her feet, perhaps never to be entirely won or lost. She gazed towards the horizon, wondering as she did every day if the Ice Captain had delivered her letter to the general in the distant wars.

The queen's gown was pale yellow. It went with the solitude. Her favourite colour was red, but she wore it no more. It did not go with old Gravabagalinien and its haunted past. The hiss of the sea demanded yellow, to her mind.

When she was not swimming, she left Tatro on the beach to play and walked below the high-tide line. Her lady-in-waiting reluctantly followed. Tough grasses grew from the sand. Some formed clumps. A step or two farther inland and other plants ventured. A little white daisy with armoured stem was among the first. There was a small plant with succulent leaves, almost like a seaweed. MyrdenInggala did not know its name, but she liked to pick it. Another plant had dark leaves. It straggled among the sand and grasses in insignificant clusters but, on occasions where conditions were right, raised itself into striking bushes with a lustrous sheen.

Behind these first bold invaders of the shore lay the litter of the tide line. Then came a haggard area, punctuated with tough, large-flowered daisies. Then less adventurous plants took over, and the beach was banished, though inlets of sand seamed the land for some way.

"Mai, don't be unhappy. I love this place."

The dawdling lady put on a sullen expression. "You are the most beautiful and fateful lady in Borlien." She had never spoken to her mistress in this tone before. "Why could you not keep your husband?"

The queen made no answer. The two women continued along the shore, some way apart. MyrdemInggala walked among the lustrous bushes, caressing their tips with her hand. Occasionally, something under a bush would hiss and recoil from her step.

She was aware of Mai TolramKetinet, trailing dolefully behind her, hating exile. "Keep up, Mai," she called encouragingly. Mai did not respond.

XI

JOURNEY TO THE
NORTHERN CONTINENT

The old man wore an ankle-length keedrant which had seen better days. On his head was a scoop-shaped hat, which protected his scrawny neck as well as his bald pate from the sun. At intervals, he lifted a shaking hand to his lips to puff at the stem of a veronikane. He stood all alone, waiting to leave the palace for good.

At his back was a coach of light build, loaded with his few personal belongings. Two hoxneys were harnessed between the shafts. It needed only a driver, and then SartoriIrvrash could be gone.

The wait afforded him a chance to look across the parade to a corner where an old bent slave with a stick was encouraging a mountain of papers to burn. That bonfire contained all the papers ransacked from the ex-chancellor's suite, including the manuscripts which formed "The Alphabet of History and Nature."

The smoke rose into a pallid sky from which light ash occasionally fell. Temperatures were as high as ever, but a grey

overcast covered everything. The ash was born on an easterly airstream from a newly erupting volcano some distance from Matrassyl. That was of no interest to SartoriIrvrash; it was the black ashes ascending which occupied his attention.

His hand trembled more violently and he made the tip of his veronikane blaze like a small volcano.

A voice behind him said, "Here are some more of your clothes, master."

His slave woman stood there, a neatly wrapped bundle offered to him. She gave him a placatory smile. "It's a shame you have to go, master."

He turned his worn face fully to her, stepped a pace nearer to look into her face.

"Are you sorry to see me go, woman?"

She nodded and lowered her gaze. Well, he thought, she enjoyed it when we had a little rumbo—and to think I never bothered to ask. I never thought of her enjoyment. How isolated I have been in my own feelings. A good enough man, learned, but worth nothing because I had no feelings for others. Except for little Tatro.

He didn't know what to say to the slave woman. He coughed.

"It's a bad day, woman. Go inside. Thank you."

She gave him a last eloquent glance before turning away. SartoriIrvrash thought to himself, Who knows what slave women feel? He hunched his shoulders, irritated with her, and with himself, for showing feeling.

He scarcely noticed when the driver appeared. He took in only a youthful figure, head shrouded against the heat in a kind of Madi hood, so that its face could scarcely be seen.

"Are you ready?" this figure called, as it swung itself up into the driver's seat. The two hoxneys shuffled as the weight adjusted against their straps.

Still SartoriIrvrash lingered. He pointed with his kane towards the distant bonfire. "There goes a whole lifetime's learning." He was mainly addressing himself. "That's what I can't forgive. That's what I shall never forgive. All that work . . ."

With a heavy sigh, he climbed aboard the coach. It began at once to roll forward, towards the palace gates. There were

those in the palace who loved him; fearing the king's wrath, they had not dared to emerge and wave him farewell. He set his face firmly to the front, blinking his eyes rapidly.

The prospects before SartoriIrvrash were dim. He was thirty-seven years and eight tenners old—well past middle age. It was possible that he could get a post as advisor at the court of King Sayren Stund, but he detested both the king and Oldorando, which was far too hot. He had always kept himself apart from his own and his dead wife's relations in Matrassyl. His brothers were dead. There was nothing for it but to go and live with his daughter; she and her husband dwelt in a dull southern town near the Thribiat border.

There he would sink from human ken and attempt to rewrite his life's work. But who would print it, now that he had no power? Who would read it if it were not printed? In despair, he had written to his daughter, and now intended to catch a boat that would take him south. The coach proceeded briskly downhill. At the bottom of the hill, instead of turning towards the docks, it swerved to the right and rattled up a narrow alley. Its hubs on its left side screamed as they rubbed against the walls of the houses.

"Take care, you fool, you've gone wrong!" said Sartori-Irvrash, but he said it to himself. Who cared what happened?

The equipage rattled down a back road under the brow of a cliff and entered a small neglected courtyard. The driver jumped energetically down and closed the courtyard gates, so that they could not be seen from the street. He looked in at the ex-chancellor.

"Would you care to climb down? There's someone waiting to see you." He swept off his elaborate headgear in a mock bow.

"Who are you? What have you brought me here for?"

The boy opened the carriage door invitingly.

"Don't you recognise me, Rushven?"

"Who are you? Why—Roba, it's you!" he said in some relief—for the thought had occurred to him that Jandol-Anganol might be planning to kidnap and murder him.

"It's me or a hoxney, for I move at speed these days. That's how it's all secrecy. I'm a secret even from myself. I have vowed to be revenged on my cursed father again, since he ban-

ished my mother. And on my mother, who left without a farewell to me.''

As he allowed the boy to help him out, SartoriIrvrash surveyed him, anxious to see if he looked as wild as his words. RobaydayAnganol was now just twelve years old, a smaller and thinner edition of his father. He was toasted brown by the sun; red scars showed on his torso. Smiles came and went like twitches over his face, as though he could not decide whether he was joking or not.

''Where have you been, Roba? We've missed you. Your father missed you.''

''Do you mean the Eagle? Why, he nearly caught me. I've never cared for court life. I care even less now. My father's crime has set me free. So I am a hoxney-brother. A Madiassister. I will never become king, and he will never again become happy. New lives, new lives, and one for you, Rushven! You first introduced me to the desert, and I will not desert you. I'm going to take you to someone important, human, not father or hoxney.''

''Who? What's all this about? Wait!''

But Roba was striding off. SartoriIrvrash looked doubtfully at the coach loaded with all his worldly goods and then decided he had better follow. Walking fast, he entered a dim hall only a step or two behind the king's son.

The house was built according to a pattern suited to its overshadowed location: it stretched up to the light like a plant growing between boulders. The old man was panting by the time Roba led them off the shaking wooden stairs and into a room on the third floor, the only room on that level. SartoriIrvrash broke into prolonged coughing and collapsed on a stool someone offered him.

There were three people awaiting them in the room, and he observed that they seized on the opportunity also to cough. A certain rickety elegance in their structure, a certain sharpness of bone structure, marked them out as Sibornalese. One of them was a woman, elegantly dressed in a silk chagirack, the northern equivalent of a charfrul, its delicate fabric patterned with large black and white formal flowers. Two men stood behind her in the shadows. SartoriIrvrash recognised her immediately as Madame Dienu Pasharatid, wife of the am-

bassador who had disappeared the day that Taynth Indredd
had introduced matchlocks into the palace.

He bowed to her and apologised for his coughing.

"We are all doing it, Chancellor. It is the volcano making
our throats sore."

"I believe my throat is sore through grief. You must not call
me by my old title." He would not ask her to what volcano she
referred, but she saw uncertainty in his face.

"The volcanic eruption in the Rustyjonnik Mountains. Its
ash carries this way."

She regarded him with sympathy, letting him recover from
the stairs. Her face was large and plain. Although he knew her
for an intelligent woman, there was an unpleasant asperity
about her mouth, and he had often been guilty of avoiding her
company.

He looked about. The walls were covered with thin paper
which had peeled in places. One picture hung there, a pen-and-
tint drawing of what he recognised as Kharnabhar, the holy
mountain of the Sibornalese. The only window, which was to
one side, lighting Dienu Pasharatid's face in profile, provided
a view of rocky cliff from which creepers hung; the vegetation
had a coating of gray ash. Roba sat cross-legged on the floor,
sucking a straw and smiling from one to another of the party.

"Madame, what do you want with me? I must go to catch a
boat before further disasters befall me," SartoriIrvrash said.

She stood before him and clutched her hands behind her
back, while gently moving her weight from one foot to another.

"We ask you to forgive us for getting you here in such an
unusual way, but we wish to enlist your aid—for which aid, we
will pay generously."

She outlined her proposal, turning occasionally to the men
for confirmation. All Sibornalese were profoundly religious,
believing, as he knew, in God the Azoiaxic, who existed before
life and round whom all life revolves. The members of the ambassadorial contingent held the religion of Akhanaba in low
regard, considering it little better than a superstition. They
were therefore shocked but not surprised when JandolAnganol made the decision to break his marriage and contract
another.

Sibornalese—and the Azoiaxic through them—regarded the bond between woman and man as an equal decision to be held through life. Love was a matter of will, not whim.

SartoriIrvrash sat nodding automatically through this part of the speech, recognising its sententious tone as characteristic of the northern continentals and longing to be on his way.

Roba, not even listening, winked at the ex-chancellor and said confidentially, "This is the house where Ambassador Pasharatid used to meet a lady of the town. It's an historical whorish house—but for you this lady will only talk."

SartoriIrvrash hushed him.

Ignoring the interruption, Madame Dienu said that her party felt that he alone, Chancellor SartoriIrvrash, had pretension to knowledge in the Borlienese court. They felt that the king had treated him almost as badly as—possibly worse than—the queen. Such injustice distressed them, as it would all members of the Church of the Formidable Peace. She was now returning home. They invited SartoriIrvrash to join them, in the assurance that he would be given good accommodation in Askitosh and a good advisory position in the government, as well as freedom to complete his life's work.

He felt the trembling which so often overcame him return. Temporising, he asked, What sort of advisory post?

Oh, advice on matters Borlienese, upon which he was such an expert. And they were preparing to leave Matrassyl on the hour.

So overwhelmed was he by this offer that SartoriIrvrash did not enquire why this sudden haste. Gratefully, he accepted.

"Excellent!" exclaimed Madame Dienu.

The two men behind her now showed an almost ancipital ability to change from stillness to intense activity without intervening stages. They were immediately gone from the room, to promote shouting on all floors and a galumphing on all stairs, as luggage and people hastened down into the courtyard below. Carriages emerged from shelters, hoxneys from stables, stable boys with harness from tackrooms. A procession was assembled in less time than a Borlienese could have drawn on a pair of boots. Prayers were briskly said, all standing round in a circle, and then they were away, leaving an empty house behind them.

They drove north through the warren of the old town, circled the great semisubterranean Dome of Striving, and were soon on the road north with the Takissa gleaming on their left-hand side. Roba yippeed and sang as they went.

Weeks of travel followed.

A feature of the first part of their journey was the pervading greyness caused by the volcanic ash. Mount Rustyjonnik, always a source of grumbling and occasional runs of lava, was in full eruption. The country in the path of its ash became a land of the dead. Trees were killed by the substance, fields covered with it, streams clogged with it. After rain, it turned to paste. Birds and animals died or fled the area. Human families and phagors trudged away from their blighted homes.

Once the Sibornalese party had crossed the River Mar, the blight grew less. Then it faded. They entered Mordriat—a name of terror in Matrassyl. The reality was peaceful. Most of the tribes smiled beneath sheltering layers of braffista turbans, their chief item of apparel.

Guides were engaged to guarantee their safety, thin villain-ous-looking men who abased themselves at every sunrise and sunset. Round their campfire at night, the head Pointer of the Way, as he called himself, explained to the travellers how the ornamentation on his braffista indicated his rank in life. He boasted of the numerous ranks below his.

None listened more eagerly than SartoriIrvrash. "Strange, this human propensity to create ranks in society," he observed to the rest of the party.

"A propensity the more noticeable the nearer the bottom of the pile one descends," said Madam Dienu. "We avoid such demeaning gradations in my land. How you will enjoy seeing Askitosh. It is a model for all communities."

SartoriIrvrash had some reservations about that. But he found a restful quality in the steady severity of Madame Dienu after years of dealing with a changeable king. As the wilder-ness grew more arid, his spirits rose; equally, Roba's madness grew calmer. But when the others slept, SartoriIrvrash could not. His bones, which had become accustomed to a goosedown mattress, could not adapt to a blanket and hard ground. He lay looking up at the stars and the lightning flickering between them, full of an excitement he had not

known since he and his brothers were children. Even his bitterness against JandolAnganol abated somewhat.

The weather continued dry. The coaches made fair progress
over the low hills. They arrived at a small trading town called
Oysha—"Quite probably a corruption of the Local Olonets
word 'osh,' meaning simply 'town,' " SartoriIrvrash explained to the company. Explanations that could be attached
to things made the journey more enjoyable. However the word
was derived, Oysha the Takissa, rushing down from the east,
met up with its formidable tributary, the Madura. Both rivers
had their sources high in the limitless Nktryhk. Beyond Oysha
to the north stretched the Madura Desert.

In Oysha, the coaches were exchanged for kaidaw geldings.
The Pointer volubly made the deal, during which much striking of foreheads took place. The kaidaw was a reliable animal
when it came to crossing deserts. The rust-coloured brutes
stood in the dusty market square of Oysha, indifferent to the
deal being negotiated beside them.

The ex-chancellor sat on a chest while the trading was in
progress. He mopped his brow and coughed. The outfall from
Mount Rustyjonnik had given him a sore throat and fever he
could not shake off. He stared at the long haughty faces of the
kaidaws—those legendary steeds of the warrior phagors in the
Great Winter. It was hard to see in these slow beasts the whirlwind which, with phagors astride it, had brought destruction
upon Oldorando and other Campannlatian cities in the time of
cold.

In the Great Summer, the animals stored water in their
single hump. This made them suitable for desert conditions.
They looked meek enough now, but excited SartoriIrvrash's
sense of history.

"I should purchase a sword," he told RobaydayAnganol.
"I was quite a swordsman in my younger day."

Roba turned a cartwheel. "You turn the year upside down,
now that you are free of the Eagle. You're right to defend
yourself, of course. In those hills lives the accursed Unndreid
—our herdsmen here sleep with his multitudinous daughters
every night. Murder's as frequent hereabouts as scorpions."

"The people seem friendly."

Roba squatted before SartoriIrvrash and put on a cunning

leer. "Why are they outwardly so friendly? Why is Unndreid now armed to the teeth with Sibornalese bang-bangs? Have you discovered why the big black Io Pasharatid left the court so suddenly?"

He took SartoriIrvrash's arm and led him behind one of the coaches for privacy, where only the guileless eyes of the kaidaws were upon them.

"Even my father cannot buy friendship or love. These Sibornalese buy friendship. It's their way. They'd trade their mothers for peace. They have been greasing their safe passage to Borlien by presenting the chiefs along the route with matchlocks, as they say. I say there is no match for them. Even Akhanaba's favourite king, JandolAnganol, son of VarpalAnganol, father of a Madi-lover—but not so mad in that direction as he—even that monarch of Matrassyl was no match for matchlocks. They did for him in the Battle of the Cosgatt. Did you ever see the wound in his thigh?"

"It kept your father abed. I saw only its effects, not the wound."

"He goes without a limp. Lucky not to go without a hardon! That wound was a kiss from Sibornal."

Lowering his voice, SartoriIrvrash said, "You well know that I never trusted the Sibs. When the matchlocks were demonstrated in court, I advised that no Sibs should be present. My word went unheeded. It was shortly after the demonstration that Io Pasharatid disappeared."

Roba lifted a cautionary finger and wagged it slowly. "Disappeared because his swindles were then revealed—revealed to his wife, our fair companion, and his own ambassadorial staff. There was a local young lady involved, who acted as go-between . . . and whom I also go between, on occasions . . . that's how I know all about Io Pasharatid."

He laughed. "The matchlocks which Taynth Indredd had in his possession—which he presented so arrogantly to my eaglefather—which my eagle-father took so pusillanimously, because he would take a plague scab from a beggar if it was offered—those matchlocks were sold to Taynth Indredd cheap by Pasharatid. Why cheap? Because they were not his to sell, in which case he could not avoid making a profit. The guns were the property of his government, intended to buy friend-

ship with such as the rogues you see here, and with such as
Dervlish the Skull, who has proved his friendship a thousand
times over.''

"Unusual behaviour for a Sib. Especially one in high office.''

"High office, low character. It was because of the young
lady. Did you never see the way he eyed my fair mother—I
mean, she who was my mother before she went away without
farewell?''

"Pasharatid would have been put to death if your father
had discovered his crime. I assume he is now back in Sibornal.''

RobaydayAnganol shrugged eloquently. "We are following
him. Madame Dienu is after his blood. To understand his lust
for other ladies, simply contemplate union with her. Would
you couple with a matchlock? . . . He'll be busy concocting a
lying tale, to cover his sins. She will arrive and seek to destroy
it. Ah, Rushven, no drama like a family drama! They will
have old Io locked up in the Great Wheel of Kharnabhar,
mark my words. It was a place of religion, now they lock up
criminals there. Well, monks are also prisoners. . . . What a
drama to come. You know the old saying, 'More than an arm
up a Sibornalese sleeve.' I almost wish I were coming with
you, to see what happens.''

"But you are coming! My dear boy!''

"Ah, unky, no affection! Not for Anganols! No protests.
I'm leaving you here. You go north with Madame. I go back
south with this coach. I have my parents to look after . . . my
ex-parents. . . .''

SartoriIrvrash's face showed his distress. "Don't leave me,
lad, not with these villains. I shall be dead in no time.''

Making funny running-away gestures, the prince said,
"Well, that's escaping from being human, isn't it? I'm going
to be a Madi in no time. Another escape, another escapade.
It's the Ahd for me.''

He jumped forward and kissed SartoriIrvrash on his bald
pate.

"Good luck in your new career, old uncle. Green things will
grow from us both!''

He leaped into the coach, cracked his whip over the hox-

neys, and was away at a great pace. The tribesmen fell back in
alarm, cursing him in the name of the sacred rivers. A cloud of
dust swallowed the speeding vehicle.

The Madura Desert: Matrassyl began to seem a long way
off. But the stars came nearer overhead and, on clear nights,
the sickle of YarapRombry's Comet blazed like a signpost on
their way.

SartoriIrvrash stood shivering in the small hours when the
fire had died and the other travellers were sleeping. He could
not entirely lose his fever. He thought of BillishOwpin. His
story of having come from another world seemed more likely
here than it had done at the palace.

He walked by the tethered kaidaws and encountered the
Pointer of the Way, standing silently smoking. The two men
talked in low voices. The kaidaws uttered sniggering grunts.

"The animals are quiet enough," SartoriIrvrash said. "History pictures them as almost unmanageable brutes. To be rid-
den only by phagors. I've never seen a phagor riding one, any
more than I have ever seen a cowbird with a phagor. Perhaps
history was wrong on that point, too. I've spent a lifetime trying to disentangle history from legend."

"Perhaps they aren't so different," the Pointer said. "I
can't read a single letter, so I have no strong opinion in the
matter. But we smoke these kaidaws when they're mere
calves—puff a veronikane up their nostrils. It seems to make
them calm.

"I'll tell you a tale, since you can sleep no more than I." He
sighed heavily in preparation for the burden of narrative.
"Many years ago now, I went eastwards with my master,
through the provinces controlled by Unndreid, up into the
wilderness of the Nktryhk. It's a different world up there, very
harsh world, with little air to breathe, yet people remain fit."

"Less infection at high altitudes," commented Sartori-
Irvrash.

"That's not what the people of the Nktryhk say. They say
that Death is a lazy fellow who doesn't readily bother to climb
mountains. I'll tell you one thing. Fish is a popular food.

Often the fish may be caught in a river a hundred or more miles away. Yet it doesn't decay. You catch a fish here at dawn, it's bad by Freyr-set. Up in the Nktryhk, it remains good to eat for a small year.''

He leaned over the back of one of the patient kaidaws and smiled. "It was fine up there when you got used to it. Cold by night, of course. No rain, never. And there, in the high valleys, is land ruled only by fuggies. They're not as submissive as here. I tell you, it's a different world. The fuggies ride kaidaws, ride them like the wind—aye, and have cowbirds to sail at their shoulders. My understanding is that they come down and invade the lowlands when snow falls here, whenever that may be. When Freyr fails.''

Nodding his head with interest and some disbelief, Sartori-Irvrash said, "But there can be few phagors at those altitudes, surely? What can they eat, apart from your ever-fresh fish? There's no food.''

"That isn't so. They grow crops of barley in the valleys— right up to the snowbanks. All they need is irrigation. Every drop of water and urine is precious. There's a virtue in that thin air—they have crops of barley that ripen in three weeks.''

"Half a tenner from sowing? Incredible.''

"Nevertheless it is so," said the Pointer. "And the phagors share the grain and never quarrel or use money. And the white cowbirds drive out all other winged things bar the eagles. I saw it with my own eyes, when I stood no higher than this quadruped's shoulders. I mean to go back one day—no king or laws there.''

"I'll make a note of all that, if you don't mind," said Sar-toriIrvrash.

As he wrote, he thought of JandolAnganol among his abandoned buildings.

After the Madura, the long desolation of Hazziz. Twice they had to pass through strips of vegetation, stretching from one bleak horizon to another like god's hedges. Trees, shrubs, a riot of flowers, drew a line across the face of the grasslands.

"This is/will be the uct," said Dienu Pasharatid, employing

a translation of a Sibish continuous present tense. "It stretches across the continent from east to west, following the lines of Madi migration."

In the uct, they saw Others. Madis were not the only beings to use the verdant road. The Pointer of the Way shot an Other from a tree. It fell to the ground almost at their feet, its eyebrows still twitching with shock. They roasted it later over the campfire.

One day rain fell, closing across the grasslands like a snake's jaw. Freyr climbed higher into the sky than it managed in Matrassyl. SartoriIrvrash still wished to travel only by dimday, according to upper class Borlienese custom, but the other travellers would have none of that.

The nights spent sleeping in the open were over. The ex-chancellor surprised himself by regretting their passing. Sibornalese settlements were becoming more frequent, and in them the party stayed overnight. Each settlement was built to the same plan. Smallholdings lay inside a circle, with guard houses posted every so many paces along the perimeter. Between the smallholdings, roads like spokes of a wheel led in to one or more rings of dwellings which formed the hub. Generally, barns, stores, and offices encircled a church dedicated to the Formidable Peace, standing at the geometrical center of the wheel formation.

Grey-clad priests-militant ruled these settlements, supervising the arrival and departure of the travelling party, which was always given free food and accommodation. These men, who sang the praises of God the Azoiaxic, wore the wheel symbol on their garb and carried wheel locks. They did not forget that they were in territory traditionally claimed by Pannoval.

When it was almost too late, SartoriIrvrash noticed that the Pointer of the Way and his men were not allowed inside the Sibornalese settlement. Touching his braffista, their guide was taking his pay from one of the ambassadorial staff and making off, heading southwards.

"I must bid him farewell," said SartoriIrvrash. Dienu Pasharatid thrust a hand before him. "That is not necessary. He has been paid and he will leave. Our way ahead is clear."

"But I liked the man."

"But he is of no further use to us. The way is safe now,

moving from settlement to settlement. They believe superstitious things, these barbarians. The Pointer told me he could lead us this far only because his tribe's land-octave came this way."

Pulling at his whiskers uncomfortably, SartoriIrvrash said, "Madame Dienu, sometimes old habits enshrine truth. The preference for one's own land-octave is entirely dead. Men and women prosper best when they live along whatever land-octave they were born on. Practical sense lies behind such beliefs. Such octaves generally follow geological strata and mineral deposits, which influence health."

She flicked a smile on and off her boney face. "Naturally, we expect primitive peoples to hold primitive beliefs. It is that which anchors them to primitivism. Things are continuously better where we are going." This last sentence was evidently a direct translation into Olonets of one of many Sibish tenses.

Being of such high rank, Dienu Pasharatid addressed SartoriIrvrash in Pure Olonets. In Campannlat, Pure Olonets, as opposed to Local Olonets, was spoken only by high castes and religious leaders, mainly within the Holy Pannovalan Empire; it was becoming increasingly the prerogative of the Church. The main language of the northern continent was Sibish, a dense language with its own script. Olonets had made little headway against Sibish, except along some southern coasts where trade with the Campannlatian shore was common.

Sibish deployed multiple tenses and conditionals. It had no *y* sound. The substituted *i* was pronounced hard, while *ch*'s and *sh*'s were almost whistled. One result of this was to make a native of Askitosh sound sinister when speaking to a foreigner in the latter's own language. Perhaps the entire history of the continuous northern wars rested on the mockery that Sib-speakers made of a word like "Matrassyl." But behind the brief pursing of the lips involved lay the blind driving force of the climate of Helliconia, which discouraged unnecessary opening of the mouth for half the Great Year.

The travellers left their kaidaws at the southernmost settlement, where the Pointer went his way, and posted northwards from settlement to settlement on hoxneys.

After the twelfth settlement, they progressed up a slope which grew gradually steeper. It climbed for some miles. They

were forced to dismount and walk beside their steeds. At the top of the rise stood a line of young rajabarals, high and thin, their bark of the translucence of celery. When the trees were gained, SartoriIrvrash laid a hand against the nearest tree. It was soft and warm, like the flank of his hoxney. He gazed up into the plumes high above him, stirring in the breeze.

"Don't look upward—look ahead!" said one of his companions.

On the other side of the crest lay a valley, sombre in its blue shades. Beyond it was a darker blue: the sea.

His fever had gone and was forgotten. He smelt a new smell in the air.

When they reached the port, even the northerners showed excitement. The port had a defiantly Sibish name, Rungobandryaskosh. It conformed to the general layout of the settlements they had passed, except that it consisted only of a semi-circle, with a great church perched centrally on the cliff, a beacon light on its tower. The other half of the circle, symbolically, lay across the Pannoval Sea in Sibornal.

Ships lay in nearby docks. Everything was clean and shipshape. Unlike most of the races of Campannlat, the Sibornalese were natural seafarers.

After a night in a hostel, they rose at Freyr-rise and embarked with other travellers on a waiting ship. SartoriIrvrash, who had never been on anything larger than a dinghy before, went to his small cabin and fell asleep. When he woke, they were preparing to sail.

He squinted out of his square porthole.

Batalix was low over the water, spreading a pathway of silver across it. Nearby ships were visible as blue silhouettes, without detail, their masts a leafless forest. Near at hand, a sturdy lad rowed himself across the harbour in a rowing boat. The light so obscured detail that boy and boat became one, a little black shape where body went forward as oars went back. Slowly, stroke by stroke, the boat was dragged through the dazzle. The oars plunging, the back working, and finally the dazzle yielding (and soon composing itself again), as the rower won his way to the pillars of a jetty.

SartoriIrvrash recalled a time when he as a lad had rowed his two small brothers across a lake. He saw their smiles, their

hands trailing in the water. So much had been lost since then. Nothing was without price. He had given so much for his precious "Alphabet."

There were sounds of bare feet on deck, shouted orders, the creak of tackle as sails were raised. Even from the cabin, a tremor was felt as the wind started to catch. Cries from the dock, a rope snaking fast over the side. They were on their way to the northern continent.

It was a seven-day voyage. As they sailed north-northwest, the Freyr-days grew longer. Every night, the brilliant sun sank somewhere ahead of their bows, and spent progressively less time below the horizon before rising somewhere to the north of northeast.

While Dienu Pasharatid and her friends lectured Sartori-Irvrash on the bright prospects ahead, visibility became dimmer. Soon they were enveloped in what one sailor, in the ex-chancellor's hearing, called "a regular Uskuti up-and-downer." A thick brown murk descended like a combination of rain and sandstorm. It muffled the ship's noises, covering everything above and below decks in greasy moisture.

SartoriIrvrash was the only person to be alarmed. The captain of the vessel showed him that there was no need to fear.

"I have sufficient instruments to sail through an underground cavern unharmed," he said. "Though of course our modern exploring ships are even better equipped."

He showed SartoriIrvrash into his cabin. On his desk lay a printed table of daily solar altitudes, to determine latitude, together with a floating compass, a cross-staff, and an instrument the captain called a nocturnal, by which could be measured the elevation of certain first magnitude stars, and which indicated the number of hours before and after midnight of both suns. The ship also had the means to sail by dead reckoning, with distance and direction measured systematically on a chart.

While SartoriIrvrash made notes of these matters, there was a great cry from the lookout, and the captain hurried on deck, cursing in a way the Azoiaxic One would hardly have commended.

Through the drizzle loomed brown clouds and, somewhere in the clouds, men were bellowing. The clouds became shrouds and sails. At the last possible minute, a ship as big as their own slid by, with hardly a foot of leeway between hulls. Lanterns were seen, faces—mainly savage and accompanied by shaking fists—and then all were gone, back into the hanging soup. The Sibornal-bound ship was alone again in its sepia isolation.

Passengers explained to the foreigner that they had just passed one of the Uskut "herring-coaches," fishing with curtain nets off the coast. The herring-coach was a little factory, since it carried salters and coopers among its crew, who gutted and packed the catch at sea, storing it in barrels.

Thoroughly upset by the near collision, SartoriIrvrash was in no mood to listen to a eulogy on the Sibornalese herring trade. He retired to his damp bunk, still wrapped in his coat, and shivered. When they landed in Askitosh, he reminded himself, they would be on a latitude of 30° N, and only five degrees south of the Tropic of Carcampan.

On the morning of the seventh day of the voyage, the banks of fog rolled back, though visibility remained poor. The sea was dotted with herring-coaches.

After a while, a sluggish stain on the horizon resolved itself into the coastline of the northern continent. It was no more than a ruled line of sandstone dividing almost waveless sea from undulating land.

Moved by something like enthusiasm for the sight of her homeland, Madame Dienu Pasharatid delivered SartoriIrvrash a brief geography lesson. He saw how the water was dotted with small ships. Uskutoshk had been forced to become a maritime nation because of the advance of ice southwards from the Circumpolar Regions—these regions being mentioned with hushed tones. There was little land for cultivation between sea and ice. The seas had to be harvested and sea lanes opened to the two great rich grain prairies of the continent—which she indicated as being distant with a sweep of her arm.

How distant, he asked.

Pointing westward and yet more westward, she named the

nations of Sibornal, pronouncing their titles with varied inflections, as if she knew them personally, as if they were personages standing on a narrow strip of land glaring southwards, with cold draughts from the Circumpolar Regions freezing their backs—and all with a strong inclination to march down into Campannlat, SartoriIrvrash muttered to himself.

Uskutoshk, Loraj, Shivenink, where the Great Wheel was situated, Bribhar, Carcampan.

The grainlands were in Bribhar and Carcampan.

Her roll call ended with a finger pointing to the east.

"And so we have rounded the globe. Most of Sibornal, you see, is isolated in the extreme, caught between ocean and ice. Hence our independence. We have mountainous Kuj-Juvec coming after Carcampan—it is scarcely populated by humans —and then the troubled region of Upper Hazziz, leading into the Chalce Peninsula; then we are safe back in Uskutoshk, the most civilized nation. You arrive at a time of year when we have both Freyr and Batalix in the sky. But for over half the Great Year, Freyr is eternally below the horizon, and then the climate becomes severe. That's the Weyr-Winter of legend. . . . The ice moves south, and so do the Uskuts, as we call ourselves, if we can. But many die. Many die." She used a future-continuous tense.

Warm though it was, she shivered at the thought. "Some other people's lifetimes," she murmured. "Fortunately, such cruel times are still far away, but they are hard to forget. It's a race memory, I suppose. . . . We all know that Weyr-Winter will come again."

From the docks, they were escorted to a solid four-wheeled brake with a canopy. Into this vehicle they climbed after human slaves had piled in their baggage. Four yoked yelk then dragged them off at a good pace, along one of the radial roads leading away from the quayside.

As they passed under the shadow of an immense church, SartoriIrvrash tried to sort out the impressions that thronged in on him. He was struck by the fact that much of the wagonette in which they rode was not of wood but metal: its axles, its sides, even the seats on which they sat, all were metal.

Metal objects were to be seen on every side. The people

crowding in the streets—not jostling and shouting like a
Matrassyl crowd—carried metal pails or ladders or assorted
instruments to the ships; some men were encased in gleaming
armoured jackets. Some of the grander buildings on the way
flaunted iron doors, often curiously decorated, with names in
raised relief upon them, as if the occupants intended to live on
there perpetually, whatever happened in the Circumpolar
Regions.

A haze in the sky warded off the heat of Freyr, which, to the
visitor's eye, stood unnaturally high in the sky at noon. The
atmosphere of the city was smokey. Although Sibornal's
forests were thin in comparison with the riotous jungles of the
tropics, the continent had extensive lignite and peat beds, as
well as metal ores. The ores were smelted in small factories in
various parts of the city. Each metal was located in a definite
area. Its refiners, its workers, and its ancilliary trades were
grouped about it, and its slaves about them. Over the last
generation, metals had become less expensive than wood.

"It's a beautiful city." One of the men leaned over to
favour the visitor with this observation.

He felt small, sniffed a small sniff, and said nothing.

From the wagonette, he could see how Askitosh's half-
wheel plan worked. The great church by the harbour was the
axle. After a semicircle of buildings came a semicircle of
farms, with fields, then another semicircle of buildings, and so
on, though various living pressures had in some places broken
down what to Borlinese eyes was an unnatural symmetry.

They were delivered to a large plain building like a box, in
which slitlike windows had been cut. Its double entrance doors
were of metal; on them, in raised relief, were the words *1st.
Conventional, Sector Six*. The conventional proved to be a cross
between a hotel, a monastery, a nunnery, a school, and a
prison, or so it appeared to SartoriIrvrash, as he explored the
cell-like room he was given, and read the rules.

The rules declared that two meals were served per day, at
twenty minutes past four and at nineteen, that prayers were
held every hour (voluntary) in the church on the top floor,
that the garden was open during dimday for relaxed walking
and meditation, that instructions (whatever they were) might

be had at all times, and that permission was needed before visitors left the establishment.

Sighing, he washed himself and settled down on the bed, letting gloom overcome him. But Uskutoshkan hospitality, like most things Uskutoshkan, was brisk, and in no time came a brisk rap at his door and he was conducted along a corridor to a banquet.

The banquetting hall was long and low, lit by slit windows, from which the activities of the street could be glimpsed in small vertical sections. The floor was uncarpeted, yet a touch of luxury, even grandeur, was added to the chamber by an enormous tapestry on the rear wall which depicted, upon a scarlet background, a great wheel being rowed through the heavens by oarsmen in cerulean garments, each smiling blissfully, towards an astonishing maternal figure from whose mouth, nostrils, and breasts sprang the stars in the scarlet sky.

So struck was SartoriIrvrash by the details of this tapestry that he itched to make a note or even a sketch; but he was thrust forward and introduced to twelve personages who stood waiting to receive him. Each was named for him in turn by Madame Dienu Pasharatid. None shook his proffered hand: it was not the habit in that country to touch the hands of anyone outside one's own family or clan.

He tried to grasp the complex names, but the only one to remain in his head was Odi Jeseratabhar, and that because it belonged to a Priest-Militant Admiral who wore a blue-and-grey striped uniform and was female. And moreover was beautiful in an austere way, with two fair tresses plaited and wound about her head to finish as two blond horns sticking forward with an impressive yet comical air.

All concerned smiled in an affable way upon their guest from Campannlat, and assembled themselves at the table with great noise of metal chairs scraping on the bare floor. As soon as they were seated, silence fell, and the greyest member of the dozen rose to say grace. The rest placed their forefingers on foreheads in the attitude of prayer. SartoriIrvrash did the same. The grace began, intoned in dense Sibish, with dextrous use of continuous present, conditional-eternal, past-into-present, transferential, and other tenses, to carry the message

of thanks all the way to the Azoiaxic One. The length of the
prayer was perhaps intended to be proportional to the distance.

It was over at last, and a meal of many minute courses,
mainly vegetarian except for fish, and relying heavily on assorted raw and steamed seaweeds, was served by slave
wenches. Fruit juices and an alcoholic drink called yoodhl,
with a seaweed base, were served.

The one exceptional course, the only one which Sartori-
Irvrash could say he really enjoyed, was a spitted creature
brought on with ceremony, which he guessed to be a pig. It
was presented still on its spit and covered with a creamy sauce.
Of this, he was given a small portion of breast. He was told it
was "treebries." Only some days later did he discover that
treebries was roast Nondad. It was a prized Uskutoshki delicacy, rarely served except to distinguished visitors.

While the banquet was still in progress, Dienu Pasharatid
came round behind SartoriIrvrash's chair and spoke to him.

"Soon, the Priest-Militant Admiral will address us. What
she says may alarm you. Do not be alarmed. I know you are
not given to fear. Equally, I know you are not given to malice,
so do not think ill of me because of my part in this."

The ex-chancellor was immediately alarmed and dropped
his knife. "What is going to be said?"

"An important announcement which will affect your country's destiny and mine. Odi Jeseratabhar will give you the
details. Just remember, I was forced to bring you here in order
to clear my name of any stain shed on it by my husband's actions. Remember that you hate JandolAnganol and all will be
well."

She left him and returned to her seat. He found himself
unable to take another mouthful of food.

Once the complex meal was finished and spirit served, the
speeches began.

First came a welcoming speech from a local panjandrum,
couched in almost comprehensible terminology. Then Madame Dienu arose.

After a brief preliminary, she came to her point. Making an
oblique reference to her husband, she said she felt she had to
atone for his departure from diplomatic procedures. There-

fore, she had rescued Chancellor SartoriIrvrash from the melancholy position in which he found himself and had brought him here.

Their distinguished visitor was in a position to do them, and Uskutoshk, and indeed the entire northern continent, a service which would go down in history and secure for his name a place in their annals. What that service was, their loved and respected Priest-Militant Admiral, Madame Odi Jeseratabhar, would now announce.

Premonitions of bad things made SartoriIrvrash feel even worse than the yoodhl had done. He longed for a veronikane but, seeing that nobody else at the table smoked, was smoking, was about to smoke, or was even employing the conditional-eternal to smoke, desisted, and gripped the table instead, as the Admiral rose.

Since she was making a speech, she employed a kind of Mandarin Priest-Militant Sibish.

"Priests-Militant, War Commissions members, friends, and our new ally," began the lady imposingly, tossing her blond horns, "time is always short, so I will/am cut my speech accordingly. In only eighty-three years, Freyr will be/is at its strongest, and in consequence the Savage Continent and its barbarous nations are/should in dire array, prophesying doom for themselves. They are/were incapable of facing the future as we in Uskutoshk—rightly, to my mind—pride ourselves in doing/done/continuing.

"Of the chief nations of that unhappy continent, Borlien in particular is/will in trouble. Unfortunately, our old enemy, Pannoval, continues/grows strong. A random factor not calculated has recently/now become apparent, with our arms trading growing beyond control, owing to delinquent ambassadors. We shall not dwell on that incident.

"Soon, the warlike nations of the Savage Continent will be making imitations of our weapons. We must/can act before that is allowed to happen to any great extent, while we have supremacy.

"As those of my friends on the War Commission already know, our plan is nothing less than to take over Borlien."

Her words struck the banqueters to silence. Then a great murmur of acclamation arose. Many eyes turned towards

where SartoriIrvrash sat, white-faced.

"We have not/will not enough troops to hold down all of Borlien by force. Our plan is to annex and subdue by means provided unwittingly by the Borlienese king, JandolAnganol. Once we subdue Borlien, we can strike at Pannoval from the south as well as the north."

The banqueters began clapping before the fair Admiral had finished. They smiled first at each other and then at Sartori-Irvrash, who kept his gaze firmly on the finely turned lips of the Admiral.

"We have a fleet ready to sail," said those lips. "We anticipate that Chancellor SartoriIrvrash will sail with it, to play his vital role. His reward will be great."

Again applause, rationed to a few hand claps.

"The fleet will sail westward. I shall be in command aboard the *Golden Friendship.* We intend/shall sail round the coast of Campannlat, finally approaching the Bay of Gravabagalinien, where Queen MyrdemInggala is/will exiled, from the west. The chancellor and I will stop to conduct the queen from that place of exile, while the rest of the fleet intend/will sail on to bombard Ottassol, Borlien's largest port, until it capitulates/has capitulated.

"The queen is/was/will well-loved by her people. Sartori-Irvrash will proclaim a new government for Ottassol under the queen, with himself as prime minister. No battle need be fought."

"You will/should appreciate the feasibility of this plan. Our distinguished ally and the barbarian queen, descended from the Thribriat Shannana, are both united in a hatred of King JandolAnganol. The queen will be happy to be reinstated. She will of course be under our supervision.

"Once Ottassol is/can secure, our boats and soldiery will move upriver to take over the capital, Matrassyl. My understanding, based on agents' reports, is that we shall/can find allies there, notably the queen's old father and his faction. The king's insecure rule will be easily ended. His life the same. The world can do without such phagor lovers.

"With Borlien fallen into our hands, we execute a sabre slash northwards, right across the Savage Continent, from Ottassol in the south to Rungobandryaskosh.

"We are hastening matters forward now that you are here. Rest, friends, for action lies ahead, action of a most glorious sort. We plan that a good part of the fleet will/can/should sail at Freyr-rise, two days from now, God willing.

"A great future dawns/will dawn."

This time, the applause was unrationed.

XII

THE DOWNSTREAM
PASSENGER TRADE

"The brute, unchanging ignorance of the people. . . . They labour and do not improve their lot. Or they don't labour. It makes no difference. They're interested in nothing beyond their own village—no, beyond their own belly buttons. Look at them, idle lot! If I were that stupid, I'd still be a pedlar in Oldorando City Park . . ."

The philosopher making these comments was sprawling among cushions, with cushions behind his head and another under his bare feet. By his right hand, he had a glass of his favourite Exaggerator, to which crushed ice and lemon had been added, while his left arm was wrapped about a young woman with whose left breast he was idly toying.

The audience to whom he was making these comments—excluding the young woman, whose eyes were closed—were two in number. His son leaned against the rail of the boat on which they were travelling, his eyes half closed and his mouth half open. This youth had a bunch of yellow-blue gwing-gwings by

his side to eat and occasionally spat a gwing-gwing stone at other river traffic.

Propped up against the fo'c'sle where he was shaded from the sun lay a pallid young man who sweated a good deal and muttered still more. He was covered by a striped sheet, beneath which he moved his legs restlessly; he was running a fever and had been ever since the boat left Matrassyl on its journey south. This being one of his less lucid intervals, he scarcely seemed any more capable than the gwing-gwing eater of receiving the older man's wisdom.

This did not deter the older man.

"At that last stop we made, I asked one old fool who was leaning against a tree if he thought it was getting hotter, year by year. All he said was, 'It's always been hot, skipper, since the day the world was made.' 'And what day might that be?' I asked him. 'In the Ice Age, as I heard tell.' That was his reply. In the Ice Age! They've no sense. Nothing gets through to them. Take religion. I live in a religious country, but I don't believe in Akhanaba. I don't believe in Akhanaba because I have reasoned things out. These natives in these villages, they don't believe in Akhanaba—not because they have reasoned things out as I have, because they don't reason . . ."

He interrupted himself to take a firmer grasp on the left breast and a long drink of the Exaggerator.

". . . They don't believe in Akhanaba because they're too stupid to believe. They worship all kinds of demons, Others, Nondads, dragons. They still believe in dragons. . . . They worship MyrdemInggala. I asked my manager to show me round the village. In almost every hut, there hung a print of MyrdemInggala. No more like her than I am, but *intended* for her. . . . But, as I say, they're interested in nothing beyond their own belly buttons."

"You're hurting my bips," the young lady said.

He yawned and covered his mouth with his right hand, wondering absently why he enjoyed the company of strangers so much more than that of his own family: not just his rather stupid son, but his uninteresting wife and overbearing daughter. It would suit him to sail for ever down the river with this girl and this youth who claimed to come from another world.

"It's soothing, the sound of the river. I like it. I'll miss it
when I'm retired. There's proof that Akhanaba doesn't exist.
To make a complicated world like ours, with a steady supply
of living people coming and going—rather like a supply of
precious stones dug from the earth, polished, and sold off to
customers—you would need to be really clever, god or no god.
Isn't that so? Isn't it?"

He pinched with his left finger and thumb, so that the girl
squealed and said, "Yes, if you say so."

"I do say so. Well, if you were so clever, what pleasure
would it give you to sit up above the world and look down at
the stupidity of these natives? You'd go out of your mind with
the monotony of it, generation after generation, getting no
better. 'In the Ice Age . . .' By the beholder . . .'"

Yawning, he let his eyelids close.

She jabbed him in the ribs. "All right, then. If you're so
clever, tell me who did make the world. If it wasn't Akhanaba,
who was it?"

"You ask too many questions," he said.

Ice Captain Muntras fell asleep. He woke only when the
Lordryardry Lady was preparing to moor for the night at
Osoilima, where he was to enjoy the hospitality of the local
branch of the Lordryardry Ice Trading Co. He had been enjoying the hospitality of each of his trading posts in turn, so
that the journey downriver from Matrassyl had taken longer
than was usually the case—almost as long as the upriver
journey, when the boats of his ice trading fleet were towed
against the stream by teams of hoxneys.

One reason had caused the shrewd Ice Captain, in his
younger days, to establish an outpost at Osoilima, and that
reason loomed over them as the *Lady* tied up. It towered three
hundred feet above the crests of the brassims which flourished
hereabouts. It dominated the surrounding jungle, it lorded it
over the wide river, it pondered on its reflection in the water.
And it drew pilgrims from the fourteen corners of Campannlat, eager for reverence—and ice. It was the Osoilima Stone.

The local manager, a grey-haired man with a broad Dimariam accent, by name Grengo Pallos, came aboard and shook

his employer's hand warmly. He helped Div Muntras supervise passenger disembarcation. As phagors unloaded some bales of goods marked OSOILIMA, Pallos returned to the Ice Captain.

"Only three passengers?"

"Pilgrims. How's trade?"

"Not good. Have you nothing more for me?"

"Nothing. They've grown lazy in Matrassyl. Upheavals at court. Bad for trade."

"So I hear. Spears and money never rattle together. Bad about the queen. Still, if we unite with Oldorando, it may encourage more pilgrims here. Hard times, Krillio, when even the devout say it's too hot to travel. Where will it all end, I ask myself. You're retiring at the right time."

The Ice Captain drew Pallos aside. "I've got a special case here, and I don't know what to make of him. He's sick, his name's BillishOwpin. He claims to have come from another world. Maybe he's mad, but what he has to say is very interesting, if you can take it in. He thinks he's dying. But I say he's not. Could your old woman give him some special attention?"

"As good as done. We'll discuss the cost of accommodation in the morning."

So Billy Xiao Pin was helped ashore. Also ashore went the young lady, by name AbathVasidol, who was getting a free cruise down to Ottassol. Her mother, an old friend of the captain's, by name of MettyVasidol, kept a house on the outskirts of Matrassyl.

After the two traders had had a drink, they went to see Billy, now installed in the modest establishment ruled over by Pallos's wife.

He was feeling better. He had been scrubbed down the backbone with a block of Lordryardry ice, a sovereign remedy for all ills. The fever had gone, he was no longer coughing or sneezing—as they left Matrassyl, his allergy vanished. The captain told him he was not going to die.

"I shall die soon, Captain, but I am grateful for your kindness, all the same," said Billy. After the horrors of Matrassyl, it was bliss to be in the care of the Ice Captain.

"You won't die. It was that filthy volcano, Mount Rusty-

jonnick, pouring out its poison. Everyone in Matrassyl fell sick. Same symptoms as you—weepy eyes, sore throat, fever. You are fine now, fit to be on your feet. Never give in.''

Billy coughed weakly. ''You might be right. My life may have been prolonged by sickness. I shall surely die of helico virus, since I have no immunity to it, but the volcano may have postponed that fate for a week or two. So I must make the most of life and freedom. Help me to stand up.''

In no time, he was walking about the room, laughing, stretching his arms.

Muntras and the manager's wife stood by, smiling at him. ''What a relief, what a relief!'' said Billy. ''I was beginning to hate your world, Captain. I thought Matrassyl was going to be the death of me.''

''It's not a bad place when you get to know it.''

''But religious!''

Muntras said, ''Where you have mankind and phagors together, you will have religion. The clash of two unknowns generates that kind of thing.''

The wisdom of this remark impressed Billy, but Pallos's wife ignored it and took a firm grip on his upper arm.

''Why, you're fine,'' she said. ''I'll wash you, and you'll feel completely fit again. Then we'll get some scoff into you, that's what you need.''

Muntras said, ''Yes, and I've another remedy for you, Billyish. I'll send in this pleasant young lady, Abath, daughter of an old friend of mine. Very nice willing girl. Half an hour of her company will do you a power of good.''

Billy regarded him quizzically, and his cheeks grew red. ''I told you I am of completely different stock from you, not being born on Helliconia. . . . Would it work? Well, we're identical physically. Would the young lady *mind* . . . ?''

Muntras laughed heartily. ''She'd probably prefer you to me. I know how you're set on the queen, Billish, but don't let that put you off. Use a little imagination, and Abath will be equal to the queen in every way.''

Billy's face was a study in red. ''Earth, what an experience. . . . What can I say? Yes, send her in, please, and let's see if it works . . .''

As the traders went out, Pallos laughed, rubbing his hands

together, and said, "He certainly shows an experimental spirit. Will you charge him for the girl?"

Knowing Pallos's mercenary nature, Muntras ignored this question. Perhaps catching the snub, Pallos asked hastily, "All his talk of dying—do you think he comes from another world? Is that possible?"

"Let's have a drink, and I'll show you something he gave me." He summoned up Abath, gave her a kiss on the cheek, and sent her in to see Billish.

The evening shadows were taking on a velvet intensity. Batalix was in the western sky. The two men sat companionably on Pallos's verandah with a bottle and a lantern between them. Muntras brought up his heavy fist, placed it on the table, and opened it.

In his palm lay Billy's watch, with its three dials, where small figures flickered busily:

$$11:49:2 \qquad 19:06:52 \qquad 23:15:43$$

"It's a beauty. How much is it worth? Did he sell it to you?" Pallos prodded it.

Muntras said, "It's unique. According to Billish, it tells the time here in Borlien—this centre dial—and the time on the world he comes from, and the time on another world he does not come from. In other words, you could say this jewel is proof of his farfetched tale. To make a complicated watch like this, you'd need to be really clever. Not mad. More like a god. . . . Not but what I can't rid my mind of the notion he *is* mad. Billish says the world which made this timepiece, the world he comes from, rides above us, looking down on the stupidity of the natives. And it's a world made entirely by men like us. No gods involved."

Pallos took a sip of Exaggerator and shook his head. "I hope they can't read my trading figures."

A mist was creeping in from the river. A mother was calling her small boy home, warning him that greebs would crawl out of the water and eat him in a single gulp.

"King JandolAnganol had this elegant timepiece in his hand. He took it for an evil omen, that was plain. Pannoval, Oldorando, and Borlien have to unite, and it's only their hrat-

tocking religion that unites them. The king is committed on
such a course that he can't allow one element of religious
doubt . . ."

He tapped the timepiece with a plump finger. "This amazing jewel is an element of doubt, right enough. A message of
hope or fear, depending who you are." He tapped his breast
pocket. "Like other messages I have entrusted to me. The
world's changing, Grengo, I tell you, and not before time."

Pallos sighed and took a sip from his tumbler.

"Do you want to see my books, Krillio? I warn you takings
are down on last year."

The Ice Captain looked across the top of the lantern at
Pallos, whose face the light made cadaverous.

"I'm going to ask you a personal question, Grengo. Have
you any curiosity? I show this timepiece, I tell you it came
from another world. There's this odd feller Billish, getting his
first ever rumbo on this earth—what could be going through
his harneys? Doesn't all this waken your sense of mystery?
Don't you want to know more? Isn't there something beyond
your ledgers?"

Pallos scratched his cheek and then worked down to his
chin, setting his head to one side to do so. "All those stories
we listened to as kids. . . . You heard that woman call to her
son that a greeb would get him? There's not been a greeb seen
at Osoilima since I came here, and that's getting on for eight
years. All killed for their skins. I wish I could trap one. The
skins are worth a good price. No, Billish is telling you a story,
boss. How would men go about making a *world?* Even if it
was true, what then? It wouldn't help my figures, would it
now?"

Muntras sighed, shuffling his chair round so as to be able to
peer down into the mist, perhaps hoping that a greeb would
emerge to prove Pallos wrong.

"When young Billish comes off the kooni, I think I'll take
him up to the top of the Stone, if he's strong enough. Ask
your old woman to get us some supper, will you?"

Muntras sat where he was when the local manager had gone.
He lit a veronikane and remained smoking contentedly, absently watching the smoke ascend to the rafters. He did not
even wonder where his son was, for he knew: Div would be in

the local bazaar. Muntras's thoughts were much further away.

Eventually, Billy and Abath appeared, holding hands. Billy's face was only just wide enough to accommodate his grin. They sat down at the table without speaking. Without speaking, Muntras offered the Exaggerator bottle. Billy shook his head.

It was easy to see that he had undergone an emotional experience. Abath looked as composed as if she had just returned from church with her mother. Her features resembled a younger Metty's, but there was a lustre about her which Metty had lacked for many a day. Her gaze was bold, where Metty's was slightly furtive, but there was, thought Muntras, who considered himself a judge of human nature, the same kind of reserve to her as to her mother. She was escaping some kind of trouble in Matrassyl, which might account for her guarded manner. Muntras was content just to admire her in her light dress, which emphasised her generous young breasts and echoed the chestnut brown of her hair.

Perhaps there was a god. Perhaps he kept the world going, despite its idiocy, because of beauty like Abath's . . .

At length, Muntras exhaled smoke and said, "So, don't they go in for trittoming between man and woman on your world, Billish?"

"We are taught to trittom, as you call it, from the age of eight. It's a discipline. But down here—I mean with Abath— it's . . . the reverse of discipline . . . it's real. . . . Oh, Abathy . . ." Exhaling her name as Muntras exhaled smoke, he seized her and began to kiss her passionately, breaking off only to utter endearments. She responded in a minor key.

Billy shook Muntras's hand. "You were right, my friend, she is the equal of the queen in every way. Better."

The captain said, "Perhaps all women are equal and it is only in the imagination of men that differences lie. Remember the old saying, 'Every rumbo romps home to the same rhythm. . . .' You have a very vivid imagination, so I imagine that you found her a very good trittom in consequence. . . . Are koonis in our world as deep as in yours?"

"Deeper, softer, richer . . ." He fell to kissing the girl again.

The captain sighed. "Enough of that. Passion is as boring as drunkenness in other men. Go away, Abath. I want some

sense out of this young man, if possible. . . . Billish, if you have managed to see over the top of your own prodo since we landed, you may have noticed the Osoilima Stone. You and I are going to ascend it. If you are well enough to mount Abath, you are well enough to mount the Stone."

"Very well, if Abath can come too."

Muntras gazed at him with an expression at once a scowl and a grin. "Tell me, Billish boy—you're really from Pegovin in Hespagorat, aren't you? They're great jokers there."

"Look." He sat down facing the captain. "I'm what I say —from another world. Born and brought up there, recently landed in the space-vehicle I described to you between fever fits. I would not lie to you, Krillio, because I owe you too much. I feel I owe you more than life."

A dismissive gesture. "You owe me nothing. People shouldn't owe others anything. Remember, I was a beggar. Don't think too much of me."

"You've worked with devotion and built up a great enterprise. Now you are the friend of a king. . . ."

Filtering a little smoke between pursed lips, Muntras said stonily, "That's what you think, is it?"

"King JandolAnganol? You are a friend of his, aren't you?"

"I have dealings with his majesty, let's say."

Billy looked at him with a half-grin. "But you don't like him greatly?"

The Ice Captain shook his head, smoked, and said, "Billish, you don't care much for religion, no more than I. But I must warn you that religion is strong in Campannlat. Take the way his majesty threw your timepiece back at you. He is very superstitious and that's the king of the land. If you showed that object to the peasants of Osoilima, they would riot if you caught them at the wrong moment. They might make you a saint or they might kill you with pitchforks."

"But why?"

"It's the irrational. People hate things they don't understand. One madman can change the world. I tell you this only for your own good. Now. Come on." He stood up, sweeping his lecture away and laying a hand on Billy's shoulder. "The girl, the meal, my manager, the Stone. Practicalities."

What he demanded was done, and soon they were ready for the climb. Muntras discovered that Pallos had never been to the top of the Stone, despite living at the bottom of it for eight years. He was laughed into coming along as escort and marched beside them with a Sibornalese matchlock over one shoulder.

"Your figures can't be too bad if you can afford such artillery," Muntras said suspiciously. He trusted his managers no more than he trusted the king.

"Bought to protect your property, Krillio, and every roon of it hard earned. It isn't as though the pay's good, even when trade's good."

Their way lay along a track that ran back from the wharf to the small town of Osoilima. The mist was less thick here, and the few lights round the central square gave a semblance of cheer. Many people were about, attracted by a cooler breeze that had sprung up with sunset. Stalls selling souvenirs, sweets, or savoury waffles were doing fair business. Pallos pointed out one or two houses where pilgrims lodged which ordered Lordryardry ice regularly. He explained that most of the people wandering about, throwing their money away, were pilgrims. Some came here, drawn by a local tradition, to free slaves, human or phagor, because they had grown to believe it wrong to own another life. "Fancy giving away a valuable possession like that!" he exclaimed, disgusted with the foolishness of his fellow men.

The base of the Osoilima Stone was just by the square—or rather, the town and its square had been built close against the Stone. Closest of all was a hostelry, bearing the name The Freed Slave, where the Ice Captain bought four candles for the party. They went through its garden and began the ascent. Talipots grew by the Stone; they had to push away the stiff leaves in order to climb. Summer lightning flickered round them.

Others were already ascending. Their whispers sounded from above. The steps had been carved in the stone a long while ago. They spiralled round and round the rock, with never a hint of railing for security. The guiding lights of their candles flickered before their faces.

"I'm too old for this sort of thing," Muntras grunted.

But their slow progress led eventually to a level platform, and an arch led them into the top of the rock, where a dome had been hollowed. They could rest their elbows on the parapet and gaze in safety at the spread of mist-shrouded forest all round.

The sounds of the town reached them and the continuous noise of the Takissa. Music was playing somewhere—a double-clouth or, more likely hereabouts, binnaduria, and drums. And all about the forest, where rolls of mist allowed, they could make out dim lights.

"That's what they say," Abath chirped up. " 'Not an acre habitable, not an acre uninhabited.' "

"True pilgrims stay up here all night to watch the dawns," Muntras told Billy. "In these latitudes, there's never a day of the year when both suns aren't visible at some time. Different from where I come from."

"On the Avernus, Krillio, people are very scientific," said Billy, hugging Abath. "We have ways of imitating reality with video, 3D tactiles and so on, just as a portrait imitates a real face. As a result, our generation doubts reality, doubts if it exists. We even doubt if Helliconia is real. I don't suppose you understand what I mean . . ."

"Billish, I've travelled most of Campannlat, as a trader and before that as a beggar and pedlar. I've even been right far to the west, to a country called Ponipot beyond Randonan and Radado, where the continent ends. Ponipot is perfectly real, even if no one in Osoilima believes in its existence."

"Where is this Avernus world of yours then, Billish?" Abath asked him, impatient with the way the men talked. "Is it above us somewhere?"

"Mm . . ." The sky above was fairly clear of cloud. "There's Ipocrene, that bright star. It's a gas giant. No, Avernus is not risen yet. It is below us somewhere."

"Below us!" the girl gave a smothered laugh. "You are mad, Billish. You ought to stick to your story. *Below*! Is it a sort of fessup?"

"Where's this other world, Earth? Can you see that one, Billish?"

"It's too far away to see. Besides, Earth doesn't give out light like a sun."

"But Avernus does?"

"We see Avernus by light reflected from Batalix and Freyr."

Muntras thought.

"So why can't we see Earth by light reflected from Batalix and Freyr?"

"Well, it's too far away. It's difficult to explain. If Helliconia had a moon, it would be easier to explain—but in that case, Helliconian astronomy would be much more advanced than it is. Moons draw men's eyes to the sky better than suns. Earth reflects the light of its own sun, Sol."

"I suppose Sol is too far away to see. My eyes are not what they were anyway."

Billy shook his head and searched the northeastern sky. "It's somewhere over there—Sol and Earth, and Sol's other planets. What do you call that long straggly constellation, with all the faint stars at the top?"

Muntras said, "In Dimariam, we call that the Night Worm. Bless me, I don't see it very clear. Round these parts, they call it Wutra's Worm. Isn't that right, Grengo?"

"It's no good asking me the names of the stars," Pallos said, and sniggered as if to say, "But show me a gold ten-roon piece and I'll identify it for you."

"Sol is one of the faint stars in Wutra's Worm, about where its gills are."

Billy spoke jokingly, being slightly uneasy in the role of lecturer after his years as one of the lectured. As he spoke, the lightning was there again, laying them out momentarily for examination. The pretty girl, her mouth slightly open, staring vaguely where he was pointing. The local manager, bored, gazing into blackness, thumb tucked comfortably into the muzzle of his matchlock. The burly old Ice Captain, flattened hand up to his receding hairline, peering toward infinity with determination written over his countenance.

They were real enough—Billy was becoming used now, since he had been with Muntras and Abathy, to the idea of a *real* reality, abhorrent though it might have been to his Advisor on the Avernus, caught in an *unreal* reality. His nervous system had been jarred into life by new experiences, textures, stinks, colours, sounds. For the first time, he lived fully.

Those who looked down on him would consider him in hell; but the freedom moving throughout his frame told him he was in paradise.

The lightning was gone, sunk to nothing, leaving a moment of pitch before the mild night world returned to existence.

Billy wondered, Can I convince them about Avernus, about Earth? But they'll never convince me about their gods. We inhabit two different thought-*umwelts*.

And then came a questioning of darker tone. What if Earth was a figment of Avernian imagination, the god Avernus otherwise lacked? The devastating effects of Akhanaba and his battles against sin were apparent everywhere. What evidence was there for Earth's existence—anything more than that fuzzy patch where Sol glimmered in the Worm to the northeast?

He postponed the uncomfortable question for some future time to listen to what Muntras was saying.

"If Earth is so far, Billish, how can the people there be watching us?"

"That's one of the miracles of science. Communication over very long distances."

"Could you write down for me how you do it, when we get to Lordryardry?"

"Do you mean to say that people out there—real people like us—" said Abath, "could be watching us even now? Seeing us big-like, not down the gullet of a worm?"

"It's more than possible, my darling Abath. Your face and your name may already be known to millions of people on Earth—or rather, that is to say *will* be known when a thousand years have passed, for that's how long it takes communications to get from Avernus to Earth."

Unimpressed by figures, she could think of only one thing. Putting her hand to her mouth, she moved her mouth closer to Billy's ear. "You don't suppose they will see us having a go on the bed, do you?"

Overhearing the remark, Pallos laughed and pinched her bottom. "You charge extra for anyone watching, don't you, girl?"

"You mind your own scumbing business," Billy told him.

Muntras pursed his lips. "What possible pleasure can they get, watching us in all our native stupidity?"

"What distinguishes Helliconia from thousands of other worlds," said Billy, returning to something like a dry lecturer's tone, "is the presence here of living organisms."

As they were digesting his remark, a noise reached them from the mist and the jungle, a prolonged shrilling, distant but clear.

"Was that an animal?" asked the girl.

"I believe it was a long horn blown by phagors," said Muntras. "Often a danger sign. Are there many free phagors hereabouts, Grengo?"

"There could be. The freed phagor slaves have learned men's ways and live quite comfortably in their own jungle settlements, I hear tell," said Pallos. "They never get very bright in the harneys, though—you can charge them a good high price for broken ice."

"They buy ice off you, phagors?" asked Abath, in surprise. "I thought it was only King JandolAnganol's Phagorian Guard that got treated to ice!"

"Well, they bring in things to Osoilima to trade—gwing-gwing stone necklaces, skins, and suchlike, so then they've the money to pay me for ice. They crunch it straightaway, standing in my store. Disgusting! Like a man drinking liquor."

Silence descended on them. They stood quiet, peering out at the night, under the limitless vault of stars. To their imaginations, the wilderness seemed almost as limitless, and it was from there that the occasional sound came—once a cry, as if even those rejoicing in newfound freedom suffered. From the stars came only the uninsistent signals of light and, from the great Stone below them, darkness.

"Well, the phagors won't worry us," said Muntras, curtly, breaking in on their speculations. "Billish, over where Sol is, over in that direction somewhere lies the Eastern Range, what people call the High Nktryhk. Very few people visit it. It's almost inaccessible, and only phagors live there, legend has it. When you have been riding on your Avernus, have you ever seen the High Nktryhk?"

"Yes, Krillio, often. And we have simulations of it in our

recreation centres. The Nktryhk peaks are generally wreathed in cloud, so that we watch through infrared. Its highest plateau—which covers the top of the range like a roof—is over nine miles high, and protrudes into the stratosphere. It is a most impressive sight—awesome, to be true. Nothing lives on the very highest slopes, not even phagors. I wish I had brought a photograph to show you, but such things are heavily discouraged.''

"Can you explain to me how to make—photogiraffes?''

"Photographs. I'll try, when we reach Lordryardry.''

"Good, let's go down, then, and never mind hanging about for Akhanaba to appear. Let's get some food and sleep, and we will be off promptly in the morning, before noon.''

"Avernus will be up in an hour. It will make a transit of the whole sky in about twenty minutes.''

"Billish, you've been ill. You must be in bed in an hour. Food, then bed—alone. I must be your father on Earth—I mean to say, on Helliconia. Then if your parents watch us, they will be happy.''

"We don't really have parents, only clans,'' Billy explained, as they went under the arch and prepared to descend. "Extra-uterine birth is practised.''

"I will much enjoy your drawing me a picture of how you manage *that,*'' the Ice Captain said.

They spiralled back to the ground, Billy clutching Abathy's hand.

Downriver, the scenery changed. First one bank, then the other, became the scene of intensive cultivation. The jungles were left behind. They had entered the land of the loess. The *Lordryardry Lady* slipped into Ottassol almost before its passengers realised, unused as they were to cities which had withdrawn their existence underground.

As Div supervised the unloading of goods onto the quay, Ice Captain Muntras took Billy below decks and into a now empty cabin.

"You're feeling well?''

"Excellent. It can't last. Where's Abathy?''

"Listen to me, Billish, I want you to stay quiet here while I transact a little business in Ottassol. I must see an old friend or two. And I have an important letter to deliver. There are clever Johnnies here, not just country bumpkins. I don't wish anyone to know of your existence, you understand?"

"Why's that?"

Muntras looked him in the eye. "Because I'm an old bumpkin myself and I believe your tale."

Billy smiled with pleasure. "Thank you. You have more sense than SartoriIrvrash or the king."

They shook hands.

The bulk of the Ice Captain seemed almost to fill the little cabin. He leaned forward confidentially. "Remember how those two treated you, and do as I say. You stay in this cabin. No one must know of your existence."

"While you go ashore and get drunk again. Where's Abathy?"

A big hand came up in a cautionary gesture. "I'm getting old and I want no fuss. I will not get drunk. I will return as soon as possible. I want to get you safe to Lordryardry, where you will be well looked after, you and that magical timepiece of yours. There, you can tell me about the vessel that brought you here, and other inventions. But first I have some business to transact, and that letter to deliver."

Billy became more anxious. "Krillio, where is Abathy?"

"Don't make yourself ill again. Abathy has gone. You know she was travelling only as far as Ottassol."

"She's left without saying good-bye? Without a kiss?"

"Div was jealous, so I hustled her away. I'm sorry. She sent you her love. She's got a living to make, like everyone else."

"A living to make . . ." Speech failed him.

Muntras took the opportunity to slip nimbly out of the cabin and lock the door from the outside. He pocketed the key, smiling as he did so.

"I'll be back soon," he said reassuringly as Billy started to hammer on the door. He climbed the companionway stairs, crossed the deck, and strolled down the gangplank. Across the wharf was a tunnel leading into the loess. A notice above it read LORDRYARDRY ICE TRADING CO. TRANSIT GOODS ONLY.

This was a modest wharf. The main Lordryardry wharf was half a mile farther downstream, where the seagoing ships tied up, and a grander affair entirely. But here few eyes pried, and security was good. Muntras walked down the tunnel and entered a checking office.

Two clerks, alarmed to see the owner arrive, stood up, hiding playing cards under ledgers. The other occupants of the office were Div and Abath.

"Thank you, Div. Will you take these clerks away and let me have a moment alone with Abathy?"

In his sullen way, Div did as instructed. When the door had closed behind the three men, Muntras locked it and turned to the girl.

"Sit down, my dear, if you like."

"What do you want? The journey's over—at long last—and I ought to be on my way." She looked huffy and at the same time anxious. The sight of the locked door worried her. In a way she had of drawing down her mouth in displeasure, Muntras recognised her mother's gesture.

"Don't be cheeky, young lady. You've behaved properly till now, and I'm pleased with you. In case you don't realise it, Captain Krillio Muntras is a valuable ally for a young slip of a thing like you, old though I am. I'm pleased with you, and I intend to reward your for how amiable you were with me and Billish."

She relaxed slightly.

"I'm sorry. It's just that you were making a—a bit of a mystery of it. I mean, I would have liked to have said good-bye to Billish. What is wrong in his harneys?"

As she was talking, he was removing some silver pieces from his body belt. He held them out to her, smiling. Abath came closer and, as she reached out to take the money, he grasped her wrist tightly with his other hand. She gave a cry of pain.

"Now, girl, you can have this money, but first I'm going to get a confidence out of you. You know that Ottassol is a big port?"

He squeezed her wrist till she hissed, "Yes."

"You know there are therefore many foreigners in this big port?"

Squeeze. Hiss.

"You know among those foreigners are people from other continents?"

Another squeeze. Another hiss.

"Like Hespagorat, for instance?"

Squeeze and hiss.

"And even far Sibornal?"

Squeeze, hiss.

"Including people of the Uskut race?"

Squeeze—pause—hiss.

Although it seemed from the furrowing of Muntras's brow that this catechism was not over, he let go of the wrist, which had grown red during interrogation. Abath took the silver coins and tucked them into a pocket in the roll of luggage she had by her, making no comment beyond a dark look.

"Sensible girl. Take what you can in life. And I am correct in thinking that you had some dealings with a certain man of Uskut race, in Matrassyl, in the way of the usual commodities. Isn't that so?"

She looked defiant again and stood alertly as if thinking of attacking him.

"What usual commodities might those be?"

"The ones you and your mother trade in, my dear—money and kooni. Look, it is no secret to me, because I had the word off your mother and have kept it under my palm ever since. It's been so long that I need you to remind me of the name of that man of Uskut race with whom you exchanged those commodities."

Abath shook her head. Tears gleamed in her eyes. "Look, I thought you were a friend. Forget it! The feller's left Matrassyl anyhow, and gone back to his own country. He got into trouble. . . . That's why I came south, if you want to know. My mother should have held her slanje tongue."

"I see. Your money supply ran out—or ran away. . . . Now, I just want to hear you pronounce his name, and then you're free."

She put her hands up to her face and said into them, "Io Pasharatid."

A moment's silence.

"You did aim high, my little fillock. I hardly believed it. The ambassador of Sibornal, no less! And not only kooni but

guns involved. Did his wife know?''

"What do you think?" She was defiant again. She outshone her mother.

He became brisk. "Very well. Thank you, Abathy. You now are clear that I have a hold on you. You have a hold on me. You know about Billish. Nobody else must know about Billish. You must keep quiet and never mention his name, not even in your sleep. He was just one more customer. Now he has gone, and you've been paid.

"If you mention Billish to anyone, I shall slip a little note to the Sibornalese representative here, and you will be in trouble. In this religious land, intercourse between Borlinese ladies and foreign ambassadors is strictly illegal. It always leads to blackmail—or murder. If word gets out about you and Pasharatid, you'll never be seen again. Do we understand each other?"

"Oh, yes, you hrattock! Yes."

"Good. That's sensible. My advice is to keep your mouth and your legs closed. I'm going to take you to a friend of mine whom I have to see. He's a scholar. He needs a housemaid. He will pay you regularly and well. I'm not a natural bully, Abathy, although I enjoy getting my way. So I am doing you a favour—for your mother's sake as well as yours. You'd soon go to the bad on your own in Ottassol."

He paused to see what she said, but she merely watched him with untrusting eyes.

"Remain with my scholarly friend in his comfortable home, and you will have no need to turn into a whore. You can probably find a good husband—you're pretty and not a fool. It's a disinterested offer."

"And your friend'll keep an eye on me for you, I suppose?"

He looked at her and pushed his lips forward in a pout. "He's recently married and won't molest you. Come. We'll go and see him. Wipe your nose."

Ice Captain Muntras called a one-wheeled sedan. He and AbathVasidol climbed in and off went the sedan, pulled by two veterans of the Western Wars, who had between them

two-and-a-half arms, three legs, and about the same number of eyes.

In this style, they creaked through the underground lanes of Ottassol and eventually entered Ward Court, where daylight shone down brightly from the square of sky overhead. At the bottom of a flight of steps was a solid door with a sign above. They climbed out of the cramped conveyance, the veterans accepted a coin, and Muntras rang the doorbell.

It was hardly to be expected of a man in his profession that Bardol CaraBansity, deuteroscopist, should show surprise, whoever called on him; but he did raise an eyebrow at the girl while shaking the hand of his old acquaintance.

Over wine, which his loving wife served, CaraBansity professed himself delighted to instal AbathVasidol in his household.

"I don't suppose you will wish to carry hoxney carcasses about, but there are less alarming jobs to be done. Good. Welcome."

His wife appeared less delighted by the new arrangement, but said nothing.

"Then, sir, I shall be off, with grateful compliments to you both," said Muntras, rising from his chair.

CaraBansity rose too, and this time there was no mistaking his surprise. Of recent years, the Ice Captain had developed leisurely habits. When delivering his fresh ice—of which the CaraBansity household and its corpses consumed a fair share—the trader generally settled in for a long pleasant talk. This haste must have some meaning, thought CaraBansity.

"In gratitude for the introduction to this young lady, I will at least ride with you back to your ship," he said. "No, no, I insist."

And he did insist, to such effect that the discomfited Muntras found himself in no time with his knees pressed against the deuteroscopist's knees and their noses almost touching, and nowhere to cast his regard except into the eyes in front of his, as they jolted in a sedan towards the TRANSIT GOODS ONLY warehouse.

"Your friend SartoriIrvrash," the Ice Captain said.

"Well, I trust?"

"No. The king's dismissed him and he's disappeared."

"Sartori disappeared! Where?"

"If people knew where, it would not count as a disappearance," said Muntras humourously, dislodging one knee.

"What happened, for beholder's sake?"

"You've heard about the queen of queens, of course."

"She came through here on her way to Gravabagalinien. According to the newsletter, five thousand hats were mislaid, having been thrown carelessly into the air as she arrived at the royal dock."

"JandolAnganol and your friend fell out over the Massacre of the Myrdolators."

"And then he disappeared?"

Muntras nodded his head so gently that their noses scarcely touched.

"Into the palace dungeons, where others have gone?"

"Very likely. Or was clever enough to flee the city."

"I must discover what has happened to his manuscripts."

Silence between them.

When the sedan chair reached the warehouse, Muntras said, resting his hand on the other's sleeve, "You are too kind, but there is no need for you to get out."

Looking as confused as possible, CaraBansity climbed out nevertheless. "Come, I know your ruse. A good one. My wife can become better acquainted with your pretty AbathVasidol while you and I have a quiet farewell drink aboard your boat, eh? Don't think I didn't grasp your scheme."

"No, but—" While Muntras was anxiously paying off the sedan men, the deuteroscopist was marching in his ponderous way towards the dock where the *Lordryardry Lady* was tied up.

"I expect you have a bottle of the Exaggerator aboard?" inquired CaraBansity cheerfully, as Muntras caught up with him. "And how did you acquire this young lady you have so kindly deposited with me?"

"She's a friend of an old friend. Ottassol's a dangerous place for innocent young girls like Abathy."

There lay the *Lordryardry Lady*, with two phagor guards nearby, wearing armbands bearing the name of the company.

"I'm sorry, but I cannot let you aboard, my friend," said

Muntras, stepping into CaraBansity's path, so that once more their eyes almost touched.

"Why, what's the matter? I thought this was your last trip?"

"Oh, I shall be back . . . I live only just across the sea . . ."

"But you are always terrified of pirates."

Muntras took a deep breath. "I will tell you the truth, and keep it under your palm. I have a case of plague on board. I should have declared it to the port authorities but I didn't, being anxious to get home. I cannot let you on board. Definitely. It would endanger your life."

"Mm." CaraBansity wrapped a meaty fist round his chin, looking at Muntras from under his brow. "In my trade, I'm familiar with disease and probably immune to it. For the sake of the Great Exaggerator, I'll take the risk."

"No, sorry. You're too good a friend to lose. I will see you again soon when I'm in less of a hurry, and we'll drink ourselves under the table . . ." Talking in a distracted manner, he shook CaraBansity's hand and almost ran from him. Pounding up the ship's gangplank, he called out to his son and anyone else aboard that they were going to sail immediately.

CaraBansity stood on the quay, watching until the Ice Captain disappeared below decks. He then turned slowly on his heel and began walking away.

At a certain point into the lanes, he stopped short, snapped his fingers, and began to laugh. He thought that he had solved the minor mystery. To celebrate a further success to deuteroscopy, he turned into the next court and walked into a tavern where he was not known.

"A half-Exaggerator," he ordered. A treat for himself, a reward. People gave themselves away with talk without knowing it, for the underlying reason that they hated the feeling of guilt and therefore betrayed themselves. With that understanding, he recalled what Muntras had said in the sedan.

"Into the palace dungeons . . ." "Very likely." "Very likely" means neither yes nor no. Of course. The Ice Captain had rescued SartoriIrvrash from the king and was smuggling him to safety into Dimariam. The matter was too dangerous for Muntras to tell even SartoriIrvrash's friend in Ottassol. . . .

Sipping the fuming drink, he let his mind wander over the

possibilities which this secret knowledge opened up.

In his long and colourful career, Ice Captain Muntras had had to play some tricks on friend and enemy alike. Many mistrusted him; yet towards Billy he felt strong paternal affection, reinforced perhaps by the difficulties he experienced with his own son, the weak-minded Div. Muntras liked Billy's helplessness and valued the store of startling knowledge which seemed so much a part of Billy. Billy was indeed a herald from another world; Muntras did not doubt it. He was determined to protect the strange creature from all comers.

But before setting sail for his homeland of Dimariam, he had a small piece of business to attend to. His leisurely journey down the Takissa had not made Muntras forget his promise to the queen. At his main wharf in Ottassol, he summoned to his office one of his captains, the man who sailed the coastal trader *Lordryardry Lubber*, and laid MyrdemInggala's letter before him.

"You're bound for Randonan, yes?"

"As far as Ordelay."

"Then you will deliver this document to the Borlienese general, Hanra TolramKetinet, of the Second Army. You are personally responsible for putting it into the general's hands. Understand?"

At the main wharf, the Ice Captain transferred Billy onto the fine oceangoing *Lordryardry Queen*, the pride of his fleet. The ship was capable of transporting 200 tons of finest block ice. Now, on its homeward journey, it carried cargoes of timber and grain. Together with an excited Billy and a sullen Div.

A favouring breeze filled the sails until the cordage strained and sang. The prow swung southwards like the needle of a magnet, pointing to distant Hespagorat.

The shores of Hespagorat, together with the doleful animals which inhabited them, were familiar sights to everyone aboard the Earth Observation Station. They were watched with extra

attention as the fragile wooden ship bearing Billy Xiao Pin approached them.

Drama was not a feature of life aboard Avernus. It was avoided. Emotion: superfluous, as "On the Prolongation of One Helliconian Season Beyond the Human Life-span" had it. Yet dramatic tension was evident, especially among the youth of the six great families. Everyone was forced into the situation of disagreeing or agreeing with Billy's actions.

Many said that Billy was ineffectual. It was more difficult to admit that he showed courage and considerable ability to adapt to different conditions. Under the arguments that raged was a wistful hope that Billy might somehow convince people on Helliconia that they, the Avernians, existed.

True, Billy appeared to have persuaded Muntras. But Muntras was not considered to be important. And there were indications that Billy, having convinced Muntras, would take no further steps in that direction, but merely, selfishly, enjoy his remaining days before the helico virus attacked him.

The great disappointment was that Billy had failed where JandolAnganol and SartoriIrvrash were concerned. It had to be admitted that they had on their minds matters of more immediate concern.

The question that few people on the Avernus asked was, What, effectively, could the king and his councillor have done had they taken the trouble to understand Billy and come to believe in the existence of his "other world"? For that question led to the reflection that Avernus was far less important to Helliconia than Helliconia was to Avernus.

Billy's successes and failures were compared with those of previous Helliconia Holiday winners. Few winners had done much better than Billy, if truth were told. Some had been killed as soon as they arrived on the planet. Women had fared worse than men: the noncompetitive atmosphere on the Avernus favoured equality of the sexes; on the ground, matters were conducted differently, and most women winners ended their lives in slavery. One or two strong personalities had had their stories believed, and in one case a religious cult had grown round this Saviour from the Skies (to quote one of his titles). The cult had died when a force of Takers eradicated the

villages where the believers lived.

The strongest personalities to descend had concealed their origins entirely and lived by their wits.

One characteristic all winners shared. Despite often severe warnings from their Advisors, all had enjoyed or at least attempted sexual intercourse with the Helliconians. The moths always headed for the brightest flame.

Billy's treatment merely strengthened a general aversion among the families to the religions of Helliconia. The consensus was that those religions got in the way of sensible, rational living. The inhabitants—believers and unbelievers alike—were seen as struggling in the toils of falsehood. Nowhere was there an attempt to be placid and view one's life as an art form.

On distant Earth, conclusions would be different. The chapter in the long cavalcade of history which concerned JandolAnganol, SartoriIrvrash, and Billy Xiao Pin would be watched with a grief superior to any on the Avernus, a grief in which detachment and empathy were nicely balanced. The peoples of Earth, for the most part, had developed beyond that stage where religious belief is suppressed, or supplanted by ideology, or translated into fashionable cults, or atrophied into a source of references for art and literature. The peoples of Earth could understand how religion allowed even the labouring peasants their glimpse of eternity. They understood that those with least power have most need of gods. They understood that even Akhanaba paved the way for a religious sense of life which needed no God.

But what they most thoroughly understood was that the reason why the ancipital race was untroubled by the perturbations of religion was that their eotemporal minds would not rise to such disquiet. The phagors could never aspire to a moral altitude where they would abase themselves before false gods.

The materialists of the Avernus, a thousand light-years from such thinking, admired the phagors. They saw how Billy had been better received below than in Matrassyl Palace. Some wondered aloud whether the next winner of a Helliconia Holiday should not throw in his lot with the ancipitals and hope to lead them to overthrow mankind's idols.

This conclusion was reached after long hours of well-conducted argument. Underlying it was jealousy of the freedom of Helliconian mankind even in its fallen state—a jealousy too destructive to be faced within the confines of the Earth Observation Station.

XIII

A WAY TO BETTER WEAPONRY

The little year advanced, though seasonal effects were virtually obliterated under the great flood of Freyr's summer. The Church celebrated its special days. Volcanoes erupted. The suns swung over the bent backs of the peasants.

King JandolAnganol grew thin from waiting for his bill of divorcement to arrive. He planned another campaign in the Cosgatt, to defeat Darvlish and regain a measure of popularity. He camouflaged his inner anguish with constant nervous activity. Wherever he went, the phagor runt Yuli followed —together with other shades which vanished as the king turned his eagle gaze towards them.

JandolAnganol prayed, suffered a flagellation at the hands of his vicar, bathed, dressed, and strode out to the courtyard of the palace where the hoxneys were stabled. He wore a rich keedrant with forms of animals embroidered on it, silk trousers, and high leather boots. Over the keedrant he buckled

leather armour trimmed with silver embellishments.

His favourite steed, Lapwing, was saddled. He mounted her. Yuli ran up, yipping and calling him Father; JandolAnganol pulled the creature up behind him. They set off at a trot into the hilly parkland behind the palace. Accompanying the king at a respectful distance went a detachment of the First Phagorian Guard—in whom, during these dangerous times, JandolAnganol reposed more trust than ever before.

The warm wind was on his cheek. He breathed deep. Everything about was dusted with grey in honour of distant Rustyjonnik.

"It's zzhoodin' today," called Yuli.

"Yes, shooting."

In a dell where brassims sent up their leathery branches, a target had been established. Several men in dark clothes were busy making arrangements. They became immobile as the king arrived, testifying to his power to freeze blood by his very majesty. The Phagorian arrived silently and formed a line, blocking the mouth of the dell.

Yuli jumped from Lapwing and scampered about, insensitive to occasion. The king remained in his saddle, brow ominous, as if he had power to freeze himself.

One of the frozen figures moved forward and saluted the king. He was a small thin man of unusual physiognomy, who wore the harsh sacklike garb of his trade.

His name was SlanjivalIptrekira. The name was regarded as rude and funny. Possibly it was this life's handicap which caused SlanjivalIptrekira in middle age to sport a great amount of gingerish side-whisker, reinforced by a phagor-ear moustache. This lent his otherwise mild aspect a ferocity, as well as creating a countenance with more sideways than vertical dimension.

He licked his lips nervously as he endured the hawkish gaze of the sovereign. His unease was occasioned, not by the innuendo of his name, but by the fact that he was Royal Armourer and Chief Ironmaster of the Ironmakers Corps. And by the fact that six matchlocks built under his direction in imitation of a Sibornalese artillery piece were about to be tested.

This was his second testing. An earlier six prototypes, tested half a tenner previously, had all failed to work. Hence the lick-

ing of the lips. Hence a tendency of SlanjivalIptrekira's knees to concatenate.

The king remained upright in the saddle. He raised a hand in signal. Figures came to life.

Six phagor sergeants were delegated to test the guns one by one. They marched forward, bovine faces expressionless, heavy shoulders set, their great shaggy bulks contrasting with the scraggy anatomies of the armourers.

SlanjivalIptrekira's new weapon bore the outward appearance of the original. The metal barrel was four feet long. It was bedded into a wooden stock which curved down to a foot further two feet long. The barrel was bound to the stock with copper bands. The striking mechanism was forged of the best quality iron that the foundries of the Ironmakers Corps could produce. Silver chasing, decorated with religious symbols, had been added to the stock. As in the original, the weapon was loaded from the muzzle end by means of a ramrod.

The first phagor sergeant came up with the first weapon. He held it while an armourer primed it. The sergeant knelt, his lower leg turning forward instead of back, in a posture no human could achieve. At the muzzle end of the piece, a tripod supported part of the weight. The sergeant took aim.

"Ready, sire," said SlanjivalIptrekira, looking anxiously from weapon to majesty. The king gave an almost imperceptible nod.

The striker came down. The powder fizzled. With a mighty explosion, the gun blew to pieces.

The sergeant fell backwards, giving a guttural cry. Yuli ran squealing into the bushes. Lapwing shied. Birds flew screaming from the trees.

JandolAnganol steadied his mare.

"Try Number Two."

The sergeant was helped away, his face and chest leaking ichor. He made a small bleating noise. A second sergeant took his place.

The second gun exploded more violently than the first. Splinters of wood struck the king's chest armour. The sergeant had part of his jaw blown away.

The third gun would not fire. After repeated attempts, the

ball rolled from its muzzle to the ground. The Royal Armourer laughed nervously, face ashen. "Better luck next time," he said.

There was better luck with the fourth gun. It went off as intended, and the ball buried itself near the edge of the target. It was a large target designed for archery and stood only two dozen paces away, but the firing was accounted a success.

The fifth gun cracked dismally along its barrel. The sixth gun fired its ball, although the target was missed.

The armourers stood close together, studying the ground at their feet.

SlanjivalIptrekira came to the king's horse. He saluted again. His moustache trembled.

"We make some progress, sire. Our charges are perhaps too strong, sire."

"On the contrary, your metals are too weak. Be back here again in a week's time with six perfect weapons, or I'll flay every member of your corps, from you downwards, and drive you skinless into the Cosgatt."

He took one of the ruined guns, whistled up Yuli, and galloped away towards the palace, across the grey sward.

The innermost part of the palace-fortress—its heart, if palace-fortresses have hearts—was stifling. The sky above was overcast, and an echo of it was to be found on the ground, in every corner, on every ledge, cornice, moulding, nook and cranny, where the exhalations of distant Rustyjonnik refused to be swept away. Only when the king had passed through a thick wooden door, and then a second as thick as the first, did he escape the ash.

As the steps wound downwards, dark and cold thickened about him to embrace him like a soaked rug as he entered the subterranean set of chambers reserved for royal guests.

JandolAnganol strode through three interconnecting rooms. The first was the most fearful; it had served as a guard room, a kitchen, a mortuary, and a torture chamber, and still contained equipment relating to those earlier roles. The second was a bedroom, containing merely a bunk, though it too had served as a mortuary, and looked better suited to that pur-

pose. In the end room sat VarpalAnganol.

The old king remained wrapped in a blanket, his feet against a grate in which smouldered a log fire. A high grille in the wall behind him allowed light to filter in and define him as a darkish lump on top of which a wispy skull was perched.

These things JandolAnganol had seen many times. The shape, the blanket, the chair, the grille, the floor, even the log that never burned properly in the dank atmosphere—all these did not alter through the years. It seemed as if only here, throughout his whole kingdom, could he look on enduring things.

Making a noise suggesting that he might need to clear his throat, the old king half-turned in his chair. His expression was half vacant, half crazy.

"It's I—Jan."

"I thought it was that same path again . . . where the fish jumped. . . . You . . ." He struggled to disentangle himself from his thoughts. "That's you, Jan? Where's Father? What time is it?"

"Nearly fourteen, if that's of any interest to you."

"Time's always of interest." VarpalAnganol gave a ghostly chuckle. "Isn't it time that Borlien bumped into Freyr?"

"That's an old wives' tale. I've something to show you."

"What old wife? Your mother's dead, lad. I haven't seen her for . . . or was she here? I forget. It may warm this palace up a bit . . . I thought I smelt burning."

"It's a volcano."

"I see. A volcano. I thought it might be Freyr. Sometimes my thoughts wander. . . . Do you want to sit down, lad?" He began struggling to his feet, but JandolAnganol pushed him back into the chair.

"Have you found Roba yet? He's born now, isn't he?"

"I don't know where he is—he's out of his wits, certainly."

The old king gave a cackle. "Very shrewd. Sanity can drive you mad, you know. . . . You remember how the fish used to jump in that pool? Well, there always was something wild about Roba. Almost a man now, I suppose. If he's not here, he can't shut you up, can he? Nor can you marry him off. What's her name? Cune. She's gone, too."

"She's in Gravabagalinien."

"Good. I hope he doesn't kill her. Her mother was a fine woman. What about my old friend Rushven? Is Rushven dead? I don't know what you do up there half the time. If you can halve time."

"Rushven's gone. I told you. My agents report that he has fled to Sibornal, much good that will do him."

Silence fell between them. JandolAnganol stood with matchlock in hand, reluctant to break into his father's rambling thoughts. He was getting worse than ever.

"Perhaps he'll see the Great Wheel of Kharnabhar. It's their sacred symbol, you know." With a struggle, and only by letting his blanket slip, he managed to screw his stiff old neck round to look at his son. "It's their sacred symbol, I said."

"I know it."

"Then try and answer when I speak to you. . . . What about that other fellow, the Uskuti, yes, Pasharatid? Did they catch him?"

"No. His wife left too, a tenner ago."

The old man sank back into the chair, sighing. His hands twitched nervously at the blanket. "Sounds to me as if Matrassyl's almost empty."

JandolAnganol turned his face away, towards the grey square of light. "Just me and the phagors."

"Did I ever tell you what Io Pasharatid used to do, Jan? When he was allowed to come and see me? Curious behaviour for a man of the northern continent. They are very self-controlled—not passionate, like the Borlienese."

"Did you scheme with him to overthrow me?"

"I just sat here while he dragged a table through, a heavy table. He used to put it under that little window. Did you ever hear such a thing?"

JandolAnganol began to pace about the cell, darting his gaze into the corners as if seeking a way of escape.

"He wanted to admire the view from your luxurious apartment."

The figure in the chair gave a bleat of laughter. "Precisely so. Admiring the view. Well put. A good phrase. And the view was of . . . well, if you get the table yourself, lad, you will see. You will see the windows of MyrdemInggala's apartments, and her verandah . . ." He broke off for a dry cough which

rattled in his throat. The king paced faster. "You get a view of
the reservoir where Cune used to swim naked with her ladies-
in-waiting. Before you sent her away this was, of course. . . ."

"What happened, Father?"

"Well, that's what happened. I told you but you didn't
listen. The ambassador used to climb on to that table and
watch your queen with nothing on, wearing only a piece of
muslin. . . . Very . . . very unorthodox behaviour for a Sibornalese. A Uskuti. Or for anyone really."

"Why didn't you tell me this at the time?" He stood confronting the ancient shape of his father.

"Heh. You would have killed him."

"I should have killed him. Yes. No one would have blamed
me."

"The Sibornalese would have blamed you. Borlien would
have been in worse trouble than it is already. You will not
learn diplomatic sense. That's why I didn't tell you."

JandolAnganol began to pace. "What a calculating old
slanje you are! Surely you must have hated what Pasharatid
was doing?"

"No . . . what are women for? I have no objection to hate.
It keeps you alive, keeps you warm of nights. Hate is what
brings you down here. You came down here once, I forget
what year it was, to talk about love, but I only know about—"

"Enough!" cried JandolAnganol, stamping his boot on the
flags. "I shall never speak of love again, to you or anyone.
Why do you never help me? Why didn't you tell me what
Pasharatid was up to? Did he ever meet secretly with Cune?"

"Why don't you grow up?" Spite entered his voice. "I expect he crept in to her warm nest every night . . ."

He cringed away, expecting a blow from his son's raised
hand. But JandolAnganol squatted by the chair instead.

"I want you to look at something. Tell me what you would
do."

He lifted the homemade matchlock which had cracked
along the barrel and placed it on his father's knee.

"It's heavy. I don't want it. Her garden's all neglected
now . . ." The ex-king pushed it so that it fell on the floor.
JandolAnganol let it lie there.

"That gun was made by SlanjivalIptrekira's corps. The

barrel split on firing. Out of six guns I had him make, only one
worked properly. Of the previous batch, none has worked.
What has gone wrong? How is it that our weapon-makers'
corps, which claims to trace its foundation back for centuries,
cannot make a simple gun?''

The old heap in the chair remained silent for a while, pulling
ineffectually at its blanket. Then it spoke.

"Things don't get better for being old. Look at me. Look at
the figure behind you. . . . It may be that too many institutions
are too old. . . . What was I going to say? Rushven told me
that the various trades corps were founded to exist through the
Great Winter, to hand on their knowledge in secret from
generation to generation, so that their arts survived the black
centuries until spring.''

"I have heard him say as much. . . . What follows?''

VarpalAnganol's wheezy voice strengthened. "Why, what
follows spring is summer. What follows seasons is that the
corps perpetuate themselves, maybe losing a little knowledge
from one generation to another but not gaining new knowledge. They become hidebound. . . . Try to imagine what those
centuries of darkness and frost were like—much like being
stuck down in this hole for eternity, I imagine. Trees died. No
wood. No charcoal. No fires for smelting properly. . . . Probably it's the smelting process at fault, by the look of that barrel. The furnaces . . . they may need renewing. Better
methods, as the Sibornalese have . . .''

"I'll flog them all for their idleness. Then perhaps we'll see
some results.''

"Not idleness, tradition. Try chopping Slanji's head off and
then offering rewards. That will encourage innovation.''

"Yes. Yes, possibly.'' He picked up the gun and made for
the door.

The old man called feebly to him. "What do you want the
guns for?''

"The Cosgatt. The Western Wars. What else?''

"Shoot the enemies nearest your doorstep first. Teach
Unndreid a lesson. Darvlish. Then you'll be safer to fight farther away.''

"I don't need your advice on how to wage war.''

"You're afraid of Darvlish.''

"I'm afraid of no one. Of myself, sometimes."

"Jan."

"Yes?"

"Ask them to send me logs which burn, will you?" He began to cough rackingly.

JandolAnganol knew he was only shamming.

To show himself properly humble, the king went to the great dome in the main square of Matrassyl. Archpriest BranzaBaginut greeted him at the North Door.

JandolAnganol prayed publicly among his people. Without thought, he took with him his pet runt, who stood patiently by his master while the latter prostrated himself for an hour. Instead of pleasing his people, JandolAnganol displeased them by taking a phagor into the presence of Akhanaba.

His prayer, however, was heard by the All-Powerful, who confirmed that he should take VarpalAnganol's advice regarding the Ironmakers Corps.

Yet JandolAnganol vacillated. He had enough enemies without taking on one of the corps, whose power in the land was traditional, and whose chiefs were represented on the scritina. After private prayer and scourging, he went lengthily into pauk, to be counselled by the fessup of his grandfather. The battered grey cage floating in obsidian comforted him. Again, he was encouraged to act.

"To be holy is to be hard," he said to himself. He had promised the scritina that he would devote himself wholeheartedly to his country. So it should be. Matchlocks were necessary. They would compensate for lack of manpower. Matchlocks would bring back the golden age.

Accompanied by a mounted troop of the Royal First Phagorian Guard, JandolAnganol went to the quarters of the Ancient Corps of Ironmakers and Swordsmen and demanded admittance. The great shadowy place opened up to him. He entered their quarters, which led into the rock. Everything here spoke of long-dead generations. Smoke had come like age to blacken everything.

He was greeted by officers with ancient halbards in some kind of uniform, who tried to bar his way. Chief Ironmaster

SlanjivalIptrekira came running with ginger whiskers bristling—apologising, yes, bowing, yes, but stating firmly that no nonmenber of the corps (barring possibly the odd woman) had ever entered these premises, and that they had centuries-old charters showing their rights.

"Fall back! I am king. I will inspect!" shouted JandolAnganol. Giving a command to the phagorian guard, he moved forward. Still mounted on their armoured hoxneys, they surged into an inner courtyard, where the air stank of sulphur and tombs. The king climbed from his mount, going forward surrounded by a strong guard while other soldiers waited with the hoxneys. Corpsmen came running, paused, scurried this way and that, dismayed at the invasion.

Red in the face, SlanjivalIptrekira still fell back before the king, protesting. JandolAnganol, showing his teeth in a holy snarl, drew his sword.

"Run me through if you will," shouted the armourer. "You are for ever cursed for breaking in here!"

"Rhhh! You lurk underground like miserable fessups! Out of my way, slanje!"

He pressed forward. The invading party went in under grey rock, thrusting into the entrails of the establishment.

They came to the furnaces, six of them, pot-bellied, made of brick and stone, patched and repatched, towering up to a murky roof, where ventholes in the rock showed as blackened cavities. One of the furnaces was working. Boys were shovelling and kicking fuel into a gleaming eye of heat, as fire roared and raged. Men in leather aprons drew a tray of red-hot rods from the furnace door, set them on a mutilated table, and stepped back, tight-lipped, to see what the excitement was.

Further into the chamber, men were kneeling by anvils. They had been hammering away at iron rods. Their din stopped as they stood to see what was happening. At the sight of JandolAnganol, blank amazement covered their faces.

For a moment, the king too was stopped. The terrible cavern astonished him. A captive stream gushed along a trough to work the enormous bellows placed by the furnace. Elsewhere were piled timbers and instruments as fearful as any used in torture. From a separate side cavern came wooden tubs bearing iron ore. Everywhere, blacksmiths, iron smelters,

craftsmen—half naked—peered at him with pink-rimmed eyes.

SlanjivalIptrekira ran before the king, his arms raised, waving, fists clenched.

"Your Majesty, the ores are being reduced by charcoal. It is a sacred process. Outsiders—even royal personages—are not allowed to view these rites."

"Nothing in my kingdom is secret from me."

"Attack him, kill him!" cried the Royal Armourer.

The men carrying glowing iron bars lifted them with thick leather gloves. They looked at each other, then set them down again. The king's person was sacred. Nobody else moved.

With perfect calm, JandolAnganol said, "Slanji, you have uttered a treasonable command against your sovereign, as all those here bear witness. I will have every member of the corps executed without exception if anybody dares make a move against my royal person."

Brushing past the armourer, he faced two men at a table.

"You men, how old are these furnaces? For how many generations has metalcraft continued in this manner?"

They could not answer for fear. They wiped their blackened faces with their blackened gloves, which effected no improvement in their appearance.

It was SlanjivalIptrekira who answered, in a subdued voice. "The corps was founded to perpetuate these sacred processes, Your Majesty. We but do as we are bid by our ancestors."

"You are answerable to me, not to your ancestors. I bid you make good guns and you failed." He turned to the corpsmen who had gathered silently in the fumous chamber.

"You men, all, and apprentices. You carry out old methods. Those old methods are obsolete. Haven't you the wits to understand? There are new weapons available, better than we can make in Borlien. We need new methods, better metals, better systems."

They looked at him with dark faces and red-rimmed eyes, unable to understand that their world was ending.

"These rotten furnaces will be demolished. More efficient ones will be built. They must have such furnaces in Sibornal, in the land of the Uskuti. We need furnaces like the Sibornalese. Then we shall make weapons like the Sibornalese."

He summoned up a dozen of his brute soldiery and commanded them to destroy the furnaces. The phagors seized crowbars and commenced without question to carry out their orders. From the live furnace, when its wall was broached, molten metal burst forth. It flashed across the floor. A young apprentice fell screaming under its flood. The metal set fire to wood shavings and timber. The corpsmen shrank away aghast.

All the furnaces were broken. The phagors stood by for further orders.

"Have them built anew, according to directions I shall send you. I will have no more useless guns!" With these words, he marched from the building. The corpsmen came to themselves and threw buckets of water over their blazing premises. SlanjivalIptrekira was arrested and jostled off into captivity.

The following day, the Royal Armourer and Ironmaster was tried before the scritina and convicted of treason. Even the other corpsmasters could not save SlanjivalIptrekira. He had ordered his men to attack the person of his king. He was executed in the public view, and his head exhibited to the crowd.

Enemies of the king in the scritina, and not his enemies only, nor only in the scritina, were nevertheless angered that he had ventured into premises by long tradition sacrosanct. This was another mad act which would never have been committed had Queen MyrdemInggala been near to keep his madness under control.

JandolAnganol, however, sent a messenger to Sayren Stund, King of Oldorando, his future father-in-law. He knew that the destruction of the city of Oldorando, when it had been overcome by phagor invasion, had resulted in the craft corps' being reformed, and their equipment renewed. Their foundries should therefore be more advanced than Borlien's. He remembered at the last moment to send his neighbour a gift for Simoda Tal.

King Sayren Stund sent JandolAnganol a dark hunchbacked man called Fard Fantil. Fard Fantil came with credentials showing him to be an expert in iron furnaces who understood new methods. JandolAnganol sent him to work immediately.

Immediately, a delegation from the Ironmakers Corps, ashen of face, came before the king to complain of Fard Fantil's ruthlessness and sullen ways.

"I like sullen men," roared JandolAnganol.

Fard Fantil had the premises of the guild moved to a hillside outside Matrassyl. Here the timber was available for charcoal and the supply of running water was constant. The water was necessary to power stamping mills.

No one in Borlien had ever heard of stamping mills. Fard Fantil explained in supercilious fashion that this was the only way to crush ore effectively. The corpsmen scratched their heads and grumbled. Fard Fantil cursed them. Furious at being turned out of their town quarters, the men did all they could to sabotage the new establishment and bring the foreigner into disgrace. The king still received no guns.

When Dienu Pasharatid disappeared from the court so unexpectedly, following her husband to Uskutoshk, she had left behind some Sibornalese staff. These JandolAnganol had imprisoned. He ordered an Uskut brought before him and offered him his freedom if he would design an effective iron smelter.

The cool young man had perfect manners, so perfect that he made a flourish whenever he addressed the king.

"As your majesty knows, the best smelters come from Sibornal, where the art is advanced. There we use lignite instead of charcoal for fuel, and forge the best steel."

"Then I wish you to design a smelter for use here, and I shall reward you."

"Your majesty knows that the wheel, that great basic invention, came from Sibornal, and was not known in Campannlat until a few centuries ago. Also many of your new crops are from the north. Those furnaces which you destroyed—even that design came from Sibornal during a previous Great Year."

"Now we wish for something more up-to-date." JandolAnganol restrained his temper.

"Even when the wheel was brought to Borlien, Your Majesty, full use was never made of it, not only for transport, but in milling, pottery, and irrigation. You have no windmills in Borlien as we have in Sibornal. It has seemed to us, Your

Majesty, that the nations of Campannlat have been slow to adopt the arts of civilisation."

It was noticeable that about the king's jaw a roseate flush mounted as the sun of his anger was dawning.

"I'm not demanding windmills. I want a furnace capable of producing steel for my guns."

"Your majesty possibly intends to say guns imitated from the Sibornalese model."

"No matter what I intend to say, what I do say is that I require you to build me a good furnace. Is that understood, or do you only speak Sibish?"

"Forgive me, Your Majesty, I had thought you understood the position. Permit me to explain that I am not an artisan but an ambassadorial clerk, nimble with figures but not with bricks and suchlike. I am if anything less able to build a furnace than your majesty."

Still the king received no guns.

The king spent an increasing amount of time with his phagor soldiery. Knowing the necessity for repeating everything to them, he impressed upon them every day that they would accompany him in strength to Oldorando, in order to make a grand display in the foreign capital on the occasion of his marriage.

Places were delegated in the palace grounds where king and phagor guard met on equal terms. No human entered the phagorian barracks. To this rule the king subscribed, as VarpalAnganol had before him. There was no question of his venturing beyond a certain point in the way he had invaded the traditional quarters of the Ironmakers Corps.

His chief phagor major was a gillot by name Ghht-Mlark Chzarn, addressed by JandolAnganol as Chzarn. They conversed in Hurdhu.

Knowing the ancipital aversion to Oldorando, the king explained once more why he required the presence of the First Phagorian at his forthcoming marriage.

Chzarn responded.

"Speech has been made with our ancestors in tether. Much speech has formed in our harneys. It is delivered that we make

a goance with your sovereign body to Hrl-Drra Nhdo in the
land Hrrm-Bhhrd Ydohk. That goance we make at command.''

"Good. It is good we make goance together. I rejoice that
those in tether are in agreement. Have you further to say?''

Ghht-Mlark Chzarn stood impassive before him, her deep
pink eyes almost level with his. He was aware of her smell and
of the barely audible sound of her breathing. His long acquaintance with phagors told him that more speech was to
come. The members of the guard behind her were equally impassive, pressing together, coat against coat. An occasional
fart broke from their ranks.

Impatient man though JandolAnganol was, something in
the deliberation of phagors—in that intense impression that
what they said came not from them only but rather from a
great distance, relayed from some ancestral store of understanding to which he could never have access—soothed him.
He stood before his major almost as still as she before him.

"Further sayance.'' Ghht-Mlark Chzarn went through a
formula with which the king was familiar. Before a new subject could be broached, linkages with those in tether must be
sustained. Thus was aneotic thought endured.

They confronted each other, as tradition demanded, in a
military room called the Clarigate; humans entered at one end,
phagors at the other. The walls were painted by phagors in
swirling greens and greys. The ceiling was so low that its
beams were scarred by tracks of ancipital horn points—possibly a deliberate device to emphasise the fact that the
Phagorian Guard were never dehorned.

One god only protected the king, Akhanaba, the All-Powerful; many demons tormented him. Phagors were not among
those demons; he was accustomed to the steady calculation of
their speech, never regarding them—as did his fellow men—as
either slow-witted or convoluted in thought.

And in these days of his inner torment, he found a new factor to admire about his guard. They were not sexually preoccupied. He considered that the streams of lubricious thought
which occupied the minds of men and women at court—and
his own mind, despite applications of god and rod—were absent from ancipital harneys.

There was a periodicity to phagor sexuality. Gillots came into oestrus every forty-eight days, while the stalluns performed the sexual act every three weeks. Coitus was joined without ceremony and not always privately. Because of this lack of shame in what to humans was an act more secret than prayer, the ancipital race was a symbol of lust. The goat foot, the erect horns, were emblems of rut to humanity. Tales of stalluns raping women—and on occasion men—were common and could lead to drumbles and purges in which many phagors were killed.

When the phagor major arrived at her thought, it was brief. "In our goance to Hrl-Drra Nhdo in the land Hrrm-Bhhrd Ydohk, it is delivered your ancipital host must make great presence. So your power burn bright before Hrl-Drra Nhdo people. Commendation comes that that host on parade must have carriance of . . ." A long pause while the concept struggled through into speech. ". . . Of new weapons."

With considerable pain, JandolAnganol said, "We need the new hand artillery from Sibornal. As yet, we cannot produce them in Borlien."

Beads of condensation stood on the walls of the Clarigate. The heat was overpowering. Chzarn made a gesture the king knew well, signifying "Stand."

He repeated his statement. She repeated the "Stand" gesture.

After consultation both with those living and with those in tether, the phagor major declared that the needed weapons would be obtained. Although the king understood the struggle phagors underwent to verbalise the aneotic, he was compelled to ask them how the weapons would be obtained.

"Much speech has form in our harneys," said Chzarn, after another pause.

There was an answer. She switched to Eotemporal to be clear in her tenses. An answer would be delivered, was even now about to be delivered, but must nevertheless wait upon another time, another tenner. His power would be made great in Hrl-Drra Nhdo. Hold horns high.

He had to be content with that.

For farewell, JandolAnganol leant forward, hands to side, neck extended. The gillot also leaned forward, her head pro-

truding over dugs and great barrel of body. Unhorned head met horned head, foreheads touched, harneys were together. Then both parties turned smartly away.

The king left by the Humans Only door of the Clarigate.

Excitement moved in his eddre. His Phagorian would provide their own arms. What faithfulness was theirs! What devotion, deeper than that of human beings! He did not reflect on other possible intrepretations of Chzarn's speech.

Briefly, he thought of the happy days when his flesh invaded Cune's delectable queme flesh; but those times of ease and venery were dead. His concern must now be with these creatures, who would help him rid Borlien of its enemies.

Chzarn and the phagor soldiery departed from the Clarigate in a spirit different from the king's. They could scarcely be said to have an alteration of mood. Blood flow hastened or slowed in response to breathing; so much was true.

What was spoken in the Clarigate was reported by Ghht-Mlark Chzarn to the Matrassyl Kzahhn, Ghht-Yronz Tharl himself. The kzahhn reigned under his mountain, unknown even to the king. At this time of evil, when Freyr flew nearer down the air-octaves with his scorching breath, the ancipitals generally despaired. The ichor became sluggish in their veins. Lowland components allowed themselves to fall wholly under human subjugation. But a sign had been given them and hope stirred in their eddre.

To Kzahhn Ghht-Yronz Tharl had been brought a remarkable Son of Freyr, a captive of the disgraced chancellor, by name Bhrl-Hzzh Rowpin. Bhrl-Hzzh Rowpin came from another world and knew almost as much about the Catastrophe as the ancipitals did. To them under the mountain, Bhrl-Hzzh Rowpin had delivered ancient truths which other Sons of Freyr rejected. The things he spoke had gone unheeded by the chancellor and by the king; but the component of Ghht-Yronz Tharl heeded them and determination took form in their harneys.

For the speech of the strange Son of Freyr reinforced voices from tether which sometimes seemed to grow faint.

The Sons of Freyr were badly made, with poor componentalism. So it was with the king, as the faithful spy Yuli reported. For the weak king now offered them a chance to strike

back against their traditional enemy. By seeming to obey him, they could stamp their hurt and harm against Hrl-Drra Nhdo, ancient Hrrm-Bhrrd Ydohk. It was a hate-place cursed long ago by one of the Great Ones now only a keratinous image, the Crusading Kzahhn, Hrr-Brahl Yprt. Red ichor would flow there again.

Courage was needed. Be valiant. Hold horns high.

For the required hand artillery, they had only to follow favourable air-octaves. The phagors were on occasion allies of the Nondads and aided them against the Sons of Freyr. The Nondads struggled against the Sons of Freyr called Uskuts. Uskuts—shame to speak of it—devoured dead bodies of Nondads, denying them the comfort of the Eighty Darknesses. . . . The Nondads would with their light fingers take hand artillery from the Uskat race. And the hand artillery would bring dismay to the Sons of Freyr.

So it came about. Before another tenner passed, King JandolAnganol was armed with Sibornalese matchlocks— weapons supplied not by his allies in Pannoval or Oldorando, not forged by his own armourers, but brought by devious routes as a gift from those who were his enemies.

In such a fashion, a better way of killing spread slowly across Helliconia.

Belatedly, after many disputes, Fard Fantil the hunchback established his weapon factory outside Matrassyl. The newly acquired weapons served as models. After much cursing of his work force, the hunchback produced native matchlocks which did not blow up and fired with some accuracy.

By then, Sibornalese manufacturers had improved their designs and perfected a wheel-lock piece, which fired the powder pan by means of a revolving flint wheel rather than the old untrustworthy fusee.

Made confident by his new armoury, the king buckled on his breastplate, saddled Lapwing, and rode forth to war. Once more he led an ahuman army against his enemies, the rag and bobtail of Driat tribes who terrorised the Cosgatt under Darvlish the Skull.

The two forces met only a few miles from where Jandol-

Anganol had sustained his wound. This time, the Eagle of
Borlien was more experienced. After a day-long conflict, victory was his. The First Phagorian followed him blindly. The
Driats were killed, routed, thrown into ravines. The survivors
scattered among the tawny hills from which they had emerged.

For the last time, the vultures had reason to praise the name
of Darvlish.

The king returned in triumph to his capital, with the head of
Darvlish mounted high on a pole.

The head was placed above the gate of Matrassyl palace,
there to fester until Darvlish was in reality nothing but a skull.

*Billy Xiao Pin was by no means the only male among the in-
habitants of Avernus to dream of Queen MyrdemInggala.
Such private things were seldom admitted even to friends.
They emerged only indirectly in that evasive society—for instance, in a general execration of King JandolAnganol's latest
behaviour.*

*The sight of the Thribriatan warlord's head on Jandol-
Anganol's gatepost was enough to provoke a howl of protest
from this faction.*

*One of its spokesmen said, "This monster tasted blood with
the death of the Myrdolators. Now he is accumulating the
weapons for which he traded the queen of queens. Where will
he stop? Plainly, we should check him now, before he plunges
all Campannlat into war.*

*Just as JandolAnganol was enjoying some of the popularity
he hoped for in Borlien, he roused unusual opprobrium on the
Avernus.*

*The complaints brought against him had been heard before
of other tyrants. It was more convenient to blame the leader
than the led; the illogic of that position was seldom remarked.
Shifting conditions, shortages of foodstuffs and materials,
guaranteed that Helliconian history was a constant series of
bids for power, of dictators gaining wide support.*

*The suggestion that Avernus should move in to put an end
to one particular oppression or another was also far from new.
Nor was intervention an entirely idle threat.*

When Earth's colonising starship entered the Freyr-Batalix

system in 3600 A.D., it established a base on Aganip, the inner planet closest to Helliconia. On Aganip, 512 colonists were landed. They had been hatched aboard the starship during the final years of its voyage. The information encoded in the DNA of fertilized human egg cells had been stored in computers during the voyage. It was transferred into 512 artificial wombs. The resultant babies—the first human beings to walk the ship during its one-and-a-half millennium flight—were reared by surrogate mothers in several large families.

The young humans ranged in age from fifteen to twenty-one Earth years old when they landed on Aganip. The construction of the Avernus was already in process. Automation and local materials were used.

Owing to more than one near disaster, the ambitious construction program had taken eight years. During that hazardous period, Aganip was used as a base. When the job was complete, the young colonists were ferried aboard their new home.

The starship then left the system. The inhabitants of the Avernus were alone—more alone than any humans had ever been before.

Now, 3,269 Earth years later, the old base was a shrine, occasionally visited by the enlightened. It had become part of Avernian mythology.

There were minerals on Aganip. It would not be impossible to shuttle to the planet and there construct a number of ships with which to invade Helliconia. Not impossible. But unlikely, for there were no technicians trained for such a project.

The hotheads who whispered of such things had to work against the whole ethos of the Earth Observation Station, which was strictly non-interventionist.

Also, the hotheads were male. They had to contend with the female half of the population, who admired the troubled king. The women watched JandolAnganol defeat Darvlish. It was a great victory. JandolAnganol was a hero who suffered much for his country, shortsighted though that aim might be. He was a tragic figure.

The sort of intervention this female faction dreamed of was to descend to Borlien and be by JandolAnganol's side, day and night.

*   *   *

And when these events at last reached Earth?

There would be much nodding of approval at Jandol-Anganol's choice of which piece of Darvlish's anatomy to exhibit. Not the Skull's feet, which had carried the man into skirmish after skirmish. Not his genitals, which had fathered so many bastards to create future trouble. Not his hands, which had silenced many a foe. But his head, where all the other mischief had been co-ordinated.

XIV

WHERE FLAMBREG LIVE

White shadows filled the city of Askitosh. They lay entangled among grey buildings. When a man walked along the pale roads, he took on their pallor. This was the famous Uskuti "silt-mist," a thin but blinding curtain of cold dry air which descended from the plateaux standing behind the city.

Overhead, Freyr burned like a gigantic spark in the void. Sibornalese dimday reigned. Batalix would rise again in an hour or two: At present only the greater star remained. Batalix would rise and sink before Freyr-set and—in this early spring season—would never attain zenith.

Wrapped up in a waterproof coat, SartoriIrvrash looked upon this phantasmal city as it slipped from view. It sank away into the silt-mist, became bare bones, and then was gone entirely. But the *Golden Friendship* was not entirely alone in the mist. From forwards, a well-muffled observer could make out the jolly boat ahead with the ancipital rowers straining as they pulled the warship out of harbour. At hand, too, were glimpses of other spectral ships, their sails hanging limp or

flapping like dead skin, as the Uskuti fleet started on its mission of conquest.

They were out in the sullen channel when a blur on the eastern horizon marked Batalix-rise. A wind got up. The striped sails above them began to stir and tighten. Not a sailor on board but felt a lightening in spirit; the omens were right for a long voyage.

Sibornalese omens meant little to SartoriIrvrash. He shrugged his thin shoulders under his padded keedrant and went below. On the companionway, he was overtaken by Io Pasharatid, the ex-ambassador to Borlien.

"We shall do well," he said, nodding his head wisely. "We set sail at the right time and the omens are fulfilled as decreed."

"Excellent," said SartoriIrvrash, yawning. The seagoing priests-militant of Askitosh had mustered every deuteroscopist, astromancer, uranometrist, hieromancer, meteorologician, metempiricist, and priest they could lay hands on to determine the tenner, week, day, hour, and minute on which the *Golden Friendship* should most auspiciously sail. The birth signs of the crew and the wood of which the keel was made had been taken into account. But the most persuasive sign lay in the heavens, where YarapRombry's Comet, flying high in the northern night sky, was timed to enter the zodiacal constellation of the Golden Ship at six-eleven and ninety seconds that very morning. And that was the precise time when the hawsers were cast off and the rowers began to row.

It was too early for SartoriIrvrash. He did not contemplate the long and hazardous voyage with cheer. His stomach felt queasy. He disliked the role that had been thrust upon him. And, to crown his discomfort, here was Io Pasharatid, marching about the ship and being suspiciously friendly, as if no disgrace had ever befallen him. How did one behave to a man like that?

It seemed that Dienu Pasharatid could arrange anything. Perhaps because of her cunning appropriation of JandolAnganol's ex-chancellor into her plans, and the designs of her war commission, she had saved her husband from prison. He had been allowed to sail with the soldiery of the *Golden Friendship* as a hand-artillery captain—perhaps in an under-

standing by the powers-that-be that a long sea voyage in a 910-ton carrack was as bad as a prison sentence, even a sentence in the Great Wheel of Kharnabhar.

Despite this narrow escape from justice, Pasharatid was more arrogant than ever. He boasted to SartoriIrvrash that, by the time they reached Ottassol, he would command the soldiery; so he stood every chance of commanding the Ottassol garrison.

SartoriIrvrash lay on his bunk and lit a veronikane. He was immediately hit by seasickness. It had not troubled him on the way to Askitosh. Now it made up for lost time.

For three days, the ex-chancellor declined all rations. He woke on the fourth day feeling superlatively well and made his way on deck.

Visibility was good. Freyr was eyeing them across the waters, low to the north of northeast, somewhere in the direction from which the *Golden Friendship* had come. The shadow of the ship danced across the smalts of the fresh sea. The air was steeped in light and tasted wonderful. SartoriIrvrash stretched up his arms and breathed deep.

No land was to be seen. Batalix was set. Of the ships which had escorted them from harbour as guard of honour, only one remained, sailing two leagues to leeward with its flags streaming in the wind. Almost lost in blue distance was a cluster of herring-coaches.

So delighted was he at being able to stand without feeling wretched, so loud was the song of canvas and shrouds, that he scarcely heard the greeting addressed to him. When it was repeated, he turned and looked up into the faces of Dienu and Io Pasharatid.

"You've been ill," said Dienu. "My sympathies. Unfortunately, Borlienese are not good sailors, isn't that so?"

Io said quickly, "At least you feel better now. There's nothing like a good long voyage for the health. The journey is approximately thirteen thousand miles, so with favouring winds we should be there in two tenners and three weeks—off Ottassol, that is."

He devoted himself over the next few days to taking SartoriIrvrash on a tour of the ship, explaining its working in the last detail. SartoriIrvrash made notes of what little interested

him, wishing in his Borlienese heart that his own country had
such expertise in nautical matters. The Uskuti and other nations of Sibornal had guilds and corps which were in general
principle similar to those of the civilised Campannlatian nations; but their maritime and military guilds excelled all others
in numbers and efficiency, and had/would (for the tense
was condition-eternal-subjunctive) triumphantly survived the
Weyr-winter. Winter, Pasharatid explained, was especially
severe in the north. Over the coldest centuries, Freyr remained
always below the horizon. The winter was always in their
hearts.

"I believe that," said SartoriIrvrash solemnly.

In Weyr-winter, even more than in the Great Summer, the
peoples of the ice-bound north depended on the seas for survival. Sibornal therefore had few private ships. All ships
belonged to the Priest-Sailors Guild. Emblems of the guild
decorated the sails of the ship, making of its functionalism a
thing of some beauty.

On the main sail rode the device of Sibornal, the two concentric rings joined by two undulant spokes.

The *Golden Friendship* had a fore-, main-, and mizzen-
mast. An artemon projecting over the bowsprit was raised
only in favouring winds, to speed progress. Io Pasharatid
explained exactly how many square feet of sail could be
hoisted at any time.

SartoriIrvrash was not entirely averse to being bored by a
stream of facts. He had devoted much of his life trying to
ascertain what was speculation, what fact, and to have a constant flow of the latter was not without attraction. Nevertheless, he speculated as to why Pasharatid should go to such
lengths to show friendship; it was hardly a predominant Sibornalese characteristic. Nor had it been in evidence in Matrassyl.

"You stand in danger of tiring SartoriIrvrash with your
facts, dear," said Dienu, on the sixth day of their voyage.

She left them where they were standing, tucked back at the
highest point of the poop, behind a pen containing female
arang. Not a foot of deck but was used for something—rope,
stores, livestock, cannon. And the two companies of soldiers
they had aboard were forced to spend most of the day, wet or

fine, standing about on deck, impeding the movements of the sailors' guildsmen.

"You must miss Matrassyl," said Pasharatid, speaking firmly into the wind.

"I miss the peace of my studies, yes."

"And other things as well, I imagine. Unlike many of my fellow Uskuts, I enjoyed my time in Matrassyl. It was very exotic. Too hot, of course, but I did not mind that. There were fine people with whom I came in contact."

SartoriIrvrash watched the arang fighting to turn round in their pen. They provided milk for the officers. He knew that Pasharatid was coming to his point at last.

"Queen MyrdemInggala is a fine lady. It is a shame that the king has exiled her, do you not think?"

So that was it. He waited before replying.

"The king saw that his duty lay in serving his country . . ."

"You must feel bitter at his treatment of you. You must hate him."

When SartoriIrvrash did not reply to that, Pasharatid said, or rather, shouted quietly in his ear, "How could he bear to give up a lady as lovely as the queen?"

No response.

"Your countrymen call her 'the queen of queens,' is that not correct?"

"That is correct."

"I never saw anyone so beautiful in my life."

"Her brother, YeferalOboral, was a close friend of mine."

This remark silenced Pasharatid. He appeared almost about to terminate the conversation when, with a burst of feeling, he said, "Just to be in Queen MyrdemInggala's presence—just to see her—made a man—affected a man like . . ."

He did not finish his sentence.

Weather conditions were changeable. A complex system of high and low pressure areas brought fogs, hot brownish rains, such as they had encountered on the voyage across to Sibornal—"regular Uskuti up-and-downers"—and periods of clarity where the featureless coastlines of Loraj could sometimes

be glimpsed to starboard. Still they made good time, with
pursuing winds either warm from the southwest or chilly from
west of northwest.

Boredom drove SartoriIrvrash to become familiar with
every part of the ship. He saw how the men were so cramped
that they slept on deck on coils of rope, or on bins below deck,
their heels propped high on the bulkheads. There was not an
inch of spare space.

Day by day, the smell of the ship grew stronger. To perform
their solid excretions, the men pulled off their trousers and
worked their way along a spar set over the side of the ship, on
which they had to balance, with a rope coming down from the
yardarm to hold onto. Urination was performed to leeward,
over the rail—and in dozens of other places, judging by olfac-
tory evidence. The officers fared almost as badly. The women
enjoyed better privacy.

After almost three weeks at sea the course was changed
from due west to west by northwest, and the *Golden Friendship* and its companion sailed into Persecution Bay.

Persecution Bay was a great and melancholy indentation
over one thousand miles long and five hundred miles deep on
the coast of Loraj. Even at its mouth, the sea slackened, while
day by day the wind dropped and the temperature fell. Soon
they moved through a pearly haze, broken only by the shouts
of the duty man calling the depth. They travelled now by dead
reckoning.

Impatience seized SartoriIrvrash. He retired to his kennel of
a cabin to smoke and read. Even those occupations were
unsatisfactory, for his stomach howled like a lost dog.
Already, ship's rations were causing him, a thin man at the
best of times, to tighten his belt. Men's rations were salted
fish, onions, olive or fish oil with bread every morning, soup
at midday, and a repetition of breakfast for the evening meal,
with hard cheese substituted for fish. A mug of fig wine or
yoodhl was served to each man twice a week.

The men supplemented this diet with fresh-caught fish,
hooked over the side. Officers fared little better, apart from
an issue of pungent arang milk occasionally, to which was
added brandy for those on watch. The Sibornalese complained

at this diet in no more than a routine way, as if inured to it.

Moving forward at five knots, they crossed the line of 35°N, thus leaving the tropics for the narrow northern temperate zone. On that same day, they heard fearsome crashings through the mist, and a series of huge waves set the ship rocking. Then silence again. SartoriIrvrash poked his head out of his cabin and enquired of the first seaman who passed what it was.

"Coast," said the man. And in a fit of communicativeness added a further word, "Glaciers."

SartoriIrvrash nodded in satisfaction. He turned back to his notebook, which was, for want of better occupation, becoming a diary.

"Even if the Uskuti are not civilised, they are enlarging my knowledge of the world. As is well known among scholars, our globe is set between great bands of ice. To the extreme north and the extreme south are lands consisting only of ice and snow. The miserable continent of Sibornal is especially loaded with this bothersome stuff, which may account for the dead hearts of its people. Now it seems they steer towards it, as if drawn by a magnet, instead of sailing on towards the warmer seas.

"What the purpose of this deviation might be, I shall not enquire—not wishing to risk further lectures from my personal demon, Pasharatid. But it may at least permit me to glimpse that horrid expanse which makes up the alpha and omega of the world."

In the night came a ferocious storm which was on them without warning. The *Golden Friendship* could only heave to and weather it out. Immense waves burnt against the hull, sending spray high into the spars. There were also ominous knockings which resounded through the ship, as if some giant of the deep was asking to be admitted aboard—so thought the ex-chancellor of Borlien, as he clung terrified to his bunk.

He doused the single whale-oil light in the cabin, as orders demanded. In the noisy dark he lay, by turns cursing JandolAnganol and praying to the All-Powerful. The giant of the deep by now had firm hold of the ship in both hands and was rocking it as some maniac might rock a cradle, in an attempt

to pitch the baby out upon its nose. To his later astonishment, SartoriIrvrash fell asleep while this decanting process was at its height.

When he roused, the ship was silent again, its movement barely discernible. Beyond the porthole lay more mist, lit by meagre sunshine.

Moving to the companionway, past sleeping soldiers, he stared up at the sky. Tangled among the rigging was a pallid silver coin. He looked upon the face of Freyr. Back to memory came the fairy story he had enjoyed reading in the queen of queens' company to TatromanAdala, about the silver eye in the sky that had sailed away at last.

The duty man called soundings. On the sea floated floes of ice, many carved into absurd forms. Some resembled stunted trees or monstrous fungi, as if the god of ice had taken it into his head to devise grotesque counterparts to living nature. These were the things that had come knocking at the heights of the storm, and it was a cause for gratitude that few bergs were half as big as the ship. These mysterious forms emerged from the mist, only to recede again into abstraction.

After a while, something made SartoriIrvrash shift his attention and look up. Across a narrow stretch of water were two phagor heads. The eyes in those heads stared not at the passing ship but at each other. . . . There were the long face with its misanthropic jaw, the eyes protected by boney ridges, the two horns curving upwards.

And yet, no sooner had he recognised the beasts than SartoriIrvrash knew he was mistaken. These were no phagors. He was seeing two wild animals which confronted each other.

The movement of the ship caused the mist to swirl apart, revealing a small island, no more than a tussock in the sea, yet with a steep little cliff on the near side. Perched on the island's barren crown stood two four-legged animals. Their coats were brown. Apart from their colour and their stance, they markedly resembled ancipitals.

Nearer view diminished the resemblance. These two animals, for all that they were challenging each other, had none of the stubbornness, the independent look which characterised phagor. It was, in the main, the two horns which had caused SartoriIrvrash to jump to the wrong conclusion.

One of the animals turned its head to look at the ship. Seizing the instant, the other animal lowered its forehead and rammed forward with a powerful shoulder movement. The sound of the blow reached the ship. Though the animal had moved no more than three feet, the whole weight of its body from its rear legs on was behind the butt.

The other animal staggered. It tried to recover. Before its head could go down, a second butt came. Its rear feet slipped. It fell backwards, struggling. It struck the water with a great splash. The *Golden Friendship* drifted onward. The scene was hidden in the mist.

"I expect you recognise them," said a voice at SartoriIrvrash's elbow. "They're flambreg, of the bovidae family."

Priest-Militant Admiral Odi Jeseratabhar had scarcely spoken to SartoriIrvrash during the voyage. He had, however, lost no chance in observing her about her duties. She had a good head and carried herself well. Despite the severe lines of her face, her manner was animated, and the men responded willingly to her orders. The inflections of her voice and her uniform proclaimed her to be a grand person; yet her approach was informal, conveying even a hint of eagerness. He liked her.

"This is a desolate shore, ma'am."

"There are worse. In primitive times, Uskotoshk used to land its convicts here and leave them to fend for themselves." She smiled and shrugged, as if dismissing past follies. Her blond plaits escaped from under the flat nautical cap she wore.

"Did the convicts survive?"

"Indeed. Some intermarried with the local population, the Loraji. In an hour, some of us will be going ashore. To compensate for my discourtesy in ignoring you so far, I invite you to come along as my guest. You can see what Persecution looks like."

"I would be glad to do so." He realised as he spoke how excellent it would be to escape the ship for a while.

The *Golden Friendship,* with the *Union* close behind, was inching through the silent waters. As the mist cleared, a solemn shoreline of cliff was revealed, without colour. At a place where the cliffs were eroded, the land fell to meet the ocean. Towards this point the ships slowly headed, tracing a

course through a number of small islands, little more than congregations of stones. Gravel spits also barred the way. From one spit, the ribs of an ancient wreck protruded. But eventually the *Friendship*'s anchor was lowered, and the jolly boat after it. The shouts of the sailors sounded hollow against the desolation.

Odi Jeseratabhar chivalrously helped SartoriIrvrash down the side of the ship. The Pasharatids followed, then six men armed with heavy wheel locks. The phagor rowers bent over their oars, and the boat moved between confining spits towards a ruined jetty.

The phagorlike flambreg were the possessors of the scene. Two large males were fighting with locked horns on a stoney beach, their hoofs clashing on broken shells. Males had small manes; otherwise the sexes could scarcely be distinguished. As with other Helliconian species, there was little sexual dimorphism, owing to the more marked seasonal dimorphism. Both male and female flambreg varied in colour from black to shades of russet, with white underparts. They stood four feet or more high at the shoulder. All wore smooth horns sweeping upwards. Face markings varied.

"This is their mating season," said the Priest-Militant Admiral. "Only the fury of rut drives the beasts to venture into the icy water."

The boat slid against the jetty and the party climbed out. There were sharp stones underfoot. In the distance, detonations could be heard, as ice fell from a glacier into the sea. The cloud overhead was iron grey. The phagor rowers stayed huddled in the boat, clutching their oars, unmoving.

An army of crabs rushed out to surround the landing party, raising their asymmetrical arms in menace. They did not attack. The musketeers killed some with gun butts, whereupon their fellows set on them and wrenched them apart. No sooner was this feast begun, and the crabs off guard, than toothed fish jumped from the shallow water, seized one of the crustacea apiece, and sank away from view.

Lining up smartly in this idyllic spot, the marksmen worked in pairs with their weapons, one aiming, one supporting the muzzle. Their targets were some female flambreg who milled about on the shore a few yards away, oblivious to the party

from the *Golden Friendship*. The guns went off. Two females fell, kicking.

The marksmen changed positions and guns. A further three shots. This time, three cows fell kicking. The rest of the herd fled.

Men and phagors now splashed through shallow water and over spits, shouting, cheered on by cries from the ships, where the rails were lined with men watching the sport.

Two of the flambreg were not dead. One marksman carried a short-bladed knife. With this, he slit their spinal cords as they tried to stagger to their feet and run.

Great white birds came winging in upon the scene, to hover above the men on an updraught, their heads flicking this way and that as they scented death. They swooped, fanning the men with their wings and raking one with long talons.

The sailors fought off both crabs and birds as the knifeman went about his work. With one long stroke, he opened up the bellies of the dead animals. Reaching inside, he pulled forth their bowels and livers, casting them aside to steam on the shore. With quick chopping movements, he severed the hind legs from the trunks. Golden blood oozed up his arm. The birds screamed overhead.

Phagors carried the legs and carcasses back to the jolly boat.

Another round of killing took place. Meanwhile, the Pasharatids had brought a sledge from the boat. Four sturdy phagors seized up the traces and pulled it to the shore. Sartori-Irvrash was invited to follow.

"We will give you a short trip to view the country," Jeseratabhar said, with a tight smile. He thought that this was their excuse to seize a respite from the ship. He fell in beside her, matching her pace.

A strong smell of farmyard met them. The flambreg were cantering about as if nothing had happened, while the white birds fought for offal. Following the sledge, the humans laboured up the slope. They saw other animals resembling flambreg, but with shaggier, greyer coats and ringed horns. These were yelk. Dienu Pasharatid said disdainfully that yelk should have been shot instead of flambreg. Red meat was better than yellow.

No one responded to this comment. SartoriIrvrash glanced at Io. The man's face was closed. He seemed entirely remote. Was he possibly thinking about the queen?

They made their way up between immense boulders deposited by a vanished glacier. On some boulders were scratched ancient names and dates, where convicts had sought to memorialise themselves.

The party reached more level ground. Breathing deeply, they surveyed the panorama. The two ships lay on the fringes of a black sheet of water to which the shelves of a black sky came down. Small icebergs stood here and there; some, caught in a current, moved rapidly towards the sombre distance and could be mistaken for sails. But there was no other human life.

On their other hand lay the land of Loraj, which stretched into the Circumpolar Regions. The mists were still dispersing, to reveal a plain almost without feature. In its very blankness was a grandeur of a kind. Beneath their feet, the ground was grassless, stamped with the imprints of thousands upon thousands of hoofprints.

"These plains belong to the flambreg, the yelk, and the giant yelk," Dienu Pasharatid said. "And not just the plains, but the whole land."

"It's not a place for men and women," said Io Pasharatid.

"Flambreg and yelk look similar, yet differ anatomically," said Odi Jeseratabhar. "The yelk are necrogenes. Their young are born from their corpses and feed on their carrion instead of milk. Flambreg are viviparous."

SartoriIrvrash said nothing. He was still shaken from the slaughter on the shore. The guns were still firing. The object of the ships' putting in to Persecution was precisely to obtain fresh meat.

The four phagors now pulled the four humans along in the sledge. The plain proved to be sodden, pitted with ponds and muskegs. Progress was slow. To the north stretched low mustard-coloured hills, their flanks patched with dwarf spruce and other hardy trees. The trees had less success on the plain, where their branches were weighed down with the clumsy nests of birds, built from sticks and driftwood. The leaves of the trees were fouled with white droppings.

The ships and the sea sank from view. The air was chill, less

loaded with sea taint. A stink of rutting animals lay over the ground. The sound of firing died in the distance. They travelled for almost an hour without speaking, relishing the great space about them.

The Priest-Militant Admiral called a halt beside a striated ochre boulder. They climbed from the sledge, marching about separately, swinging their arms. The boulder loomed over them. The only sounds were bird cries and the sough of the wind, until they detected a distant rumbling.

To SartoriIrvrash, the rumble suggested only a distant glacier breaking. He dismissed it in his pleasure at having ground beneath his feet again. The women, however, looked gravely at each other and climbed without speaking to stand on top of the boulder. They scanned the landscape and gave cries of alarm.

"You, brutes, draw the sledge close under the rock," Odi Jeseratabhar called in Hurdhu to the phagors.

The rumble became a thunder. The thunder rose from the earth, from everywhere. Something was happening to the low slopes to the west. They were in motion. With the terror of someone faced with a natural event beyond the scope of his imagination, SartoriIrvrash ran to the rock and began to climb. Io Pasharatid helped him scramble to a shoulder where there was room for all four of them. The phagors stood against the boulder, milts flicking up their nose slots.

"We'll be safe here till they pass," said Odi Jeseratabhar. Her voice shook.

"What is it?" SartoriIrvrash asked.

Through a thin haze, the distance was rolling itself up like a rug and tumbling towards them. They could only watch in silence. The rug resolved itself into an avalanche of flambreg, advancing on a wide front.

SartoriIrvrash tried to count them. Ten, twenty, fifty, a hundred—it was impossible. The front of the advance was a mile wide—two, five miles wide, and comprised herd after herd of animals. Endless ranks of yelk and flambreg were converging on the plain where the boulder stood.

The ground, the rock, the very air, vibrated.

Necks extended, eyes glaring, saliva flowing free from open mouths, the herds came on. They wove their living streams

about the boulder, joined them at its far side, and passed on. White cowbirds sailed above them, keeping pace with no more than an occasional dip of a wing.

In their excitement, the four humans stretched out their arms, screamed, waved, cheered with exhilaration.

Beneath them was a sea of hoofed life stretching back to and beyond the horizon. Not a single beast looked up at the gesticulating humans; each knew that to miss its footing meant death.

The human exhilaration soon faded. The four sat down, huddling close. They looked about with increasing listlessness. Still the herd passed. Batalix rose, Batalix set in concentric aureoles of light. Still there was no sign of the end of the herd. The animals continued to flow by in their thousands.

Some flambreg detached themselves from the stampede to mill about by the bay. Others plunged straight into the sea. Still others galloped in a trance over the cliffs to their death. The main body of animals thundered down into the dip and up the other side, heading towards the northeast. Hours passed. The animals continued with their monotonous drumbeats of noise.

Overhead, magnificent curtains of light unfolded and flashed, rising to the zenith. But the humans became despondent: the life which had exhilarated them earlier now depressed them. They huddled together on their ledge. The four phagors stood pressed against the wall of rock, the sledge before them for protection.

Freyr sloped shallowly towards the horizon. Rain began to fall, at first uncertainly. The lights overhead were extinguished as the fall became heavier, soaking the ground and changing the sound of the hoofbeats.

Icy rain fell for hours. Once it had established itself, it prevailed like the herd, with no variation to its monotony.

The darkness and noise isolated SartoriIrvrash and Odi Jeseratabhar slightly from the others. They clung together for protection.

The hammer of animals and elements penetrated him. He crouched with his brow against the rib cage of the admiral, expecting death, reviewing his life.

It was the loneliness that did it, he thought. A deliberate

loneliness, lifelong. I allowed myself to drift away from my brothers. I neglected my wife. Because I was so lonely. My learning sprang from that awful sense of loneliness: by my learning I set myself further apart from my fellows. Why? What possessed me?

And why did I tolerate JandolAnganol for so long? Did I recognise a torment in him similar to mine? I admire JandolAnganol—he lets the pain come to the surface. But when he took hold of me, it was like a rape. I can't forgive that, or the deliberate wanton accursed burning of my books. He burnt my defences. He'd burn the world down if he could. . . .

I'm different now. Severed from my loneliness. I will be different, if we escape. I like this woman Odi. I'll show it.

And somewhere in this ghastly wilderness of life I will find the means to bring JandolAnganol low. For years, I swallowed insults, ate bitterness. Now—I'm not too old—I'll see to it for everyone's sake that he is brought low. He brought me low. I'll bring him low. It's not noble, but my nobility has gone. Nobility's for scum.

He laughed and the cold froze his front teeth.

He discovered that Odi Jeseratabhar was weeping, and possibly had been for some while. Boldly, he clutched her to him, inching his way across their perch until his rough cheek was against hers. Every inch was accompanied by the limitless drumming of hoofs across a dark void.

He whispered almost random words of consolation.

She turned so that their mouths were almost touching. "To me falls blame for this. I should have foreseen it might happen . . ."

Something else she said, snatched away by the storm. He kissed her. It was almost the last voluntary gesture left him. Warmth lit inside him.

The journey away from JandolAnganol had changed him. He kissed her again. She responded. They tasted a mutual rain on their lips.

Despite their discomfort, the humans slipped into a sort of coma. When they woke, the rain had faded to no more than a drizzle. The herd was still passing the rock. Still it stretched to the far horizon on either side. They were forced to relieve their bladders by crouching at one edge of the boulder. The phagors

and the sledge had been swept away while they were asleep. Nothing remained.

What caused them to rouse was an invasion of flies which arrived with the herd. As there was more than one kind of animal in the great stampede, so there was more than one kind of animal among the flying invasion; all kinds were capable of drawing blood. They settled in their thousands on the humans, who were forced to fold themselves into a small huddle and cover themselves with cloaks and keedrants. Any skin exposed was instantly settled on and sucked till it bled.

They lay in stifling misery, while beneath them the great boulder shook as if still traveling on the glacier which had deposited it on the plain. Another day went by. Another dimday, another night.

Batalix rose again to a scene of rain and mist. At last the force of the herd slackened. The main body had gone by. Stragglers still passed, often mother flambreg with yearlings. The torment of flies lessened. Towards the northeast, the thunder of the disappearing herd still sounded. Many flambreg still milled about along the coastline.

Trembling and stiff, the humans climbed and slid to the ground. There was nothing for it but to make their way back to the shore on foot. With the stench of animal in their nostrils, they staggered forward, assailed by flies every inch of the way. Not a word passed between them.

The ship sailed on. They left Persecution Bay. The four who had been stranded in the midst of the stampede lay below decks in a fever induced by exposure and the bites of the flies.

Through SatroriIrvrash's delirious brain travelled the herd, ever on, covering the world. The reality of that mass presence would not go away, struggle against it as he would. It remained even when he recovered.

As soon as he was strong enough, he went without ceremony to talk to Odi Jeseratabhar. The Priest-Militant Admiral was pleased to see him. She greeted him in a friendly fashion and even extended a hand, which he took.

She sat in her bunk covered only by a red sheet, her fair hair wild about her shoulders. Out of uniform, she looked gaunter

than ever, but more approachable.

"All ships sailing long distances call in at Persecution Bay," she said. "They pick up new victuals, meat chiefly. The Priest-Sailors Guild contains few vegetarians. Fish. Seal. Crabs. I have seen the flambreg stampedes before. I should have been more alert. They draw me. What do you think of them?"

He had noticed this habit in her before. While weaving a spell of Sibish tenses about herself, she would suddenly break out with a question to disconcert the listener.

"I never knew there were so many animals in the world . . ."

"There are more than you can imagine. More than anyone can/should imagine. They live all around the skirts of the great ice cap, in the bleak Circumpolar lands. Millions of them. Millions and millions."

She smiled in her excitement. He liked that. He realised how lonely he was when she smiled.

"I assume they were migrating."

"Not that, to the best of my knowledge. They come down to the water, but do not stay. They travel at all times of the year, not just in spring. They may simply be driven by desperation. They have only one enemy."

"Wolves?"

"Not wolves." She gave a wolflike grin, glad to have caught him out. "Flies. One fly in particular. That fly is as big as the top joint of my thumb. It has yellow stripes—you can't mistake it. It lays its eggs in the skin of the wretched bovidae. When the larvae hatch, they burrow through the hide, enter the bloodstream, and eventually lie in pockets under the skin on the back. There the grubs grow big, in a sore the size of a large fruit, until eventually they burst out of their crater and fall to the ground to begin the life cycle again. Almost every flambreg we kill has such a parasite—often several.

"I have seen individual animals run in torment till they dropped, or cast themselves off tall cliffs, to escape that yellow-striped fly."

She regarded him benevolently, as if this account gave her some inward satisfaction.

"Madame, I was shocked when your men shot a few cows on the shore. Yet it was nothing. I see now. Nothing."

She nodded.

"The flambreg are a force of nature. Endless. Endless. They make humanity appear as nothing. The estimated population of Sibornal is twenty-five million at present. There are many times—perhaps a thousand times—that number of flambreg on the continent. As many flambreg as there are trees. It is my belief that once all Helliconia consisted only of those cattle and those flies, ceaselessly coming and going throughout the continents, the bovidae perpetually suffering a torment they perpetually tried to escape."

Before this vision, both parties fell silent. SartoriIrvrash returned to his cabin. But a few hours later, Odi Jeseratabhar sought him out. He was embarrassed to receive her in his stinking cubbyhole.

"Did my talk of unlimited flambreg make you gloomy?" There was coquetry in her question, surely.

"On the contrary. I am delighted to meet with someone like you, so interested in the processes of this world. I wish they were more clearly understood."

"They are better understood in Sibornal than elsewhere." Then she decided to soften the boast by adding, "Perhaps because we experience more seasonal change than you do in Campannlat. You Borlienese can forget the Great Winter in Summer. One sometimes fears/fearing when alone that, if next Weyr-Winter becomes just a few degrees colder, then there will be no humans left. Only phagors, and the myriad mindless flambreg. Perhaps mankind is—a temporary accident."

SartoriIrvrash contemplated her. She had brushed her hair free to her shoulders. "I have thought the same myself. I hate phagors, but they are more stable than we. Well, at least the fate of mankind is better than that of the ceaselessly driven flambreg. Though we certainly have our equivalents of the yellow-striped fly . . ." He hesitated, wanted to hear more from her, to test her intelligence and sensibilities. "When I first saw the flambreg, I thought how closely they resembled ancipitals."

"Closely, in many respects. Well, my friend, you pass for learned. What do you make of that resemblance?" She was testing him, as her pleasantly teasing manner indicated. By

common consent, they sat down side by side on his bunk.

"The Madis resemble us. So do Nondads and Others, though more remotely. There seems to be no family connection between humans and Madis, though Madi-human matings are sometimes fertile of offspring. Princess Simoda Tal is one such sport. I never heard that phagors mate with flambreg." He gave a dry laugh at his uncertainty.

"Supposing that the genethlic divinities who shape us have made a family connection, as you call it, between humankind and Madikind? Would you then accept that there was a connection between flambreg and phagors?"

"That would have to be determined by experiment." He was on the brink of explaining his breeding experiments in Matrassyl, then decided to reserve that topic for another time. "A genetic relationship implies outward similarities. Phagors and flambreg have golden blood as a protection against cold . . ."

"There is proof without experiment. I do not believe as most people do that every species is created separately by God the Azoiaxic." She lowered her voice as she said this. "I believe the boundaries blur with time, as the boundary between human and Madi will blur again when your Jandol-Anganol weds Simoda Tal. You see where I lead?"

Was she secretly an atheist, as he was? To SartoriIrvrash's amazement, the thought gave him an erection. "Tell me."

"I have not heard of phagors and flambreg mating, that's true. However, I have good reason to believe that once this world held nothing but flambreg and flies—both in countless and mindless millions. Through genetic change, ancipitals developed from flambreg. They're a refined version. What do you think? Is it possible?"

He tried to match her manner of argument.

"The similarities may be several, but they are mainly surface ones, apart from blood colour. You might as well say men and phagors are alike because both species talk. Phagors stand erect like us. They have their own cast of intelligence. Flambreg have nothing of the kind—unless galloping madly back and forth across a continent is intelligent."

"The phagorian ability to walk upright and use language came after the two bloodlines divided. Imagine that phagors

developed from a group of flambreg which . . . which found
an alternative to ceaseless flight as a way of dealing with the
fly problem."

They were gazing at each other with excitement. He longed
to tell Odi of his discovery regarding hoxneys.

"What alternative?"

"Hiding in caves, for instance. Going underground. Free of
the fly torment, they developed intelligence. Stood upright to
see further and then had forefeet free to use tools. In the dark,
language developed as a substitute for sight. I'll show you my
essay on the subject one day. Nobody else has seen it."

He laughed to think of flambreg performing such tricks.

"Not over one generation, dear friend. Over many. Endless
generations. The cleverer ones would win. Don't laugh." She
tapped his hand. "If this did not happen in past time, then let
me ask you this. How is it that the gestation period for gillots
is one Batalix-year—while the gestation period for a flambreg
cow is exactly the same length of time? Doesn't that prove a
genetic relationship?"

Sailing on, the two ships passed the lowly ports of the southernmost coast of Loraj, which lay inside the tropics. From the
port of Ijivibir, a caravel of 600 tons named the *Good Hope*
sailed out to join the *Golden Friendship* and the *Union*. It
made a brave sight, with its sails painted in vertical stripes.
Cannon were fired from the flagship in greeting, and the
sailors gave a cheer. On an empty ocean, three vessels were
many more than two.

Another occasion was marked when they had reached the
most westerly point of their course at a longitude of 29° East.
The time was ten to twenty-five. Freyr was below the horizon,
trawling an apricot glow above. The glow dissolving the
horizon seemed to radiate from the hazy water. It marked the
grave from which the great sun would presently rise. Somewhere concealed in that glow lay the sacred country of
Shivenink; somewhere in Shivenink, high in the mountains
that ran all the way from sea to North Pole, was the Great
Wheel of Kharnabhar.

A bugle sounded All Hands. The three ships clustered.

Prayers were said, music played, all stood to pray with finger to forehead.

Out of the apricot haze came a sail. By a trick of the light, it appeared and disappeared like a vision. Birds screamed about its masts, newly away from land.

It was an all-white ship, sails white, hull fresh with white-wash. As it drew nearer, firing a gun in salute, those aboard the other ships saw that it was a caravel, no bigger than the *Good Hope;* but on its mainsail stood the great hierogram representing the Wheel itself, inner and outer circles connected by wavy lines. This was the *Vajabhar Prayer,* named after Shivenink's chief port.

The four ships tacked close, like four pigeons nestling together on a branch. A bark of orders from the Priest-Militant Admiral herself. Bowsprits turned, cordage creaked, artemons filled. The little fleet began to sail southwards.

Colours in the water changed to a deeper blue. The ships were leaving the Pannoval Sea astern and entering the northern margins of the vast Climent Ocean. Immediately, they struck rough weather. They had a hard time of it, combatting mountainous seas and hazardous storms, in which they were bombarded by gigantic hailstones. For days, they saw neither sun.

When at last they reached calmer waters, Freyr's zenith was lower than before, and Batalix's somewhat higher. To port lay the cliffs of Campannlat's westernmost redoubt, Cape Findowel. Once they had rounded Findowel they sailed into the nearest anchorage along the coast of the tropical continent, there to rest for two days. The carpenters repaired the storm damage, the members of the Priest-Sailors Guild stitched sails or else swam in a warm lagoon. So welcome was the sight of men and women disporting themselves naked in the water—the puritanical Sibornalese were curiously unprudish on this occasion—that even SartoriIrvrash ventured into the water in a pair of silken underpants.

When he rested afterwards on the beach, sheltering from the power of both suns, he watched the swimmers climb out one by one. Many of the *Good Hope*'s crew were women, and sturdily built. He sighed for his youth. Io Pasharatid climbed out beside him and said to him quietly, "If only that beautiful

queen of queens were here, eh?''

"What then?'' He kept watching the water, hoping that Odi would emerge naked.

Pasharatid dug him in the ribs in an un-Sibornalese way.

"What then, you say? Why, then this seeming paradise would be paradise indeed.''

"Do you suppose that this expedition can possibly conquer Borlien?''

"Given the fortune of war, I'm sure of it. We are organised and armed, in a way JandolAnganol's forces will never be.''

"Why, then the queen will come under your supervision.''

"That reflection had not escaped me. Why else do you think I have this sudden enthusiasm for war? I don't want Ottassol, you old goat. I want Queen MyrdemInggala. And I intend to have her.''

XV

THE CAPTIVES OF THE QUARRY

A man was walking with a pack slung over one shoulder. He wore the tattered remains of a uniform. Both suns beat down on him. Streams of sweat ran down into his tunic. He walked blindly, rarely looking up.

He was traversing a destroyed area of jungle in the Chwart Heights in eastern Randonan. All round were blackened and broken stumps of trees, many still smouldering. On the few occasions when the man looked about him, he could see nothing but the trail and blackened landscape all round. Palls of grey smoke rose in the distance. It was possible that tropical heat had started the blaze. Or perhaps a spark from a matchlock had been the cause of the death of a million trees. For many tenners battles had been fought over the area. Now soldiers and cannon were gone, and the vegetation likewise.

Everything about the man's posture expressed weariness and defeat. But he kept on. Once he faltered, when one of his shadows faded and disappeared. Black cloud, rolling up, had blotted out Freyr. A few minutes later, Batalix too was

swallowed. Then the rain came down. The man bowed his head and continued to walk. There was nowhere he could shelter, nothing he could do but submit to nature.

The downpour continued, increasing in ferocity by sudden fits. The ashes hissed. More and more of the resources of the heavens were called in, like reserves being brought into a battle.

Bombardment by hail was the next tactic. The hailstones stung the weary man into a run. He took what refuge he could in a hollow tree stump. Falling back against the crumbling wood, he exposed a stronghold of rickybacks. Deprived of their little fortress, the crustaceans climbed through veritable Takissas of liquid ash, seeking refuge with their puny antennae waving.

Unaware of this catastrophe, the man stared forth from under the brim of his hat, panting. Several bent figures staggered through the murk. They were the remnants of his army, the once celebrated Borlienese Second Army. One man passed obliviously within inches of the tree stump, dragging a terrible wound which bled afresh under the hailstones. The shelterer wept. He had no wound, except for a bruise on his temple. He had no right to be alive.

Like an uncomforted child, his weeping turned to exhaustion; he slept despite the hail.

The dreams that terminated sleep were full of hail. He felt their smart on his cheek, woke, saw that the sky was again clear. He started up, yet still the stones struck his face, his neck. As he gasped with vexation, a stone flew into his mouth. He spat it out, turning in bewilderment.

The gnarled, broomlike plants nearby had been burnt by fire. Fire had hardened their seedcases, ripening their seeds with its flame. In a new day's warmth, the cases untwisted. They made a small noise, like the parting of moist lips. Their seeds were shot out in all directions. The ashy ground would provide fertile conditions for growth.

He laughed, suddenly pleased. Whatever folly mankind got up to, nature went on its uncheckable way. And he would go on his way. He patted his sword, adjusted his hat, hitched his pack, and started walking southeastwards.

He emerged from the devastated area towards noon. The

way wound down between thickets of shoatapraxi. Over centuries, the road the soldier travelled had been by turns river,
dried bed, ice track, cattle trail, and highway. No man could
trace its usages. Humble flowers grew beside its banks, some
sprung from parent plants which had seeded far away. The
banks became higher on either side. He staggered between
them, hampered by shifting gravels underfoot. When they
crumbled away at last, under the brow of a hill, he saw cottages standing in fields.

The prospect did little to reassure him.

The fields had long been untended. The cottages were dere-
lict. Many roofs had fallen in, leaving end-walls pointing like
old fists to the sky. Hedges topping the banks on either side of
the track had collapsed from the weight of dust that had been
thrown up. Dust had spread over adjoining fields, over cottages and outbuildings, over abandoned pieces of luggage
which dotted the view. Everything was rendered in the same
greyish tone, as if created all from one material.

Only a great army passing could have raised so much dust,
the man with the pack thought. The army had been his. The
Second Army had then been marching forward into battle. He
was now returning silently in defeat.

His footsteps deadened, General Hanra TolramKetinet
walked down the meandering street. One or two furtive
phagors peered at him from the ruins, the long masks of their
faces without expression. He did not remember this village; it
was just one more village they had marched through on just
one more hot day. As he reached the end of the street and the
sacred pillar which defined the local land-octave, he saw a
wedge-shaped copse which he thought he recalled, a copse
which his scouts had reconnoitred for enemy. If he was right,
there was a sizeable farmhouse beyond it, in which he had
slept for a few hours.

The farmhouse remained intact. It was surrounded by out-
houses which had been damaged by fire.

TolramKetinet stood by the gateway, peering in. Both yard
and house were silent except for the buzz of flies. Sword in
hand, he moved forward. Two slaughtered hoxneys lay in an
open stall, bodies black with flies. Their stench met his nostrils.

Freyr was high, Batalix already westering. Conflicting
shadows lent the house a drab air as he moved towards it. The
windows were dimmed with dust. There had been a woman
here, the farmer's woman, with four small children, he recalled. No man. Now there was only the buzz of silence.

He set his pack down by the front doorstep and kicked the
door open with his foot.

"Anyone there?" He hoped some of his men might be
resting in the rooms.

No response. Yet his alerted senses warned him that there
was a living thing in the building. He paused in the stone hall.
A tall pendulum clock, with its twenty-five illuminated hours,
stood silent against one wall. Otherwise, the impression was
one of the poverty common to an area which has long been in
a war zone. Beyond the hall everything lay in shadow.

Then he marched determinedly forward, down the passage,
and into a low-ceilinged kitchen.

Six phagors stood in the kitchen. They stood motionless,
as if awaiting his return. Their eyes glowed deep pink in the
shade. Beyond them, through a window, grew a patch of
bright yellow flowers; catching the sun, they made the beast
shapes indeterminate. Yellow reflections rested on shoulders,
on long cheekbones. One of the brutes retained its horns.

They came towards him, but TolramKetinet was ready. He
had picked up their scent in the hall. They held spears, but he
was a practised swordsman. They were swift, but they got in
each other's way. He drove the blade up under their rib cages,
where he knew their eddre were. Only one of the ancipitals
lunged with its spear. He half-severed its forearm with a single
blow. Gold blood flew. The room filled with their heavy sick
breathing. All died without making any other sound.

As they fell, he saw by their blazes that they had been
trusted members of his guard. Catching the Sons of Freyr in
disorder, they had taken a chance and reverted to type. A less
wary soldier would have fallen into their ambush. Indeed, one
had done so recently. At the back of the kitchen, spread out
on a table, was a Borlienese corporal, his throat neatly bitten
out.

TolramKetinet went back into the courtyard and leaned
against a warm outer wall. After a short while, his nausea

passed. He stood breathing in the warm air, until the stench of nearby decay drove him from the courtyard.

He could not rest here. When his strength returned, he picked up his pack and resumed his silent march along the road leading towards the coast. Towards the sea and its voices.

The forest closed about him. The road south led through twisted columns of spirax trees, with their double entwined trunks. Through their avenues walked TolramKetinet. This was not dense tangled jungle. Little grew on its floor, for little sunlight penetrated down to the ground. He walked as in a lofty building, surrounded by pillars of amazing design.

Above spread other layers of the forests which separated Borlien from Randonan. The shrub layer, through which large creatures sometimes crashed. The understory, where Others swung and called, occasionally dropping to the floor, to snatch at a fungus before swarming up to the safety of the branches. The canopy, the true roof of the jungle, decked with flowers TolramKetinet could not see, and birds he could only hear. The emergent layer, formed by the tallest trees, which reared above the canopy, home of predatory birds which watched and did not sing.

The solemnity of the rain forest was such that it appeared to those who ventured into it to be much more permanent than savannah land or even desert. It was not so. Of the 1825 small Helliconian years which made one Great Year, the elaborate jungle organism was able to sustain itself for less than half that period. Closely examined, every single tree revealed, in root, trunk, branch, and seed, the strategies it employed to survive when climate was less clement, when it would endure solitary in a howling waste, or wait in a case, petrified, beneath snow.

The fauna regarded the various layers of their home as unchanging. The truth was that the whole intricate edifice, more marvellous than any work of man, had come into being only a few generations ago in response to the elements, springing up like a jack-in-the-box from a scattering of nuts.

In this hierarchy of plants was a perfect order which appeared random only to an untutored eye. Everything, animal or insect or vegetable, had its place, generally a horizontal zone, to call its own. The Others were rare exceptions to this

rule. Phagors had taken refuge in the forest, often living in huts contrived in the angles between high-kneed roots, and Others had gravitated into their company, to play a role somewhere between pet and slave.

Often, settlements of a dozen or more phagors, with their runts, were established about the base of a large tree. TolramKetinet gave such places a wide berth. He deeply mistrusted the phagors, and feared the sorties made by their Others, who came rushing out like watchdogs when strangers were near, brandishing sticks.

Men sometimes lurked in these settlements. A small human hut was to be seen next to—and little to be distinguished from—an ancipital hut. These men, near-naked, were evidently accepted by the phagors as large versions of Others. It was as though the brown-pelted Others, in their alliance with the phagors, gave a licence to the men to live in lowly harmony with them.

Most of the men were deserters from units of the Second Army. TolramKetinet spoke to them, trying to persuade them to join him. Some did so. Others threw sticks. Many admitted that they hated the war and rejoined their old commander only because they were sick of the jungle with its secretive noises and slender diet.

After a day of marching along the aisles of the rain forest, they fell back into their old military roles again and accepted as if with relief the ancient disciplines of command. Tolram-Ketinet also changed. His stance had been that of a defeated man. Now he pulled his shoulders back and took on something of his old swagger. The lines of his face tightened; he could again be recognised as a young man. The more men there were to take orders, the more easily he gave orders, and the more right they seemed. With the mutability of the human race, he became what those about him regarded him as being.

So the small force arrived at the Kacol River.

Powered by their new spirit, they launched a surprise raid and took the shantytown of Ordelay. With this victory, fighting spirit was entirely restored.

Among the craft on the Kacol was an ice ship, flying the flag of the Lordryardry Ice Trading Company. When the town was invaded, this vessel, the *Lordryardry Lubber,* tried to make its

escape downstream, but TolramKetinet intercepted it with a group of men.

The terrified captain protested that he was a neutral and claimed diplomatic immunity. His business in Ordelay was not merely to trade in ice but to hand a letter to General Hanra TolramKetinet.

"Do you know where this general is?" demanded Tolram-Ketinet.

"Somewhere in the jungle, losing the king's war for him."

With a sword at his throat, the captain said that he had sent a paid messenger to deliver the message; there his obligations ended. He had carried out Captain Krillio Muntras's instructions.

"What said the contents of the letter?" TolramKetinet demanded.

The man swore he did not know. The leather wallet which contained it was sealed with the seal of the queen of queens, MyrdemInggala. How would he dare tamper with a royal message?

"You would never rest until you found out what was in it. Speak, you scoundrel!"

He needed encouragement. When crushed under an upturned table, the captain admitted that the seal of the wallet had come unstuck on its own. He had happened to notice, without meaning to, that the queen of queens was being sent into exile by King JandolAnganol, to a place on the north coast of the Sea of Eagles called Gravabagalinien; that she feared for her life; and that she hoped that she might one day see her good friend the general delivered from the dangers of war into her presence. She prayed that Akhanaba would guard him from all ills.

When he heard this, TolramKetinet became pale. He went away and looked over the side of the boat at the dark-flowing river, so that his soldiers should not see his face. Expectations, fears, desires, woke in him. He uttered a prayer that he might be more successful in love than in war.

TolramKetinet's party put the battered captain of the *Lubber* ashore and commandeered his boat. They caroused for a day in town, stacked the ice ship with provisions, and sailed for the distant ocean.

*   *   *

High above the jungle, the Avernus sailed in its orbit. There were those on the observation satellite, unfamiliar with the varieties of warfare practised on the planet below, who asked what kind of force could have defeated the Borlienese Second Army. They looked in vain for a set of swaggering Randonanese patriots who had repelled the invasion of their homeland.

There was no such force. The Randonanese were semi-savage tribes who lived in harmony with their environment. Some tribes cultivated patches of cereal. All lived surrounded by dogs and pigs which, when young, were allowed to suckle indiscriminately at the breasts of nursing mothers if they so desired. They killed for the pot and not for sport. Many tribes worshipped Others as gods, although that did not stop them killing such gods as they encountered swinging among the branches of the great forest home. Such was the mould of their mind that numbers of them worshipped fish, or trees, menses, spirits, or patches of double daylight.

In their humility, the tribes of Randonan tolerated the tribes of phagors, which were torpid, and consisted mainly of itinerant woodmen or fungusmongers. The phagors, in their turn, rarely attacked the human tribes, though the customary tales were told of stalluns carrying off human women.

The phagors brewed their own drink, raffel. On certain occasions, they brewed a different potion, which the Randonanese tribes called vulumunwun, believing it to be distilled from the sap of the vulu tree and from certain fungi. Unable to concoct vulumunwun themselves, they obtained it by barter from phagors. Then a feast would be held far into the night.

On these occasions, a great spirit often spoke to the tribes. It told them to go out and make sport in the Desert.

The tribes would bind their gods, the Others, to bamboo chairs and carry them away through the jungle on their shoulders. The whole tribe would go, babies, pigs, parrots, preets, cats, and all. They would cross the Kacol and enter what was officially Borlien. They would invade the richly cultivated lands of the central Borlienese plain.

This was the land the Randonanese called the Desert. It was

open to the skies; the suns blazed down. It had no great trees, no dense shrub, no secret places, no wild boar, no Others. In this godless place—with a final libation of vulumunwun—they dared make sport, setting fire to or despoiling the crops.

The plainsmen of Borlien were sturdy dark men. They hated the pale lizards who materialised like ghosts out of nowhere. They rushed from their little villages and drove off the invaders with any weapon that came to hand. Often they lost their own lives in the process, for the tribesmen had blow tubes from which they blew feathered thorns tipped with poison. Maddened, the farmers would leave their homes and burn down the forests. So it had finally come to war between Borlien and Randonan.

Aggression, defense, attack, and counterattack. These moves became confused in the enantiodromia which, in human minds, constantly turns all things into their opposites. By the time the Second Army deployed its platoons in the jungle-clad mountains of Randonan, the little tribesmen had themselves become, in the eyes of their enemies, a formidable military force.

Yet what had defeated TolramKetinet's expedition was no armed opposition. The defence of the tribes was to slide away into the jungle, shrieking through the night barbaric insults at the invaders, just as they heard the Others do. Like the Others, they took to the trees, to rain darts or urine down on the general's men. They could not properly wage war. The jungle did that for them.

The jungle was full of diseases to which the Borlienese army was not immune. Its fruits brought torrential dysenteries, its pools malarias, its days fevers, and its insects a sordid crop of parasites which fed on the men from the outside in or from the inside out. Nothing could be properly fought; everything had to be survived. One by one, or in batches, Borlienese soldiers succumbed to the jungle. With them went King Jandol-Anganol's ambitions for victory in the Western Wars.

As for that king, so distant from his army disintegrating in Randonan, he was suffering from difficulties almost as elaborate as the mechanisms of the jungle. The bureaucracies

of Pannoval were more enduring than the jungle and so had
longer to develop their entanglements. The queen of queens
had been gone from JandolAnganol's capital for many weeks,
and still his bill of divorcement had not arrived from the
capital of the Holy Empire.

As the heat intensified, Pannoval stepped up the drumble
against the ancipital species living on its lands. Fleeing phagor
tribes sought refuge in Borlien, against the general wishes of
the mass of people, who both hated and feared the shaggies.

The king felt differently. In a speech given in the scritina, he
welcomed the refugees, promising them land in the Cosgatt on
which they would be allowed to settle if they would join the
army and fight for Borlien. By this means, the Cosgatt, now
safe from the shadow of Darvlish, could be cultivated at low
cost, and the newcomers effectively removed from the presence of the Borlienese.

This human hand extended to the phagors pleased no one in
Pannoval or Oldorando, and the bill of divorcement was again
delayed.

But JandolAnganol was pleased with himself. He was suffering enough to appease his conscience.

He put on a bright jacket and went to see his father. Again
he walked through the winding ways of his palace and down
through the guarded doors to the cellarage where he kept the
old man. The chambers of the prison seemed more dank than
ever. JandolAnganol paused in the first chamber which had
once served as mortuary and torture chamber. Darkness
enclosed him. The sounds of the outer world were stilled.

"Father!" he said. His own voice sounded unnatural to his
ears.

He went through the second chamber and into the third,
where pallid light filtered in. The log fire smouldered as usual.
The old man, wrapped as usual in his blanket, sat before the
fire as usual, chin resting on chest. Nothing down here had
altered for many years. The only thing that had altered now
was that VarpalAnganol was dead.

The king stood for a while with one hand on his father's
shoulder. Thin though it was, the flesh was unyielding.

JandolAnganol went and stood under the high barred window. He called to his father. The skull with its wispy hair

never moved. He called again, louder. No movement.

"You're dead, aren't you?" said JandolAnganol, in tones of contempt. "Just one more betrayal. . . . By the beholder, wasn't I miserable enough with her gone?"

No answer came. "You've died, haven't you? Gone away to spite me, you old hrattock . . ."

He strode over to the fireplace and kicked the logs all over the cell, filling it with smoke. In his fury, he knocked the chair over, and the frail body of his father fell to the stones, remaining in its huddled position.

The king stooped over this tiny effigy, as if contemplating a snake, and then, with a sudden movement, fell to his knees—not to engage in prayer, but to seize the body by its dry throat and pour a flood of words upon it, in which the accusation that this dead thing had long ago turned his mother against him, quenching her love, was repeated in many forms, hissed forth with spiteful examples, until the words died and the king remained there bent over the body, wrapped in heavy coils of smoke. He beat the flagstones with his fist, then crouched motionless.

The logs strewn across the floor were extinguished by damp, each one by itself. At last, red-eyed, the king took himself away from the darkened place, going upwards with a hurried pace as if pursued, up to warmer regions.

Among the many denizens of the palace was an ancient nurse who lived in the servants' quarters and was bedridden most of the day. JandolAnganol had not entered the servants' quarters since he was a child. He found his way without hesitation through the mean corridors and confronted the old woman, who jumped out of bed and clung to one of its posts in terror. She glared at him aghast, pulling hair before her eyes.

"He's dead, your master and lover," JandolAnganol said, without expression. "See that he is prepared for burial."

Next day, a week of mourning was declared, and the Royal First Phagorian Guard paraded through the city in black.

The common people, starved of excitement by their poverty, were quick to spy upon the king's mood, at second or third hand if need be. Their connections with the palace were close, if subterranean. All knew someone who knew someone

who was in the royal employ; and they smelt out JandolAnganol's alternating moods of excitement and despair.
Bareheaded under the suns, they flocked to the holy ground
where VarpalAnganol, with the pomp due to a king, was to be
buried on his correct land-octave.

The service was presided over by the Archpriest of the
Dome of Striving, BranzaBaginut. The members of the scritina were there, housed in a stand erected for the occasion,
and draped with the banners of the house of Anganol. These
worthies showed on their faces more the heaviness of disap-
proval of the living king than grief for the dead one; but they
attended nevertheless, fearing the consequences if they did
not, and their wives attended them, for the same reason.

JandolAnganol made an isolated figure as he stood by the
open grave. He gave an occasional darting glance round, as if
hoping for sight of Robayday. This nervous glance became
more frequent as the body of his father, wrapped in a gold
cloth, was placed on its side in the place dug for it. Nothing
went down with him. All present knew what waited below, in
the world of the gossies, where material things were needed no
more. The only concession to the rank of the departed was
when twelve women of the court came forward to cast flowers
down upon the still form.

Archpriest BranzaBaginut closed his eyes and chanted.

"The seasons in their processes bear us away to our final octaves. As there are two suns, the lesser and the greater, so we
have two phases of being, life and death, the lesser and the
greater. Now a great king has gone from us into the greater
phase. He who knew the light has gone down into the
dark . . ."

And as his high voice silenced the whispering of the crowd,
who strained forward eagerly as the dogs which also attended
the ceremony were straining their noses toward the grave, the
first handfuls of earth were thrown.

At that moment, the king's voice rang out. "This villain
ruined my mother and myself. Why do you pray for such a
villain?"

He took a great leap across the lips of the pit, pushed the
Archpriest aside, and ran, still shouting, towards the palace,
the shoulders of which loomed above the hill. Beyond sight of
the crowd, he ran still, and would not stop until he was at his

stables and on his hoxney and riding madly out into the
woods, leaving Yuli to mewl far behind.

The disgraceful episode, this insult to the established
religion by a religious man, delighted the common population
of Matrassyl. It was talked about, laughed over, praised, condemned, in the rudest hut.

"He's a joker, is Jandol," was often the carefully considered verdict, arrived at in taverns after a long evening's drinking, where death was not regarded with much affection. And
the reputation of the joker rose accordingly, to the vexation of
his enemies on the scritina.

To the wrath not only of the joker's enemies but to that of a
slender young man, bronzed of skin and dressed in rags, who
attended the burial and witnessed the king's departure.
Robayday had been not far away, living on a fisherman's
island among the reedy waters of a lake, when news of his
grandfather's death reached him. He had returned to the
capital with the alertness of a deer which attempts a closer inspection of a lion.

Seeing the joker's retreat, he was emboldened to follow and
leaped on a hoxney, taking a track that had been familiar to
him since his youth. He had no intention of confronting his
father and did not even know what was in his own mind.

The joker, who had anything but humour on his mind, took
a path he had not taken since SartoriIrvrash had been expelled. It led to a quarry, hidden by the soft waxy stems of
young rajabaral trees; these saplings, with hundreds of years
of growth in them, were scarcely recognisable as the redoubtable wooden fortresses they would become when the summer
of the Great Year yielded once more to winter. His fever over,
the king tied Lapwing to a young tree. He rested a hand on the
smooth wood, and his head on his hand. To his mind came a
memory of the queen's body and of the cadency which had
once lit their love. Such good things had died, and he had not
known.

After a while in silence, he led Lapwing past the stump of
the parent rajabaral, as black as an extinct volcano. Ahead
stood the wooden palisade which barred entry to the quarry.
No one challenged him. He pushed his way in.

All was untended in the forecourt. Weeds thrived. The
lodge was in disrepair; a short neglect was leading it to a long

decay. An old man with a straggling white beard came forward and bowed low to his majesty.

"Where's the guard? Why isn't the gate locked?" But there was carelessness in his challenge, which he uttered over one shoulder, in the act of approaching the cages ahead.

The old man, accustomed to the king's moods, was too wise to adopt a matching carelessness, and followed with a lengthy explanation of how all but he were withdrawn from the quarry once the chancellor was disgraced. He was alone and still tended the captives, hoping thereby to incur the king's pleasure.

Far from showing pleasure, the king clasped his hands behind his back and assumed a melancholy face. Four large cages had been built against the cliffs of the quarry, each divided into various compartments for the greater comfort of its prisoners. Into these cages JandolAnganol sent his dark regard.

The first cage contained Others. They had been swinging there by hands, feet, or tails as a way of passing time; when the king moved towards their prison, they dropped down and came running to the bars, thrusting out their handlike paws, oblivious to the exalted status of their visitor.

The occupants of the second cage shrank away at the stranger's approach. Most of them flitted into their compartments, out of sight. Their prison was built on rock, so that they could not tunnel into the earth. Two of their number came forward and stood against the bars, looking up into JandolAnganol's face. These protognostics were Nondads, small elusive creatures often confused with Others, to whom they bore a resemblance. They stood waist-high to a human and their faces, with protruding muzzles, resembled Others. Scanty loincloths covered their genitals; their bodies were covered with light sandy hair.

The two Nondads who came forward addressed the king, flitting nervously about as they did so. A strange amalgam of whistles, clicks, and snorts served them for language. The king regarded them with an expression between contempt and sympathy before passing on to the third cage.

Here were imprisoned the more advanced form of protognostic, the Madis. Unlike the occupants of the first two cages, the Madis did not move when the king approached.

Robbed of their migratory existence, they had nowhere to go; neither the settings of the suns nor the comings and goings of kings held meaning for them. They tried to hide their faces in their armpits as JandolAnganol regarded them.

The fourth cage was built of stone, rough-hewn from the quarry, as a tribute to the greater firmness of will of its occupants, which were human—mainly men and women of Mordriat or Thribriatan tribes. The women slunk back into the shadows. Most of the men pressed forward and began eloquently to implore the king to release them, or at worst to allow no more experiments on them.

"There's nothing for it now," said the king to himself, moving about as restlessly as those imprisoned.

"Sir, the indignities we have suffered . . ."

Ash from Rustyjonnik still lay in odd corners, where weeds thrust from it, but the eruptions had ceased as suddenly as they began. The king kicked at the ash, raising a small dust storm with his boots.

Although he was most interested in the Madis and studied them from all angles, sometimes squatting to do so, he was too restless to remain in one place. Madi males struggled forward with one of their females, naked, and offered her to him as a condition of their release.

JandolAnganol broke away in disgust, his face working.

Bursting from behind the stone cage into the sunlight, he came face to face with RobaydayAnganol. Both became rigid like two cats, until Roba began to gesticulate, arms and fingers spread. Behind him came the white-haired old guard, shuffling his feet and complaining.

"Imprisoning them for the good of their sanity, mighty king," said Roba.

But JandolAnganol moved swiftly forward, flung an arm about his son's neck, and kissed him on the lips, as though he had decided on this approach a while ago.

"Where have you been, my son? Why so wild?"

"Can a boy not grieve among leaves, but must come to court to do so?" His words were indistinct as he backed away from his father, wiping his mouth with the back of his hand. As he bumped into the third cage, his other hand went behind him to support himself.

Immediately, one Madi reached out and grasped his fore-

arm. The naked female who had been offered to the king bit him savagely in the ball of his thumb. Roba screamed with pain. The king was at once at the cage with his sword drawn. The Madis fell back and Roba was released.

"They're as hungry for royal blood as Simoda Tal," said Roba, hopping about with his hands clutched between his legs. "You saw how she bit me in the balls! What a stepmotherly act was there!"

The king laughed as he sheathed his sword.

"You see what happens when you put your hand in other people's affairs."

"They're very vicious, sir, and certain they've been wronged," said the old guard from a safe distance.

"Your nature inclines toward captivity as frogs incline towards pools," Roba told his father, still skipping. "But free these wretched beings! They were Rushven's folly, not yours —you had greater follies afoot."

"My son, I have a phagor runt I care for, and perhaps he cares for me. He follows me for affection. Why do you follow me for abuse? Cease it, and live a sane life with me. I will not harm you. If I have wounded you, then I regret it, as you have long given me cause to regret it. Accept what I say."

"Boys are particularly difficult to bring up, sir," commented the guard.

Father and son stood apart, regarding each other. JandolAnganol had hooded his eagle gaze, and appeared calm. On Roba's smooth face was a smouldering rage.

"You need another runt following you? Haven't you captives enough in this infamous quarry? Why did you come up here to gloat over them?"

"Not to gloat. To learn. I should have learned from Rushven. I need to know—what Madis do. . . . I understand, boy, that you fear my love. You fear responsibility. You always have. Being a king is all responsibility . . ."

"Being a butterfly is a butterfly's responsibility."

Irritated by this remark, the king again took to pacing before the cages. "Here was all SatoriIrvrash's responsibility. Maybe he was cruel. He made the occupants of these four cages mate with each other in prescribed combinations in order to see what resulted. He wrote all down, as was his fashion. I burnt it all—as is my fashion, you will add. So, then.

"By his experiments, Rushven found a rule which he called a cline. He proved that the Others in Cage One could some-times produce progeny when mated with Nondads. Those progeny were infertile. No, the progeny of the Nondads breed-ing with Madis were infertile. I forget details. Madis could produce progeny when mated with the humans in Cage Four. Some of those progeny are fertile.

"He carried on his experiments for many years. If Others and Madis were forced to copulate, no issue resulted. Humans mating with Nondads produce no issue. There is a grading, a cline. These facts he discovered. Rushven was a gentle person. He did what he did for the sake of knowledge.

"You probably blame him, as you blame everyone but yourself. But Rushven paid for his knowledge. One day, two years ago—you were absent then, in the wilds as usual—his wife came to this quarry to feed the captives, and the Others broke out of their cage. They tore her to pieces. This old guard will tell you . . ."

"It was her arm I found first, sir," said the guard, pleased to be mentioned. "The left arm, to be partic'lar, sir."

"Rushven certainly paid for his knowledge. Roba, I have paid for mine. The time will come when you too have to pay a price. It won't always be summer."

Roba tore leaves from a bush as if he would destroy the bush, and wrapped the leaves about his wounded hand. The guard went to help him, but Roba kicked him away with a bare foot.

"This stinking place . . . these stinking cages . . . the stink-ing palace. . . . Taking notes of dirty little ruttings. . . . Once, look, before kings were born, the world was a big white ball in a black cup. Along came the great kzahhn of all ancipitals and mated with the queen of all the humans, split her open with his enormous prodo. and filled her right up with golden spume. That rumbo so shook the world that it jarred it out of its winter frigidity and caused the seasons—"

He could not finish the sentence, so overcome was he by laughter. The old guard looked disgusted and turned to the king.

"I can assure you, sir, the chancellor never carried out no such experiment here, to my certain knowledge."

The king remained rigid, eyes bright with contempt, not

moving until his son's outburst was over. He turned his back
to him then, before speaking.

"We have no need of that, and no need of quarrelling, not
in a time of grief. Let us return together to the palace. You can
ride behind me on Lapwing, if you wish."

Roba fell to his knees and covered his face with his hands.
He made noises that were not weeping.

"Perhaps he's hungry," suggested the guard.

"Get out, man, or I'll slice your head off."

The guard fell back. "I still feed them faithfully every day,
Your Majesty. Bring all the food up from the palace, and I'm
not as young as I was."

JandolAnganol turned back towards his kneeling son.
"You know your grandfather is now one with the gossies?"

"He was tired. I saw his grave yawn."

"I do my best, sir, but really I need a slave to assist me . . ."

"He died in his sleep—an easy death, for all his sins."

"I said he was tired. Self-demented, mother-tormented,
granddad-fermented . . . that's three blows you've struck.
Where next?"

The king folded his arms and tucked his hands into his armpits. "Three blows! You child—they're my one wound. Why
do you plague me with nonsense? Stay and comfort me. Since
you're unfit to marry even a Madi, stay."

Roba put his hands on the dirt before him and began slowly
to get to his feet. The guard seized his chance to say, "They
don't copulate any more, sir. Only among themselves, each
cageful, as a way of passing time."

"Stay with you, Father? Stay with you as Grandfather
stayed, in the bowels of the palace? No, I'm going back to
the—"

As he was speaking, the guard shuffled forward in supplicatory fashion and interposed himself between Jandol-
Anganol and his son. The king struck him a blow which sent
him staggering into a bush. The captives began a great to-do,
hammering on their bars.

The king smiled, or at least showed his teeth, as he attempted to approach his son. Roba backed away. "You'll never
understand what your grandfather did to me. You'll never
understand his power over me—then—now—perhaps for ever

—because I have no power over you. I could succeed only by putting him away.''

"Prisons flow like glaciers in your blood. I'm going to be a Madi, or a frog. I refuse to be human as long as you claim that title.''

"Rob, don't be so cruel. See sense. I—am about to—have to—marry a Madi girl soon. That's why I came to inspect the Madi here. Please stay with me.''

"Trittom your Madi-slave woman! Count progeny! Measure, make notes! Write it down, suffer, lock up the fertile ones, and never forget that there is one running loose about Helliconia fit to send you to an eternal prison. . . .''

As he spoke, the youth was backing away, fingers trailing on the ground. Then he turned and darted away into the bushes. A moment later, the king spied his figure climbing over the quarry cliff. Then he was gone.

The king went and leaned against the trunk of a tree, closing his eyes.

It was the whimpering of the guard which roused him. He went over to where the old man sprawled, and assisted him to his feet.

"Sorry for that, sir, but perhaps a small slave, now I'm getting past it . . .''

Rubbing his forehead with a weary gesture, JandolAnganol said, "You can answer some questions, slanje. Tell me, please, which way is it that Madi women prefer copulation? From the rear, like animals, or face to face, like humans? Rushven would have told me.''

The guard rubbed his hands on his tunic and laughed. "Oh, both ways, sir, to my observation, and I've seen it many times, working here with no help. But mainly from the rear, as do the Others. Some say as they mate for life, others as they are promiscuous, but cage life is different.''

"Do the Madi sexes kiss each other on the lips like humans?''

"I've not seen that, sir, no. Only humans.''

"Do they lick genitals before congress?''

"That is prevalent in all cages, sir. A lot of licking. Licking and sucking mostly, I'd say, very dirty.''

"Thank you. Now you may release the prisoners. They have

served their purpose. Set them free."

He left the quarry with a slow step, one hand on his sword, one on his brow.

Soft bars of shadow cast by the rajabarals moved across him as he headed back for the palace. Freyr was near to setting. The sky was yellow. Concentric haze aureoles of brown and orange, created by volcanic dust particles, encompassed the sun. It lay near the horizon like a pearl in a corrupt oyster. And the king said to Lapwing, "I can't trust him. He's wild, just as I was. I love him but I'd be better advised to kill him. If he had the sense to work with his mother forming an alliance in the scritina against me, I'd be finished. . . . I love her, but I'd be better advised to kill her, too. . . ."

The hoxney made no response. It moved towards the sunset with no ambition but to get home.

The king became aware of the vileness of his own thoughts.

Looking up at the flaring sky, he saw there the evil his religion taught him to see. "I must chasten myself," he said. "Aid me, O All-Powerful One!"

He stuck a spur in Lapwing's flank. He would go and see the First Phagorian Guard. They raised no difficult moral issues. With them he felt at peace.

The brown aureoles triumphed over the yellow. As Freyr disappeared, the oyster became ashen from its extremities inwards, changing minute by minute as the Batalix sunlight caught it. Its beauty lost, it became just a cloud formation among jumbled cloud as Batalix itself sloped westward. Akhanaba could be saying—and in no enigmatic fashion— that the whole complex scheme of things was about to end.

JandolAnganol returned to his silent palace, to find there an envoy from the Holy Pannovalan Empire. Alam Esomberr, all smiles, awaited his pleasure.

His bill of divorcement had arrived at last. He had but to present it to the queen of queens and he would be free to marry his Madi princess.

XVI

THE MAN WHO MINED A GLACIER

Summer of the small year had yielded to autumn in the southern hemisphere. The monsoons were gathering along the coasts of Hespagorat.

While on the pleasant northern coast of the Sea of Eagles Queen MyrdemInggala swam in the blue waters with her dolphins, on the dull southern coast of that same sea, where it merged with the waters of the Scimitar Sea, the Avernian prize-winner, Billy Xiao Pin, lay dying.

The port of Lordryardry was sheltered from open sea by the Lordry islands, two dozen in number, some of which were used as whaling stations. On these islands, and along the low-lying coasts of Hespagorat, marine iguanas lived in dense colonies. Wattled, warted, armoured, these inoffensive beasts grew to twenty feet in length and were sometimes to be seen swimming out to sea. Billy had observed them as the Ice Captain's *Lordryardry Lady* brought him to Dimariam.

Ashore, the beasts swarmed over rocks and marshes and each other. Something in their slothful movements and sudden

327

scurries marked them out as conspirators with the soggy weather which closed in on the Dimariamian shores at this time of small year; where cold air flowed northwards from the polar ice cap to meet the warm air above the oceans, banks of fog formed, enveloping everything in humid overcast.

Lordryardry was a small port of eleven thousand people. It owed its existence almost entirely to the enterprise of the Muntras family. One of its noteworthy features was that it lay at a latitude of 36.5° South, a degree and a half outside the wide tropical zone. Only eighteen and a half degrees farther south lay the polar circle. Beyond that circle, in the realms of eternal ice, Freyr was never to be seen during the long centuries of summer. In the Great Winter, Freyr would reappear, to remain for many lifetimes dominating the vacant world of the pole.

This Billy was told as he was driven by a traditional sledge from the ship to the ice captain's house. Krillio Muntras recounted such facts with pride, though he fell silent as his home drew near.

The room of the house to which Billy was carried was white. Its windows were framed with white curtains. As he lay locked in illness, Billy could look through trees, over town roofs, to a prospect of white mist. In that mist, an occasional mast loomed.

Billy knew he was shortly to embark on another mysterious journey. Before his ship sailed, he was tended by Muntras's self-effacing wife, Eivi, and by his formidable married daughter, Immya. Immya, he was told, had a high standing in the community as a healer.

After a day's rest, Eivi's and Immya's ministrations took effect, or else Billy enjoyed a remission. The encroaching stiffness partially left him. Immya wrapped him in blankets and helped him into the sledge. Four giant horned dogs, asokins, were harnessed up, and the family drove Billy inland to see the famous Lordryardry Glacier.

The Lordryardry Glacier had carved itself a bed between two hills. The leading face of the glacier fell into a lake which drained into the sea.

Billy observed that Krillio Muntras's manner changed subtly in the presence of his daughter. They were affectionate

together, but the respect he showed Immya was not entirely
matched by the respect in which she held him—so Billy
judged, going less by the way they spoke than by the way
Muntras held his backbone and drew in his broad stomach in
Immya's presence, as if he felt he must contain himself when
her sharp eyes were on him.

Muntras began to describe the workings at the glacier face.
When Immya modestly prompted him on the number of men
working there, he asked her without rancour to give the account herself. Which she did. Div stood behind his father and
his sister, scowling; though he, as the son, was to inherit the
ice company, he had nothing to contribute to the narrative,
and soon slunk off.

Immya was not only the chief medical practitioner of
Lordryardry; she was married to the chief lawyer of the town
the Muntras clan had founded. Her husband, referred to
always as Lawyer in Billy's presence, as if that had been his
baptismal name, stood as the spokesman and justice of the
town against the capital, Oiishat. Oiishat lay to the west, on
the frontier between Dimariam and Iskahandi. Oiishat cast
envious eyes on the prosperous new Lordryardry, and devised
ways of securing some of its wealth by taxation—schemes
which Lawyer constantly foiled.

Lawyer also foiled Muntras's local laws, which had been
improvised to benefit the Muntras family rather than their
workers. So Krillio was of two minds about his son-in-law.

Krillio's wife evidently felt differently. She would hear no
complaint about her daughter or the Lawyer. Though submissive, she was impatient with Div, whose behaviour—adversely
affected by his mother's dislike—became loutish in the home.
"You should reconsider," she told Muntras one day, when
they were both standing by Billy's bedside, after another
example of Div's awfulness. "Hand over the company to Immya and Lawyer, and then everything will prosper. Under
Div, it will be in ruin within three years. That girl has a proper
grasp of things."

Certainly Immya had a grasp of things Hespagoratean. She
had never ventured beyond the confines of the continent on

which she was born, despite frequent opportunities to do so, as if she preferred to have her front doorstep guarded by the myriad scaley watchdogs which patrolled the shores of Dimariam. But locked in her broad bosom were metaphorical maps, histories, and compass bearings of the southern continent.

Immya Muntras had a good plain square face built like her father's, a face capable of confronting glaciers. She stood foursquare to the ice face as she delivered her account of the family trade, in which she took great pride.

At this spot, they were far enough inland to be free of the coastal fog. The great wall of ice to which Muntras owed his wealth glittered in the sun. Where the glacier lay more distant, Batalix created in its hollows caverns of sapphire. Even its reflection in the lake at its foot gave off diamond glints.

The air was hard, fresh, and alive. Birds skimmed over the lake surface. Where the pure waters yielded to banks of blue flowers, insects were busy in their thousands.

A butterfly with a head shaped like a man's thumb settled on the three-faced watch on Billy's wrist. He stared at it with uncertain gaze, trying to interpret the meaning of the creature.

Things roared overhead, he knew not what. He could hardly look up. The virus was in his hypothalamus, in his brain stem. It would multiply irresistibly; no poultice could check it. Soon he would be locked immobile, like a phagor ancestor in tether.

He felt no regret. Regret only for the butterfly, leaving his hand and making off. In order to live a real life, of a kind his Advisor would not understand, sacrifices were called for. He had glimpsed the queen of queens. He had lain with beautiful Abathy. Even now, incapacitated, he could see distant bays of glacier where the light, conjuring powder- and thunder-blues, made of the ice more a colour than a substance. The excellence of nature had been tasted. Of course it had a price.

And Immya was explaining about the great blocks of ice which rattled overhead. At the ice face, men worked on scaffolding, cleaving the ice with saws and axes. They were Lordryardry's glacier miners. As the blocks fell off, they fell into an open funnel, and from there slipped into the shoot. The shoot, timber-built, was constructed with sufficient slope to keep the blocks of ice moving.

Great tombstones of ice travelled slowly down the shoot, which rumbled in every section as they passed over its stressed wooden legs. The tombstones made their way along two miles of shoot to the docks of Lordryardry.

At the docks, the tombstones were sawn into smaller blocks and loaded into the reed-insulated hulls of the ships of the company's fleet.

So the snows which had once fallen in the polar regions south of 55°, to be compressed and squeezed sluggishly down into the narrow temperate zone, were made to serve the useful purpose of cooling those who lived in far tropics. Here was where nature stopped and Captain Krillio Muntras took over.

"Please take me home," Billy said.

Immya's ready flow of figures ceased. Her tale of tonnages, the length of various voyages, the demand-related costings upon which their little empire was founded: these stopped. She sighed and said something to her father, but a fresh ice-load rumbling overhead erased her words. Then the lines of her face relaxed and she smiled.

"We'd better take Billy home," she said.

"I saw it," he said indistinctly. "I saw it."

And when almost half a Great Year had passed, when Helliconia and its sister planets had journeyed far from Freyr and were once again facing the slow furies of another winter, Billy's huddled form in the old wooden sledge was seen by millions of people on distant Earth.

Billy's presence on Helliconia represented an infringement of terrestrial orders. Those orders had stated that no human being was to land on Helliconia and disrupt the web of its cultures.

Those orders had been formulated over three thousand years earlier. In terms of cultural history, three thousand years was a long period of time. Since then, understanding had deepened—thanks largely to an intensive study of Helliconia undertaken by most of the population. There was a much better grasp of the unity—and therefore the strength—of planetary biospheres.

Billy had entered the planetary biosphere and had become

*part of it. The terrestrials saw no conflict. Billy's elements
comprised the atoms of dead star matter no different from the
elements comprising Muntras or MyrdemInggala. His death
would represent a final union with the planet, a merging
without dissolution. Billy was mortal. The atoms of which he
was constituted were indestructible.*

*There would be a measured sorrow for the winking out of
another human consciousness, for the loss of another identity,
unique, irreplaceable; but that was hardly a cause for tears on
Earth.*

*The tears were shed long before that on the Avernus. Billy
was their drama, their proof that existence existed, that they
themselves had the ancient power of biological organisms to
be moved in response to the environment. Tears and cheers
were the order of the day.*

*The Pin family, in particular, abandoned their usual passiv-
ity and threw a small family storm. Rose Yi Pin, by turns
laughing and howling, was the centre of passionate attention.
She had a marvellous time.*

The Advisor was mortified.

The fresh air visited Billy's body and bathed his lungs. It
allowed him to see every detail of the flashing world. But its
vividness, its sounds, were too much. He shut his eyes. When
he managed to open them again, the asokins were moving
briskly, the sledge bumped, and coastal pallors had begun to
veil the view.

To compensate for earlier humiliations, Div Muntras insisted on driving the sledge. He threw the reins over his right
shoulder, gripping them under his left arm while clutching the
sledge handle with his left hand. In his right hand he flourished a whip, which he cracked above the asokins.

"Go steady, Div, lad," Muntras growled.

As he spoke, the sledge struck a hummock of coarse grass
and overturned. They were travelling under the shoot, where
the ground was marshy. Muntras landed on his hands and
knees. He snatched up the reins, looking blackly at his son but
saying nothing. Immya, forming her mouth into the shape of a
stretcher, straightened the sledge and lifted Billy back into it.

Her silence was more expressive than words.

"It wasn't my fault," said Div, pretending to have hurt his wrist. His father took up the reins and silently motioned his son round to the back runners. They then proceeded at a sedate pace home.

The rambling Muntras house was built on one floor only. That floor was on many levels connected by steps or short flights of stairs, owing to the rocky terrain. Beyond the room in which Muntras and Immya placed Billy was the courtyard in which Muntras paid his workers every tenner.

The courtyard was ornamented with smooth boulders, carved from polar mountains which no human had ever seen and delivered to the coast via the glaciers. Compressed into the striations of each stone was a past chthonic history everyone in Lordryardry was too busy to decipher—though electronic eyes aboard the Avernus had done so. Beside each boulder grew tall trees whose trunks forked close to the ground. Billy could see these trees from his couch.

Muntras's wife, Eivi, greeted them on their return and fussed round her husband, as now she fussed about Billy. He was glad when she left him alone in the bare wooden room, to stare out at the bare outlines of the trees. His eyesight became fixed. The slow madness crept on him, moving his limbs, twisting his arms outward until they stretched above his head as rigidly as the wooden branches outside.

Div entered the room. The lad came in cautiously, pushing the door shut behind him and moving quickly to Billy's side. He stared down wide-eyed at Billy in his locked posture. The hand of Billy's left arm was bent back on itself, so that the knuckles almost touched the forearm and his watch cut into his skin.

"I'll take your watch off for you," Div said. He unstrapped it clumsily and laid it on a table out of Billy's line of sight.

"The trees," Billy said, through gritted teeth.

"I want a word with you," said Div threateningly, clenching his fists. "You remember on the *Lordryardry Lady,* that girl AbathVasidol? The Matrassyl girl?" he asked of Billy, sitting near him, speaking low, looking at the door as he did so. "That really beautiful girl with beautiful chestnut hair and big breasts!"

"The trees."

"Yes, the trees—they're apricot trees. Father distils his Exaggerator from the fruit of those trees. Billish, that girl Abathy, you remember her, Abathy?"

"They're dying."

"Billish, you're dying. That's why I want to talk to you. You remember how Father humiliated me with that girl? He gave her to *you*, Billish, rot you. That was his way of humiliating me, as he always tries to humiliate me. You understand? Where did my father take Abathy, Billish? If you know, tell me. Tell me, Billish. I never did you any harm."

His elbow joints creaked. "Abathy. Summer ripeness."

"I won't hold it against you because you're foreign rubbish. Now listen. I want to know where Abathy is. I love her. I shouldn't have come back here, should I? Being humiliated by my father and that sister of mine. She'll never let me take over the company. Billish, listen, I'm leaving. I can make it on my own—I'm no fool. Find Abathy, start my own trade. I'm asking you, Billish—where did Father take her? Quick, man, before they come."

"Yes." The stark gesturing trees at the window were trying to spell out a name. "Deuteroscopist."

Div leant forward, grasping Billy's knotted shoulders. "CaraBansity? He took Abathy to CaraBansity?"

From the dying man came a whispered affirmative. Div let him fall back as if he were a plank of wood. He stood flicking his fingers, muttering to himself. Hearing a sound in the passage, he ran to the window. He balanced his bulk momentarily on the sill. Then he jumped out and was gone.

Eivi Muntras returned. She fed Billy with fragments of a delicate white meat from a bowl. She forced and coaxed; he ate ravenously. In the world of the sick, Eivi was perfectly in command. She bathed his face and brow with a sponge. She drew a gauze curtain over the window to cut down the light. Through the gauze, the trees became ghost trees.

"I'm hungry," he said, when all the food was gone.

"I'll bring you some more iguana soon, dear. You liked it, didn't you? I cooked it in milk especially."

"I'm hungry," he screamed.

She left, looking distressed. He heard her talking to other

people. His neck contorted, cords standing out on it as his hearing paid out like a harpoon to fix on what was said. The words made no sense to him. He was lying upside down, so that the sentences entered his ear the wrong way up. When he flipped himself over, everything was perfectly audible.

Immya's voice said, in impartial tones, "Mother, you are being silly. These homemade nostrums cannot cure Billish. He has a rare disease which we scarcely know of except in history books. It is either bone fever or the fat death. His symptoms are unclear, possibly because he comes from that other world as he claims, and therefore his cellular composition may differ in some way from ours."

"I don't know about that, Immya dear. I just think that a little more meat would be good for him. Perhaps he'd like a gwing-gwing . . ."

"He may go into a state of bulimia, coupled with an overactive disposition. Those would be symptomatic of fat death. In that case, we would have to tie him down to the bed."

"Surely that won't be necessary, dear? He's so gentle."

"It is not a case of his disposition, Mother, but of the disposition of his disease." That was a male voice, charged with half-concealed contempt, as if a practical point were being explained to a child. It belonged to Immya's husband, Lawyer.

"Well, I don't know about that, I'm sure. I just hope it isn't catching."

"We don't believe that either fat death or bone fever is infectious at this time of the Great Year," said Immya's voice. "We think Billish must have been with phagors, with whom these illnesses are generally associated."

There was more of the kind, and then Immya and Lawyer were in the room, gazing down at Billy.

"You may recover," she said, bending slightly at the waist to deliver her words and releasing them one by one. "We shall take care of you. We may have to tie you down if you get violent."

"Dying. Inevitable." With a great effort, he pretended not to be a tree and said, "Bone fever and fat death—I can explain. Just one virus. Germ. Different effects. According to time. Of Great Year. True."

Further effort was beyond him. The rigors set in. Yet for a

moment he had it all in mind. Although it had not been his
subject, the helico virus was a legend on the Avernus, though a
dying one, confined to video-texts, since its last outbreak in
pandemic form had occurred several lifetimes before those
now alive on the station. Those who now looked down helplessly on him from above were witnessing an old story brought
back into currency only as the conclusion to every Helliconian
Holiday.

The visitations of the virus caused immense suffering but
were fortunately confined to two periods in the Great Year: six
local centuries after the coldest time of that year, when planetary conditions were improving, and in the late autumn, after
the long period of heat into which Helliconia had now entered.
In the first period, the virus manifested itself as bone fever;
in the second, as fat death. Almost no one escaped these
scourges. The mortality rate of each approached fifty percent.
Those who survived became, respectively, fifty percent lighter
or fifty percent heavier in body weight, and thus were better
equipped to face the hotter and colder seasons.

The virus was the mechanism by which human metabo-
lisms adjusted to enormous climatic changes. Billy was being
changed.

Immya was silent, standing by Billy's bedside. She folded
her arms over her grand bosom.

"I don't understand you. How do you know such things?
You're no god, or you would not be ill . . ."

Even the sound of voices drove him deeper into the entrails
of a tree. He managed again. "One disease. Two . . . opposed
systems. You as doctor understand."

She understood. She sat down again. "If it were so . . . and
yet—why not? There are two botanies. Trees that flower and
seed only once in 1825 small years, other trees that flower
and seed every small year. Things that are divided yet
united . . ."

She closed her mouth tightly as if afraid of releasing a
secret, aware that she stood on the brink of something beyond
her understanding. The case of the helico virus was not exactly
similar to that of Helliconia's binary botanies. Yet Immya was

correct in her observations on the divergent habits of plant life. At the time of Batalix's capture by Freyr, some eight million years previously, Batalix's planets had been bathed in radiation, leading to genetic divergences in multitudinous phyla. While some trees had remained flowering and fruiting as before—so that they attempted to produce seed 1825 times during the Great Year, whatever the climatic conditions— others had adapted a metabolism better geared towards the new regime, and propagated themselves only once in 1825 small years. Such were the rajabarals. The apricot trees outside Billy's window had not adapted and were, as it happened, dying off in the unusual heat.

Something in the lines which formed about Immya's mouth suggested she was attempting to chew over these weighty matters; but she switched instead to a contemplation of Billy's remarks. Her intelligence told her that if the statement proved true, it would be of great importance—if not immediately, then a few centuries ahead, when, the scanty records suggested, fat death pandemics were due.

Thinking so far into the future was not a local habit. She gave him a nod and said, "I will think about it, Billish, and bring your perception before our medical society when next we meet. If we understand the true nature of this malady, perhaps we can find a cure."

"No. Disease essential for survival . . ." He could see that she would never accept and he could never explain his point. He compromised by forcing out, "I told your father."

The remark deflected her interest from medical questions. She stared away from him, swathing herself in silence, seeming to shrink into herself. When she spoke again, her voice was deeper and harsher, as if she too had to communicate from within an imprisonment.

"What else did you do with my father? In Borlien. Was he drunk? I want to know—did he have a young woman on the boat from Matrassyl? Did he have carnal knowledge of her? You must tell me." She leaned over him, to grasp him as her brother had done. "He's drinking now. There was a woman, wasn't there? I ask you for my mother's sake."

The intensity with which these words were spoken frightened Billy; he strove to sink deeper into the tree, to feel the

rough bark gripping his eddre. Bubbles came from his mouth.

She shook him. "Did he have carnal knowledge? Tell me. Die if you will, but tell me."

He tried to nod.

Something in his distorted expression confirmed her guess. A look of vindictive satisfaction came on her face.

"Men! That's how they take advantage of women. My poor mother has suffered from his debauchery for years, poor innocent thing. I found out years ago. It was an awful shock. We Dimariamians are respectable people, not like the inhabitants of the Savage Continent, which I hope never to have to visit . . ."

As her voice died, Billy attempted an inarticulate protest. It served to rekindle the fire of Immya's animosity. "And what about the poor innocent girl involved? And her innocent mother? I long ago made that brother of mine, the bane of my life, confess to me everything my father does. . . . Men are pigs, ruled by lust, unable to keep faith . . ."

"The girl." But Abathy's name became entangled with the knots in his larynx.

Gloaming enveloped Lordryardry. Freyr sank to the west. Bird songs became fewer. Batalix took up a position low on the horizon, where it could glare across the water at the scaley things piled on the shore. Mists thickened, obscuring the stars and the Night Worm.

Eivi Muntras brought Billy some soup before she retired to bed. As he drank, terrible hungers rose from his very eddre. His immobility was overcome, he sprang at Eivi, bit her shoulder and tore flesh from it. He ran about the room screaming. This was the bulimia associated with the late stages of fat death. Other members of the family came running, slaves brought lights. Billy was cursed and cuffed and strapped down to his bed.

For an hour he was left, while the sound of ministrations came from the other end of the house. He endured visions of eating Eivi whole, of sucking her brains. He wept. He imagined that he was back on the Avernus. He imagined he was eating Rose Yi Pin. He wept again. His tears fell like leaves.

Boards creaked in the corridor. A dim lamp appeared, behind it a man's face floating as if on a stream of darkness. The Ice Captain, breathing heavily. Fumes of Exaggerator entered the room with him.

"Are you all right? I'd have to throw you out if you weren't dying, Billish." He steadied himself, breathing heavily. "I'm sorry it's come to this . . . I know you're some kind of angel from a better world, Billish, even when you bite like a devil. A man's got to believe there's a better world somewhere. Better than this one, where no one cares about you. Avernus . . . I would take you back there, if I could. I'd like to see it."

Billy was back in his tree, his limbs part and parcel of its agonised branches.

"Better."

"That's right, better. I'm going to sit in the courtyard, Billish, just outside your window. Have a drink. Think about things. It'll soon enough be time to pay the men. If you want me, just give a call."

He was sorry that Billish was dying, and the Exaggerator made him sorry for himself. It was puzzling the way he always felt more comfortable with strangers, even with the queen of queens, than he did with his own family. With them he was constantly at a disadvantage.

He settled himself down outside the window, placing a jug and glass on the bench beside him. In the milky light, the stones resembled sleeping animals. The albic climbing the walls of the house opened its blooms, the blooms opened their beaks like parrots; a tranquil scent floated on the air.

After his plan to bring Billish here in secrecy had succeeded, he found himself unable to proceed further. He wanted to tell everyone that there was more to life than they knew, that Billish was a living example of that truth. It was not just that Billish was dying; Muntras suspected, somewhere in a cold corner of his being, that there might be less to life than he knew. He wished he had remained a wanderer. Now he was back home for good. . . .

After a while, sighing, the Ice Captain pulled himself to his feet and peered through the open window. "Billish, are you awake? Have you seen Div?"

A gurgle in response.

"Poor lad, he's not really fit for the job, that's the truth . . ." He sat down again on the bench, groaning. He took up his glass and drank. Too bad Billish didn't like Exaggerator.

The milky light thickened. Dusk-moths purred among the albic. In the sleeping house at his back boards creaked.

"There must be a better world somewhere . . ." Muntras said, and fell asleep with an unlit veronikane between his lips.

The sound of voices. Muntras roused. He saw his men gathering in the court to be paid. It was daylight. Dead calm prevailed.

Muntras stood and stretched. He looked in through the window at Billish's contorted form, motionless on the couch.

"This is assatassi day, Billish—I'd forgotten, with you here. The monsoon high tide. You ought to see this. It's quite a local event. There'll be celebrations tonight, and no half measures."

From the couch came a single word, forced from a locked jaw. "Celebrations."

The workmen were rough, dressed in rough overalls. They cast their gaze down on the worn paving stones in case their master took offence at being discovered asleep. But that was not Muntras's way.

"Come on, men. I'll not be paying you out much longer. It'll be Master Div's turn. Let's get it over with promptly, and then we'll prepare for the festivities. Where's my pay clerk?"

A small man with a high collar and hair brushed in the opposite direction to anyone else's came darting forward. He had a ledger under his arm and was followed by a stallun carrying a safe. The clerk made a great business of pushing through the workers. This he did with his eyes constantly on his employer and his lips working as if he was already calculating what each man should be paid. His arrival caused the men to shuffle into a line to await their modest remuneration. In the unusual light, their features were without animation.

"You lot are going to collect your wages, and then you're going to hand it over to your wives or get drunk as usual,"

Muntras said. He addressed the men near him, among whom he saw only common-hire labourers and none of his master craftsmen. But at once a mixture of indignation and pity seized him and he spoke louder, so that all could hear. "Your lives are going by. Here you're stuck. You've been nowhere. You know of the legends of Pegovin, but have you ever been there? Who's been there? Who's been to Pegovin?"

They leaned back against the rounded stones, muttering.

"I've been all over the world. I've seen it all. I've been to Uskutoshk, I've visited the Great Wheel of Kharnabhar, I've seen old ruined cities and sold junk in the bazaars of Pannoval and Oldorando. I've spoken with kings and queens as fair as flowers. It's all out there, waiting for the man who dares. Friends everywhere. Men and women. It's wonderful. I've loved every minute of it.

"It's bigger than you can ever imagine, stuck here at Lordryardry. This last voyage, I met a man who came from another world. There's more than just this world, Helliconia. There's another circling around us, Avernus. And others beyond that, worlds to be visited. Earth, for instance."

All the while he was speaking, the little clerk was laying out his effects on a table under one of the barren apricot trees and removing the key to the safe from an inner pocket. And the phagor was setting the safe down just where needed and flicking an ear as it did so. And the men were shuffling forward to the edge of the table and making their line more definite by moving closer to each other. And other men were coming up, directing suspicious looks at their boss, and joining the rear of the line. And the comfortable seriality of the world was being maintained under the purple clouds.

"I tell you there are other worlds. Use your imagination." Muntras struck the table. "Don't you feel the wanderlust occasionally? I did when I was a young 'un, I tell you. Inside my house even now I have a young man from one of these other worlds. He's ill or he'd come out and speak to you. He can tell you miraculous things that happen lifetimes away."

"Does he drink Exaggerator?"

The voice came from within the ranks of the waiting men. It stopped Muntras in full burst. He paced up and down the line, red of face. Not an eye met his.

"I'll prove what I'm saying," Muntras shouted. "You'll have to believe me then."

He turned and stamped into the house. Only the clerk showed some impatience, drumming his little fingers on the plank table, staring about, pulling his sharp nose, and looking up at the heavy sky.

Muntras ran in to where Billy was, terribly distorted, without motion. He seized Billy's petrified wrist, only to find that the watch had gone.

"Billish," he said. He went over to the invalid, looked down at him, called his name more gently. He felt the cold skin, tested the twisted flesh.

"Billish," he said again, but now it was merely a statement. He knew that Billish was dead—and he knew who had stolen the watch, that three-faced timepiece which King Jandol-Anganol had once held. There was only one person who would do such a thing.

"You'll never miss your timepiece now, Billy," Muntras said aloud.

He covered his face with a slab of hand and uttered something between a prayer and a curse.

For a moment more, the Ice Captain stood in the room, looking up at the ceiling with his mouth open. Then, recalling his duties, he walked over to the window and gave his clerk a sign to start paying out the men's wages.

His wife entered the room with Immya, her shoulder bandaged.

"Our Billish is dead," he said flatly.

"Oh dear, and on assatassi day, too . . ." Eivi said. "You can hardly expect me to be sorry."

"I'll see his body is conveyed to the ice cellar, and we will bury him tomorrow, after the feast," Immya said, moving over to observe the contorted body. "He told me something before he died which could be a contribution to medical science."

"You're a capable girl, you look after him," Muntras said. "As you say, we can bury him tomorrow. A proper funeral. Meanwhile, I'll go and look to the nets. As a matter of fact, I feel miserable, as if anyone cares."

* * *

Taking no heed of the jabbering women who were stringing up lines of net on poles, the Ice Captain walked along the water's edge. He wore high thick boots and kept his hands in his pockets. Occasionally, one of the black iguanas would jump up against him like an importuning dog. Muntras would knee it down again without interest. The iguanas wallowed among thick brown ropes of kelp which swirled in the shallow water, sometimes kicking to get free of the coils. In places, they were banked on top of each other, indifferent to how they lay.

To add to the melancholy abandonment of their postures, the iguanas were commensal with a hairy twelve-legged crab, which scurried in its millions among the forms which kept watch on the breakers. The crabs devoured any fragment of food—seal or seaweed—dropped by the reptiles; nor were they averse to devouring infant iguanas. The characteristic noise of the Dimariamian seashore was a crunch and scrabble of armoured legs against scales; the ritual of their lives was playing out against this clamour, which was as endless as the sound of the waves.

The Ice Captain took no notice of these saturnine occupants of the shore, but stared out to sea, beyond Lordry, the whaling island. He had checked at the harbour and been told that a light sailing dinghy had been stolen overnight.

So his son was gone, taking the magic watch, either as talisman or for trade. Had sailed away, without so much as a good-bye.

"Why did you do it?" Muntras asked half aloud, staring over the purple sea on which a dead calm prevailed. "For the usual reasons a man leaves home, I suppose. Either you couldn't bear your family any longer, or you just wanted adventure—strange places, amazements, strange women. Well, good luck to you, lad. You'd never have made the world's foremost ice trader, that's certain. Let's hope you aren't reduced to selling stolen rings for a living. . . ."

Some of the women, humble worker's wives, were calling to him to come behind the nets before high tide. He gave them a salute and trudged away from the milling iguana bodies.

Immya and Lawyer would have to take over the company. Not his favourite people, but they'd probably run the whole concern better than he ever did. You had to face facts. It was no use growing bitter. Although he had never been comfortable with his daughter, he recognised that she was a good woman.

At least he'd stand by a friend and see that BillishOwpin got a proper burial. Not that either Billish or he believed in any of the gods. But just for their own two sakes.

He trudged towards the safety of the nets, where the workmen stood.

"You were all right, Billish," he muttered aloud. "You were nobody's fool."

The Avernus had company in its orbit about Helliconia. It moved among squadrons of auxiliary satellites. The main task of these auxiliaries was to observe sectors of the globe the Avernus itself was not observing. But it so happened that the Avernus, on its circumpolar orbit, was itself above Lordryardry and travelling north at the time of Billy's funeral.

The funeral was a popular event. The fact is, human egos being frail, other people's deaths are not entirely unpleasureable. Melancholy itself is among the more enjoyable of emotions. Almost everyone aboard the Avernus looked in: even Rose Yi Pin, although she watched the event from the bed of her new boyfriend.

Billy's Advisor, dry-eyed, gave a homily in one hundred measured words on the virtues of submission to one's lot. The epitaph served also as an epitaph to the protest movements. With some relief, they forgot difficult thoughts of reform and returned to their administrative duties. One of them wrote a sad song about Billy, buried away from his family.

There were now a good many Avernians buried on Helliconia, all winners of Helliconia Holidays. A question often asked aboard the Earth Observation Station was, How did this affect the mass of the planet?

On Earth, where the funeral of Billy provoked less interest, the event was seen more detachedly. Every living being is created from dead starmatter. Every living being must make

*its solitary journey upward from the molecular level towards
the autonomy of birth, a journey which in the case of humans
takes three-quarters of a year. The complex degree of organi-
sation involved in being a higher life-form cannot be forever
sustained. Eventually, there is a return to the inorganic.
Chemical bonds dissolve.*

*That had happened in Billy's case. All that was immortal
about him was the atoms from which he was assembled. They
endured. And there was nothing strange about a man of terrestrial stock being buried on a planet a thousand light-years
away. Earth and Helliconia were near neighbours, composed
of the same debris from the same long defunct stars.*

*In one detail that correct man, Billy's Advisor, was incor-
rect. He spoke of Billy going to his long rest. But the entire
organic drama of which mankind formed a part was pitched
within the great continuing explosion of the universe. From a
cosmic viewpoint, there was no rest anywhere, no stability,
only the ceaseless activity of particles and energies.*

XVII

DEATH-FLIGHT

General Hanra TolramKetinet wore a wide-brimmed hat and
an old pair of trousers, the bottoms of which were stuffed into
the tops of a pair of knee-length army boots. Across his naked
chest he had slung a fine new matchlock firearm on a strap.
Above his head he waved a Borlienese flag. He waded out to
sea towards the approaching ships.

Behind him, his small force cheered encouragement. There
were twelve men, led by an able young lieutenant, Gortor-
Lanstatet. They stood on a spit of sand; behind them, jungle
and the dark mouth of the River Kacol. Their voyage down
from Ordelay—from defeat—was over; they had navigated,
in the *Lordryardry Lubber*, both rapids and sections of the
river where the current was so slight that out from the depths
came tuberous growths, fighting like knots of reproducing eels
to gain the surface and release a scent of carrion and julip.
That scent was the jungle's malediction.

On either bank of the Kacol, the forest twisted itself into
knots, snakes, and streamers no less forbidding than the ten-
tacles which rose from the river depths. Here the forest indeed

looked impenetrable; there were visible none of the wide aisles down which the general, half a tenner ago, had walked in perfect safety, for the river had tempted to the jungle's edge a host of sun-greedy creepers. The jungle, too, had become more dwarfish in formation, turning from rain forest proper to monsoon forest, with the heavy heads of its canopy pressing low above the heads of the Borlienese troops.

Where river at last delivered its brown waters into sea, foetid morning mists rose from the forest, rolling in ridge beyond ridge up the unruly slopes that culminated in the Randonanese massif.

The mist had been something of a motif of their journey, preluded from the moment when—in undisputed possession of the *Lubber* at Ordelay—they had prized open the hatches, to be greeted by thick vapours pouring from the boat's cargo of melting ice. Once the ice was cast overboard, the new owners, investigating, had discovered secret lockers full of Sibornalese matchlocks, wrapped in rags against the damp: the *Lubber* captain's secret personal trade, to recompense himself for the dangerous voyages he undertook on behalf of the Lordryardry Ice Trading Company. Freshly armed, the Borlienese had set sail on the oily waters, to disappear into the curtains of humidity which were such a feature of the Kacol.

Now they stood, watching their general wade towards the ships, on a sandbar that stood out like a spur from a small rocky and afforested island, Keevasien Island, which lay between river and sea. The dark green tunnel, the stench, the insect-tormented silences, the mists, were behind them. The sea beckoned. They looked forward to rescue, shading their eyes to gaze seawards against a brilliance accentuated by the hazy morning overcast.

Rescue could hardly have been more timely. On the previous day, when Freyr had set and the jungle was a maze of uncertain outlines as Batalix descended, they had been seeking a mooring between gigantic roots red like intestines; without warning, a tangle of six snakes, none less than seven feet long, had dropped down from branches overhead. They were pack snakes which, with rudimentary intelligence, always hunted together. Nothing could have terrified the crew more. The man who stood at the wheel, seeing the horrible things land close to him and rapidly disentangle themselves, hissing in

fury, jumped overboard without a moment's thought, to be
seized by a greeb which a moment before had resembled a
decaying log.

The pack snakes were eventually killed. By that time, the
boat had swung side on into the current, and was grinding
against the Randonanese bank. As they attempted to regain
control, their rudder hit an underwater obstruction and broke.
Poles were brought forth, but the river was becoming both
wider and deeper, so the poles did not serve. When Keevasien
Island loomed through the dusk they had no power to choose
either the port, the Borlienese, stream, or the starboard, the
Randonanese, stream. The *Lubber* was carried helplessly
against the rocks on the northern point of the island; with
its side stove in, it was beached in the shallows. The current
tugged at it, threatening to wash it away. They grabbed some
equipment and jumped ashore.

Darkness was coming in. They stood listening to the repeti-
tive boom of the surf like distant cannon fire. Because of the
great fear of the men, TolramKetinet decided to camp where
they were for the brief night, rather than attempt to reach
Keevasien, which he knew was close.

A watch was set. The night around them was given to
subterfuge and sudden death. Small insects went shopping
with large headlights, moths' wings gleamed with terrifying
sightless eyes, the pupils of predators glowed like hot stones;
and all the while the two streams of the river surged close by,
eddying phosphorescence, the heavy drag of water moaning its
way into their dreams.

Freyr rose behind cloud. The men woke and stood about
scratching mosquito bites which covered their bodies. Tolram-
Ketinet and GortorLanstatet drove them into action. Climbing
the rocky spine of the island, they could look across the
eastern arm of the river to the open sea and the Borlienese
coast ahead. There, protected from the sea by afforested cliff,
lay the harbour of Keevasien, the westernmost town of their
native land of Borlien, once home of the legendary savant
YarapRombry.

A purplish cast to the light obscured the truth from them for
a while; they looked on broken roofs and blackened walls for
some moments before saying—almost in one voice—"It's
been destroyed!"

Phagor herds, denizens of the monsoon forest, had bartered their volumunwun with the Randonanese tribes. The great spirit had spoken to the tribes. The tribes caught Others in the trees, bound them to bamboo chairs, and progressed through the jungle to burn down the port. Nothing had escaped the flames. There was no sign of life, except for a few melancholy birds. The war was still being waged; the men could not avoid being at once its agents and its victims.

In silence, they made their way to the south side of the island, climbing down on a sandy spit to get free of the spikey undergrowth that choked the interior.

Open sea was before them, ribbed with brown where the Kacol joined it, ultimately blue. Long breakers uncurled against the steep slope of the beach, flashing white. To the west they could see Poorich Island, a large island which served as a marker between the Sea of Eagles and the Narmosset Sea. Round the angle of Poorich were sailing four ships, two carracks and two caravels.

Seizing up the Borlienese flag which had been stored among a selection of flags in the *Lubber*'s lockers, TolramKetinet walked forward into the foam to meet them.

Dienu Pasharatid was on watch on the *Golden Friendship* as it made for a safe anchorage with its fleet in the mouth of the Kacol. Her hands tightened on the rail; otherwise she gave no sign of the elation she felt on beholding, as Poorich Island slid behind, the coast of Borlien emerge from the morning mists.

Six thousand sea miles had fallen astern since they repaired the ships and sailed on from the pleasant anchorage near Cape Findowel. In that time, Dienu had communed much with God the Azoiaxic; the limitless expanses of ocean had brought her closer than ever before to his presence. She told herself that her involvement with her husband Io was over. She had had him transferred to the *Union*, so that she no longer had to look at him. All this she had done in a cool Sibornalese way, without showing resentment. She was free to rejoice again in life and in God.

There was the beautiful breeze, the sky, the sea—why, as she strove to rejoice, did misery invade her? It could not be because she was jealous of the relationship which had

grown—like a weed, she said to herself, like a weed—between
her Priest-Militant Admiral and the Borlienese ex-chancellor.
Nor could it be because she felt the slightest spark of affection
for Io. "Think of winter," she told herself—using an Uskuti
expression meaning, "Freeze your hopes."

Even the communion with the Azoiaxic, which she was
unable to break off, had proved disconcerting. It seemed that
the Azoiaxic had no place for Dienu Pasharatid in his bosom.
Despite her virtue, he was indifferent. He was indifferent
despite her seemly behaviour, her circumspection.

In this respect at least, the Dweller, the Lord of the Church
of the Formidable Peace, had proved dismayingly to resemble
Io Pasharatid himself. And it was this reflection, rather than
consolation, which pursued her over the empty leagues of sea.
Anything was welcome by way of distraction. So, when the
coast of Borlien appeared, she turned briskly from the wheel
and summoned the bugler to sound "Good Tidings."

Soon the rails of the four ships were crowded with soldiers,
eager for a first glimpse of the land they were planning to invade and subjugate.

One of the last passengers to arrive on deck was Sartori-
Irvrash. He stood for a while in the open air, clapping his
clothes and breathing deep to disperse a smell of phagor. The
phagor was gone; only her bitter scent remained—that, and a
fragment of knowledge.

After the *Golden Friendship* had left Findowel, it sailed
southeastwards across the Gulf of Ponipot, past ancient lands,
and through the Cadmer Straits, the narrowest stretch of
water between Campannlat and Hespagorat. These were lands
that legends told of; some said that humans had come into
being here, some that language was first spoken here. Here
was Ponipot, the Ponpt that little Tatro read about in her fairy
tales, Ponipot almost uninhabited, gazing towards the setting
of the suns, with its old mouldering cities whose names were
still capable of stirring men's hearts—Powachet, Prowash,
Gal-Dundar on the frigid Aza River.

Past Ponipot, to be becalmed off the rocky spines of
Radado, the land of high desert, the southern tail of the Bar-
riers, where it was said that under one million humans lived—
in contrast to the three and a quarter million in neighbouring
Randonan—and certainly fewer humans than phagors: for

Radado formed the western end of a great ancipital migratory route which stretched across the whole of Campannlat, the ultima Thule to which the creatures came in the summer of every Great Year, to go about their unfathomable rituals, or simply to squat motionless, staring across the Cadmer Straits towards Hespagorat, towards a destination unknown to other life forms.

Becalmed or otherwise, in those long hot days on the stationary ship, SartoriIrvrash had been content. He had escaped from his study into the wide world. During dimdays, there were long intellectual conversations to be enjoyed with the lady Priest-Militant Admiral, Odi Jeseratabhar. The two of them had become closer. Odi Jeseratabhar's first intricacy of language had dissolved into something less formal. The involuntary proximities enforced by their narrow quarters had become wished for, treasured. They turned into circumspect lovers. And the circumnavigation of the Savage Continent had become a circumnavigation also of souls.

Sitting together on deck during that enchanted becalmment, the aging lovers, Borlienese and Uskuti, surveyed the almost unmoving sea. The Radado mainland hung mistily in the background. Nearer at hand, Gleeat Island lay to port. Away to starboard, three other islands, submerged mountain peaks, seemed to float on the bosom of the water.

Odi Jeseratabhar pointed to starboard. "I can almost imagine I can make out the coast of Hespagorat—the land called Throssa, to be precise. All around us is the evidence that Hespagorat and Campannlat were once joined by a land bridge, which was destroyed in some upheaval. What do you think, Sartori?"

He studied the hump of Gleeat Island. "If we can believe the legends, phagors originated in a distant part of Hespagorat, Pegovin, where the black phagors live. Perhaps the phagors of Campannlat migrate to Radado because they still hope to discover the ancient bridge back to their homeland."

"Have you ever seen a black phagor in Borlien?"

"Once in captivity." He drew on his veronikane. "The continents keep their separate kinds of animals. If there was once a land bridge, then we might expect to find the iguanas of Hespagorat on the coast of Radado. Are they there, Odi?"

With a sudden inspiration, she said, "I think they are not,

because the humans might have killed them off—Radado is a barren place; anything serves as food. But what about Gleeat? While we are becalmed, we have time to spare, time in which we might add to the fund of human knowledge. You and I will go on an expedition in the longboat and see what we find."

"Can we do that?"

"If I say so."

"Remember our near disaster on the Persecution Bay expedition?"

"You thought I was crazy then."

"I think you're crazy now."

They both laughed, and he clutched her hand.

The Admiral summoned the bo'sun. Slaves were set to work. The longboat was launched. Odi Jeseratabhar and SartoriIrvrash climbed aboard. They were rowed two miles across the island, over a sea of glass. With them went a dozen armed soldiers, delighted at this chance to leave the hated confines of the ship.

Gleeat Island measured five miles across. The ship's boat beached on a steep sandy shelf at the southeast corner. A guard was set on it, while the rest of the expedition moved forward.

Iguanas basked on the rocks. They showed no fear of the humans, and several were speared to be taken back to the ship as welcome addition to the diet. They were puny beside the giant black iguanas of Hespagorat. These rarely attained more than five feet in length. Their colour was a mottled brown. Even the crabs that lived commensally with them were small and had only eight legs.

As SartoriIrvrash and Odi Jeseratabhar were searching the rocks for iguana eggs, the party came under attack. Four phagors rushed from cover, spears in hand, and fell on them. They were ragged beasts, their coats in tatters, their ribs showing.

With surprise on their side, the phagors managed to kill two of the soldiers, bearing the men down into the water with the force of their charge. But the other soldiers fought back. Iguanas scattered, gulls rose screaming, there was a brief pursuit over the rocks, and the scrimmage was finished. The phagors were dead—except for a gillot whose life Odi Jeseratabhar spared.

The gillot was larger than her companions and covered in a dense black coat. With her arms bound firmly behind her, she was made captive and taken back in the boat to the *Golden Friendship*.

Odi and Sartori embraced each other in private, congratulating themselves on confirming the truth of the old legend of the land bridge. And on surviving.

A day later, the monsoon winds blew, and the fleet was on its way eastwards again. The coast of Randonan was now passing in all its wild splendour on the port side; but Sartori-Irvrash spent most of his time below decks, studying their captive, whom he called Gleeat.

Gleeat spoke only Native Ancipital, and that in a dialect. Knowing no Native, or even Hurdhu, SartoriIrvrash had to work through an interpreter. Odi came down into the cramped dark hold to see what he was doing, and laughed.

"How can you bother with this smelly creature? We have proved our point, that Radado and Throssa were once connected. God the Azoiaxic was on our side. The small colony of iguanas isolated on Gleeat Island are an inferior strain, isolated from the main body of iguanas on the southern continent. This creature, living among white phagors, probably represents some kind of survival of the Hespagorat-Pegovin black strain. Doubtless they're dying out on such a small island."

He shook his head. While admiring her quick brain, he perceived that she reached conclusions too hastily.

"She claims that her party were on a ship which was wrecked on Gleeat in an earlier monsoon."

"That's clearly a lie. Phagors do not sail. They hate water."

"They were slaves on a Throssan galley, she says."

Odi patted his shoulder. "Listen, Sartori, it's my belief that we could have proved that the two continents were once linked just by looking at the old charts in the chartroom. There's Purporian on the Radado shore and a port called Popevin on the Throssa shore. 'Poop' means 'bridge' in Pure Olonets, and 'Pup' or 'Pu' the same in Local Olonets. The past is locked up in language, if one knows how to look."

Although she laughed, he was vexed by her superior Sibornalese style. "If the smell is overcoming you, dear, you had better go back on deck."

"We shall soon be approaching Keevasien. A coastal town. As you know, 'ass' or 'as' is Pure Olonets for 'sea'—the equivalent of 'ash' in Pontpian." With that burst of knowledge, smiling, she retired, climbing the ladder to the quarter-deck in practical fashion.

He was surprised next day to find that Gleeat was wounded. There was a golden pool of blood on the deck where she lay. He questioned her through the interpreter. Although he watched her closely, he could detect nothing resembling emotion when she answered.

"No, she is not wounded. She says she is coming on oestrus. She has just undergone her menstrual period." The interpretor looked his distaste but made no personal comment, being of inferior rank.

Such was his hatred for phagors—but it was gone now, like much else from his past life, he realised—that SartoriIrvrash had always neglected their history, just as he had refused to learn their language. Such matters he had left to Jandol-Anganol—JandolAnganol with his perverse trust in the creatures. However, the sexual habits of phagors had been a target for prurient jest to the very urchins in the Matrassyl streets; he recalled that the female ancipital, neither human nor beast, delivered something like a one-day menstrual flow from the uterus as prelude to the oestral cycle when she came on heat. It might be memories of those old whispers which caused him to imagine that his captive emitted a more pungent odour on this occasion.

SartoriIrvrash scratched his cheek. "What was that word she used for catamenia? Her word in Native?"

"She calls oestrus 'tennhrr' in her language. Shall I have her hosed down?"

"Ask her how frequently she comes into oestrus."

The gillot, who remained tied, had to be prodded before she gave answer. Her long pink milt flicked up one of her nostrils. She finally admitted to having ten periods in a small year. SartoriIrvrash nodded and went on deck for some fresh air. Poor creature, he thought; a pity we can't all live in peace. The human-ancipital dilemma would have to be resolved one day, one way or another. When he was dead and gone.

They drove before the monsoon all that night, the next day, and the night following. The rains were frequently so thick

that those aboard the *Golden Friendship* could not make out their sister ships. The Straits of Cadmer were left behind. All about them was the grey Narmosset, its waves streaked with long spittles of white. The world was a liquid one.

During the fifth night, they encountered a storm, and the carrack almost stood on its beam ends. The hollies and orange trees growing along the waist were all lost overboard, and many feared that the ship would founder. The seamen, always superstitious, approached their captain and begged that the captive phagor be cast overboard, since it was well known that ancipitals aboard ship brought bad luck. The captain agreed. He had tried almost everything else.

SartoriIrvrash was awake, despite the late hour. It was impossible to sleep in the storm. He protested against the captain's decision. No one was in any mood to listen to his arguments; he was a foreigner, and in danger of being thrown overboard himself. He went and hid while Gleeat was dragged from her foul hold and thrown into the raging waters.

Within an hour, the worst of the wind died. By the time of false light, when Poorich was just visible ahead, nothing more than a fresh breeze prevailed. By dawn, the other three vessels were disclosed, miraculously unharmed and not too far distant —God the Azoiaxic was good. Soon, the mouth of the Kacol, where Keevasien lay, could be discerned through purplish coastal mists.

An unnatural gloom hovered about the hinges of the horizon. The sea all round the Sibornalese fleet was alive with dolphins, darting just below the surface. Flocks of sea and land birds numbering many hundreds circled overhead. They uttered no cry, but the beat of their myriad wings sounded like a downpour in which no rain fell. The flocks did not serve as the call "Good Tidings" rolled out from ship to coast.

As the wind died, the cordage slackened and slapped against the masts. The four ships closed as they approached the shore.

Dienu set a spyglass to her eye and stared at where a strip of island lay among the breaking waves. She saw men standing on the strip, and counted a dozen. One was coming forward. During the days of the monsoon, they had skirted the coasts of

Randonan; here Borlien commenced—enemy territory. It was important that news of the fleet's coming was not flashed ahead to Ottassol; surprise counted for much, in this as in most warlike enterprises.

The light improved, minute by minute. The *Golden Friendship* exchanged signals with the *Union,* the *Good Hope,* and the white caravel, the *Vajabhar Prayer,* alerting them to danger.

A man in a wide-brimmed hat was wading out into the foam. Behind him, at the mouth of the river, a boat could be seen, hull half-hidden. There was always the possibility that they were moving into an ambush and, getting too far in, would lose the wind and be trapped. Dienu stood tense at the rail of the quarterdeck; for a moment, she wished that her faithless Io were with her; he was always so quick to make up his mind.

The man in the surf unfurled a flag. The stripes of Borlien were revealed.

Dienu summoned artillerymen to line the landward rail.

The distance between ship and shore diminished. The man in the surf had halted, up to his thighs in water. He was waving the flag in an assured manner. The mad Borlienese . . .

Dienu instructed the artillery captain. He saluted, went down the companion ladder to give orders to his men. The men worked in pairs, one operating the wheel lock, the other supporting the muzzle.

"Fire!" shouted the artillery captain. A pause, and then a volley of shots.

So began the battle of Keevasien sandbar.

The *Golden Friendship* was close enough for Hanra TolramKetinet to make out the faces of the soldiery along its rail. He saw the artillerymen taking aim at him.

By now, the insignia on the sails had revealed that these were Sibornalese vessels, surprisingly far from home. He wondered if his opportunist king had concluded a treaty to bring Sibornal into the Western Wars on Borlien's side. He had no reason to believe them hostile—until the weapons were raised.

The *Friendship* swung almost side on to him, to present the

artillery men with the best line of fire. He estimated that its draught would allow it to come no farther in. The *Union* was ahead of its flagship, curving round to TolramKetinet's left, getting uncomfortably close to the east end of Keevasien Island. He heard shouted orders coming across the water, as the *Union*'s main and mizzen sails were taken in.

The two smaller ships, which had sailed closer to the Randonanese shore, were cutting in to his right. The *Good Hope* was still battling against the broad brown flood from the Western arm of the Kacol, the white *Vajabhar Prayer* was past—could indeed be said to be almost behind him, though still some distance away. On all these ships except the *Good Hope,* he could see the glint of gun barrels, pointing towards him.

He heard the artillery captain's order to fire. TolramKetinet dropped his flag, turned about, plunged into the water, and commenced swimming strongly back to the sand spit.

GortorLanstatet was already providing him with covering fire. He got his men down behind a shale ridge and directed half of his fire power at the flagship, half at the white caravel, the *Vajabhar Prayer.* The latter was still coming in fast, heading towards their position. The lieutenant had with him a good crossbowman; he directed him and another man to prepare a pitch fire-thrower.

Lead balls smacked in the water round the general. He swam underwater, coming up for air as infrequently as he could. He was aware of dolphins milling about close by, but they made no attempt to interfere with him.

Suddenly the firing stopped. He surfaced and looked back. The white caravel which bore the hierogram of the Great Wheel upon its sails had unwisely cut between him and the *Golden Friendship.* The Shiveninki soldiery, crowding on the topmost deck, were preparing to fire on the defenders of the spit.

Waves burst over him. The shore was unexpectedly steep. TolramKetinet grasped hold of a root and hauled himself among bushes, working forward a few feet into cover and then collapsing. He lay breathing heavily, his face against the brown sand. He was unhurt.

Before his inward view rose a memory of the lovely face of Queen MyrdemInggala. She was speaking seriously. He re-

membered how her lips moved. He was a survivor. He would win for her sake.

Yes, he was not clever. He should not have been made general. He did not possess the natural ability to command men which Lanstatet had. But.

Since he had received the queen of queen's message in Ordelay—the first time she had ever addressed him on a personal level, even at secondhand—he had thought of the king's intention to divorce her. TolramKetinet feared the king. His allegiance to the crown was divided. Although he understood the dynastic necessity for JandolAnganol's action, that royal decision had altered TolramKetinet's feelings. He told himself that the attraction he felt for the queen was treasonable. But the queen in exile was a different matter; treason no longer entered the question. Nor did loyalty to a king who had sent him off out of jealousy to die in a Randonanese jungle. He got to his feet again, and ran for GortorLanstatet's besieged strip.

His Borlienese troops gave him a cheer as TolramKetinet threw himself down among them. He embraced them as he peered out to seaward over the shingle ridge.

In a minute, the scene had changed in certain dramatic respects. The *Golden Friendship* had taken in its sails and lowered fore and aft anchors. It lay about two hundred yards offshore. A lucky fire bolt from the crossbow had set part of its bow and the artemon mast alight. As sailors fought the blaze, two longboats full of soldiers were pulling away from the ship; one of the boats—though the information would have been lost on TolramKetinet—was led by Admiral Odi Jeseratabhar, who stood rigid in the stern; SartoriIrvrash had insisted on accompanying her and sat rather ignominiously at her feet.

The *Union* had almost beached itself away to the left of the small island, and was embarking troops into the shallows; they waded doggedly ashore. Rather nearer was the *Vajabhar Prayer,* stuck in the shallows with sails hanging limp, and a boat full of soldiery making inexpertly for the shore. This boat was the nearest target, and matchlock fire was causing some damage to it.

Only the *Good Hope* had not changed position. Caught in the flow of the outpouring Kacol, it remained with all sail hoist, bowsprit pointing towards Keevasien Island, con-

tributing nothing to the struggle.

"They must believe they are facing the entire Keevasien garrison," GortorLanstatet said.

"We certainly need that garrison, poor devils. If we stay here we'll be slaughtered."

There was no way in which thirteen men, poorly armed, could defend themselves against four boatloads of troops armed with wheel locks.

It was then that the sea rose, opened, and rained assatassi.

From one end of the Sea of Eagles to the other, assatassi flew like darts from sea to shore.

Fisherfolk who understood the sea kept this day and the following one for celebration and feasting. It was a day which occurred only once early every summer during the Great Summer, at the time of high tide. In Lordryardry, nets were ready. In Ottassol, tarpaulins were spread. In Gravabagalinien, the queen's familiars had warned her to stay away from the deadly shore. What was a feast of plenty for the knowledgeable became a rain of death for the ignorant.

Swimming in from far mid-ocean, shoals of assatassi headed for land. Their migrations during the Great Summer spanned the globe. Their feeding grounds were in the distant reaches of the Ardent Sea, where no man had visited. On reaching maturity, the shoals started their long swim eastwards, against the flow of ocean currents. Through the Climent Sea they went, and on through the narrow gates of the Straits of Cadmer.

This narrowing brought the shoals into greater proximity. The enforced closeness, together with the onset of monsoon weather in the Narmosset Sea, brought a changed behaviour pattern. What had been a long leisurely swim, without apparent aim, became a race—a race which was destined to end in the death-flight.

But for that actual flight, that desired death along thousands of miles of coast, another factor was necessary. The tide had to be right.

Throughout the centuries of winter, Helliconia's seas were all but tideless. After apastron and the darkest years, Freyr again began to make its influence felt. As its gigantic mass

beckoned the chill planet back towards the light, so too it stirred the seas. Its pull on the ocean mass was now, only 118 Earth years from periastron, considerable. The time in the small year had arrived when the combined mass of Batalix and Freyr worked together. The result was a sixty percent increase in tidal strength over the winter situation.

The narrow seas between Hespagorat and Campannlat, the strong flow of the current to the west, conspired to make the spring tides mount and break suddenly with dramatic force. On that phenomenal flow of water shoreward, the shoals of assatassi launched themselves.

The ships of the Sibornalese fleet found themselves first with no water under their draught, and then battered by a tidal wave rising precipitously and without warning from the sea. Before the crews could realise what had hit them, the assatassi were there. The death-flight was on.

The assatassi is a necrogenetic fish, or more properly fish-lizard. It reaches a length of eighteen inches at maturity; it has two large multifacetted eyes; but what chiefly distinguishes it is its straight bill of bone, supported by a boney cranium. On its death-flight the assatassi reaches speeds high enough for this bill to penetrate a man to the heart.

Off Keevasien, the assatassi broke from the surface a hundred yards further out than the *Golden Friendship*. So full did the air become with them that those which flew low enough to skim the water and those who gained heights of fifty feet alike formed part of a solid body of fast-moving fish-lizard. They gleamed like a myriad of sword blades. The air became a sword blade.

The flagship was raked by assatassi from stem to stem. Anyone standing on deck was struck. The seaward side of the ship was covered with creatures, hanging skewered by their bills. So with the three other ships. But it was the boats, already waterlogged by the tide, which suffered most. All their company was wounded, and many were killed outright. The boards were stove in. All four boats began to sink.

Cries of pain and terror sounded—lost beneath the shriek of birds who plunged down to snatch a meal from the air.

The first wave of assatassi lasted for two minutes.

Only TolramKetinet's men survived without injury. The tidal wave had washed right over them, so that they were still

prostrate and half-conscious when the assatassi came over.

When the bombardment ceased, they looked up to see chaos all round. Sibornalese troops were struggling in the water, where large predatory fish were closing in. The *Good Hope* appeared to be drifting helplessly out to sea, its main mast shattered. The fire in the masts of the *Golden Friendship* was raging unchecked. All round, rocks and trees were covered with smashed bodies of fish. Many assatassi had impaled themselves by their bills high up in branches or trunks of trees, or were lodged in inaccessible crannies in the rocks. The death-flight had taken many fish a long way inland. The sombre jungle overhanging the mouth of the Kacol were now interpenetrated by fish-lizards which would be rotten before Batalix-set.

Far from being some morbid fancy, assatassi behaviour was proof of the versatility by which species were perpetuated. Like the otherwise dissimilar biyelk, yelk, and gunnadu, which covered the icy plains of Campannlat in winter, the assatassi were necrogenes and gave birth only through death.

Assatassi were hermaphrodite. Formed in too rudimentary a way to carry within them the normal apparatus of reproduction, assatassi propagation involved destruction. Germination budded within their gut, taking the form of threadlike maggots. Embedded safely within the parental intestine, the maggots survived the impact of the death-flight and lived to feed on the carrion thus provided.

They ate their way to the outside world. There the maggots metamorphosed into a legged larval stage, closely resembling miniature iguana. In the autumn of the small year, the miniature iguanas, hitherto land-bound, made their way back to the great parent sea, fading down into it, sinking into it as tracelessly as grains of sand, to replenish the cycle of assatassi life.

So startling was the sudden turn in events that Tolram-Ketinet and Lanstatet stood up on their spit to look about them. The huge wave which had drenched all the foreshore was the prelude to an onrushing flood which set the Sibornalese struggling ashore into difficulties.

The first wave had rushed up the Kacol. Its spent waters were now returning, bringing black muds which stained the sea with their eddies. More ominously, to TolramKetinet's

left, a stream of bodies was making sodden progress out from
the river mouth, accompanied by screaming seabirds. The
general's guess was that these were the slaughtered dead of
Keevasien, about to find burial.

The incoming wave had overturned the *Golden Friendship*'s
longboat. Those who did not stay submerged long enough rose
to meet the clouds of fish-lizard.

SartoriIrvrash found himself struggling in the water with
the wounded, among whom he soon saw Odi Jeseratabhar.
One of her cheeks was torn, and a fish-lizard was embedded in
the flesh of the back of her neck. Many of the wounded were
being attacked by predatory gulls. SartoriIrvrash himself was
uninjured. Fighting his way over to Odi, he lifted her in his
arms and began to wade ashore. The water kept getting
deeper.

His face came close to the assatassi embedded in her neck,
his eye close to its great boney eye from which all life had not
yet faded.

"How can mankind ever build up bulwarks against nature,
when it keeps flooding in like a deluge, indifferent to what
it carries away?" he said to himself. "So much for you,
Akhanaba, you hrattock!"

It was all he could do to keep the unconscious Odi's head
above water. There was a spit of land only a few yards distant,
yet still the water rose about him. He cried in fear—and then
on the spit he saw a man who resembled JandolAnganol's
hated general, TolramKetinet.

TolramKetinet and GortorLanstatet were studying the
Sibornalese ship, the *Vajabhar Prayer,* which lay only a short
distance to their right. The tidal wave had flung it ashore, but
a swirling rebate of waters from the Kacol floated it again.
Apart from the assatassi peppering its starboard side, it was in
good order. The crew, thoroughly demoralised, were throwing
themselves ashore and making off into the bushes to safety.

"The ship's ours for the taking, Gortor. What do you say?"

"I'm no sailor, but there's a breeze rising from on shore."

The general turned to the twelve men with him.

"You are my brave comrades. None of you lacks courage.
If one of you had lacked courage for a moment, we all would

have perished. Now we have one last exploit before we are safe. There is no help for us at Keevasien, so we must sail along the coast. We are going to borrow this white caravel. It's a gift—though a gift we may have to fight for. Swords ready. Follow me!''

As he ran down the strand, his force following, he almost bumped into a bedraggled man struggling for the shore with a woman in his arms. The man called his name.

"Hanra! Help!''

He saw in astonishment that it was the Borlienese chancellor, and the thought came, Here must be another that JandolAnganol has cheated. . . .

He halted his party. Lanstatet dragged SartoriIrvrash from the flood, two of the men took hold of the woman between them. She was moaning and returning to consciousness. They dashed on to the *Vajabhar Prayer*.

The crew and soldiery of the Shiveninki vessel had suffered casualties. Some were killed; any wounded by the assatassi were mostly ashore. Birds darted over the ship, eating fish-lizards caught on the rigging. There remained a handful of soldiers with their officers to put up a fight. But TolramKetinet's party swarmed up the seaward side of the vessel and took them on. The opposition was already demoralised. After a halfhearted engagement, they surrendered and were made to jump ashore. GortorLanstatet took a party of three below, to round up any hiding and get them off the ship. Within seven minutes of boarding, they were ready to sail.

Eight of the men pushed the caravel. Slowly, the ship swung about and the sails filled, torn though they were by the fish-lizards.

"Move! Move!'' shouted TolramKetinet from the bridge.

"I hate ships,'' GortorLanstatet said. He fell on his knees and prayed, hands above his head. There was an explosion, and water sprayed all over them.

Their piracy had been seen from the *Golden Friendship*. A gunner was firing one of the cannon at them from a range of two hundred yards.

As the *Prayer*, at no more than walking pace, glided out of the shelter of the overhanging jungle, a stronger breeze caught it. Without needing to be told, two gunners among the

Borlienese manned one of the cannon on the gundeck. They fired it once at the *Golden Friendship;* then the angle between the ships became so acute that the muzzle of the cannon could not be turned sufficiently in the square gunport to aim at the flagship.

The gun crew in the flagship were faced with the same problem. One more ball flew over, landing in the undergrowth of the island, then silence. The eight men in the water swarmed up boarding nets and climbed on deck cheering as the *Prayer* gathered way.

The island foliage slid away to port. Trees were being attacked by the scavenging birds, devouring impaled assatassi, while the hornets and bees they disturbed buzzed savagely round them. The *Prayer* was about to pass the Uskuti ship, *Union,* still beached with its bows into the land.

"Can you blow it up as we pass?" GortorLanstatet shouted down to the gundeck.

The gunners ran to port, opened the gunport, primed the clumsy cannon. But now they were moving too fast, and the gun could not be made ready in time.

The disgraced Io Pasharatid was among the crew and soldiery on the *Union* who had deserted ship to flee from the death-flight into the island jungle. He went first. His desertion owed more to calculation than panic.

Alone among the Sibornalese in the fleet, he had once visited Keevasien. That had been during his tour of duty as ambassador to the Borlienese court. While he had no love of the place, it was in his mind that he might purchase supplies there to eke out the boredom of ship's rations. His calculation was that he might take off two hours during the general panic without being missed.

Seeing the burnt-out ruins of the town had changed his mind. He returned to the scene of action in time to witness the *Vajabhar Prayer* gliding by his own ship, with Hanra Tolram-Ketinet, favourite of the queen of queens, standing on its quarterdeck.

Io Pasharatid was not entirely sunk in self-interest, though in this instant jealousy played some part in his actions. He ran forward, rallying the men who crouched among the bushes, driving them back aboard the *Union.* The tidal wave had set it on a strip of beach, unharmed.

After some manoeuvring with oars, assisted by the flood tide, they floated the carrack free of the beach. The sails were trimmed and, slowly, her bows drifted round towards the open sea.

Signal flags were run up, reporting that the *Union* was in pursuit of the pirate. The signal was intended for the eyes of Dienu Pasharatid on the *Golden Friendship;* but she would never read another signal. Hers was one of the first human deaths occasioned by the death-flight of the assatassi.

Only when they were out of the bay and a fresh west wind was carrying them slowly against the prevailing ocean stream, did TolramKetinet and SartoriIrvrash take the chance to embrace each other.

When they had given each other some report of their adventures, TolramKetinet said, "I have little to be proud of. Since I am a soldier, I cannot complain where I am sent. My generalship has been such that my forces dissolved without my being able to fight a single battle. It is a disgrace I shall always live with. Randonan swallows men whole."

The ex-chancellor said, after a moment, "I am grateful for my travels, which were no more planned than yours. The Sibornalese used me, but from the experience has come something valuable. More than valuable."

He made a gesture indicating Odi Jeseratabhar, whose wound was now dressed, and who sat on the deck listening to the men talking, her eyes closed.

"I'm getting old and the loves of the old are always funny to mere youths like you, Hanra. No, don't deny it." He laughed. "And something more. I realise for the first time how fortunate our generations are to live at this period of the Great Year, when heat prevails. How did our ancestors survive the winter? And the wheel will turn, and again it will be winter. What a malign fate, to grow up as Freyr is dying and know nothing else. In parts of Sibornal, people don't see Freyr at all during the centuries of winter."

TolramKetinet shrugged. "It's chance."

"But the enormous scale of growth and destruction. . . . Perhaps our mistake is to think ourselves apart from nature. Well, I know of old that you are less than enthralled by such

speculations. One thing I must say. I believe I have resolved one question of such revolutionary nature . . ."

He hesitated, stroking his damp whiskers. Smiling, Tolram-Ketinet urged him to go on.

"I believe I have thought what no man has ever thought. This lady has inspired me. I need to get to Oldorando or Pannoval to lay my thought before the powers of the Holy Pannovalan Empire. My deduction, I should call it. There I shall certainly be rewarded, and Odi and I can then live comfortably."

Scrutinising his whiskery face, TolramKetinet said, "Deductions that are paid for! They must be valuable."

The man's a fool and I always knew it, thought the ex-chancellor, but he could not resist the chance to explain.

"You see," SartoriIrvrash said, lowering his voice so that it could hardly be heard for the slap of the canvas above them, "I could never abide the ancipital race, unlike my master. There lay much of our difference. My thought, my deduction, weighs very much against the ancipitals. Hence it will be rewarded, according to the terms of the Pannovlan Pronouncement."

Rising from her chair, Odi Jeseratabhar took Sartori-Irvrash's arm and said to TolramKetinet and Lanstatet, who had joined them, "You may not know that King Jandol-Anganol destroyed all the chancellor's life's work, his 'Alphabet of History and Nature.' It's a crime not to be forgotten. The chancellor's deduction, as he modestly names it, will revenge him on JandolAnganol, and perhaps allow us both to work together on reassembling the 'Alphabet.' "

Lanstatet said sharply, "Lady, you're our enemy, sworn to destroy our native land. You should be below decks in irons."

"That's past," said SartoriIrvrash, with dignity. "We're simply wandering scholars now—and homeless ones at that."

"Wandering scholars . . ." It was too much for the general, so he asked a practical question. "How are you to get to Pannoval?"

"Oldorando would suit me—it is nearer, and I hope to arrive before the king, if he is not already there, to cause him maximum botheration before he weds the Madi princess. You have no love of him either, Hanra. You'll be the ideal person to take me there."

"I'm going to Gravabagalinien," said TolramKetinet grimly, "if only this tub will sail us there, and we are not overtaken by our enemies."

All looked back. The *Vajabhar Prayer* was now in open sea, making laboured progress eastwards along the coast. The *Union* had emerged from Keevasien Bay, but lay far astern. There was no immediate danger of its catching them.

"You will see your sister Mai in Gravabagalinien," SartoriIrvrash told the general. The general smiled without replying.

Later in the day, distantly, they saw the *Good Hope* also in pursuit, with a jury-rigged main mast. The two pursuing vessels were lost in haze as thunderheads towered from the western sea, their edges cast in copper. Lightning darted silently in the belly of the cloud.

A second wave of assatassi rose from the sea, like a wing unfurling, to cast itself upon the land. The *Prayer* was too far from the coast to suffer ill effect. Only a few of the flying fish-lizard darted past the vessel. The men looked on complacently at what that morning had struck them dumb. As they crawled towards Gravabagalinien, thunderous darkness fell and tiny splinters of light showed ashore, where natives were feasting on the dead invaders.

And something without identity made its way towards the place where the queen of queens resided in her wooden palace: a human body.

RobaydayAnganol had stolen a ride downriver from Matrassyl to Ottassol, keeping ahead of his father. Wherever he went now, he went with a special haste in his gait, half-looking back; did he but know it, this aspect of a man pursued made him resemble his father. He thought of himself as pursuing. Vengeance against his father filled his mind.

In Ottassol, instead of going to the underground palace which his father was due to visit, he went to an old friend of SartoriIrvrash's, the deuteroscopist and anatomist, Bardol CaraBansity. CaraBansity was feeling no great goodwill for the king or his strange son.

He and his wife had staying with them a society of deuteroscopists from Vallgos. He offered Robayday a bed in a house

he maintained near the harbour, where, he said, a girl would look after his needs.

Robayday's interest in women was sporadic. However, he immediately found the woman in CaraBansity's harbour house attractive, with her long brown hair and a mysterious air of authority, as if she knew a secret shared by nobody else.

She gave her name as Metty, and he remembered her. She was a girl he had once enjoyed in Matrassyl. Her mother had assisted his father when the latter was wounded after the Battle of the Cosgatt. Her real name was Abathy.

She did not recognise him. No doubt she was a lady with many lovers. At first, Robayday did not enlighten her. He remained inert and let her come to him. To impress, she spoke of a scandalous connection with Sibornalese officials in Matrassyl; he watched her expression as she spoke, and thought of how different her view of the world was, with its clandestine comings and goings.

"You do not recognise me, for I am hard to recognise, yet there was a day when you wore less kohl on your eyes when we were close as tongue to teeth . . ."

Then she spoke his name and embraced him, exhibiting delight.

Later, she said she had cause to be grateful to her mother, to whom she sent back money regularly, for teaching her how to behave with men. She was cultivating a taste for the highborn and powerful; she had been shamefully seduced, she said, by CaraBansity, but now she hoped for better things. She kissed him.

She allowed her charfrul to slip and reveal her pale legs. Seeing cruelty everywhere, Robayday saw only the spider's trap. Eagerly, he entered it. Later, they lay together and kissed, and she laughed prettily. He loved her and hated her.

All his impulses screamed to him to hurry on to Oldorando, yet he remained with her for another day. He hated her and he loved her.

The second evening in her house. He thought that history would cease if he remained for ever. She again let down her beautiful hair and hitched up her skirt, climbing onto the couch with him again.

They embraced. They made love. She was a well of delight. Abathy was starting to undress him for more prolonged enjoy-

ment when there was a thumping at her door. They both sat up, startled.

A more violent thump. The door burst open, and in blundered a burly young fellow dressed in the uncouth Dimariamian fashion. It was Div Muntras, in bull-like quest of love.

"Abathy!" he cried. She yelled by way of reply.

After sailing alone to Ottassol, Div had traced his way to her by diligent enquiry. He had sold everything he possessed, except for the talismanic watch stolen from Billish, which reposed safe in his body belt. And here, at the end of the trail, he found the girl who had dominated his thoughts ever since she idled voluptuously with his father on the deck of the *Lordryardry Lady* trittoming with another man.

His face altered into the image of rage. He raised his fists. He bellowed and charged forward.

Robayday jumped up and stood on the couch, his back to the wall. His face was dark with anger at the intrusion. That the king's son should be shouted at—and at such a moment! He had no thought but to kill the intruder. In his belt was a dagger shaped from a phagor horn, a sharp two-sided instrument. He drew it.

Div was further enraged by the sight of the weapon. He could soon dispose of this slight lad, this meddler.

Abathy screamed at him, but he paid no heed. She stood with both hands to her pretty mouth, eyes wide in terror. That pleased Div. She would be next.

He rushed to the attack, landing on the couch with a leap. He received the point of the horn just below his lowest rib. The tip grated against the rib as it slid in. His charge ensured that it went into his flesh to the hilt, penetrating the spleen and the stomach, at which point the handle broke off in his opponent's hand.

A long baffled groan escaped Div. Liquids gushed over the wall as he fell against it and slipped to the floor.

Raging, Robayday left the girl to weep. He fetched two men who disposed of the corpse by tossing it into the Takissa.

Robayday ran from the city, as if pursued by mad dogs. He never returned to the girl or to the room. He had an appointment which he had been in danger of forgetting, an appointment in Oldorando. Over and again, he wept and cursed along the road.

Carried by the current, turning as it went, the body of Div Muntras drifted among the shipping to the mouth of the Takissa. No one saw it go, for most folk, even slaves, were indulging in a grand assatassi fry. Fish moved in to give the corpse their attention as the sodden mass was taken into the maw of the sea, to become part of the progression of waters westwards, towards Gravabagalinien.

That evening, when the suns sank, simple people came down to the beaches and headlands. In all the countries whose boundaries were lapped by the Sea of Eagles, in Randonan, Borlien, Thribriat, Iskahandi, and Dimariam, crowds gathered by the water's edge.

The great assatassi feast was ending. Here was a time to pause and give thanks for such blessings to the spirit who dwelt in the waters.

While women sang and danced on the sand, their menfolk waded into the sea bearing little boats. The boats were leaves, on which short candles burned, giving off a sweet scent.

On every beach, as dusk drew in, whole navies of leaves were launched. Some still floated, burning dim, long after darkness had fallen, forming panoramas reminiscent to the superstitious of gossies and fessups suspended in their more permanent darkness. Some were carried far out to sea before their feeble flames were quenched.

XVIII

VISITORS FROM THE DEEP

Anyone advancing on Gravabagalinien could see from a distance the wooden palace which was the queen's refuge. It stood without compromise, like a toy left on a beach.

Legend said that Gravabagalinien was haunted. That at some distant time in the past a fortress had stood in place of the flimsy palace. That it had been entirely destroyed in a great battle.

But nobody knew who fought there, or for what reason. Only that many had died, and had been buried in shallow graves where they fell. Their shades, far from their proper land-octaves, were still reputed to haunt the spot.

Certainly, another tragedy was not being acted out on the old unhallowed ground. For the time had come round when King JandolAnganol arrived in two ships with his men and phagors, and with Esomberr and CaraBansity, to divorce his queen.

And Queen MyrdemInggala had descended the stairs and had submitted to the divorce. And wine had been brought, and much mischief had been permitted. And Alam Esomberr,

the envoy of the C'Sarr, had made his way into the ex-queen's chamber only a few hours after he had conducted the ceremony of divorcement. And then had come the announcement that Simoda Tal had been slain in far Oldorando. And this sore news had been delivered to the king as the first rays of eastern Batalix painted yellow the peeling outer walls of the palace.

And now an inevitability could be discerned in the affairs of men and phagors, as events drew towards a climax in which even the chief participants would be swept helplessly along like comets plunging into darkness.

JandolAnganol's voice was low with sorrow as he tore the hairs from his beard and head, crying to Akhanaba.

"Thy servant falls before thee, O Great One. Thou has visited sorrow upon me. Thou hast caused my armies to go down in defeat. Thou hast caused my son to forsake me. Thou hast caused me to divorce my beloved queen, MyrdemInggala. Thou hast caused my intended bride to be assassinated. . . . What more must I suffer for Thy sake?

"Let not my people suffer. Accept my suffering, O Great Lord, as a sufficient sacrifice for my people."

As he rose and put on his tunic, the pallid-chopped Abstrog-Athenat said casually, "It's true that the army has lost Randonan. But all civilised countries are surrounded by barbaric ones, and are defeated when their armies invade them. We should go, not with the sword, but with the word of God."

"Crusades are in the province of Pannoval, not a poor country like ours, Vicar." Adjusting his tunic over his wounds, he felt in his pocket the three-faced timepiece he had taken from CaraBansity in Ottassol. Now as then, he felt it to be an object of ill omen.

AbstrogAthenat bowed, holding the whip behind him. "At least we might please the All-Powerful by being more human, and shunning the inhuman."

In sudden anger, JandolAnganol struck out with his left hand and caught the vicar across the cheek with his knuckles.

"You keep to God's affairs and leave worldly matters to me."

He knew what the man meant. His reference had been to purging phagors from Borlien.

Leaving his tunic open, feeling its fabric absorb the blood of his latest scourging, JandolAnganol climbed from the subterranean chapel to the ground floor of the wooden palace. Yuli jumped up to welcome him.

His head throbbed as if he were going blind. He patted the little phagor and sank his fingers into its thick pelage.

Shadows still lay long outside the palace. He scarcely knew how to face the morning: only yesterday he had arrived at Gravabagalinien and—in the presence of the envoy of the Holy C'Sarr, Alam Esomberr—he had divorced his fair queen.

The palace was shuttered as it had been the day previously. Now men lay everywhere in the rooms, still in drink-sodden sleep. Sunlight cut its way into the darkness in a crisscross of lines, making it seem like a woven basket that he walked through, heading for the doorway.

When he flung the door open, the Royal First Phagorian Guard stood on duty outside, its ranks of long jaws and horns unmoving. That was something worth seeing anyway, he told himself, trying to dispel his black mood.

He walked in the air before the heat rose. He saw the sea and felt the breeze, and heeded them not. Before dawn, while he still slept heavily from drink, Esomberr had come to him. Beside Esomberr stood his new chancellor, Bardol CaraBansity. They had informed him that the Madi princess he intended to marry was dead, killed by an assassin.

Nothing was left.

Why had he gone to such trouble to divorce his true wife? What had possessed his mind? There were severances the hardiest could not survive.

It was his wish to speak to her.

A delicacy in him restrained him from sending a messenger up to her room. He knew that she was there with the little princess Tatro waiting for him to leave and take his soldiers with him. Probably she had heard the news the men had brought in the night. Probably she feared assassination. Probably she hated him.

He turned in his sharp way, as if to catch himself out. His new chancellor was approaching with his heavy, determined tread, jowls jolting.

JandolAnganol eyed CaraBansity and then turned his back on him. CaraBansity was forced to skirt him and Yuli before making a clumsy bow.

The king stared at him. Neither man spoke. CaraBansity turned his cloudy gaze from the king's.

"You find me in an ill mood."

"I have not slept either, sire. I deeply regret this fresh misfortune which has visited you."

"My ill mood covers not only the All-Powerful but you, who are not so powerful."

"What have I done to displease you, sire?"

The Eagle drew his brows together, making his gaze more hawklike.

"I know you are secretly against me. You have a reputation for craftiness. I saw that gloating look you could not conceal when you came to announce the death of—you know who."

"The Madi princess? If you so distrust me, sire, you must not take me on as your chancellor."

JandolAnganol presented his back again, with the yellow gauze of his tunic patterned red with blood like an ancient banner.

CaraBansity began to shuffle. He stared up abstractedly at the palace and saw how its white paint was peeling. He felt what it was to be a commoner and what it was to be a king.

He enjoyed his life. He knew many people and was useful to the community. He loved his wife. He prospered. Yet the king had come along and snatched him up against his will, as if he were a slave.

He had accepted the role and, being a man of character, made the best of it. Now this sovereign had the gall to tell CaraBansity that he was secretly against his king. There was no limit to royal impertinence—and as yet he could see no way to escape following JandolAnganol all the way to Oldorando.

His sympathy with the king's predicament left him.

"I meant to say, Your Majesty," he began in a determined voice, and then became alarmed by his own temerity, looking at that bloody back. "This is just a trifling matter, of course, but, before we set sail from Ottassol, you took from me that interesting timepiece with three faces. Do you happen to have it still?"

The king did not turn or move.

He said, "I have it here in my tunic."

CaraBansity took a deep breath and then said, much more feebly than he intended, "Would you return it to me, please, Your Majesty?"

"This is no time to approach me for favors, when Borlien's standing within the Holy Empire is threatened." He was the Eagle as he spoke.

They both stood, watching Yuli root in the bushes by the palace. The creature pissed after the retromingent fashion of his species.

The king began to walk with measured pace in the direction of the sea.

I'm no better than a damned slave, said CaraBansity to himself. He followed.

With the runt skipping beside him, the king speeded his step, speaking rapidly as he went, so that the portly deuteroscopist was forced to catch up. He never mentioned the subject of his timepiece again.

"Akhanaba had favoured me and set many fruits in my life's way. And always to those fruits an additional flavour was given when I saw that more were promised—tomorrow, and the day after tomorrow, and the day after that. Whatever I wished, I might have more of.

"It's true I suffered setbacks and defeats, but that within a general atmosphere of promise. I did not allow them to disturb me for long. My personal defeat in the Cosgatt—well, I learnt from it and put it behind me, and eventually won a great victory there."

They passed a line of gwing-gwing trees. The king snatched down a gwing-gwing, biting into it to the stone as he spoke, letting the juice run down his chin. He gestured, clutching the despoiled fruit.

"Today, I see my life in a new light. Perhaps all that was promised me I have already received . . . I am, after all, more than twenty-five years." He spoke with difficulty. "Perhaps this is my summer, and in future when I shake the bush no fruit will fall. . . . Can I any longer rely on plenty? Doesn't our religion warn us that we must expect times of famine? Fah!—Akhanaba is like a Sibornalese, always obsessed with the winter to come."

They walked along the low cliffs separating land from

beach, where the queen was accustomed to swim.

"Tell me," said JandolAnganol carelessly, "if you as an atheist do not have a religious construction to put to the case —how do you see my difficulties?"

CaraBansity was silent, setting his beefy red face towards the ground as if guarding it against the king's abrasive look. Work up your courage, he told himself.

"Well? Come, say what you will. I have no spirit! I have been flogged by my whey-visaged vicar . . ."

When CaraBansity stopped walking, the king followed suit.

"Sire, I recently to oblige a friend took into my establishment a certain young lady. My wife and I entertain many people, some alive, some dead; also animals for dissection, and phagors, either for dissection or for bodyguards. None caused as much trouble as that certain young lady.

"I love my wife, and ever continue to do so. But I lusted after that certain young lady. I had a contempt for her, yet I lusted after her. I despised myself, and yet I lusted after her."

"But did you have her?"

CaraBansity laughed, and for the first time in the king's presence, his face lightened. "Sire, I had her much as you have that gwing-gwing, the fruit par excellence of dimday. The juice, sire, ran down. . . . But it was khmir and not love, and once the khmir was quenched—though that was certainly a process . . . that was summer process, sire—once it was quenched, I loathed myself and wanted nothing more of her. I established her apart and told her never to see me again. Since when, I learn that she has taken to her mother's profession, and caused the death of at least one man."

"What's all this to me?" asked the king with a haughty look.

"Sire, I believe the activating principle of your life to be lust rather than love.

"You tell me in religious terms that Akhanaba has favoured you and put many fruits in your path. In my terms, you have taken what you would, done what you would, and so you wish to continue. You favour ancipitals as instruments of your lust, not caring that phagors are in reality never submissive. Nothing really can stand in your way—except the queen of queens. She can stand in your way because she alone in the world commands your love, and perhaps some respect. That is

why you hate her, because you love her.

"She stands between you and your khmir. She alone can contain your—duality. In you as in me, and perhaps as in all men, the two principles are divided—but the division in you is as great as your state is great.

"If you prefer to believe in Akhanaba, believe now that he has by these supposed setbacks given you warning that your life is about to go wrong. Make it right while the chance is offered."

They stopped on the cliff, ignoring the dull thunders of the sea, and stood face to face, both of them tense. The king heard his chancellor out with never a movement, while Yuli rolled in coarse grass nearby.

"How would you suggest that I make my life right?" A less self-assured man than CaraBansity would have taken fright from his tone.

"This is my advice, Your Majesty. Do not go to Oldorando. Simoda Tal is dead. You no longer have reason to visit an unfriendly capital. As a deuteroscopist, I warn you against it." Under his grizzled eyebrows, CaraBansity kept careful note of the effect of his words on JandolAnganol.

"Your place is in your own kingdom, never more so than now, while your enemies have not forgotten the Massacre of the Myrdolators. Return to Matrassyl.

"Your rightful queen is here. Fall before her and ask forgiveness. Tear up Esomberr's bill before her eyes. Take back what you love most. Your sanity lies in her. Reject the cozzening of Pannoval."

The Eagle glared out to sea, eyes rapidly blinking.

"Live a saner life, Majesty. Win back your son. Kick out Pannoval, kick out the phagor guard, live a sane life with your queen. Reject the false Akhanaba, who has led you—"

But he had gone too far.

Matchless fury seized the king. A rage filled him until he was rage personified. He hurled himself bodily upon CaraBansity. Before this anger beyond reason, CaraBansity quailed and fell an instant before the king was on him. Kneeling on his prostrate body, the king drew his sword. CaraBansity screamed.

"Spare me, Your Majesty! Last night I saved your queen from vile rape."

JandolAnganol paused, then stood, sword point directed at the quaking body huddled by his feet. "Who would dare touch the queen when I was near? Answer?"

"Your Majesty . . ." The voice trembled slightly, the lips uttering it were pressed almost to the ground; yet what it said was clear. "You were drunk. And Envoy Esomberr went into her room to ravish her."

The king breathed deep. He sheathed his sword. He stood without movement.

"You base commoner! How could you understand the life of a king? I do not go back along the path I have once trod. You may possess life, which is mine to take, but I have a destiny and shall follow on where the All-Powerful leads.

"Crawl back to where you belong. You cannot advise me. Keep out of my way!"

Yet he still stood over the grovelling anatomist. When Yuli came snuffling up, the king turned suddenly away and strode back to the wooden palace.

The guard roused at his shout. They were to be away from Gravabagalinien within the hour. They would march for Oldorando as planned. His voice, his cold fury, stirred up the palace as if it were a nest of rickybacks disturbed by the lifting of a log. Esomberr's vicars could be heard within, calling to each other in high voices.

This commotion reached the queen in her chambers. She stood in the middle of her ivory room, listening. Her bodyguard was at the door. Mai TolramKetinet sat with two maids in the anteroom, clutching Tatro. Thick curtains were drawn across the windows.

MyrdemInggala wore a long flimsy dress. Her face was as pale as the shadow of a cowbird's wing on snow. She stood breathing the warm air into her lungs and out again, listening to the sound of men and hoxneys, of curses and commands below. Once she went to the curtains; then, as if disdaining her own weakness, withdrew the hand she had raised and returned to where she waited before. The heat brought out beads of perspiration which clung to her forehead like pearls. She heard the king's voice once distinctly, then not again.

As for CaraBansity, he climbed to his feet when the king had gone. He walked down to the bay where he could not be

seen, to recover his colour. After a while, he began to sing. He
had his liberty back, if not his timepiece.

In his pain, the king went to a small room in one of the
rickety towers and bolted the door behind him. Dust drifting
down gave phantom substance to slices of gold shining in
through a lattice. The place smelt of feathers, fungus, and old
straw. On the bare boards of the floor were pigeon droppings,
but the king, ignoring them, lay down and cast himself by an
effort of will into pauk.

His soul, detached from his body, became tranquil. Like a
moth wing, it sank into the velvety darkness. The darkness remained when all else had gone.

This was the paradox of the limbo in which the soul now
drifted rudderless: that it extended everywhere and was an
endless domain, while at the same time being as familiar to
him as the dark space under the bedclothes to a child.

The soul had no mortal eyes. It saw with a different vision.
It saw beneath it, through the obsidian, a host of dim lights,
stationary but seeming to move in relation to each other
because of the soul's descent. Each light had once been a living
spirit. Each was now drawn to the great mother-principle
which would exist even when the world was dead, the original
beholder, the principle even greater than—or at least apart
from—such gods as Akhanaba.

And the soul moved in particular to one light that attracted
it, the gossie of its father.

The spark that had once been no less a personage than
VarpalAnganol, King of Borlien, resembled only a tentative
sketch of sunshine on an old wall, with its ribs, its pelvis,
scarcely drawn. All that remained of the head which had worn
the crown was the suggestion of a stone, with ambers faintly
connotating eye sockets. Beneath this little cockleshell—visible through it—were fessups like trails of dust.

"Father, I come before you, your unworthy son, to beg
your forgiveness for my crimes to you." So spoke the soul of
JandolAnganol, hanging where no air was.

"My dear son, you are welcome here, welcome whenever
you can find time to visit your father, now among the ranks of

the dead. I have no reproach for you. You were always my
dear son."

"Father, I shall not mind your reproaches. Rather, I welcome your most bitter rebukes, for I know how great is my sin
against you."

The silences between their speeches were immeasurable
because no breath was exhaled.

"Hush, my son, nobody needs to talk of sin among this
company. You were my loving son, and that suffices. No more
need be said. Grieve not."

When it seemed time to speak, a dusty fire, the mere death
of a candle flame, issued from where a mouth had been. Its
smoke could be seen ascending between the cage of the ribs
and up the stack of the throat.

The soul spoke again. "Father, I beg you to pour your
wrath upon me for all that I did against you in your life, and
for causing your death. Lessen my guilt. It is too much to
bear."

"You are innocent, my son, as innocent as the wave that
splashes on the shore. Feel no guilt for the happiness you
brought into my life. Now in the residue of that life, I have no
wrath to bring against you."

"Father, I kept you imprisoned ten years in a dungeon of
the castle. In what way can I earn forgiveness for that act?"

The flame moved upwards, issuing as sparks.

"That time is forgotten, son. I scarcely remember a time of
imprisonment, for you were always there to speak with me.
Those occasions were cherished, for you asked advice of
me—which I freely gave, as far as it was in my capacity."

"It was a melancholy place."

"It gave me time to think over the failings of my own life, to
prepare myself for what was to come."

"Father, how your forgiveness wounds me!"

"Come closer, my boy, and let me comfort you."

But for the living to touch the dead was forbidden in the
realm of the original beholder. If that ultimate duality was
breached, then both were consumed. The soul floated lightly
away from the thing that hung before it in the abyss.

"Comfort me with more advice, Father."

"Speak."

"First of all, let me know whether that tormented son of

mine has fallen among you. I fear the instability of his life."

"I shall welcome the boy when he arrives, never worry—but as yet he still journeys in the world of light."

After a moment, the soul communicated again.

"Father, you perceive my position among the living. Advise me where I am to go. Am I to return to Matrassyl? Should I remain in Gravabagalinien? Or shall I continue to Oldorando? Where does my most fruitful future lie?"

"In each place there are those who await you. But there is one who awaits you in Oldorando whom you know not. That one holds your destiny. Go to Oldorando."

"Your advice will guide my actions."

From among the sparkling battalions of the dead, the soul rose, slowly at first, and then with a great urgency. Somewhere, a drum was sounding. The sparks dissolved below, sinking back into the original beholder.

The inanimate anatomy on the floor in the belfry began slowly to move. Its limbs twitched. It sat up. Its eyes opened in a blank face.

The only living thing to meet its gaze was Yuli, who crawled nearer and said, "My poor king in tether."

Without answering, JandolAnganol ruffled the runt's fur and let it snuggle against him.

"Oh, Yuli, what a thing is life."

After a minute, he patted the ancipital across the shoulders. "You're a good boy. No harm in you."

As the creature snuggled against him, the king felt an object against his side, and drew from his pocket the watch with three faces which he had taken from CaraBansity. Whenever he looked at it, his thoughts became troubled, yet he could not find it in himself to throw it away.

Once, the timepiece had belonged to Billy, the creature who claimed to come from a world not ruled by Akhanaba. It was necessary to banish Billy from consciousness (as one banished the thought of those damned Myrdolators), for Billy was a challenge to the whole elaborate structure of belief by which the Holy Pannovalan Empire stood. Sometimes, the fear came to the king that he might become bereft of his religious faith, as he had become bereft of so much else. Only his faith and

this humble inhuman pet were left to him.

He groaned. With a great effort, he got to his feet again.

Within the hour, King JandolAnganol was at the head of his force, riding Lapwing with Envoy Alam Esomberr beside him. Behind came the king's captains, then Esomberr's party, and after them the body of the First Royal Phagorian Guard, ears atwitch, scarlet eyes fixed ahead, marching as their kind had done many centuries before towards the city of Orlando.

The king's departure from the wooden palace, with all its underlying sense of anxiety, made a due impression on the watchers on the Avernus. They were glad to divert their attention from the sight of the king in pauk. Even the devoted female admirers of his majesty felt uncomfortable at the sight of him lying prone with his spirit away from his body.

Throughout the human population of Helliconia, pauk, or pater-placation, came as naturally as spitting. It had no particular religious significance, although it often existed alongside religion. Just as women became pregnant with future lives, so people were pregnant with the lives of those who had gone before them.

On the Avernus, the mysterious Helliconian practice of pauk was regarded as a religious function roughly equivalent to prayer. As such, it embarrassed the six families. The families suffered no inhibitions concerning sex: constant monitoring had ensured that long since; for them love and the higher emotions were no more than side effects of daily functions, to be ignored where possible; but religion was particularly difficult to deal with.

The families regarded religion as a primitive obsession, an illness, an opiate for those who could not think straight. They hoped perpetually that SartoriIrvrash and his kind would become more militant in their atheism and bring about the death of Akhanaba, thus contributing to a happier state of affairs. They neither liked nor understood pauk. They wished it did not happen.

On Earth, other opinions prevailed. Life and death could be perceived as an inseparable whole; death was never feared where life was properly lived. The terrestrials regarded with the liveliest interest the Helliconian activity of pauk. During

*the first years of contact with Helliconia, they had regarded
the trance state as a kind of astral projection of the Helliconian soul, rather similar to a state of meditation. Later, a
more sophisticated viewpoint had developed; understanding
grew that the people of Helliconia possessed an ability peculiar
to them, to shift beyond and return from the boundary set between life and death. This continuity had been given them in
compensation for the remarkable discontinuities of their
Great Year. Pauk had evolutionary value, and was a point of
union between the humans and their changeable planet.*

*For this reason, the terrestrials were particularly interested
in pauk. They had at this period discovered their own unity
with their own planet, and related that unity to increasing empathy with Helliconia.*

In the days that followed, lassitude took the queen of
queens and laid her low.

She had lost the things of value which gave existence its
previous fragrance. After the storm, the flowers would never
lift their heads so high again. With her deep sense of guilt that
she had somehow failed her king went bitter anger against
him. If she had failed, it was not for want of trying, and the
years of loving bestowed on him as freely as breath were more
than wasted. Yet love remained beneath her anger. That was
the cruellest thing. She understood JandolAnganol's self-
doubt as no one else did. She was unable to break from the
bond they had once forged.

Every day, after prayer, she went into pauk, to communicate with her mother's gossie. After her prostrations, recalling
how SartoriIrvrash in particular had condemned all pater-
placation as superstition, MyrdemInggala, in a fury of doubt,
questioned whether she had visited her mother at all, whether
the phantom was not in her head, whether there could be survival for anyone after death, except in the memories of those
who had still to pass beyond that forbidding shore.

She questioned. Yet pauk was her consolation as much as
the sea. For her dead brother YeferalOborol was now among
the gossies, pouring out love for her as he sank towards the
original beholder. The queen's unspoken fear, that he had
been murdered by JandolAnganol, was proved baseless. She

knew now where the real blame lay. For all that she was grateful.

Yet she regretted not having that additional reason to hate the king. She swam in the sea among her familiars. Peace of mind forsook her each time she returned to shore. The phagors carried her back to the palace in her throne; her resentment grew as she approached its doors. The days dragged by and she grew no younger. She was scarcely on speaking terms with Mai. She ran up to her creaking chambers and hid her face.

"If you feel so badly, follow the king to Oldorando and plead with the C'Sarr's representatives there to annul your divorce," Mai said in impatient tones.

"Would you like to follow the king?" asked MyrdemInggala. "I would not."

Burnt into her memory was a recollection of how, in spendthrift times, this woman, her lady-in-waiting, had been harvested into the king's bed and the two of them, like low whores, had been pleasured by him at one and the same time. Neither woman spoke of those occasions—but they lay between them as tangibly as a sword.

Chiefly from a need to talk to someone, the queen persuaded CaraBansity to stay at the palace for a few days, and then for a day more. He pleaded that his wife awaited him back home in Matrassyl. She pleaded with him to wait a little longer. He begged to be excused, but, cunning man though he was, he found it impossible to say no to the queen. They walked every day along the shore, sometimes coming on herds of deer, and Mai trailed disconsolately behind them.

When JandolAnganol, Esomberr, and their party had been gone from Gravabagalinien for a week and two days, the queen was sitting moodily in her room, gazing to the landward side of her narrow domain. The door was thrown open and in ran TatromanAdala, shrieking a greeting.

The child came halfway across the gulf between the door and the place where her mother crouched. That mother had raised her head and looked from under her disordered hair with such venom that Tatro halted.

"Moth! Can you play?"

The mother saw how the daughter's infant face bore the features of her father's line. The genethlic divinities might

have further tragedies yet in store. The queen screamed at Tatro.

"Get out of my sight, you little witch!"

Amazement, scandal, anger, dismay passed across the child's face. It glowed red, it seemed to dissolve, it flowed with tears and sobs.

The queen of queens leaped to her sandalless feet, and rushed at the small being. Twirling it about, she thrust it forward and out of the room, slamming the door on it. Then she herself, flinging her body against a wall, hands above her head, also wept.

Later in the day, her mood lightened. She sought out the child and made a fuss of her. Lassitude gave way to a mood of elation. She put on a satara gown and went downstairs. Her portable golden throne was summoned, though the heat of midday was heavy on Gravabagalinien. Submissive hornless phagors brought it forth. Majordomo ScufBar came, and Princess Tatro with her nursemaid, and the nursemaid's maid, carrying storybooks and toys.

The small procession being assembled, MyrdemInggala mounted her throne, and they started on the way to the beach. At this hour, no courtiers accompanied them. Freyr regarded them, low over a shoulder of cliff, Batalix shone almost at zenith.

Leisurely waves, aglitter as if the world had just begun that day, came in, curling to reveal for a moment their cucumber hearts. About the stand of the Linien Rock, water gargled invitingly. Of the assatassi of the recent past there was no sign, nor would there be until next year.

MyrdemInggala stood for a while on the beach. The phagors stood silently by her throne. The princess rushed excitedly about, issuing her commands to the maids for the building of the strongest sand castle ever, a pianissimo generalissimo rehearsing her role in life. The lure of the sea was not to be resisted. With a bold swing of her arm, the queen released herself from her dress and slid the zona from under her breasts. Her perfumed body was available to the sunlight.

"Don't leave me, Moth!" Tatro shrilled.

"I shall not be long," replied her mother, and ran down the beach to plunge into the beckoning sea.

Once below the surface, the forked creature became a fish

herself, as lithe as a fish and almost as speedy. Swimming strongly she passed the dark form of the Linien Rock, to surface only when she was well out into the bay. Here the headland to the east curved round, creating a comparatively narrow passage between it and the solitary stand of rock. She called. The queen of queens was immediately surrounded by dolphins—her familiars, as she spoke of them.

They came, as she knew, in ranking order. She had only to release a spur of urine into the water, and the shapes silvered in, circling about her, closer and closer, till she could rest her arms upon two of them as securely as on the arms of her throne.

Only the privileged could touch her. They were twenty-one in number. Beyond them was an outer court, not less than sixty-four in number. Sometimes, a member of this outer court was permitted to join the inner. Beyond the outer court was a retinue whose numbers MyrdemInggala could only estimate. Possibly one thousand three hundred and forty-four. The retinue contained most of the mothers, children, and oldsters belonging to this school—or nation, as the queen thought of it.

Beyond the retinue, constantly on guard for danger, was the regiment. She rarely saw individual members of the regiment and was discouraged from approaching them, but understood that it numbered certainly as many individuals as the retinue. She also understood that in the deeps were monsters which the dolphins feared. It was the duty of the regiment to guard the retinue and the courts, and to warn them of danger.

MyrdemInggala trusted her familiars more than she trusted her human companions; yet, as in every living relationship, something was withheld. Just as she could not share with them her life on land, they had something in the deeps, some dark knowledge, they could not share with her. Because this thing was unknown, lying beyond her mind, it had its sinister music.

The inner court spoke to her with their great orchestral range of voices. Their pipings near at hand were humble and sweet—truly she was accepted as a queen below water as on land. Further out to sea, long sustained baritone chirps sounded, with basso profundo groans intermingling in a perplexing pattern.

"What is it, my sweetings, my familiars?"

They raised their smiling faces and kissed her shoulders. She knew each member of the inner court by sight and had names for them.

Something worried them. She relaxed, letting her understanding spread out like her urine through the water. She swam deep with them, out to colder water. They spiralled about her, occasionally touching her skin with their skin.

Secretly she hoped to catch a glimpse of the monsters of the true sea. She had not been exiled long enough in Gravabagalinien ever to catch a glimpse of them. However, they appeared to be telling her that this time trouble came from the west.

They had warned her of the death-flight of the assatassi. Although they lacked her time sense, she began to appreciate that whatever was coming was coming slowly but remorselessly, and would arrive soon. Strange thrills worked in her. The creatures responded to her thrills. Every shudder of her body was part of their music.

Understanding her curiosity, the dolphins guided her forward again.

She stared through the zafferine panes of the sea. They had brought her to the brink of a shallow shelf, on which seaweeds grew, bent before the overmastering current. They pushed through. Beyond was a sandy basin. Here were the multitudes of the retinue, line on line, facing westwards.

Beyond them, moving with the wary action of a patrol, was the whole force of the regiment, close together, body almost touching body, making the sea black and extending farther out than vision could penetrate. Never before had the queen been allowed such a close sight of the whole school, or realised how vast it was, how many individuals comprised it. Matching the complex ranks assembled came a tremendous harmony of noise, extending far beyond her human hearing.

She surfaced, and the court followed. MyrdemInggala could remain submerged for three or four minutes, and the dolphins needed to take breath as she did.

She glanced towards the shore. It was distant. One day, she thought, these beautiful creatures that I can love and trust will carry me away from sight of mankind. I shall be changed. She could not tell whether it was for death or life she longed.

Figures danced on the remote shore. One figure waved a

cloth. The queen's first response was, indignantly, that they were using her dress for the purpose. Then she realised that they signalled to her. It could only mean a crisis of some kind. Guiltily, her thoughts went to the little princess.

She clutched her breasts in sudden apprehension. To the inner court she gave a word of explanation, before striking back towards the shore. Her familiars followed or plunged before her in arrowhead formation, creating a favourable wake to hasten her strokes.

Her dress lay untouched on her throne, the phagors guarding it, shoulders hunched and acknowledging no excitement. One of the maids, in desperation, had ripped off her own garment to wave. She assumed it again as MyrdemInggala emerged from the water, reluctant to have anyone compare her body with the queen's.

"There's a ship," cried Tatro, eager to be first with the news. "A ship is coming!"

From the headland, using the spyglass which ScufBar brought, the queen saw the ship. CaraBansity was sent for. By the time he arrived on the scene, two further sails were sighted, mere blurs in the murk of the western horizon.

CaraBansity rubbed his eyes with a heavy hand as he returned the spyglass to ScufBar.

"Madam, to my mind the nearest ship is not from Borlien."

"Where, then?"

"In half an hour, its marking will be clearer."

She said, "You are a stubborn man. Where is the ship from? Can't you identify that insignia on its sail?"

"If I could, madam, then I would think it was the Great Wheel of Kharnabhar, and that is nonsense, because it would mean there was a Sibornalese ship very far from home."

She snatched the glass. "It is a Sibornalese ship—of good size. What could it be doing in these waters?"

The deuteroscopist folded his arms and looked grim. "You have been provided with no defences here. Let us hope it is making for Ottassol and its intentions are good."

"My familiars warned me of this," said the queen gravely.

The day wore on. The ship made slow progress. There was great excitement at the palace. Barrels of tar were rolled out to an eminence above the little bay where it was anticipated the

ship's boat would have to land if Gravabagalinien was its destination. At least the crew could be confronted by flaming tar if they proved hostile.

The air thickened towards evening. There was no doubt now about the hierogram on the sail. Batalix sank in concentric aureoles of light. People came and went in the palace. Freyr disappeared into the same hazes as its fellow and was gone. Twilight lingered, the sail glinted on the sea; it tacked now, to keep the wind.

With darkness, stars began to appear overhead. The Night Worm burned bright, with the Queen's Scar dim beside it. Nobody slept. The small community feared and hoped, knowing its vulnerability.

The queen sat in her shuttered hall. Tall candles of whale oil fluttered on the table by her side. The wine a slave had poured into a crystal glass and topped with Lordryardry ice was untouched and threw blurred gules on the table. She waited and stared across the room at the bare wall opposite, as if to read there her future fate.

Her aide de camp entered, bowing. "Madam, we hear the rattle of their chains. The anchor is going down."

The queen called CaraBansity and they went to the seashore. Several men and phagors were mustered, to ignite the tar barrels if necessary. Only one torch burned. She took it and strode with it into the dark water. To the wetting of her garments she paid no heed. Lifting the torch above her head, she advanced towards the other advancing lights. She felt immediately the smooth kiss of her familiars about her legs.

Mingled with the roar of surf came a creak of oars.

The wooden wall of the ship, its sails furled, was faintly visible as a backdrop. A boat had been let down. The queen saw men straining, barebacked, at the oars. Two men were standing amidships, one with a lantern, their faces caught in the nimbus of light.

"Who dares come ashore here?" she called.

And a voice came back, male, with a thrill in it, "Queen MyrdemInggala, queen of queens, is that you?"

"Who calls?" she asked. But she recognised the voice even as his response came across the diminishing distance between them.

"It is your general, ma'am, Hanra TolramKetinet."

He jumped from the boat and waded ashore. The queen raised her hand to those on the eminence not to fire their barrels. The general fell before her on one knee, clasping her hand on which the ring with the blue stone gleamed. Her other hand went to his head, to steady herself. In a half-circle round them stood the queen's phagor guard, their morose faces vaguely sketched in the night.

CaraBansity stepped forward with some amazement to greet the general's companion in the longboat. Taking Sartori-Irvrash in a great hug, he said, "I had reason to suppose you were in hiding in Dimariam. For once I guessed wrong."

"You're rarely wrong, but this time you were out by a whole continent," said SartoriIrvrash. "I've become a world traveller—what are you doing here?"

"I've remained here since the king left. For a while, JandolAnganol conscripted me to your old post, and almost killed me for it. I've stayed for the ex-queen's sake. She's in a doleful state of mind, poor lady."

Both men looked towards MyrdemInggala and TolramKetinet, but could see no dolefulness about either of them.

"What of her son, Roba?" asked SartoriIrvrash. "Have you news of him?"

"News and no news." CaraBansity's forehead creased in a frown. "It would be some weeks ago that he arrived at my house in Ottassol, just after the assatassi death-flight. The lad's crazed and will cause damage. I let him have a room for the night." He was about to say more, but stopped himself. "Don't mention Robay to the queen."

As the two couples stood conversing on the sand, the boat returned to the *Prayer* to transport Odi Jeseratabhar and Lanstatet ashore. When the oarsmen had dragged the boat safely above the high-tide mark, the whole party made its way up the beach to the palace, following the queen and TolranKetinet. In some of the windows of the palace, lights had been lit.

SartoriIrvrash introduced Odi Jeseratabhar to CaraBansity in glowing terms. CaraBansity became noticeably cool; he made it clear that a Sibornalese admiral was not welcome on Borlienese soil.

"I understand your feelings," Odi said faintly to CaraBan-

sity. She was pale and drawn, her lips white and her hair straggling.

A meal was prepared for the unexpected guests, during which time the general was reunited with his sister Mai and embraced her. Mai wept.

"Oh, Hanra, what's to happen to us all?" she asked. "Take me back to Matrassyl."

"Everything will be fine now," her brother said with assurance.

Mai merely looked her disbelief. She wished to be free of the queen—not to have her as sister-in-law.

They ate fish, followed by venison served with gwing-gwing sauces. They drank such wine as the king's invading force had left, chilled with the best Lordryardry ice. As the meal progressed, TolranKetinet told the company something of the suffering of the Second Army in the jungle; he turned occasionally to Lanstatet, who sat next to his sister, for confirmation of one point or another. The queen appeared scarcely to be listening, though the account was addressed to her. She ate little and her gaze, shielded under long lashes, was rarely lifted from the table.

After the meal, she seized up a candle in its pewter holder and said to her guests, "The night grows short. I will show you to your quarters. You are more welcome than my previous visitors."

The military force with Lanstatet were shown to rear accommodation. SartoriIrvrash and Odi Jeseratabhar were given a chamber near the queen's, and a slave woman to attend them and dress Odi's wounds.

When these dispositions were completed, MyrdemInggala and TolranKetinet stood alone in the echoing hall.

"I fear you are tired," he said in a low voice as they mounted the stairs. She made no answer. Her figure, ascending the steps before him, suggested not fatigue but suppressed energy.

In the corridor upstairs, slatted blinds rattled against the open windows with the stirrings of false dawn. An early bird called from a tower. Looking obliquely back at him, she said, "I have no husband, as you have no wife. Nor am I queen, though by that name I am still addressed. Nor have I been scarcely a woman since I arrived at this place. What I am, you

shall see before this night is over.''

She flung open the doors of her own bedchamber and gestured to him to enter.

He paused, questioning. ''By the beholder—''

''The beholder shall behold what she will behold. My faith has fallen from me as shall this gown.''

As he entered, she clasped the neck of her dress and pulled it open, so that her neat breasts, their nipples surrounded by large dark aureoles, sprang before his gaze. He shut the door behind him, calling her name.

She gave herself to him with an effort of will.

During what was left of the night, they did not sleep. The arms of TolramKetinet were round her body, and his flesh inside hers.

Thus was her letter, despatched by the Ice Captain, answered at last.

The next morning brought challenges forgotten in the reunions of the previous night. The *Union* and the *Good Hope* were closing in on the undefended harbour. Pasharatid was drawing near.

Despite the crisis, Mai insisted on getting her brother to herself for half an hour; while she lectured him on the miseries of life in Gravabagalinien, TolramKetinet fell asleep. She threw a glass of water over him to wake him. Staggering angrily out of the palace, he went to join the queen down by the shore. She stood with CaraBansity and one of her old women, looking out to sea.

Both suns were in different sectors of the sky, both shining the more brightly because they were about to be eclipsed by black rain clouds drawing up the slopes of the sky. Two sails glittered in the actinic light.

The *Union* was close, the *Good Hope* no more than an hour's sailing behind; the hierograms on its spread canvas were clear to behold. The *Union* had lowered its artemon, in order to allow its companion to catch up.

Lanstatet was already working with his force, unloading equipment from the *Prayer*.

''They're coming in, Akhanaba help us!'' he shouted to TolramKetinet.

"What's that woman doing?" TolramKetinet asked.

An old woman, a servitor of the queen's, a long-term house-keeper of the wooden palace, was helping Lanstatet's men unload the *Prayer*. It was her way of showing her dedication to the queen. A man above her was rolling kegs of gunpowder from the deck onto a gangplank. The old woman was directing the kegs down the slope, releasing a soldier for other duties.

"I'm helping you—what do you think?" she screamed back at the general.

Her attention was distracted. The next keg rolled off the gangplank and struck her shoulder, bowling the old woman over, pitching her face down on the shingle.

She was dragged up, faint but protesting, to lie against a chest on the beach. Blood streamed down her face. Myrdem-Inggala hurried down from the headland to comfort her.

As the queen knelt by her old servant, TolramKetinet stood over her and laid a hand on the queen's shoulder.

"My arrival has brought trouble on you, lady. That was not my intention. I am trying to regret I did not sail straight on to Ottassol."

The queen made no answer, but took the old woman's head on her lap. The latter's eyes had closed, but her breathing was regular.

"I said, lady, that I hope you don't regret that I did not sail on to Ottassol."

Distress showed in her face as she turned to him. "Hanra, I have no regrets about last night when we were together. It was my wish. I thought to be free of Jan. But it did not achieve what I hoped. For that, I am to blame, not you."

"You are free of him. He divorced you, did he not? What are you talking about?" He looked angry. "I know I'm not a very good general, but—"

"Oh, stop that!" she said impatiently. "It's got nothing to do with you. What do I care if you lost your scerming army? I'm talking about a bond, a solemn state that existed between two people for a long time. . . . Some things don't end when we hope they will. Jan and I—it's like being unable to waken —oh, I'm unable to express—"

With some annoyance, TolramKetinet said, "You're tired. I know how women get upset. Let's talk about such things later. Let's deal with the emergency first." He pointed out to sea,

and adopted a no-nonsense voice. "Judging by the nonappearance of the *Golden Friendship*, it was too badly damaged to sail. The Admiral Jeseratabhar says that Dienu Pasharatid was on it. Perhaps she has been killed, in which case Io Pasharatid on the *Union* will be full of vengeance."

"I fear that man," said MyrdemInggala. "And with excellent reason." She bent her head over the old woman.

Her general gave her a side glance. "I'm here to protect you from him, aren't I?"

"I suppose you are," she said spiritlessly. "At least your lieutenant is doing something about the matter."

JandolAnganol had seen to it that the wooden palace had no weapons with which to defend itself. But the rocks extending out to sea from the Linien Rock meant that any considerable vessel like the *Union* had to sail between the Rock and the headland, and there lay the defender's chance. GortorLanstatet had reinforced his working party on the beach with phagors. Two large cannon from the *Vajabhar Prayer*'s quarterdeck had been winched ashore and were now being manhandled onto the headland, where they would command the bay.

ScufBar and another serving man came up with a stretcher to carry the injured woman back to the safety of the palace and apply iced bandages to her wounds.

Leaving the queen's side, TolramKetinet ran to help position the cannon. He saw the danger of their situation. Apart from the phagors and a few unarmed helpers, the defending forces at Gravabagalinien numbered only his complement of thirteen who had come with him from Ordelay. The two Sibornalese ships now closing on the bay each contained possibly fifty well-armed fighting men.

Pasharatid's *Union* was turning, to present itself broadside on to the coast.

Heaving at the ropes, the men tried to get the second cannon into place.

Confronting the queen with folded arms, CaraBansity said, "Madam, I gave the king good advice which was ill taken. Let me now offer you a similar dose and hope for a kindlier reception. You and your ladies should saddle up hoxneys and ride inland, making no delay."

Her face lit with a sad smile. "I'm glad of your concern,

Bardol. *You* go. Return to your wife. This place has become my home. You know Gravabagalinien is said to be the residence of the ancient ghosts of those who were killed in a battle long ago. I would rather join those shades than leave."

He nodded. "So it may be. I shall stay too, ma'am, in that case."

Something in her expression showed him she was pleased by what he said. On impulse, she asked, "What do you make of this misalliance between our friend Rushven and the Uskuti lady—an admiral, no less?"

"She keeps quiet, but that does not reassure me. It might be safer to pack those two off. There's always more than an arm up a Sibornalese sleeve. We must use our cunning, ma'am—there's little enough else on our side."

"She appears genuinely devoted to my ex-chancellor."

"If so, she has deserted the Sibornalese cause, ma'am. And that may give this man Pasharatid another reason for coming ashore. Pack her off, for everybody's safety."

At sea, smoke billowed, concealing all but the sails of the *Union*. A moment later, explosions were heard.

The shots landed in the water at the foot of a low cliff. With a second salvo, the marksmen would be more accurate. Evidently the lookout had sighted the manoeuvring of the cannon on shore.

But the shots proved to be no more than warnings. The *Union* swung to port and began sailing straight towards the little bay.

The queen stood alone, her long hair, still unbound from the night, streaming in the wind. There was a sense in which she was prepared to die. It might be the best way of resolving her troubles. She was—to her dismay—not prepared to accept TolramKetinet, an honest but insensitive man. She was vexed with herself for putting herself under emotional obligation to him. The truth was, his body, his caresses of the night, had merely roused in her an intense longing for Jan. She felt lonelier than before.

Moreover, she divined with melancholy detachment Jan's loneliness. That she might have assuaged, had she herself been more mature.

Out to sea, monsoon rain created gulfs of darkness and slanting light. Showers burned across the waters. The clouds

loomed lower. *Good Hope* was almost lost in murk. And the sea itself—MyrdemInggala looked, and saw that her familiars were choking the waves. What she had mistaken for choppiness was the ferment of their bodies. The rain drove in at speed and dashed itself against her face.

Next second, everyone was struggling through a heavy downpour.

The cannon stuck, its wheels spun in mud. A man fell on his knees, cursing. Everyone cursed and bellowed. The fusee in its perforated tin would be doused if the downpour continued.

Hope of placing the cannon effectively was now dead. The wind veered with the storm. The *Union* was blown towards the bay.

As the ship drew level with the Linien Rock, the dolphins acted. They moved in formation, retinue and regiment. The entrance to the bay was barred by their bodies.

Sailors in the *Union*, half-blinded by rain, shouted and pointed at the teeming backs beneath their hulls. It was as if the ship ran across black shining cobbles. The dolphins wedged their bodies solid against the timbers. The *Union* slowed, groaning.

Screaming with excitement, MyrdemInggala forgot her sorrows and ran down to the water. She clapped her hands, shrieked encouragement at her agents. Sand and salt splashed over her calves, rushing beneath her dress. She plunged forward in the undertow. Even TolramKetinet hesitated to follow. The ship loomed over her and the rain lashed down.

One of her familiars reared out of the water as if he had expected her coming, seizing the fabric of her dress in his mouth. She recognised him as a senior member of the inner court, and spoke his name. In his medley of calls was an urgent message she could recognise: stay away, or gigantic things—she could not determine what—would seize her. Something far off in the deeps had her scent.

Even the queen of queens was frightened by the news. She retreated, guided by the familiar all the way. As she reached the sand, clutching her soaked dress, he sank away below the foam.

The *Union* lay only a few ship's lengths from where the queen and her followers stood. Between beach and carrack were dolphins, both courts and regiment, packed tight.

Through the driving torrents, the queen recognised the commanding figure of Io Pasharatid—and he had recognised her.

He stood tall and sinister on the streaming deck, swart-bearded, canvas jacket open to the rain, cap pitched over his eyes. He looked at her and then he acted.

In his fist was a spear. Climbing onto the rail of the ship, clutching the shrouds with one hand, he leaned forward and stabbed down repeatedly into the water. With every stab, crimson spurted up the blade of the weapon. The waters became lashed with foam. Pasharatid stabbed again and again.

To superstitious mariners, the dolphin is a sacred creature. Ally of the spirits of the deep, it can do no wrong in sailors' eyes. Harm it and one places one's own life in jeopardy.

Pasharatid was surrounded by furious mariners. The spear was wrestled from his hand and thrown away. The watchers ashore saw him borne fighting to the deck until his soldiers rushed in and pulled him free. The scrimmage continued for a while. The queen's familiars had successfully barred the way to Gravabagalinien.

The rainstorm was at its height. The waves rose higher, crashing up the beach with splendid fury. The queen screamed her victory, looking in her dishevelment much like her dead mother, the wild Shannana, until TolramKetinet dragged her back, in fear that she would hurl herself into the water again.

Lightning flashed in the storm's belly and then struck with following thunder. Cloud shifted like blown sheet, outlining the *Good Hope* suddenly in silver water. It stood off a third of a mile or less from its companion ship, as its crew fought to keep it offshore.

A line of dolphins streamed from the bay and could be seen heading beyond the *Good Hope* as if summoned by something there.

The sea convulsed. It boiled about the Lorajan vessel. Men ashore swore afterwards that the water boiled. The convulsion grew, with glimpses of things churning. Then a mass rose from the water, shook waves from its head, rose, still rose, till it towered above the masts of the *Good Hope*. It had eyes. It had a great lantern jaw and whiskers that writhed like eels. More of it came out of the sea in thick scaled coils, thicker than a man's torso. The storm was its element.

And there were more coils. A second monster appeared, this one in a rage, to judge by the darting movements of its head. Like a gigantic snake, it rose, then struck at the waves, diving, to leave sections of its roped body still agleam in the viscous air.

Its head emerged again, setting the *Good Hope* rocking. The two creatures joined forces. Careless in their obscene sport, they writhed through the water. One lashing tail smashed against the side of the caravel, breaking planking and treenails.

Then both beasts were gone. The waters lay flattened where they had been. They had obeyed the summons of the dolphins and now were making back towards the depths of the ocean. Although their appearances before the eyes of men were rare, the great creatures still formed part of the cycle of living beings which had adapted to the Great Year of Helliconia.

At this stage of their existence, the great serpents were asexual. Long past was their period of intense mating activity. Then, they had been flighted creatures, and had squandered centuries in amorous anorexy, feeding on procreation. Like giant dragonflies, they and their kind had flirted above the world's two lonely poles, free of enemies or even witnesses.

With the coming of the Great Summer, the aerial creatures migrated to the seas of the south, and in particular to the Sea of Eagles, where their appearance had led some long-dead and ornithologically unversed seamen to name an ocean after them. On remote islands like Poorich and Lordry, the creatures shed their wings. They crawled upon their bellies into the brine, and there gave birth.

In the seas the summer would be spent. Eventually the great bodies would dissolve, to feed assatassi and other marine inhabitants. The voracious young were known as scupperfish. They were not fish at all. When the chills of the long winter came to prompt them, the scupperfish would emerge onto land and assume yet another form, called by such ill names as Wutra's Worm.

In their present asexual state, the two serpents had been stirred into activity by a recollection of their distant past. The memory had been brought them by the dolphins, in the form of a scent trace, infused into the waters by the queen of queens during her menstrual period. In confused restlessness, they

coiled about each other's bodies; but no power could bring back what had gone.

Their ghastly apparition had knocked any desire for fighting from the bellies of those aboard the *Union* and the *Good Hope*. Gravabagalinien was a haunted place. Now the invaders knew it. Both ships crammed on all possible sail and fled eastwards before the storm. The clouds covered them and they were gone.

The dolphins had disappeared.

Only the waters raged, breaking high up the Linien Rock with dull booms which carried along the beach.

The human defenders of Gravabagalinien made their way back through the rain to the wooden palace.

The chambers of the palace echoed like drums under the weight of monsoon rain. The tune kept changing as the rain died, then fell with renewed vigour.

A council of war was held in the great chamber, the queen presiding.

"First, we should be clear what kind of a man we are dealing with," TolramKetinet said. "Chancellor SartoriIrvrash, tell us what you know of Io Pasharatid, and please speak to the point."

Whereupon SartoriIrvrash rose, smoothing his bald head and bowing to her majesty. What he had to say would indeed be brief but hardly pleasant. He apologised for bringing up old unhappy things, but the future was always linked with the past in ways that even the wisest among them could scarcely anticipate. He might give as an instance . . .

Catching Odi Jeseratabhar's eye, he applied himself to the point, hunching up his shoulders to do so. In the years in Matrassyl, his duty as chancellor had been to discover the secrets of the court. When the queen's brother, YeferalOboral of beloved memory, was still alive, he had discovered that Pasharatid—then ambassador from his country—was enjoying the favours of a young girl, a commoner, whose mother kept a house of ill-repute. He, the chancellor, also discovered from VarpalAnganol that Pasharatid contrived to look upon the queen's body when naked. The fellow was a scoundrel, lustful and reckless, kept in check only by his wife—whom

they had reason to believe was now dead.

Moreover, he wished to retell a rumour—perhaps more than a rumour—gathered from a guide called the Pointer of the Way, whom he befriended on his journey through the desert to Sibornal, that Io Pasharatid had murdered the queen's brother.

"I know that to be so," said MyrdemInggala, dismissively. "We have every reason to regard Io Pasharatid as a dangerous man."

TolramKetinet rose.

He adopted military postures and spoke with rhetorical flourishes, glancing across at the queen to see how his performance was being received. He said that they were now clear how Pasharatid was to be feared. It was reasonable to assume that the scoundrel was in command of the *Union* and, by dint of his connections, could enforce his orders on the commander of the *Good Hope*. He, TolramKetinet, had evaluated the military situation from the enemy's viewpoint, and estimated that Pasharatid would move as follows. One—

"Please make this brief, or the man will burst in upon us at this table," said CaraBansity. "We take it that you're as great an orator as you are a general."

Frowning, TolramKetinet said that Pasharatid would decide that two ships could never take Ottassol. His best plan would be to capture the queen and thus force Ottassol to submit to his demands. They should anticipate that Pasharatid would land somewhere to the east of Gravabagalinien, wherever a favourable beach presented itself. He would then march on Gravabagalinien with his men. He, TolramKetinet (who struck his chest as he spoke), declared that they must immediately muster their defences against this anticipated land attack. The queen's person was safe in his keeping.

After a general discussion, the queen issued orders. As she spoke, rain started to drip down on the table. "Since water is my element, I cannot complain if the roof leaks," she said.

MyrdemInggala advised that defences should be built along the perimeters of the palace grounds and that the general should draw up an inventory of all weapons and warlike impedimenta available, not forgetting the armoury of the *Vajabhar Prayer*.

Turning to SartoriIrvrash, she ordered him and Odi

Jeseratabhar to depart from the palace at once. They might have three hoxneys from the stables.

"You are kind, ma'am," said SartoriIrvrash, although the expression on his volelike face suggested he thought otherwise. "But can you spare us?"

"I can if your companion is fit to ride."

"I don't think she is fit."

"Rushven, I can spare you as Jan could spare you. You advised him on the plan of divorcement, didn't you? As for your new consort, I understand that she is or was a close friend of the villainous Io Pasharatid."

He was taken aback. "My lady, there was much botheration. . . . Many questions of policy were involved. I was paid to support the king."

"You used to claim that you supported the truth."

He searched his charfrul absentmindedly, as if looking for a veronikane, then settled for rubbing his whiskers instead.

"Sometimes the two roles coincided. I know that your kind heart and the king's spoke for the phagors in our kingdom. Yet they are the chief cause of all human troubles. In summer, we have the opportunity to rid ourselves of them when their numbers are low. Yet summer is the time we squabble among ourselves and are least capable of seeing them as our ultimate enemy. Believe me, ma'am, I have studied such histories as *Brakst's Thribriatiad*, and have learned—"

She looked at him not unfavourably, but now held up her hand.

"Rushven, no more! We were friends, but our lives have changed. Go in peace."

Unexpectedly, he ran round the table and clasped her hand.

"We'll go, we'll go! After all, I'm used to cruel treatment. But grant one request before we leave. . . . With Odi's assistance, I have discovered something of vital importance to us all. We shall go on to Oldorando, and present this discovery to the Holy C'Sarr, in the hopes that it may merit award. It will also discountenance your ex-husband, you may be pleased to hear—"

"What is your request?" she broke in angrily. "Be finished, will you? We have more important business."

"The request has to do with the discovery, ma'am. When we were all safe at the palace at Matrassyl, I used to read to

your infant daughter. Little you care for that now. I remember the charming storybook that Tatro possessed. Will you permit me to take that storybook with me to Oldorando?"

MyrdemInggala stifled something between a laugh and a scream. "Here we try to prepare for a land attack and you wish to have a child's book of fairy tales! By all means take the book as far as I'm concerned—then be off the premises, and take that ceaseless tongue of yours with you!"

He kissed her hand. As he backed to the door, Odi beside him, he gave a sly smile and said, "The rain is stopping. Fear not, we shall soon be away from this inhospitable refuge."

The queen hurled a candlestick after his retreating back.

To one side of the palace was an extensive garden, where herbs and fruit bushes grew. In the garden was an enclosure within which pigs, goats, chickens, and geese were kept. Beyond this enclosure stood a line of gnarled trees. Beyond the trees lay a low earthworks, grass-covered, which encircled marshy ground to the east—the direction from which Pasharatid's force would come if it did come.

After a businesslike survey of the ground, TolramKetinet and Lanstatet decided they must use this old line of defence.

They had considered evacuating Gravabagalinien by ship. But the *Prayer* had been inexpertly moored. During the storm, it suffered damage and could hardly be considered seaworthy.

Everything of value was unloaded from the ship. Some of its higher timbers were utilised to make a watchtower in the stoutest tree.

As the ground dried off after the storm, some of the phagors were employed to build a defensive breastwork along the top of the earthworks. Others were deployed to dig trenches nearby.

This was the scene of activity which met SartoriIrvrash and Odi Jeseratabhar as they left the settlement. They travelled one behind the other on hoxneys, with a third animal trailing, carrying their baggage. They saw CaraBansity supervising the digging of fortifications, and SartoriIrvrash halted.

"I must bid farewell to my old friend," he said as he dismounted.

"Don't be long," Odi warned. "You have no friends here because of me."

He nodded and walked over to the deuteroscopist, squaring his shoulders.

CaraBansity was working in a patch of marshy ground with some labouring ancipitals. When he looked up and saw SartoriIrvrash, his heavy face went dark, then, as if forced to it by the pressure of excitement, burst into a smile. He beckoned SartoriIrvrash over.

"Here's the past . . . these earthworks form part of an ancient fortification system. The phagors are uncovering the geometries of legend made flesh. . . ."

He walked over to a newly dug pit. SartoriIrvrash followed. CaraBansity knelt at the edge of the pit, heedless of squelching mud. An arm's length below the turf, emerging from the peaty soil, lay what SartoriIrvrash took at first to be an old black bag, pressed flat. It was or it had been a man. His body lay sprawled on its left side. Short leather tunic and boots suggested that the man had been a soldier. Half-concealed beneath his flattened form lay the hilt of a sword. The man's profile, mouth distorted by broken teeth, had been moulded by earth's pressure into a macabre smile. The flesh was a rich shining brown.

Other bodies were being uncovered. The phagors worked without interest, scratching the mud away with their fingers. From the dirt, another mummified soldier appeared, a fearful wound in his chest. The creases of his face were clear, as if in a pencil sketch. His eyeballs had collapsed, giving his expression a melancholy vacancy.

The cellar smell of soil bit into their nostrils.

"The peaty earth has preserved them," said SartoriIrvrash. "They could be soldiers who died in battle, or similar botheration. They may be a hundred years old."

"Far more than that," said CaraBansity, jumping down into the trench. He scratched up one of a number of what SartoriIrvrash had taken to be stones, and lifted it for examination. "This is probably what killed the fellow with the broken teeth. It's a rajabaral tree seed, as hard as iron. It may have been baked, which is why it never germinated. It's over six centuries since spring, when the rajabarals seeded. The at-

tackers used the seeds as cannonballs. This is where the legendary battle of Gravabagalinien was fought. We find the site because we are about to use it again for battle.''

"Poor devils!''

"Them? Or us?'' He went to the rear corner of the excavation. Lying below the body of the man with the chest wound was a phagor, partly visible. Its face was black, its coat matted and reddened by the bog water, until it resembled a compressed vegetable growth. "You see how even then men and phagors fought and died together.''

SartoriIrvrash gave a snort of disgust. "They may equally well have been enemies. You've no evidence either way.''

"Certainly it's a bad omen. I wouldn't want the queen to see these. Or TolramKetinet. He's scumber himself. We'd better cover the bodies up.''

The ex-chancellor made to turn away. "Not all of us cover up the secrets we find, friend. I have knowledge in my possession which, when I lay it before the authorities of Pannoval, will start a Holy War against the ancipital kind throughout all Campannlat.''

CaraBansity looked calculatingly at him through his heavy bloodshot eyes. "And you'll get paid for starting that war, eh? Live and let live, I say.''

"Yes, you say it, Bardol, but these horned creatures don't. Their creed is different. They will outbreed us and kill us unless we act. If you had seen for yourself the flambreg herds—''

"Don't fly into a passion. Passion always causes trouble. . . . Now, we'll get on with our job. There are probably hundreds of bodies lying under the earth about here.''

Folding his arms tightly about his chest, SartoriIrvrash said, "You give me a cold reception, just like the queen.''

CaraBansity climbed slowly out of the trench. "Her majesty gave you what you asked for, a book and three hoxneys.'' He stuck a knuckle between his teeth and stared at the ex-chancellor.

"Why are you so against me, Bardol? Have you forgotten the time when, as young men, we looked through your telescope and observed the phases of Kaidaw as it sped above us? And from that deduced the cosmic geometries under which we exist?''

"I don't forget. You come here, though, with a Sibornalese officer, a dedicated enemy of Borlien. The queen is under threat of death and the kingdom of dissolution. I have no love of JandolAnganol or of phagors, yet I wish to see them continue, in order that people may still look through telescopes.

"Overturn the kingdom, as both you and she would do, and you overturn the telescopes."

He gazed through the trees towards the sea with a bitter expression, shrugging his shoulders.

"You have witnessed how Keevasien, once a place of some culture, home of the great YarapRombry, has been carelessly erased. Culture may flourish better under old injustice than under new. That's all I say."

"It's a plea for your own way of life."

"I shall always fight for my own way of life. I believe in it. Even when it means fighting myself. Go, take that woman with you—and remember there's always more than an arm up a Sibornalese sleeve."

"Why speak to me like this? I'm a victim. A wanderer—an exile. My life's work's ruined. I could have been the Yarap-Rombry of my epoch. . . . I'm innocent."

CaraBansity shook his large head. "You're of an age when innocence is a crime. Leave with your lady. Go and spread your poison."

They regarded each other challengingly. SartoriIrvrash sighed, CaraBansity climbed back into his trench.

SartoriIrvrash walked back to where Odi Jeseratabhar waited with the animals. He mounted his hoxney without a word, tears in his eyes.

They took the trail leading northwards to Oldorando. JandolAnganol and his party had travelled that way only a few days earlier, on their way to the home of the king's murdered bride-to-be.

XIX

OLDORANDO

The suns blazed down out of a cloudless sky, flattening the veldt with their combined light.

King JandolAnganol, Eagle of Borlien, enjoyed being in the wilderness again. His way of enjoyment was not every man's. It consisted mainly of hard marches interspersed with short rests. This was not to the taste of the C'Sarr's pleasure-loving envoy, Alam Esomberr.

The king and his force, with attendant ecclesiastics, approached Oldorando from the south along one of the old Pilgrim's Ways, which led on through Oldorando to Holy Pannoval.

Oldorando stood at the crossroads of Campannlat. The migratory route of the phagors and the various ucts of the Madis ran east and west close by the city. The old salt road meandered north into the Quzints and Lake Dorzin. To the west lay Kace—slatternly Kace, home of cutthroats, craftsmen, vagabonds, and villains; to the south lay Borlien—friendly Borlien, home of more villains.

JandolAnganol was approaching a country at war, like his own, with barbarians. That war between Oldorando and Kace

had broken out because of the ineffectiveness of King Sayren Stund as much as the nastiness of the Kaci.

Faced with the collapse of the Second Army, Jandol-Anganol had made what was widely regarded as a cowardly peace with the hill clans of Kace, sending them valuable tributes of grain and veronikane in order to seal the armistice.

To the Kaci, peace was relative; they were long accustomed to internecine struggles. They simply hung their crossbows on the back of the hut door and resumed their traditional occupations. These included hunting, blood feuds, potting—they made excellent pottery which they traded with the Madi for rugs—stealing, mining precious stones, and goading their scrawny womenfolk into working harder. But the war with Borlien, sporadic though it had been, instilled in the clans a new sense of unity.

Failing by some chance to quarrel during their extensive victory celebrations—when JandolAnganol's grain tribute was converted into something more potable—the leading clans of Kace accepted as their universal suzerain a powerful brute called Skrumppabowr. As a kind of goodwill gesture on his election, Skrumppabowr had all the Oldorandans living on Kaci land slaughtered, or "staked" as the local term was.

Skrumppabowr's next move was to repair the damage done by war to irrigation terraces and to villages in the southeast. To this end, he encouraged ancipitals to come in to Kace from Randonan, Quain, and Oldorando. In exchange for their labour, he guaranteed the phagors freedom from the drumbles racking Oldorando. Being heathen, the Kaci clans saw no reason to persecute the phagors as long as they behaved themselves and never looked at Kaci women.

JandolAnganol heard of these events with pleasure. They confirmed his sense of himself as a diplomat. The Takers were less pleased. The Takers were the militants of the Holy Pannovalan Empire, with highly placed connections within the See of Pannoval itself. Kilandar IX, so it was rumoured, had been a Taker himself in his young days.

A mounted arm of Takers, striking out from Oldorando City, made a daring raid on Akace, the squalid mountain settlement which served as a capital, and slaughtered over a thousand newly arrived phagors overnight, together with a few Kaci.

This success proved less than a victory. On their way home, the Takers, rendered careless by the outcome of their raid, were ambushed by Lord Skrumppabowr's clans and slaughtered in their turn, many in sadistic ways. Only one Taker returned to Oldorando, more dead than alive, to tell the tale. A thin bamboo rod had been driven through his body from his anus; the sharp end protruded from behind the clavicle of his right shoulder. He had been staked.

Reports of this outrage reached King Sayren Stund. He declared a holy war on the barbarians and set a price on Skrumppabowr's head. Blood had since been spilt on both sides, but mainly on the Oldorandan side. At the present time, half the Oldorandan army—in which no phagors were allowed to serve—was away making forced marches among the wilderness of shoatapraxi which abounded on Kace hillsides.

The king soon lost interest in the struggle. After the murder of his elder daughter, Simoda Tal, he retreated into the confines of his palace and was rarely seen. He bestirred himself when he heard of JandolAnganol's approach, but then only at the concerted prompting of his advisors, his Madi queen, and his surviving daughter, Milua Tal.

"How are we to amuse this great king, Sayren, sweetest?" asked Queen Bathkaarnet-she, in her singing voice. "I am such a poor thing, a flower, and I am lame. A limp flower. Will you wish me to sing my songs of the Journey to him?"

"I don't care for the man, personally. He's without culture," said her husband. "Jandol will bring his phagor guard, since he can't afford to pay real soldiers. If we must endure the pestilential things in our capital, perhaps they'll amuse us with their animal antics."

Oldorando's climate was hot and enervating. The eruption of Mount Rustyjonnik had opened up a chain of volcanic activity. A sulphurous pall often hung over the land. The flags which the king ordered to be put out to greet his Borlienese cousin hung limp in the airless atmosphere.

As for the King of Borlien, impatient energy possessed him. The march from Gravabagalinien had taken the best part of a tenner, first over the loess farmlands, then across wilder country. No pace was rapid enough for JandolAnganol. Only the

First Phagorian made no complaint.

Bad news continued to reach the column. Crop failure and famine were everywhere in his kingdom; evidence of that lay all round. The Second Army was not merely defeated: it was never going to reemerge from the jungles of Randonan. Such few men as came back slunk to their own homes, swearing they would never soldier again. The phagor battalions which had survived disappeared into the wilds.

From the capital, the news was no more encouraging. JandolAnganol's ally, Archpriest BranzaBaginut, wrote that Matrassyl was in a state of ferment, with the barons threatening to take over and rule in the name of the scritina. It behoved the king to act positively, and as soon as possible.

He enjoyed being on the move, delighted in living off what game there was, rejoiced in the evening bivouac, and even tolerated days of brilliant sunshine, away from the coastal monsoons. It was as if he took pleasure from the ferment of emotions that filled him. His face became leaner, tenser, his waywardness more marked.

Alam Esomberr felt less enthusiastic. Brought up in his father's house in the subterranean recesses of Pannoval, he was unhappy in the open and mutinous about the forced pace. The dandified envoy of the Holy C'Sarr called a halt at last, knowing he had the support of his weary retinue.

It was dimday, when fat, brilliant flowers opened among the lustreless grasses, inviting the attention of dusk-moths. A bird called, hammering at its two notes.

They had left the loess farmlands behind and were traversing a farmless moor which supported few villages. For shade, the envoy's party retreated under an enormous denniss tree, whose leaves sighed in the breeze. The denniss sprouted many trunks, some young, some ancient, which propped themselves up languidly—like Esomberr himself—with gnarled elbows as they sprawled on the ground in all directions.

"What can drive you like this, Jandol?" Esomberr asked. "What are we hurrying for, except for hurrying's abominable sake? To put it another way, what fate awaits you in Oldorando better than the one you revoked in Gravabagalinien?"

He eased his legs and looked up with his amused glance into the king's countenance.

JandolAnganol squatted nearby, balancing on his toes. A

faint smell of smoke came to his nostrils, and he searched the distance for its origin. He threw small pebbles at the earth.

A group of the king's captain, the Royal Armourer, and others leant on their staffs, a short distance away. Some smoked veronikanes, one teased Yuli, prodding the creature with his staff.

"We must reach Oldorando as soon as possible." He spoke as one who wants no argument, but Esomberr persisted.

"I'm eager to see that somewhat squalid city myself, if only to soak for a few millennia in one of their famous hot springs. That doesn't mean I'm anxious to *run* all the way there. You're a changed man since your Pannoval days, Jandol—not quite such fun, if I may say so. . . ."

The king threw his pebbles more violently. "Borlien needs an alliance with Sayren Stund. That deuteroscopist who presented me with my three-faced timepiece, Bardol CaraBan-sity, said I had no business in Oldorando. A conviction seized me at that moment that I had to go there. My father supported me. His dying words to me were—as he lay dying in my arms—'Go to Oldorando.' Since that fool TolramKetinet allowed his army to be wiped out, I can only seek union with Oldorando. The fates of Borlien and Oldorando have always been linked." He flung down a final stone with violence, as if to destroy all argument.

Esomberr said nothing. He plucked a grass blade to suck, suddenly self-conscious under the king's stare.

After a moment, JandolAnganol jumped up, to stand with his feet planted apart.

"Here stand I. While I press upon the earth, the energies of the earth surge up through my body. I am of the Borlienese soil. I am a natural force."

He raised his arms, fingers tensed.

The phagors, armed with their matchlocks, lay about at a short distance, like shapeless cattle, looking over the plain. Some rooted under stone and found grubs or rickybacks, which they ate. Others stood without movement, beyond the occasional swing of the head or a flick of the ears to ward off flies. Winged things buzzed in the shade. Made uneasy, Esomberr sat up.

"I don't understand what you mean, but do enjoy yourself." His voice was dry.

The king scrutinised the horizon as he spoke. "An example for you, so that you understand well the kind of man I am. Although I may have rejected my Queen MyrdemInggala for whatever reason, nevertheless she remains mine. If I discovered that you, for instance, had dared to enter her bedchamber to consort with her while we were in Gravabagalinien, then, notwithstanding our friendship, I would kill you without compunction, and hang your eddre from this tree."

Neither of them moved. Then Esomberr rose and stood with his back to one of the trunks of the denniss. His narrow handsome face had grown as pale as a dead leaf.

"I say, did it ever occur to you that those damned phagors of yours, well armed with Sibornalese weapons, strike fear into ordinary chaps like me? That they will most likely meet with an ill reception in Sayren Stund's capital, where a holy drumble is in progress? Are you ever afraid that you might . . . well, grow to be a bit like a phagor yourself?"

The king turned slowly, with an expression denoting total lack of interest in the question.

"Watch."

He screwed his face into a mixture of grimace and smile, and snorted breath through his nose. He broke into a run, gathered himself, and leaped clear over one of the trunks of the tree, a full four feet above the ground. It was a perfect jump. He recovered himself, turned, and jumped the trunk in the opposite direction, with a force which carried him almost against Esomberr.

The king was half a head taller than the envoy. The latter, alarmed, reached for his sword, then stood without movement, tense against the king.

"I am twenty-five years of age, in fine condition, and fear neither man nor phagor. My secret is that I am capable of going with circumstances. Oldorando shall be my circumstance. I gain energy from the geometry of circumstance. . . . Do not vex me, Alam Esomberr, or forget my words about the sanctity of what was once mine. I am one of your circumstances, and not vice versa."

The envoy moved to one side, coughed as a reason for moving his hand from his sword hilt to his mouth, and managed a pale smile.

"You're terribly fit, I see that. That's tremendous. By the

beholder, but I envy you. It's a wretched nuisance that I and
my little rabble of vicars aren't in such fine trim. I've often
thought that praying vitiates the muscles. Therefore, I must
request that you proceed ahead with your party and your
favoured species—at your breakneck pace—while we follow
on behind at our own feeble pace, eh?"

JandolAnganol regarded him without change of expression.
Then he gave a fierce grimace. "Very well. The country
hereabouts is peaceful, but guard yourselves. Robbers have
scant respect for vicars. Remember you carry my bill of
divorcement."

"Strive ever onwards, if you will. I shall deliver your bill to
the C'Sarr in good time." He gave a wave of his hand and left
it dangling in front of him. The king did not take it.

Instead, JandolAnganol turned away without further word
and whistled Yuli to his side. He called the gillot leader of the
guard, Ghht-Mlark Chzarn. The ahuman columns formed up
and marched away; the humans followed more informally. In
a short while, Alam Esomberr, together with his followers,
was left standing silent under the denniss tree. Then the figures
were lost to JandolAnganol amid the shade. Soon the great
tree itself was lost in the shimmering heat of the plain.

Two days later, the king halted his force only a few miles
short of Oldorando. Wisps of smoke trailed across the rolling
landscape.

He stood by one of the aged stone pillars which dotted the
landscape. Impatient for the rear of the phagor column to
catch up, JandolAnganol traced with one finger the worn
design on the stone, a familiar pattern of two concentric
circles with curving lines running from inner to outer circle.
Just for a moment, he wondered what the pillar and its pattern
could signify; but such enigmas—presumably never capable of
resolution, any more than he expected to be told what long-
dead king had erected the stones—occupied his mind only for
a moment. His thoughts were all on what lay immediately
ahead.

They had reached a region which was in fact a hinterland of
the fabled city they were approaching.

Of that city, there was as yet no sign. The view comprised

low rolling hills, the foothills of the foothills of the Quzint Mountains, running like an armoured spine over the continent. Ahead, sprawling across the ground, was one of the ucts, threading its way into the distance on either side.

The uct here formed a tawny rather than a green line, comprising few large trees but many bushes and cyclads, entwined by gaudy mantle flowers, the seeds of which migrant tribes chewed as they progressed.

No road was as wide as this uct. Unlike a road, however, it was not to be travelled by humans. Despite the depredations of arang and fhlebiht, it had become impenetrable. The Madi tribes with their animals travelled along its edge. There, scattering seeds and droppings, the protognostics unthinkingly widened the uct. Year by year it spread, becoming a strip of forest.

Not that the strip was regular. Alien growths like shoatapraxi, introduced as burrs on the coats of animals, had prospered in places were they could take advantage of favourable soil conditions, and spread in thickets. The Madi skirted the new thickets, or else plunged through them leaving a trail later obliterated by further waves of aliens.

What was incidental became established. The uct served as a barrier. Butterflies and small animals found on one side of the barrier were not to be seen on the other. There were birds and rodents and a deadly golden snake which kept to the shelter of the uct and never ventured beyond its confines as they spread across the continent. Several kinds of Others lived their pranksome lives out in the uct.

Humans, too, recognised the existence of the uct by using it as a frontier. This uct marked the frontier between Northern Borlien and the land of Oldorando.

And that frontier was on fire.

A lava flow from a newly erupting volcano had set the uct ablaze. It had begun to burn along its length like a fusee.

Instruments on the Avernus were recording details of increasing volcanic activity on the world approaching periastron below. Data relayed to Earth concerning Mount Rustyjonnik showed that the material from the eruption rose to a height of 50 kilometres. The lower layers of this cloud were carried

*rapidly eastwards, circling the globe in 15 days. The material
rising above 21 kilometres moved westwards with the prevailing flow of the lower stratosphere, to circle the globe in 60
days.*

*Similar readings were obtained for other eruptions. Dust
clouds gathering in the stratosphere were about to double
Helliconia's albedo, reflecting the increasing heat of Freyr
away from the surface. Thus the elements of the biosphere
worked like an interrelated body or machine to preserve its
vital processes.*

*During the decades when Freyr was closest to Helliconia,
the planet would be shielded by acidic dust layers from its
worst effects.*

*Nowhere was this dramatic homeostasis observed with more
wonder and awe than on Earth.*

*On Helliconia, the forest fire was the end of the world for
many frightened creatures. To a more detached view, it was a
sign of the world's determination to save itself and its freight
of organic life.*

JandolAnganol's forces waited, tucked in a shallow valley.
A pall of smoke to the east announced the approach of the
fire. Numbers of hairy pigs and deer ran along the line of the
uct westwards to safety. Herds of slower fhlebiht followed,
setting up a massive bleating as they passed.

Families of Others went by, encouraging their young in a
human fashion. They had dark fur and white faces. Some
species were tailless. They swung deftly from branch to branch
and were gone.

JandolAnganol rose and stood in a crouch to watch the
game go by. The little runt Yuli leapt up sportively to join
him. The phagors continued to rest impassively like cattle,
chewing their day's ration of porridge and pemmican.

To the east, Madis and their flocks were fleeing before the
blaze. While some of their animals bolted for freedom or ran
in terror into the thicket, the protognostics themselves remained obedient to custom and followed the line of the uct.

"Blind fools!" exclaimed JandolAnganol.

His quick mind devised a plan. Ordering up a section of
phagorian guard, he set a trap into action. When the leading

Madis came up, a rope draped with thorn-lianas from the thickets suddenly sprang into the air before them. They came to a confused halt, sheep, asokins, and dogs milling about their legs.

Their Madi faces were as innocuous as the faces of parrots or flowers. Foreheads and jaws receded, eyes and noses were prominent, giving them a permanent look of incredulity before the world. The males had bosses on foreheads and jaws. Their hair was glossy brown. They called to each other in despairing pigeon voices.

Out leaped the phagor section from its concealment. Each phagor closed in on the frightened Madis. Each caught three or four by their arms, arms burned red by the suns and powdered by the dust of the track. They came without fight. A gillot caught the bellwether, an asokin with a can thumping against its chest. The ewes stood meekly by.

Some Madis tried to run. JandolAnganol clubbed two with his fist, sending them sprawling. They lay crying in the dirt. But others were coming up from the rear all the while, and he let them go.

His party forced their way through the uct with their bag. The dense coats of the phagors rendered them immune to thorns. Driving their captives before them, they crossed over from Borlien to Oldorando. They were safely on their way when the fire passed through the strip, travelling at a brisk walking pace, leaving ashes behind it.

It was in this manner that the royal party arrived at the city of Oldorando, more resembling shepherds than royalty. Their protognostic prisoners were torn and bleeding from the uct thicket, as were many of the humans. The king himself was covered in dust.

There was about Oldorando something almost theatrical, perhaps because at its heart lay the gaudy stage on which worship of Akhanaba the ox-faced All-Powerful was at its most resplendent. True worship is solitary; when the religious gather together, they put on pageants for their gods.

Lying in the steamy centre of Campannlat, threaded by the River Valvoral which connected it with Matrassyl and—ultimately—the sea, Oldorando was a city of travellers. Mostly they came to worship or, if not to worship, to trade.

In the physical form of the city was commemorated the long

existence of these opposed intentions. The Holyval sector of the city ran in a diagonal line from southwest to northeast, rising above the sprawl of commerce like a fretted cliff. Holyval included the Old City, with its quaint seven-storey towers, in which lived permanent religious communities. Here were the Academicians, a female order. Here, too, were pilgrims and beggars, as well as god's scum, those who beat empty breasts. Here were courts of shadow and places of prayer sunk deep into the earth. Here too stood the Dom with its attendant monasteries, and King Sayren Stund's palace.

It was generally agreed—at least by those whose lives were enclosed by Holyval—that this sector of saintliness, this diagonal of decency, ran between sewers of worldly vices.

But set in Holyval's pompous and fretted walls and forbidding ramparts were a variety of doors. Some were opened only on ceremonial occasions. Others allowed access to the Old City only for the privileged. Others admitted only women or only men (no phagors were permitted to sully Holyval). But others, and those among the most used, let even the most secular of persons to come and go as they would. Between the holy and the unholy, as between the living and the dead, was set a barrier which detained nobody from crossing it.

The unholy lived in less grand premises, although even here the rich had built their palaces along the broader boulevards. The wicked prospered, the good made their way through life as best they could. Of the city's present population of eight hundred and ninety thousand humans, almost one hundred thousand were in religious orders, and served Akhanaba. At least as many were slaves, and served believer and unbeliever alike.

It was in keeping with the shows which Oldorando loved that two messengers clad in blue and gold should wait on JandolAnganol's arrival at the south gate, with a coach in which to draw him to King Sayren Stund.

JandolAnganol refused the coach and, instead of taking the triumphal route along Wozen Avenue, paraded his dusty company into the Pauk. The Pauk was a comfortable, down-at-heels area of taverns and markets where there were traders who would buy both animals and protognostics.

"Madis don't fetch much in Embruddock," said one sturdy

dealer, using the old country name for Oldorando. "We got enough of them and, like the Nondads, they don't work well. Now your phagors would be a different question, but in this city I'm not allowed to trade in phagors."

"I'm selling only the Madis and animals, man. Your price, or I'll go elsewhere."

When a sum had been agreed on, the Madis were sold into captivity and the animals to slaughter. The king retired in satisfaction. He was now better prepared to meet Sayren Stund. Before the transaction, he had not so much as a roon piece on him. Phagors dispatched to Matrassyl for gold had not returned.

Moving in military order, the First Phagorian proceeded up Wozen Avenue, where crowds had assembled to watch them. The crowds cheered JandolAnganol as he strode along with Yuli. He was popular with the rabble of Oldorando, despite his championship of the officially deplored ancipitals. The common people contrasted a lively, eager man favourably with their fat, idle, domestic breed of monarch. The common people did not know the queen of queens. The common people had sympathy for a king whose bride-to-be had been brutally murdered—even if that bride was only a Madi, or half-Madi.

Among the common people went the religious. The clerics were out with banners. RENOUNCE YOUR SINS. THE END OF THE WORLD IS NIGH. REPENT YE WHILE TIME IS. Here as in Borlien, the Pannovalan Church played on public fears in order to bring the independent-minded to heel.

The dusty progress continued. Past the ancient King Denniss Pyramid. Through the Wozen sector. Into the wide Loylbryden Square. On the far side of the square, across a stream, Whistler Park. Facing on to square and park, the great Dom of Striving and the picturesque town palace of the king. In the centre of the square, a golden pavilion, in which was seated King Sayren Stund himself, waiting to greet his visitor.

Beside the king sat Queen Bathkaarnet-she, wearing a grey keedrant decorated with black roses, and an uncomfortable crown. Between their majesties on a smaller throne sat their one remaining daughter, Milua Tal. The three of them reposed in absurd dignity under an awning, while the rest of the court

sweated in the sun. The heat buzzed with flies. A band played. The absence of soldiers was noticeable, but several elderly officers in resplendent uniforms marched slowly about. The civil guard kept the crowd in order along the perimeters of the square.

The Oldorandan court was known for its stifling formality. Sayren Stund had done his best to soften court etiquette on this occasion, but there remained a line of advisors and church dignitaries, many of them in flowing canonicals, drawn up severely as they waited to shake JandolAnganol's hand and kiss his cheek.

The Eagle stood with his party of captains and his hunchbacked armourer, surveying them challengingly, the dust of his journey still about him.

"Your parade would do credit to a museum, Cousin Sayren," he said.

Sayren Stund was dressed, as were his officers, in a severe black charfrul to express mourning. He levered himself out of his throne and came to JandolAnganol with arms extended. JandolAnganol made a bow, holding himself stiffly. Yuli stood a pace behind him, sticking his milt up alternate nostrils, otherwise motionless.

"Greetings in the name of the All-Powerful. The Court of Oldorando welcomes you in your peaceful and fraternal visit to our capital. May Akhanaba make the meeting fruitful."

"Greetings in the name of the All-Powerful. I thank you for your fraternal reception. I come to offer my condolences and my grief at the death of your daughter, Simoda Tal, my bride-elect."

As JandolAnganol spoke, his glance, under the line of his eyebrows, was ever active. He did not trust Sayren Stund. Stund paraded him along the ranks of dignitaries, and JandolAnganol allowed his hand to be shaken and his grimy cheek to be kissed.

He saw from Sayren Stund's demeanour that the King of Oldorando bore him ill will. The knowledge was a torment. Everywhere was hatred in men's hearts. The murder of Simoda Tal had left its stain, with which he now had to reckon.

After the parade, the queen approached, limping, her hand

resting on Milua Tal's arm. Bathkaarnet-she's looks had faded, yet there was something in her expression, in the way she held her head—submissively yet perkily—which affected JandolAnganol. He recalled a remark of Sayren Stund's which had once been reported to him—why had that lodged in his memory?—"Once you have lived with a Madi woman, you want no other."

Both Bathkaarnet-she and her daughter had the captivating bird faces of their kind. Though Milua Tal's blood had been diluted with a human stream, she presented an exotically dark, brilliant impression, with enormous eyes glowing on either side of her aquiline nose. When she was presented, she gazed direct at JandolAnganol, and gave him the Look of Acceptance. He thought briefly of SartoriIrvrash's mating experiments; here if ever was a fertile cross-breeding.

He was pleased to gaze on this one bright face among so many dull ones, and said to her, "You much resemble the portrait I was sent of your sister. Indeed, you are even more beautiful."

"Simoda and I were much alike, and much different, like all sisters," Milua Tal replied. The music of her voice suggested to him many things, fires in the night, baby Tatro cooing in a cool room, pigeons in a wooden tower.

"Our poor Milua is overcome by the assassination of her sister, as we all are," said the king, with a noise which incorporated the best features of a sigh and a belch. "We have agents out far and wide, pursuing the killer, the villain who posed as a Madi to gain entrance to the palace."

"It was a cruel blow against us both."

Another compendious sigh. "Well, Holy Council will be held next week, with a special memorial service for our departed daughter, which the Holy C'Sarr himself will bless with his presence. That will cheer us. You must stay with us for that event, Cousin, and be welcome. The C'Sarr will be delighted to greet such a valued member of his Community—and it would be to your advantage to pass time with him, as you will realise. Have you met His Holiness?"

"I know his envoy, Alam Esomberr. He will arrive shortly."

"Ah. Yes. Hmm. Esomberr. A witty fellow."

"And adventurous," said JandolAnganol.

The band struck up. They proceeded across the square to the palace, and JandolAnganol found Milua Tal by his side. She looked up brightly at him, smiling. He asked her conspiratorially, "Are you prepared to tell me your age, ma'am, if I keep it a secret?"

"Oh, that's one of the questions I hear most often," she said, dismissively. "Together with 'Do you like being a princess?' Persons think me in advance of my age, and they must be right. The increased heat of the present period brings younger persons on, develops them in every way. I have dreamed the dreams of an adult for over a year. Did you ever dream you were in the powerful irresistible embrace of a fire god?"

He bent to her ear and said in a ferocious whisper, playfully, "Before I reveal to you if I am that fire god, I shall have to answer my own question. I'd put you at no more than nine years old."

"Nine years and five tenners," she replied, "but it is emotions, not years, which count."

The facade of the palace was long, and three storeys high, with massive polished columns of rajabaral rising through the marked horizontals of the upper storeys. The roof swept flamboyantly upwards, tiled with blue tiles made by Kaci potters. The palace had been first built over three hundred and fifty small years ago, after Oldorando was partially destroyed by phagor invasion; although its timbers had been renewed since, the original design was adhered to. Elaborately carved wooden screens protected the unglazed windows. The doors were of the same type of carving, but veneered in silver and backed by thick, wooden panels. A tubular gong was struck within, the doors opened, and Sayren Stund led his guests inside.

There followed two days of banquetting and empty speeches. The hot water springs for which Oldorando was famous also played their part. A service of thanksgiving was held in the Dom, attended by many high-ranking dignitaries of the Church. The singing was magnificent, the costumes impressive, the darkness in the great underground vault all that Akhanaba could desire. JandolAnganol prayed, sang, spoke, submitted to ceremony, and confided in no one.

All were uncertain of this strange man, all kept their eyes on

him. And his eyes were on all. It was clear why some called him the Eagle.

He took care to see that the First Phagorian Guard was suitably housed. For a city that hated phagors, they were well provided for. Across the Loylbryden Square from the Dom was Whistler Park, an area of green entirely surrounded by the Valvoral or its tributaries. Here were preserved brassim trees. Here also was the Hour Whistler of continent-wide fame. The geyser blew with a shrill note at every hour, with the greatest accuracy. Days, weeks, tenners, years, centuries, went by; still the Hour Whistler blew. Some said the hour's length, and the forty minutes which divided the hour, had been decided by this noise issuing from the earth.

An ancient seven-storey tower and some new pavilions stood on the margins of the park. The phagors were billeted in the pavilions. The four bridges into the park were guarded, by phagors on the inner and humans on the outer side, so that no one could get into the park to molest the ancipitals.

Crowds soon gathered to watch the ancipital soldiery across the water. These well-drilled, placid-seeming creatures were far different from the phagors of popular imagination, where they rode godlike on great rust-red steeds, travelling at godlike speeds to bring destruction among men. Those riders of the icy storm had little in common with the beasts marching dourly about the park.

As JandalAnganol left his cohorts to return to Sayren Stund, he noticed how restless they were. He spoke to Phagor-Major Chzarn, but could get from her only that the guard needed a while to settle into new quarters.

He assumed that the noise of the Hour Whistler caused them some irritation. Giving them words of reassurance, he left, the runt capering along at his side. A sulphurous volcano smell filled the air.

Milua Tal met him as he entered the silver gates of the palace. In the last two days he had grown increasingly fond of her volatile company, her cooing pigeon voice.

"Some of your friends have arrived. They say they're holy, but everyone seems to be holy here. The chief of them doesn't look holy. He's too handsome to be holy. He looks naughty to me. Do you like naughty people, King Jandol?—because I think I'm rather naughty."

He laughed.

"I think you are naughty. So are most people. Including some of the holy ones."

"So it is necessary to be exceptionally naughty to stand out from the crowd?"

"That's a reasonable deduction."

"Is that why you stand out from the crowd?"

She slipped her hand into his, and he clasped it.

"There are other reasons. Being a fire god is one."

"I find most people are terribly disappointing. Do you know, when my sister was murdered, we found her sitting upright in a chair, fully dressed. No blood visible. That was disappointing. I imagined pools of blood. I imagined people threw themselves all over the place when they were getting killed, as if they hated what was happening."

JandolAnganol asked in a hard voice, "How was she killed?"

"Zygankes, stabbed right through the heart with a fuggie horn! Father says it was a fuggie horn. Right slap through her clothes and her heart." She glanced suspiciously at Yuli, following his master, but Yuli had been dehorned.

"Were you frightened?"

She gave him a scornful look. "I never think about it. At all. Well, I think about her sitting upright, I suppose. Her eyes were still frozen open."

They entered the tapestried reception hall. Milua Tal's warning had served to alert JandolAnganol to the arrival of Alam Esomberr and his "little rabble of vicars," as Esomberr had called them. They were surrounded by a crowd of Oldorandan grandees, from whom a bumble of polite regard arose.

The eagle eye of the king, penetrating to the rear of the chamber, observed another familiar figure who, as the king arrived, was being bustled out of a rear door. The figure turned to look back as he left the room and his gaze, despite all the heads in between, met JandolAnganol's. Then he was gone, and the door closed behind him.

On the entry of the king, Esomberr broke courteously from his companions and came forward to make a bow to JandolAnganol, giving one of his mocking smiles.

"Here we are, as you see, Jandol, my somewhat ecclesias-

tical party and I. One twisted ankle, one case of food poisoning, one envoy longing for the fleshpots, otherwise all in good order. Travel-stained, of course, from a preposterously long walk across your domains . . .'' They embraced formally.

"I'm glad you are preserved, Alam. You will find the fleshpots rather gloomy here, that's my impression.''

Esomberr was eyeing the runt standing by the king's side. He made playfully to pat Yuli, and then withdrew his hand. "You don't bite, do you, thing?''

"I'm zivilised,'' said Yuli.

Esomberr raised an eyebrow. "I don't want to speak out of turn, Jandol, but will this rather stuffy crowd here, Sayren Stund and company, tolerate even a zivilised you-know-what in their midst? There's a drumble on at present—to celebrate the death of your betrothed, I gather. . . .''

"I've met no trouble yet—but the C'Sarr arrives soon. You had better get your fleshpotting in before then. By the way, I have just seen my ex-chancellor, SartoriIrvrash. Do you know anything about him?''

"Hmm. Yes, yes, I do, sire.'' Esomberr rubbed his elegant nose with a finger. "He and a Sibornalese lady came upon me and my rabble of vicars shortly after you and your phagorian infantry had trotted on ahead in your brisk, forceful manner. Both he and the Sibornalese lady were on hoxney-back. They journeyed the rest of the way with us.''

"What business has he in Oldorando?''

"Fleshpots?''

"Try again. What did he tell you?''

Alam Esomberr cast his eyes down to the floor as if seeking to recall an elusive memory. "Zygankes, travel does soften the mind . . . hm. Why, I really cannot say, sire. Perhaps you had best ask him yourself?''

"He had come from Gravabagalinien? Why was he there?''

"Sire, perhaps he wished to view the sea, as I've heard some men do before they die.''

"In that case, his wish could have been premonitory,'' said JandolAnganol, with spirit. "You are not helpful this evening, Alam.''

"Forgive me. My legs are in such shape that my head is also affected. I may be more effectual after I have bathed and dined. Meanwhile, I assure you that I am no friend of your

somewhat gaseous ex-chancellor.''

"Except that you both would rid the world of phagors.''

"So would most men if they had the courage to act. Phagors and fathers.''

They regarded each other. "We had better not get to the subject of courage,'' said JandolAnganol, and walked away.

He plunged into a group where men in grand ornamental charfruls and exotic hairpieces were conversing with King Sayren Stund, interrupting them without apology. Sayren Stund looked flustered, but reluctantly asked his audience to leave him. A space was cleared about the two kings. Immediately, a lackey came forward with a silver tray, to present glasses of iced wine. JandolAnganol turned. Only half deliberately, he knocked the tray from the man's hand.

"Tut-tut-tut,'' said Sayren Stund. "No matter, it was an accident, I saw that. Plenty more wine. And more ice, as a matter of fact, delivered now by a *lady* captain, Immya Muntras. We must accustom ourselves to such innovations.''

"Brother king, never mind the niceties of conversation. You are sheltering here in your palace a man who was my chancellor, of whom I rid myself, a man I think my enemy, since he went over to the Sibornalese cause, by name SartoriIrvrash. What does he want here? Has he brought you some secret messages from my ex-queen, as I fear?''

The King of Oldorando looked about apprehensively.

"The man you mention arrived here only twenty minutes ago, along with gentry of good character, such as Alam Esomberr. I agreed to give him shelter. He has a lady with him. I assure you they are not to be guests under this roof.''

"She is Sibornalese. I dismissed that man. I conclude that he cannot be here to do me any favours. Where will they lodge?''

"Dear brother, I hardly think that is business of mine or yours. The dusk-moth must keep to the dusk, as we say.''

"Where will he stay? Are you protecting him? Be frank with me.''

Sayren Stund had been sitting on a high chair. He rose with dignity and said, "It grows heated in here. Let us take a walk in the garden before we become overheated.'' He gestured to his wife to remain behind.

They progressed through the room amid a corridor of bows.

Only the runt Yuli followed. The gardens were lit by flam-beaux set in niches. Since almost as little air circulated as in the palace, the torches burned with a steady flame. A sulphurous smell hung about the neatly trimmed avenues.

"I do not wish to vex you, Brother Sayren," Jandol-Anganol said. "But you understand that I have unknown enemies here. I perceived just by the look of SartoriIrvrash, by his expression, that he is now my enemy, come to make trouble for me. Do you deny that?"

Sayren Stund had taken better control of himself. He was corpulent and he wheezed as he walked. He said coolly, "You appreciate that the common people of Oldorando, or Em-bruddock, as some like to say, affecting the old mode, regard men of your country—this is not a prejudice I share, you understand—as barbarians. I cannot educate them out of the illusion, not even by stressing the religion we have in com-mon."

"How does this answer my question?"

"Dear, I'm out of breath. I think I have an allergy. May I ask you if you keep that fuggie following at heel simply to of-fend me and my queen?" He indicated Yuli with a contemp-tuous gesture.

It was the turn of JandolAnganol to be at a loss.

"He's no more than—a pet hound. He follows me every-where."

"It's an insult to bring that creature into this court. It should be housed on Whistler Island with the rest of your animals."

"I tell you, it's just a favourite hound. It sleeps outside my bedchamber door at night and will bark if there's danger."

Sayren Stund stopped walking, clasped his hands behind his back, and gazed intently into a bush.

"We should not quarrel, we both have our difficulties, I in Kace, you at home in Matrassyl, if the reports that reach me are to be trusted. But you cannot bring that creature into my court—the force of the opinion of the court is against it, whatever I personally may say."

"Why did you not say this when I arrived, two days ago?"

A heavy sigh from the Oldorandan king. "You have had two days' grace. Think of it like that. The Holy C'Sarr arrives shortly, as you know. The honour of receiving him means

much, but is a grave responsibility. He will not tolerate the sight of a phagor. You are too difficult for us, Jandol. Since you have exhausted your purpose here, why do you not return to your capital tomorrow, with your troupe of animals?"

"Am I that unwelcome? You invited me to stay for the C'Sarr's visit. What poison has SartoriIrvrash poured in your ear?"

"The occasion when the Holy C'Sarr is present must pass off peacefully. Perhaps the alliance with powerful Pannoval is more important to me than to you, since my kingdom is nearer. Frankly, fuggies and fuggy-lovers are not popular in this part of the world. If you have no purpose here, then I suggest we give you godspeed tomorrow."

"If I have a purpose?"

Sayren Stund cleared his throat. "What purpose? We are both religious men, Jandol. Let us go and pray and be scourged together now, and part as friends and allies in the morning. Isn't that best? Then your visit can be sweetly remembered. I will give you a boat with which you can sail rapidly down the Valvoral and be home in no time. Can you smell the flowering zaldal? Beautiful, isn't it?"

"I see." JandolAnganol folded his arms. "Very well, then, if that is as deep as your friendship and your religion go—we shall quit your presence on the morrow."

"We shall sorrow to see you leave us. So will our queen and daughter."

"I comply with your request, and poorly I think of it. In return, answer my question. Where is SartoriIrvrash?"

The King of Oldorando showed sudden spirit. "You have no right to think poorly of my request. Do you imagine my daughter would be dead today if you had not been espoused to her? It was a political killing—she had no personal enemies, poor girl. Then you come to court with your filthy fuggies and expect to be made welcome."

"Sayren, I say truly, I grieve for the death of Simoda Tal. If I found the murderer, I would know how to deal with him. Do not increase my sorrow by laying that evil at my door."

Sayren Stund ventured to rest his hand upon the arm of his brother king.

"Do not worry yourself about—the man you mention, your ex-chancellor. We have given him a room in one of the monas-

tic hostels which lie behind this palace and the Dom. You will not have to meet with him. And we will not part foes. That would not do." He blew his nose. "Just be sure you leave Oldorando tomorrow."

They made each other a bow. JandolAnganol went slowly up to his quarters in a wing of the palace, Yuli following behind.

Indifferent tapestries hung on the walls here, the board floor was filthy. He knocked on his infantry major's door. No answer came. On inspiration, he went along to Fard Fantil's door and knocked. The Royal Armourer called to him to enter. The hunchback sat on his bed, polishing his boots; he jumped to his feet when he saw who entered. A phagor guard stood silent by the window, spear in hand.

JandolAnganol lost no time in coming to the point.

"You're the very man I want. This is your native city and you know local customs as I don't. We leave here tomorrow—yes, it's unexpected, but there's no choice. We sail to Matrassyl."

"Trouble, sire?"

"Trouble."

"He's tricky, is the king."

"I want to take SartoriIrvrash with me, prisoner. He's here, in the city. I want you to find him, overpower him, smuggle him into these quarters. We can't cut his throat—it would cause too much of a scandal. Get him here, unseen."

Fard Fantil began to pace up and down the room, clutching his brow. "We can't do such a thing. It's impossible. The law won't allow. What has he done?"

JandolAnganol smacked a fist into his palm. "I know that dangerous old crank's way of thought. He has developed some mad piece of knowledge to discredit me. It will concern the phagors somehow. Before it gets out, I must have him safe, a prisoner. We leave with him tomorrow, shut in a chest. Nobody will know. He resides in one of the hostels behind this palace. Now, I rely on you, Fard Fantil, for I know you as a good man. Do this, and I will reward you, on my word."

Still the armourer hesitated. "The law won't allow."

In a steely voice, the king said, "You have a phagor here in your chambers. I expressly forbad it. Except for my runt, all ancipitals were to be housed in Whistler Park. You merit a

flogging for disobeying my orders—and a demotion.''

"He is my personal servant, sire.''

"Will you get SartoriIrvrash for me, as I request?''

With a sullen look, Fard Fantil agreed.

The king threw a bag of gold onto the bed. It was the money he had acquired in the market, two days previously.

"Good. Disguise yourself as a monk. Go at once. Take that pet of yours with you.''

When man and phagor had gone, JandolAnganol stood for a while in the dark room, thinking. Through the window, he could see YarapRombry's Comet low in the northern sky. The sight of that bright smudge in the night brought a memory of his last encounter with his father's gossie, and its prediction that he would meet one in Oldorando who would control his destiny. Was that a reference to SartoriIrvrash? His brain, like a darting glance, looked over other possibilities.

Satisfied that he had done all that might be done in a hostile place, he returned to his quarters, where Yuli had settled himself for sleep before the door as usual. The king gave him a pat as he climbed past.

By the bed, a tray of wine and ice had been placed. Perhaps it was Sayren Stund's way of showing gratitude to a departing guest. Scowling, JandolAnganol drank off a full glass of the sweet wine, then hurled tray and pitcher into a corner.

Flinging off his clothes, he climbed in among the rugs and immediately slept. He always slept soundly. This night, his sleep was heavier than usual.

His dreams were many and confused. He was numerous things, and at last he was a fire god, paddling through golden fire. But the fire was less flame than liquid. He was a fire god of the sea, and MyrdemInggala was riding a dolphin just ahead of him. He struggled mightily. The sea clutched him.

At last he caught her. He held her tight. The gold was all about them. But the horror that had tagged along on the margins of the dream was moving in rapidly upon him. MyrdemInggala was other than he thought. An immense weight and sickliness emanated from her body. He was crying as he wrestled with her. The gold ran about his throat and eyes. She felt like—

He broke from the dream into waking. For a moment, he scarcely dared open his eyes. He was in the bed in the Oldorandan palace. He was clutching something. He was trembling violently.

Almost against his wish, his eyes opened. Only the gold from the dream remained. It stained the rugs and silken pillows. It stained him.

Crying out, he sat up, flinging back the skins that covered him. Yuli lay close against him. The runt's head had been severed. There was only the body. It was cold. Its copious golden blood had ceased to flow and lay congealing in a pool beneath the corpse, and beneath the king.

The king flung himself down on the bare floor, face to the tiles. He wept. The sobs rose from some inner recess and shook his whole stained body.

It was the custom in the Oldorandan court for a service to be held every morning at the tenth hour, in the Royal Chapel, which was under the palace. King Sayren Stund, to honour his guest, invited JandolAnganol each day to read—as was his custom—from the revered "Testament of RayNilayan." Much whispering and speculation filled the chapel on this morning, as the royal members of the faith gathered. Many doubted that the Borlienese king would appear.

The king came down the stairs from his chambers. He had washed himself over and over and dressed, not in a charfrul, but in knee-length tunic, boots, and light cloak. His face was of an extreme pallor. His hands shook. He walked deliberately, taking step by step, and was in control of himself.

As he descended the staircase, his armourer came at the run after him, and spoke.

"Sire, I had no response to my knock at your door earlier. Forgive me. I have the prisoner you named in my room, tied in the garderobe. I will watch him till the ship is ready. Tell me only what time I can smuggle him aboard."

"Plans may be changed, Fard Fantil."

The king's manner as much as his words alarmed the armourer.

"Are you ill, sire?" Said with an ill-favoured glance upwards from under his brows.

"Go back to your room." Without a backward look, the
king continued to descend, down to the ground floor and
down again to the Royal Chapel. He was the last to enter. The
introit was playing on vrach and drums. All eyes turned upon
him as he walked stiffly, like a boy on stilts, to mount into the
box beside Sayren Stund. Only Stund remained gazing
towards the altar, eyes blinking rapidly, as if unaware of
anything amiss.

The royal box was set apart, in front of the congregation. It
was an ornate affair, its carved sides decorated with silver. Six
curving steps led up to it. Ranking just below it was a plainer
box, reached by only one step, where Queen Bathkaarnet-she
sat with her daughter.

JandolAnganol took his place beside the other king, staring
ahead, and the service proceeded. Only after the long hymn of
praise to Akanaba did Sayren Stund turn and gesture to JandolAnganol, just as he had done on previous days, to read a
part of the Testament.

With slow pace, JandolAnganol descended the six steps,
walked across the black and red tiles to the lectern, turned,
and faced the congregation. Absolute silence fell. His face was
as white as parchment.

He confronted their massed stoney regard. He read curiosity, covert smiles, hatred. Nowhere did he detect sympathy,
except on the face of the nine-year-old girl, who shrank down
beside her mother. She, he observed, as he directed his full
regard at her, mustered the old Madi Look of Acceptance, as
she had when first they met.

He spoke. His voice sounded surprisingly feeble but, after a
faltering start, gathered strength.

"I wish to say—that is, Your Royal Highnesses, Nobles,
All, I would say—you must excuse me if I do not read, but instead take this opportunity to address you direct in this holy
place, where the All-Powerful hears every word, and looks
into every heart.

"I know he must look into your hearts and see how much
you wish me well. Just as much as I wish you well. My kingdom is a great and rich one. Yet I have left it to come here
almost alone—almost alone. We all are in quest of peace for
our peoples. That quest has long been mine, and my father's

before me. My life's quest is for the prosperity of Borlien. So I have sworn.

"And there is a more personal quest. I am without that thing which a man most desires, even above his service to his country. I lack a queen.

"The stone I set rolling half a year ago still rolls. My resolve was then to marry the House of Stund's daughter; that intention I shall now carry out."

He paused as if himself alarmed by what he was about to say. Every eye in the chapel lit on his face to search out the story of his life inscribed there.

"It is therefore not only in response to what His Royal Highness, King Sayren Stund, has done that I announce here, before the throne of one who is above all earthly power, that I—King JandolAnganol of the House of Anganol—intend to unite the nations of Borlien and Oldorando in a blood bond. I mean to take in marriage as soon as is possible the prized and beloved daughter of His Majesty, Princess Milua Tal Stund. The solemnisation of our nuptials will take place, Akhanaba willing, in my capital city of Matrassyl, since I am desired to leave for there today."

Many in the congregation jumped up, in order to see how Sayren Stund responded to this astonishing news. When JandolAnganol ceased speaking, they became like statues under his chill gaze, and again there was absolute silence in the chapel.

Sayren Stund had slipped gradually from his seat and could no longer be seen. The tableau was broken by a cry from Milua Tal, who recovered fast from her initial surprise and rushed across the floor to clasp JandolAnganol.

"I will stand by you," she said, "and perform as your nuptial wife in all things."

XX

HOW JUSTICE WAS DONE

Firecrackers exploded. Crowds gathered. Rathel was drunk. Prayers were said in the holier parts of the city.

The population of Oldorando City rejoiced at the news of JandolAnganol's engagement to Princess Milua Tal. They had no logical reason for rejoicing. The royal house of Stund and the church with which it was involved lived well at the populace's expense. But chances for rejoicing are few, and wisely taken.

The royal family had won general sympathy when Princess Simoda Tal was assassinated. Such horrendous events contributed to the emotional life of the people.

That the younger sister was now affianced to the man previously engaged to her dead sister was an enjoyable coup de théâtre. There was prurient speculation as to when Milua Tal experienced her first menses and—as usual—debate about the sexual habits of the Madis. Were they totally promiscuous or entirely monogamous? It was a question never settled, though most male opinion was in favour of the former alternative.

JandolAnganol met with general approval.

In the public view, he was a dashing figure, neither offensively young nor distastefully old. He had married and divorced one of the most beautiful women in all Campannlat. As to why he should now marry a girl younger than his son . . . such dynastic couplings were not rare; while the numbers of child prostitutes in East Gate and Uidok provided one easy answer to the question.

On the subject of phagors, the population was more neutral than the palace supposed. Certainly, everyone knew their folk history, and the famous time when phagor hordes destroyed the city. But that was long ago. There were no marauding fuggie bands now. Phagors had become a rare sight in Oldorando. People liked to go and view them in Whistler Park, gazing across the Valvoral at the First Phagorian Guard. They were, after a fashion, popular.

None of which appeased the bitter resentment of King Sayren Stund.

Never a determined man, he had let the moment slip by when he might have banned the match. He inwardly cursed himself. He cursed his queen. Bathkaarnet-she approved the match.

Bathkaarnet-she was a simple woman. She liked Jandol-Anganol. As she put it, singing, she "liked his looks." Although she had no fondness for the ancipital kind, she saw in the constant drumbles a sort of intolerance which might easily spill over against her own kind; indeed, the Madis were not popular in Oldorando, and incidents of violence against them were frequent. Therefore she considered that this man who protected phagors would be kind to her sole remaining daughter, a half-Madi.

More tellingly, Bathkaarnet-she knew that Sayren Stund had long had it in mind to marry off Milua Tal to Taynth Indredd, a prince of Pannoval far older and more revolting than JandolAnganol. She disliked Taynth Indredd. She disliked the thought of her daughter living in gloomy Pannoval, buried under the mountains of the Quzint. That was not a fit fate for a Madi, or the daughter of a Madi. JandolAnganol and Matrassyl appeared the better bargain.

So, in her self-effacing way, she opposed her king. He was forced to find another way to show his anger. And a way was at hand.

Outwardly, Sayren Stund preserved a pleasant demeanour. He could not admit any responsibility for the killing of Yuli. He even invited JandolAnganol to a meeting to discuss wedding arrangements. They convened in a room where fans swung from the ceiling, where potted vulus grew, and where bright Madi rugs hung on the walls in place of windows, Pannoval-style.

With Sayren Stund were his wife and an advisor in holy orders, a tall saturnine man with a face like an unshaven hatchet, who sat in the background, looked at no one, and said nothing.

JandolAnganol arrived in full uniform, escorted by one of his captains, a hearty outdoor man who looked bewildered by his new diplomatic role.

Sayren Stund poured wine and offered a glass to JandolAnganol.

The latter refused. "The fame of your vineyards is universal, but I have found the vintage makes me sleepy."

Ignoring the thrust, Sayren Stund came to the point.

"We are content that you should marry the Princess Milua Tal. You will recall that your intention was to wed my murdered daughter in Oldorando. Therefore we request you to hold the ceremony here, under the dispensation of the Holy C'Sarr himself, when he arrives."

"Sire, I understood you to say you were eager for me to leave today."

"That was a misunderstanding. We are given to understand that the tame creature of yours which caused us offence has been disposed of." As he said this, his eyes slid towards the saturnine advisor, as if for support. "We will hold festivities appropriate for you, rest assured."

"Are you certain the C'Sarr will be here in three days?"

"His messengers are already here. Our agents are in touch. His entourage has passed Lake Dorzin. Other visitors, such as Prince Taynth Indredd of Pannoval, are expected tomorrow. Your nuptials will make the occasion a solemn historic event."

Realising that Sayren Stund intended to gain advantage over him by this delay, JandolAnganol retired to a corner of the room to talk to his captain. He wished to leave immediately before more treachery could be worked. But for that he needed a ship, and ships were at the dispensation of Sayren

Stund. There was also the pressing question—as the captain reminded him—of SartoriIrvrash, bound and gagged and near suffocation in Fard Fantil's garderobe.

He addressed Sayren Stund. "Have we reason to be certain that the Holy C'Sarr will perform this office for us? He is ancient, is he not?"

Sayren Stund pursed his lips.

"Ageing, certainly. Venerable. Not, I'd say to the best of my judgement, ancient. Possibly thirty-nine and a tenner or two. But he might, of course, have an objection to the alliance, on the grounds that Borlien continues to harbour phagors and refuses to obey requests for a drumble. On that point of doctrine, I would not myself care to be dogmatic; we must naturally hear the judgement from his holy lips."

Points of anger burned on JandolAnganol's cheeks.

In a restrained voice, he said, "There is reason to believe that our beloved religion—to which none is more attached than I—began in simple phagor worship. That was when both phagors and men lived more primitively. Although ecclesiastical history seeks to hide the fact, the All-Powerful once closely resembled an ancipital in appearance. Of more recent centuries, popular images have blurred over that resemblance. Nevertheless, it is there.

"Nobody imagines nowadays that phagors are all-powerful. I know from my personal experience how docile they can be, given firm handling. Nevertheless, our religion hinges centrally upon them. Therefore it cannot be just to persecute them under the edicts of the Church."

Sayren Stund looked back for assistance to his priestly advisor. This worthy spoke, saying in a hollow voice, without looking up, "That is not an opinion which will carry weight with His Holiness the C'Sarr, who would say that the Borlienese king blasphemes against the countenance of Akhanaba."

"Quite," said Sayren Stund. "That is not an opinion which will carry weight with any of us, brother. The C'Sarr must marry you and you must keep your views to yourself."

The meeting concluded briskly. Alone with his queen and the dark advisor, Sayren Stund rubbed his chubby hands and said, "Then he will wait for the C'Sarr. We have three days to see the wedding does not take place. We need SartoriIrvrash. The phagor quarters in Whistler Park have been searched and

he is not there. He must then be still in the palace. We will have the king's quarters searched—every nook and cranny."

The dark advisor cleared his throat. "There is the question of the woman, Odi Jeseratabhar. She arrived here with SartoriIrvrash. This morning, she sought refuge in the Sibornalese ambassadorial mansion in some distress, reporting her friend's disappearance. My understanding is that she is an admiral. My agents tell me that she has not been well received. The ambassador may treat her as a traitor. Nevertheless, he will not hand her over—as yet at least."

Sayren Stund fanned himself and took some wine. "We can manage without her."

"There is another point in your majesty's favour which my ecclesiastical lawyers have produced," continued the priestly advisor. "King JandolAnganol's divorcement from Myrdem-Inggala is contained in a bill which as yet remains in the possession of Alam Esomberr. Although the king has signed it and appears to believe his divorce absolute, by an ancient enactment of Pannovalan canon law the divorce of royal personages is not absolute until the bill has physically passed into the keeping of the C'Sarr. The enactment was passed in order to delay ill-considered dynastic alliances. So at present King JandolAnganol is in a de facto state of decree nisi."

"And therefore cannot marry again?"

"Any marriage contracted before the decree is absolute would be illegal."

Sayren Stund clapped his hands and laughed. "Excellent. Excellent. He's not going to get away with this impertinence."

"But we need an alliance with Borlien," said the queen feebly.

Her husband scarcely bothered to look at her.

"My dear, we have but to undermine his position, to disgrace him, and Matrassyl will reject him. Our agents report further riots there. I may then myself step in as the saviour of Borlien, ruling over both kingdoms, as Oldorando has ruled over Borlien in the past. Have you no sense of history?"

JandolAnganol was well aware of the difficulty of his position. Whenever he felt discouraged he whipped up his anger by thinking of Sayren Stund's malice. When he had sufficiently

recovered from the shock of discovering Yuli's headless body to leave his room, he had come upon the head lying in the corridor. A few yards farther down the corridor lay the human guard he had posted, stabbed to death, his face hacked at savagely with a sword. JandolAnganol had vomited. A day later, sickness still overwhelmed him. Despite the heat, there was chill in his body.

After the meeting with Sayren Stund, he walked across to Whistler Park, where a small crowd which had gathered gave him a cheer. Association with the phagorian guard calmed him.

He inspected their premises with greater care than before. The phagor commanders trailed behind him. One of the pavilions had been designed as a kind of guest house, and was pleasantly furnished. Upstairs was a complete apartment.

"This apartment will be mine," JandolAnganol said.

"It make your place. No person in Hrl-Drra Nhdo have entry here."

"No phagors either."

"No phagors."

"You will guard it."

"It izz our understanding."

He saw no reason to worry that the commander used what was an ancient phagorian name for Oldorando, though he knew of their long and seemingly ineradicable memories. He was too used to their archaic speech habits.

As he was walking back across the park, four phagors escorting him, the earth shook. Tremors were frequent in Oldorando. This was the second he had felt since his arrival. He looked across Loylbryden Square at the palace. He wished there would be an earthquake severe enough to shake it down, but he could see that the wooden pillars along its face were designed for maximum stability.

The onlookers and loiterers seemed unworried. A waffle seller carried on business as usual. With an inward tremor, JandolAnganol wondered if the end of the world was coming, despite all the wise men said.

"Let it all end," he said to himself.

Then he thought of Milua Tal.

*   *   *

Towards Batalix-set, messengers ran to the palace to say
that Prince Taynth Indredd of Pannoval was arriving at the
East Gate earlier than anticipated. A formal invitation was
sent to JandolAnganol's party to be present at the welcome
ceremony in Loylbryden Square, an invitation he could
scarcely refuse.

Indifferent to affairs of state, or to wars in progress elsewhere, Taynth Indredd had been on a hunt in the Quzints, and
came loaded with trophies of the hunt—skins, plumes, and
ivories. He arrived in a palanquin, followed by several cages
of animals he had captured. In one cage, a dozen Others chattered at the crowd or moped dejectedly. A twelve-piece band
played lively airs as they marched, and banners flew. It was a
more impressive entry than JandolAnganol's. Nor did Taynth
Indredd have to stoop to haggling for a little money in the
marketplace.

Among the prince's retinue was one of JandolAnganol's
few friends in the Pannovalan court, Guaddl Ulbobeg. Ulbobeg looked exhausted from his journey. When the official
welcoming ceremony showed signs of turning into a prolonged
drinking bout, JandolAnganol managed to talk to the old
man.

"I'm getting too frail to undertake such expeditions,"
Guaddl Ulbobeg said. He lowered his voice to add, "And between ourselves, Taynth Indredd gets more tiresome, tenner
by tenner. I greatly desire to retire from his service. I'm thirty-
six and a quarter, after all."

"Why don't you retire?"

Guaddl Ulbobeg laid a hand on JandolAnganol's arm. The
king was moved by the unthinking friendliness of the gesture.
"With the post goes the bishopric of Prayn. Do you not recall
I am a bishop of the Holy Pannovalan Empire, bless it? Were
I to resign before being retired, I'd lose the post and all that
goes with it. . . . Taynth Indredd, by the by, is not best pleased
with you, so let me warn you."

JandolAnganol laughed. "I'm universally hated, I do
believe. How have I offended Taynth Indredd?"

"Oh, it's common knowledge that he and our pompous
friend Sayren Stund intended him to marry Milua Tal until
you put your oar in."

"You know about that?"

"I know everything. I also know I'm going to bathe and then to bed. Drink's no good to me at my age."

"We'll talk in the morning. Rest well."

The earthquakes came again in the early part of the night. This time, they were serious enough to cause alarm. In the poorer parts of the city, tiles and balconies were dislodged. Women ran out screaming into the streets. Slaves spread alarm throughout the palace.

It suited JandolAnganol well. He needed a distraction for his purposes. His captains had investigated the grounds to the rear of the palace and discovered—as was to be expected of a building which had not had to serve as a fortress for a great while—that there were many exits for those who knew. Some had been made by the palace staff for their own convenience. Although there were guards at the front, anyone could leave by the back. As JandolAnganol did.

Only to find that the palace had its own diversions. In the alley that ran outside the northeast side of the palace, a wagon, drawn by six hoxneys, arrived. Four burly men climbed down. One held the lead hoxney, while the other three set about sliding wooden bars away from a side door. They flung the door open and shouted to someone inside the wagon. When there was no answer, two of the men climbed in and, with blows and curses, dragged a bound figure out into the street. A rug had been tied over the captive's head. When he groaned too distinctly, he was fetched a blow across his shoulders.

Without hurry, the three toughs unlocked an iron door and passed into an outbuilding of the palace. The door slammed shut behind them.

JandolAnganol watched this event from the concealment of a portico. Beside him was the fragile figure of Milua Tal. From where they stood, beside the wall, they could smell the heavy fragrance of the zaldal, to which Sayren Stund had drawn JandolAnganol's attention earlier.

In the pavilion in Whistler Park, which they called the White Pavilion, they established their refuge. They would be

safe under the protection of the Phagorian Guard. The king was still preoccupied with the sight they had just witnessed in the street.

"I think your father means to kill me before I can escape from Oldorando."

"Killing's not so bad, but he's determined somehow to disgrace you. I'll find out how if I can, but he gives me only black looks now. Oh, how can kings be so difficult? I hope you won't be like that when we escape to Matrassyl. I'm so curious to see it, and to sail down the Valvoral. Boats going downstream can go at a fantastic speed, faster than birds.

"Do they have pecubeas in Borlien? I'd like some in my room, just like Moth has. Four pecubeas at least, maybe five—if you can afford it. Father says that you intend to murder me in revenge and cut my head off, but I just laughed and stuck my tongue out—have you seen how far my tongue comes out?—and said, 'Revenge for what, you silly old king-person?' and that got him so mad. I thought he'd have apolloplexy."

She chattered away happily as she examined the apartment.

Carrying their single light, JandolAnganol said, "I intend you no harm, Milua. You can believe that. Everyone thinks me a villain. I am in the hands of Akhanaba, as we all are. I do not even intend your father harm."

She sat on the bed and stared out of the window, the beakiness of her face emphasized in the shadows. "That's what I told him, or words to that effect. He was so mad, he let one thing slip. You know SartoriIrvrash?"

"I know him well."

"He's in Father's hands again. Father's men found him in that hunchback's room."

He shook his head. "No. He's still bound and gagged in a garderobe. My captains are going to bring him over here for safekeeping."

Milua Tal gave her bubbling laugh. "He fooled you, Jan. That's another man, a slave they put in there in the dark. They found the real SartoriIrvrash when everyone was greeting fat old Prince Taynth."

"By the beholder! That man has trouble for me, that man has trouble. He was my chancellor. What does he know? . . . Milua, whatever happens, I am going to face it out. I must

face it out, my honour is involved."

"Oh, zygankes, 'My honour is involved'! You sound like Father when you say that. Aren't you supposed to say you are mad about my infantile beauty or something?"

He caught at her hands. "So I may be, my pretty Milua! But what I'm trying to say is that that sort of madness is no good without something to back it. I have to survive dishonour, to outlive it, to remain uncontaminated by it. Then honour will return to me. All will respect me for surviving. Then it will be possible to form an alliance between my country and yours, as I have long desired, and I will form it with your father or with whoever succeeds him."

She clapped her hands. "I succeed him! Then we'll have a whole country each."

Despite his tension, his premonition that further ills were about to befall him, he burst into laughter, seized her, and pressed her delicate body against him.

The earth shook again.

"Can we sleep here, together?" she whispered.

"No, it would be wrong. In the morning, we go to see my friend Esomberr."

"I thought he wasn't your friend."

"I can make him be my friend. He's vain, but not a villain."

The earth tremors died. The night died. Freyr rose in strength, again hidden from sight by the yellow haze, and the temperature climbed.

That day, few persons of importance were seen about the palace. King Sayren Stund announced that he would hold no audiences; those who had lost a home or a child in the tremors wailed in vain in the stagnant anterooms, or were turned away. Nor was King JandolAnganol to be seen. Or the young princess.

On the following day, a body of Oldorandan guards, eight strong, arrested JandolAnganol.

They caught him as he descended the staircase leading from his room. He fought, but they lifted him off his feet and carried him to a place of imprisonment. He was kicked down a spiralling stone stair and thrown into a dungeon.

He lay for many minutes on the floor, beside himself with anger.

"Yuli, Yuli," he said, over and over. "I was so sick at what they did to you that I never could think through to see what danger I was in. . . . I never could think. . . ."

After some minutes of silence, he said aloud, "I was over-confident. That's always been my fault. I trusted too much that I could ride with the circumstances. . . ."

A long while later, he picked himself off the floor and looked helplessly about. A shelf against one wall served as bed and bench. Light filtered in from a high window. In one corner was a trough for sanitary purposes. He sank down on the bench, and thought of his father's long imprisonment.

When his spirits had sunk still lower, he thought of Milua Tal.

"Sayren Stund, if you harm one lash of her eyes, you slanje . . ."

He sat rigid. Eventually, he forced himself to relax and leaned with his back against the moist wall of the cell. With a roar, he jumped up and began to pace about, up and down, between wall and door.

He ceased only when he heard the scrape of boots coming down the stair. Keys rattled at the lock, and a black-clad member of the local clerisy entered between two armed guards. As he gave a scanty bow, JandolAnganol recognised him as Sayren Stund's axe-faced advisor, by name Crispan Mornu.

"Under what devious law am I, a visiting prince of a friendly country, imprisoned?"

"I am come to inform you that you are charged with murder, and will be tried for that crime tomorrow at Batalix-break, before a royal ecclesiastical court." The sepulchral voice paused, then added, "Prepare yourself."

JandolAnganol advanced in a fury. "Murder? Murder, you pack of criminals? What new scoundrelism is this? Whose murder is laid at my door?"

Crossed spears halted his advance.

The priest said, "You are charged with the murder of Princess Simoda Tal, elder daughter of King Sayren Stund of Oldorando."

He bowed again and withdrew.

The king remained where he was, staring at the door. His eagle eyes fixed upon its boards, never blinking, as if he had vowed they should never blink again until he was free.

He stayed almost motionless throughout the night. The intense active principle within him, being confined, stayed coiled within him like a spring. He maintained a defiant alertness throughout the hours of dark, waiting to leap to attack anyone who ventured to enter the dungeon.

Nobody came. No food was brought, no water. During the night there was a remote tremor—so remote it might have been in an artery rather than the earth—and a powder shower of mortar floated down to the stones. Nothing else. Not so much as a rat visited JandolAnganol.

When light seeped in to the place of confinement, he went over to the stone trough. By climbing onto it and hooking his fingers into a hollow between two stones, carved by previous prisoners, he could look out of the unglazed window. A precious breath of fresh air expired upon his cheek.

His dungeon was at the front of the palace, near to the corner by the Dom, or so he estimated. He could look across Loylbryden Square. His viewpoint was too low to see anything beyond it except the tops of trees in the park.

The square was deserted. He thought that if he waited long enough he would possibly see Milua Tal—unless she was also captive of her father.

His view was towards the west. The tiny patch of sky he could see was free of haze. Batalix cast long shadows across the cobbles. Those shadows paled and then divided into two as Freyr also rose. Then they died as the haze returned and the temperature started to mount.

Workmen came. They brought platforms and poles with them. Their manner was the resigned one of workmen everywhere: they were prepared to do the job, but not prepared to hurry over it. After a while, they set up a scaffold.

JandolAnganol went and sat down on the bench, clutching his temples between his nails.

Guards came for him. He fought them, uselessly. They put him in chains. He snarled at them. They pushed him up the stone stairs indifferently.

*   *   *

Everything had fallen out as King Sayren Stund might have wished it. In the incessant enantiodromia which afflicts all things, turning them into their opposites, he could now crow over the man who had so recently crowed over him. He bounded up and down with glee, he uttered cries of joy, he embraced Bathkaarnet-she, he threw merrily evil glances at his dejected daughter.

"You see, child, this villain you threw your arms about is to be branded a murderer before everyone." He advanced upon her with ogreish glee. "We'll give you his corpse to embrace in a day's time. Yes, just another twenty-five hours and your virginity will be safe forever from JandolAnganol!"

"Why not hang me too, Father, and rid yourself of all your daughters to worry about?"

A special chamber in the palace had been set aside to serve as the courtroom. The Church sanctified it for judiciary purposes. Sprigs of veronika, scantiom, and pellamountain—all regarded as cooling herbs—were hung to lower the stifling temperature and shed their balm into the room. Many luminaries of court and city were gathered to watch the proceedings, not all of them by any means as in accord with their ruler as he supposed.

The three main actors in the drama were the king, his saturnine advisor, Crispan Mornu, and a judge by name Kimon Euras, whose station in the Church was minister of the rolls.

Kimon Euras was so thin that he stooped as if the tautness of his skin had bent the backbone it contained; he was bald or, to be precise, without visible vestige of hair, and the skin of his face displayed a greyish pallor reminiscent of the vellums over which he had parsimonious custody. He spiderish air, as he ascended to his bench, clad in a black keedrant hanging to his spatulate feet, seemed to guarantee that he would handle mercy with a similar parsimony.

When these impressive dignitaries were settled in their places, a gong was struck, and two guards chosen for strength dragged King JandolAnganol into the chamber. He was made to stand in the middle of the room for all to see.

The division between prisoner and free is sharp in any court. Here it was more marked than usual. The king's short imprisonment had been enough to make filthy his tunic and his person. Yet he stood with his head high, darting his eagle gaze

about the court, more like a bird of prey hunting weaknesses than a man looking for mercy. The clarity which attended his movements and contours remained part of him.

Kimon Euras began a long address in a powdery voice. The ancient dusts from the documents in his charge had lodged in his larynx. He spoke marginally louder when he came to the words, ". . . cruel murder of our beloved Princess Simoda Tal, in this very palace, by the thrust of an ancipital horn. King JandolAnganol of Borlien, you are charged with being the instigator of this crime."

JandolAnganol immediately shouted in defiance. A bailiff struck him from behind, saying, "Prisoners are not allowed to speak in this court. Any interruptions and you will be thrown back in your cell."

Crispan Mornu had managed for the occasion to find a garment of deeper black than usual. The colour reflected up into his jowls, his cheeks, his eyes, and, when he spoke, into his throat.

"We intend to demonstrate that the guilt of this Borlienese king is inescapable, and that he came here with no other purpose than the destruction of Princess Milua Tal, thus ending the lineage of the House of Stund. We shall produce a copy of the instrument with which Princess Simoda Tal was cruelly dispatched. We shall produce also the actual perpetrator of the deed. We shall show that all factors point inescapably to the prisoner as the originator of the cruel plot. Bring forth the dagger."

A slave scurried forward, making a great business of his haste, and presented the article demanded.

Unable to keep out of the proceedings, Sayren Stund reached forward and grasped it before Crispan Mornu could take it.

"This is the horn of a phagor beast. It has two sharp edges, and hence cannot be confused with the horn of any other animal. It corresponds with the configurations of the wound in the late princess's breast. Poor dear girl."

"We do not attempt to pretend that this is the weapon with which the murder was committed. That weapon is lost. This is merely a similar one, newly pulled from the head of a phagor.

"I wish to remind the court, and they shall judge whether or not the fact is relevant, that the prisoner had a phagor runt for

a pet. That runt the prisoner blasphemously named after the great warrior-saint of this nation, Yuli. Whether the insult was deliberate or made through ignorance, we need not inquire.''

"Sayren Stund, your callousness will be well repaid," JandolAnganol said, and received a hearty blow for it.

When the horn dagger had been passed round, the curved figure of Kimon Euras uncurled enough to ask, "What else has the prosecution to bring against the accused by way of evidence?''

"You have seen the weapon with which the deed was done," the black voice of Crispan Mornu announced. "Now we shall show you the person who used the weapon to kill the princess Simoda Tal."

Into the court a struggling body was half-brought, half-carried. It had a rug tied about its head, and JandolAnganol thought immediately of the prisoner he had seen in the night, evicted from the wooden wagon.

This captive was tugged into the well of the court. At a word of command, the rug was wrenched from it.

The youth thus revealed seemed to consist of a fury of a tousled mane of hair, an empurpled visage, and a torn shift. When he was struck hard and began to whimper instead of struggle, he was recognisable as RobaydayAnganol.

"Roba!" cried the king, and received a chop in the kidneys which doubled him up in pain. He sank down on a bench, overwhelmed by the sight of his son in captivity—Roba, who had always feared captivity.

"This young person was apprehended by his majesty's agents in the seaport of Ottassol, in Borlien," said Crispan Mornu. "He proved difficult to track down, since he posed sometimes as a Madi, adopting their habits and style of dress. He is, however, human. His name is RobaydayAnganol. He is the son of the accused, and his wildness is widely talked of.''

"Did you murder the late Princess Simoda Tal?" demanded the judge, in a voice like tearing parchment.

Robayday burst into a fit of weeping, during which he was heard to say that he had murdered nobody, that he had never been to Oldorando before, and that he wanted only to be left in peace to lead his own miserable life.

"Did you not carry out the murder at the instigation of your

father?'' demanded Crispan Mornu, making each word sound like a small axe descending.

"I hate my father! I fear my father! I would never do his bidding."

"Why then did you murder the Princess Simoda Tal?"

"I didn't. I didn't. I am innocent, I swear."

"Whom did you murder?"

"I have murdered no one."

As though these were the very words he had waited all his life to hear, Crispan Mornu raised a mottled hand high in the air and brought up his nose until it shone in the light as if honed.

"You hear this youth claim he has murdered no one. We call a witness who will prove him a liar. Bring in the witness."

A young lady entered the court, moving freely if nervously between two guards. She was directed to take a stance beneath the judge's platform, while those in the court regarded her avidly. Her beauty and youth were appealing. Her cheeks were brightly painted. Her dark hair was strikingly dressed. She wore a tight-fitting chagirack, the floral pattern of which emphasised her figure. She stood with one hand on her hip, slightly defiant, and managed to look at once innocent and seductive.

Judge Kimon Euras curved his albaster skull forward and was perhaps rewarded by a glimpse down into her zona, for he said in a more human tone than had so far been the case, "What is your name, young woman?"

She said in a faint voice, "Please, AbathVasidol, usually called Abathy by my friends."

"I am sure you have plenty of friends," said the judge.

Untouched by this exchange, Crispan Mornu said, "This lady has also been brought here by his majesty's agents. She came not as a prisoner but of her own free will, and will be rewarded for her efforts on behalf of the truth. Abathy, will you tell us when you last saw this youth, and what the circumstances were?"

Abathy moistened her lips, which were already shining, and said, "Oh, sir, I was in my room, my little room in Ottassol. My friend was with me, my friend Div. We were sitting on the bed, you know, talking. And suddenly this man here . . .''

She paused.

"Go on, girl."

"It's too awful, sir . . ." There was a thick silence in the court, as if even the cooling herbs were drowning in the heat. "Well, sir, this man here came in with a dagger. He wanted me to go with him, and I wouldn't. I don't do such things. Div went to protect me, and this man here struck with his dagger—or horn, it was, you know—and he killed Div. He stabbed Div right in the stomach."

She demonstrated daintily on her own hypogastric region, and the court craned its collective neck.

"And what happened then?"

"Well, sir, you know, this man here took the body away and threw it into the sea."

"This is all a lie, a lying plot!" said JandolAnganol.

It was the girl who answered him, with a spurt of her own anger. She was more at home in the court now, and beginning to enjoy her role.

"It's not a lie. It's the truth. The prisoner took Div's body away and threw it into the sea. And the extraordinary thing was that a few days later it returned, the body I mean, packed in ice, to Ottassol, because I saw it in the house of my friend and protector, Bardol CaraBansity—later to become the king's chancellor for a while."

JandolAnganol emitted a strangled laugh and appealed direct to the judge. "How can anyone believe such an impossible story?"

"It's not impossible, and I can prove it," Abathy said boldly. "Div had a special jewel with three moving faces with figures, a timepiece. The figures were alive. Div kept it in a belt round his waist." She indicated the area she meant on her own anatomy, and again the collective neck was craned. "That same jewel turned up at CaraBansity's and he gave it to his majesty, who probably has it now." She pointed her finger dramatically at JandolAnganol.

The king was visibly taken aback and remained silent. The timepiece lay forgotten in his tunic pocket.

He recalled now, all too late, how he had always feared the timepiece as an alien thing, a thing of science to be mistrusted. When BillishOwpin, the man who claimed to have come from another world, had offered him the timepiece, JandolAnganol

had thrown it back to him. Mysteriously, it had returned later through the agency of the deuteroscopist. Despite his intentions, he had never rid himself of it.

Now it had betrayed him.

He could not speak. An evil spell had descended on him: that he saw, but could not say when it had begun. Not all his dedication to Akhanaba had saved him from the spell.

"Well, Your Majesty, well, brother," said Sayren Stund, with relish, "have you this jewel with living figures?"

JandolAnganol said faintly, "It is intended as a wedding gift for the Princess Milua Tal . . ."

A hubbub broke out in court. People dashed here and there, clerics called for order, Sayren Stund covered his face in order to hide his triumph.

When order was restored Crispan Mornu put another question to Abathy. "You are sure this young man, Robayday-Anganol, son of the king, is the man who murdered your friend Div? Did you ever see him again?"

"Sir, he was a great nuisance to me. He would not go away. I don't know what would have happened to me if your men hadn't arrested him."

A short silence prevailed in court while everyone contemplated what might have happened to such an attractive young lady.

"Let me put one last and rather personal question to you," Crispan Mornu said, fixing Abathy with his corpselike stare. "You are evidently a low-born woman, and yet you seem to have well-connected friends. Rumour mentions your name with that of a certain Sibornalese ambassador. What do you say to that?"

"Shame," said a voice from the court benches, but Abathy answered in an untroubled way, "I did have the pleasure of knowing a Sibornalese gentleman, sir. I like the Sibornalese for their good manners, sir."

"Thank you, Abathy, your testament has been invaluable." Crispan Mornu managed a moue which resembled a stiletto's smile. He then turned to the court, speaking only when the girl had left.

"I submit that you need no further proof. This innocent young girl has told us all we need to know. His lies to the contrary, the King of Borlien's son is revealed as a murderer. We

have heard how he murdered in Ottassol, presumably at his
father's instruction, merely to obtain some bauble to bring
here. His preferred weapon was a phagor horn; he had already
murdered Simoda Tal, using the same weapon. His father was
left to proceed here to enjoy our hospitality, to carry out his
evil designs upon his majesty's sole remaining daughter. We
have uncovered here as black a plot as ever history related. I
have no hesitation in demanding—on behalf of the court, and
on behalf of our whole nation—the death penalty for both
father and son.''

RobaydayAnganol's defiance had collapsed as soon as
Abathy had entered the court. He looked no more than an
urchin, and his voice sank to a whisper as he said, ''Please let
me go free. I'm made for life, not death, for some wild plot
where the breeze blows. I have no wild plot with my father
—that I deny, and all other charges.''

Crispan Mornu swung dramatically about and confronted
the youth.

''You still deny the murder of Simoda Tal?''

Robayday moistened his lips. ''Can a leaf kill? I'm merely a
leaf, sir, caught in the world's storm.''

''Her Majesty Queen Bathkaarnet-she is prepared to identify you as a visitor to this palace a while ago, when you came
disguised as a Madi for the express purpose of committing the
foul deed. Do you wish her majesty to come to this court to
identify you?''

A violent trembling took Robayday. ''No.''

''Then the case is proven. This youth, a prince, no less,
entered the palace and—at his father's command—murdered
our much-loved princess, Simoda Tal.''

All eyes turned to the judge. The judge turned his gaze
down to the floor before delivering judgement.

''The verdict is as follows. The hand that committed this
vile murder belongs to the son. The mind that controlled the
hand is the father's. So where lies the source of guilt? The
answer is clear—''

A cry of torment broke from Robayday. He thrust out a
hand as if physically to intercept Kimon Euras's words.

''Lies! Lies! This is a room of lies. I will speak the truth,
though it destroy me! I confess I did that thing to Simoda Tal.
I did it not because I was in league with my father the king.

Oh, no, that's impossible. We are day and night. I did what I did to spite him.

"There he stands—just a man now, not a king! Yes, just a man, while my mother remains the queen of queens. I, in league with him? I would no more kill for his sake than I would marry for his sake. . . . I declare the villain innocent. If I must die your dingy death, then never let it be said even in here that I was in league with him. I wish there was a league between us. Why help one who never helped me?"

He clutched his head as if to wrench it from his shoulders.

In the silence following, Crispan Mornu said coldly, "You might have done your father more harm by keeping silent."

Robay gave him a cold sane look. "It's the principle of evil in men I fear—and I see that principle more rampant in you than in that poor man burdened with the crown of Borlien."

JandolAnganol raised his eyes to the ceiling, as if trying to detach himself from earthly events. But he wept.

With the sound of rippling parchment, the judge cleared his throat.

"In view of the son's confession, the father is of course shown to be blameless. History is full of ungrateful sons. . . . I therefore pronounce, under the guidance of Akhanaba, the All-Powerful, that the father go free and the son be taken from here and hanged as soon as it suits the convenience of his majesty, King Sayren Stund."

"I will die in his stead and he can reign in my stead." The words came from JandolAnganol, spoken in a firm voice.

"The verdict is irreversible. Court dismissed."

Above the shuffle of feet came Sayren Stund's voice.

"Remember, we refresh ourselves now, but this afternoon comes a further spectacle, when we hear what King JandolAnganol's ex-chancellor, SartoriIrvrash, has to say to us."

XXI

THE SLAYING OF AKHANABA

The drama of the court and the humiliation of JandolAnganol had been watched by a greater audience than the king could have imagined.

The personnel of the Avernus, however, were not entirely occupied by the story in which the king played a conspicuous part. Some scholars studied developments taking place elsewhere on the planet, or continuities in which the king played merely an incidental role. A group of learned ladies of the Tan family, for instance, had as their subject the origins of long-standing quarrels. They followed several quarrels through generations, studying how the differences began, were maintained, and were eventually resolved. One of their cases concerned a village in Northern Borlien through which the king had passed on his way to Oldorando. There the quarrel originally concerned whether pigs belonging to two neighbours should drink at the same brook. The brook had gone and so had the pigs, yet two villages existed at the spot locked in hatred and still referring to the killing of neighbours as "hog-sticking." King JandolAnganol, by passing with his phagors through one village and not the other, had exacer-

452

bated the feud, and a youth had had a finger broken in a brawl that night.

Of that, the learned Tan ladies were as yet unaware. All their records were automatically stored for study, while they at present worked over a chapter in their quarrel which had taken place two centuries ago; they studied videos of an incident of indecent exposure, when an old man from one of the villages had been mobbed by men from the other village. After this squalid incident, someone had composed a beautiful dirge on the subject, which was still sung on festive occasions. To the learned Tan ladies, such incidents were as vital as the king's trial—and of more significance than all the austerities of the inorganic.

Other groups studied matters even more esoteric. Phagor lines of descent were particularly closely watched. The question of phagor mobility, baffling to the Helliconians, was by now fairly well understood on the Avernus. The ancipitals had ancient patterns of behaviour from which they were not easily deflected, but those patterns were more elaborate than had been supposed. There was a kind of "domestic" phagor which accepted the rule of man as readily as the rule of a kzahhn; but hidden from the eyes of men was a much more independent ancipital which survived the seasons much as its ancestors had done, taking what it would and moving on: a free creature, unaffected by mankind.

The history of Oldorando as a unit also had its scholars, those who were most interested in process. They followed interweaving lives of individuals in only a general way.

When the eyes of Avernus first turned towards Oldorando, or Embruddock as it was then, it was little more than a place of hot springs where two rivers met. Round the springs, a few low towers stood in the middle of an immense ice desert. Even then, in the early years of Avernian research, it was apparent that this was a place, strategically situated, with a potential for growth when the climate improved.

Oldorando was now larger and more populous than anyone in the six families had seen it before. Like any living organism, it expanded in favourable weather, contracted in adverse.

But the story was no more than begun as far as those on the Avernus were concerned. They kept their records, they transmitted a constant stream of information back to Earth;

*present transmissions could be reckoned to arrive there in the
year 7877. The intracacies of the Helliconian biosphere and its
response to change throughout the Great Year could be
understood only when at least two complete cycles had been
studied.*

*The scholars could extrapolate. They could make intelligent
guesses. But they could no more see the future than King JandolAnganol could see what was to befall that very afternoon.*

Sayren Stund had not been in better humour since before his
elder daughter died. Before the afternoon's event, which was
to humiliate JandolAnganol further, Stund ate a light meal of
Dorzin gout and called a meeting of the inner circle of his
council to impress on them how clever he had been.

"Of course it was never my intention to hang King JandolAnganol," he informed the councillors genially. The threat
of execution was simply to reduce him, as that Other of a son
of his put it, to a mere man, naked and defenceless. He thinks
he can do as he pleases. That is not so."

When he had finished talking, his prime minister rose to
make a speech of thanks to his majesty.

"We particularly appreciate your majesty's humiliation of a
monarch who cultivates phagors and treats them—well,
almost as if they were human. We in Oldorando can have no
doubt, must have no doubt, that the ancipitals are animals,
nothing more. They have all the stamp of animals. They talk.
So do preets and parrots.

"Unlike parrots, phagors are forever hostile to mankind.
We know not where they come from. They seem to have been
born in the late Cold Period. But we do know—and this is
what King JandolAnganol does not know—that these formidable newcomers must be eradicated, first from among
human society, then from the face of the earth.

"We still have the indignity of suffering JandolAnganol's
phagor brutes in our park. We all anticipate that, after this
afternoon's event, we shall be able to show gratitude once
more to King Sayren Stund for ridding us for ever both of this
pack of brutes, and of their pack master."

There was general clapping. Sayren Stund himself clapped.
Every word in the minister's speech echoed his own words.

Sayren Stund enjoyed such sycophancy. But he was not a fool. Stund still needed the alliance with Borlien; he wished to make sure he would be the senior partner to it. He hoped, too, that the afternoon's entertainment would impress the nation with whom he was already in uncomfortable alliance, Pannoval. He intended to challenge the C'Sarr's monopoly of militarism and religion; that he could do by supplying an underlying philosophy for the Pannovalan drive against the ancipital kind. Having talked to SartoriIrvrash, he foresaw that that scholar could provide precisely such a philosophy.

He had struck a bargain with SartoriIrvrash. In exchange for the afternoon's oratory and the destruction of Jandol-Anganol's authority, Sayren Stund had Odi Jeseratabhar released from the Sibornalese embassy, despite the grumbles of the Sibornalese. He promised SartoriIrvrash and Odi the safety of his court, where they could live and work in peace. The bargain had been agreed upon with glee on all sides.

The heat of the morning had overwhelmed many of those who attended the court; reports entering the palace spoke of hundreds dying of heart attacks in the city. The afternoon's diversion was therefore staged in the royal gardens, where jets of water played on the foliage and gauzes were hung from trees to create pleasant shade.

When the distinguished members of court and Church had gathered, Sayren Stund came forward, his queen on his arm, his daughter following behind. Screwing up his eyes, he gazed about for sight of JandolAnganol. Milua Tal saw him first and hastened across the lawn to his side. He stood under a tree, together with his Royal Armourer and two of his captains.

"The fellow has boldness, grant him that," Sayren Stund murmured. He had had delivered to JandolAnganol an ornate letter apologising for his mistaken imprisonment, while making excuses because the evidence was so much against him. What he did not know was that Bathkaarnet-she had written a simpler note, expressing her pain over the whole incident and referring to her husband as a "love throttler."

When his majesty was comfortably settled on his throne, a gong was struck, and Crispan Mornu appeared, shrouded as

ever in black. Evidently the minister of the rolls, Kimon
Euras, was too overcome by his morning's activities to manage anything further. Crispan Mornu was in sole charge.

Ascending the platform set in the middle of the lawn, he
bowed to the king and queen and spoke in his voice which had
about it, as a court wit once remarked, the same redolence as
the sex life of a public hangman.

"We have a rare treat this afternoon. We are to be present
at an advancement of history and natural philosophy. Of recent generations, we among the enlightened nations have come
to understand how the history of our cultures is at best intermittent. It is caused by our Great Year of 1825 small years,
and not by wars as the idle have claimed. The Great Year contains a period of intense heat and several centuries of intense
cold. These are punishments from the All-Powerful for the
sinfulness of mankind. While the cold prevails for so long,
civilisation is difficult to maintain.

"We are to hear from one who has pierced through these
disruptions to bring us news of distant matters which concern
us urgently today. In particular, they refer to our relationship
with those beasts which the All-Powerful sent to chasten us,
the phagors.

"I beg you, gentles, all, to listen well to the scholar Master
SartoriIrvrash."

Languidly polite clapping went about the lawn. On the
whole, music and tales of bawdy were preferred to intellectual
effort.

As the clapping died, SartoriIrvrash came forth. Although
he smoothed his whiskers with a familiar gesture and looked
rather furtively to left and right, he did not appear nervous.
By his side walked Odi Jeseratabhar in a flowered chagirack.
She had recovered from her assatassi wounds and carried
herself alertly. Much of her Uskuti arrogance remained in the
gaze with which she surveyed the assembly. Her expression
was gentler when she looked at SartoriIrvrash.

The latter had adopted a linen hat to cover his baldness. He
carried some books which he deposited carefully on the table
before he spoke. The magisterial calm with which he began
betrayed nothing of the consternation he was about to spread.

"I am grateful to his majesty, King Sayren Stund, for giving
me sanctuary in the Oldorandan court. In my long life,

vicissitudes have been many, and even here, even here, I have not been free of botheration from those who are the enemies of knowledge. All too often, those who hate learning are the very people on whom we should most rely to promote it.

"For many years, I served as chancellor to King Varpal-Anganol, and later to his son, who dares to be present here despite his encounter with justice this morning. By him I was unfairly dismissed from office. During my years in Matrassyl, I was compiling a survey of our world, entitled 'The Alphabet of History and Nature,' in which I sought to integrate and distinguish between myth and reality. And it is on that subject I speak now.

"When I was dismissed, all my papers were most cruelly burnt, and my life's work destroyed. The knowledge I carry in my head was not destroyed. With it, with my experiences since, and in particular with the assistance of this lady by my side, Odi Jeseratabhar, Priest-Militant Admiral of the Sibornalese fleet, I have come to understand much that was previously a mystery.

"One mystery in particular. A cosmological mystery, one which touches on our everyday lives. Bear with me, hot though it is, for I shall be as brief as possible, although I am told that is not always my habit."

He laughed and looked about him. Everywhere was attention, real or feigned. Encouraged, he plunged into his argument.

"I hope to offend no one by what I say. I speak in the belief that men love truth above all things.

"We are so bound to our human concerns that we rarely catch sight of the great business of the planet about us. It is more marvellous than we can credit. It abounds with life. Whatever the season, winged and footed life is everywhere, from pole to pole. Endless herds of flambreg, each herd numbered in millions of beasts, rove ceaselessly across the vast continent of Sibornal. Such a sight is unforgettable. Where have the beasts come from? How long have they been there? We have no answers to such questions. We can only remain mute with awe.

"The secrets of antiquity could be unlocked if only we ceased our warring. If all kings had the wisdom of Sayren Stund."

He bowed in the direction of the Oldorandan king, who smiled back, unaware of what was to come. There were scattered handclaps.

"While life was peaceful at the Matrassyl court, I was privileged in enjoying the company of MyrdemInggala, called by her subjects the queen of queens—merely because they knew not of Queen Bathkaarnet-she, of course—and her daughter, TatromanAdala. Tatro had a collection of fairy tales which I used to read to her. Although all my papers were destroyed, as I have said, Tatro's fairy tales were not destroyed, not even when her cruel father banished her to the coast. We have a copy of Tatro's book here."

At this point, Odi solemnly raised the little book aloft and held it for all to see.

"In Tatro's storybook is a tale called 'The Silver Eye.' I read it many times without perceiving its inner meaning. Only when I travelled could I grasp its elusive truth. Perhaps because the herds of flambreg reminded me strongly of primitive ancipitals."

Until this point, SartoriIrvrash's delivery, free of his old pedantry, had kept his audience listlessly attentive. Many of the audience lounging on the lawn were drumble organisers, with a natural hatred of phagors; at the word "ancipitals," they showed interest.

"There is an ancipital in the story of the Silver Eye.

"The ancipital is a gillot. Her role is advisor to a king in a mythical country, Ponpt. Well, not so mythical: Ponpt, now called Ponipot, still exists to the west of the Barrier Mountains. This gillot is superior to the king, and provides him with the wisdom whereby he rules. He depends on her as a son on a mother. At the end of the story, the king kills the gillot.

"The Silver Eye itself is a body like a sun, but silver and shining only by night. Like a close star, without heat. When the gillot is slain, the Silver Eye sails away and is lost for ever.

"What did all that signify? I asked myself. Where was the meaning of the tale?"

He leaned over the podium, hunching his shoulders and pointing at the audience in his eagerness to tell the tale.

"The key to the puzzle came when I was on an Uskuti sailing vessel. The vessel was becalmed in the Cadmer Straits.

Odi, this lady here, and I landed on Gleeat Island, where we managed to capture a wild gillot with a black pelage. The females of the ancipital species have a one-day flow of menses from the uterus as a prelude to the oestral cycle, when they go into rut. Because of my prejudice against the species, I have no knowledge of Native Ancipital or even Hurdhu, but I discovered then that the gillot's word for her period was 'tennhrr.' That was the key! Forgive me if such a subject seems too disgusting to contemplate.

"In my studies—all destroyed by the great King Jan-dolAnganol—I had noted that even phagors preserved one or two legends. They could hardly be expected to make sense. In particular, there is a legend which says Helliconia once had a sister body circling about it, just as Batalix circles about Freyr. This sister body flew away as Freyr arrived and as mankind was born. So the legend goes. And the name of the escaping body in Native is T'Sehn-Hrr.

"Why should 'tennhrr' and 'T'Sehn-Hrr' be virtually the same word? That was the question I asked myself.

"A gillot's tennhrr occurs ten times in a small year—every six weeks. We may therefore assume that this heavenly eye or moon served as a timing mechanism for the periods. But did the moon 'T'Sehn-Hrr,' supposing it existed, circle Helliconia once every six weeks? How to check on something which happened so long ago that human history has no record of it?

"The answer lay in Tatro's story.

"Her story says that the silver eye in the sky opened and shut. Possibly that means it grew bigger or smaller, according to distance, as does Freyr. It became wide open or full ten times in a year. That was it. Ten times again. The pieces of the puzzle fitted.

"You understand the unmistakable conclusion to which I was drawn?"

Gazing at his audience, SartoriIrvrash saw that indeed many of them did not understand. They waited politely for him to be done. He heard his voice rise to a shout.

"This world of ours once had a moon, a silver moon, which was lost at a time of some kind of disturbance in the heavens. It sailed away, we don't as yet know how. The moon was called T'Sehn-Hrr—and T'Sehn-Hrr is a phagor name."

He looked at his notes, he conferred briefly with Odi, as the listeners stirred. He resumed his discourse with a note of asperity in his voice.

"Why should the moon have only an ancipital name? Why is there no human record of this missing body? The answer leads us into the mazes and botherations of antiquity.

"For when I looked about, I found that missing moon. Not in the sky, but shining forth from our everyday speech. For how is our calendar divided? Eight days in a week, six weeks in a tenner, ten tenners in a year of four hundred and eighty days. . . . We never question it. We never question why a tenner is called a tenner, because there are ten of them in a year.

"But that is not the whole truth. Our word 'tenner' commemorates the time when the silver eye was open and the moon was full. It does so because humanity adopted the phagor word 'tennhrr.' 'Tenner' is 'tennhrr' is 'T-Sehn-Hrr.' "

The murmurings from the crowd were louder. Sayren Stund was plainly uncomfortable. But SartoriIrvrash held up Tatro's storybook and called for silence. So engrossed was he that he failed to see the trap opening before him.

"Hear the whole conclusion, my friends. There stands King JandolAnganol among you, and he must hear the truth as well—he who has so long encouraged the noxious ahumans to breed on his territories."

But no one was interested in JandolAnganol at present. Their angry faces turned to SartoriIrvrash himself.

"The conclusion is clear, inescapable. The ancipital race, to which we can ascribe many of our human difficulties over the ages, is not a race of new invaders, like the Driats. No. It is an ancient race. It once covered Helliconia as flambreg cover the Circumpolar Regions.

"The phagors did not emerge out of the last Weyr-Winter, as the Sibornalese call it. No. That story is based on ignorance. The real story, the fairy story, tells the truth. *Phagors long preceded mankind.*

"They were here on Helliconia before Freyr appeared— possibly long before. Mankind came later. Mankind depended on the phagors. Mankind learned language from the phagors and still uses phagor words. 'Khmir' is the Native word for 'rut.' 'Helliconia' itself is an old ancipital term."

JandolAnganol found his voice at last. The speech was such an onslaught on his religious sensibilities that he had stood as if in a trance, his mouth open, more resembling fish than eagle.

"Lies, heresy, blasphemy!" he shouted. The cry of blasphemy was taken up by other voices. But Sayren Stund had ordered his guard to see that JandolAnganol did not interrupt. Burly men closed in on him—to be met by JandolAnganol's captains with drawn swords. A struggle broke out.

SartoriIrvrash raised his voice. "No, you see your glory diminished by the truth. Phagors preceded mankind. Phagors were the dominant race on our world, and probably treated our ancestors as animals until we rebelled against them."

"Let's hear him. Who dares say the man is wrong?" shrilled Queen Bathkaarnet-she. Her husband struck her in the mouth.

The hubbub from the audience rose. People were standing and shouting or kneeling to pray. Fresh guards ran to the scene, while some court ladies tried to escape. A fight had broken out round JandolAnganol. The first stone was thrown at SartoriIrvrash. Brandishing his fist, he continued to speak.

In that courtly crowd, now moved to fury, there was at least one cool observer, the envoy Alam Esomberr. He was detached from the human drama. Unable to be deeply moved by events, he could derive only amusement from their effects.

Those on Earth, distant in time and space, viewed the scene on King Sayren Stund's lawn with less detachment. They knew that SartoriIrvrash spoke truth in general, even if his details were sometimes incorrect. They also knew that men did not love truth above all things, as he claimed. Truth had constantly to be fought for, for it was constantly being lost. Truth could sail away like a silver eye, never to be seen again.

When T'Sehn-Hrr sailed away, no human being had witnessed the event. Cosmologists on the Avernus and on Earth had reconstructed the event, and believed they understood it. In the great disruptions which had overtaken the system eight million Earth years previously, the gravitational forces of the star now called Freyr, with a mass 14.8 times that of the Sun, had wrenched T'Sehn-Hrr away from Helliconia's pull.

Calculations indicated that T'Sehn-Hrr had a radius of 1252

*km, against Helliconia's 7723 km. Whether the satellite had
been capable of supporting life was doubtful.*

*What was certain was that the events of that epoch had been
so near catastrophic that they had remained etched in the
eotemporal minds of the phagors. The sky had fallen in and
no one had forgotten it.*

*More impressive to human minds was the way in which life
on Helliconia had survived even the loss of its moon and the
cosmological events which had caused that loss.*

"Yes, I know. This sounds like sacrilege and I am sorry,"
shouted SartoriIrvrash, as Odi moved close to him and the
noise grew. "What is true should be said—and heard. Phagors
were once the dominant race and will become so again if
allowed to live. The experiments I conducted show, I believe,
that we were animals. Genethlic divinities bred mankind from
Others—Others who were ancipital pets before the upheaval.
Mankind developed from Others as phagors developed from
flambreg. As phagors developed from flambreg, they may
again cover the earth one day. They are still waiting, wild,
with kaidaws, in the High Nktryht, to descend in vengeance.
They will wipe you out. Be warned then. Increase the drumbles. Intensify them. Ancipitals must be wiped out in the summer, when mankind is strong. When winter comes, the wild
kaidaws return!

"My final word to you: We must not waste energy fighting
each other. We should fight the older enemy—and those humans who protect them!"

But the humans were already fighting each other. The most
religious members of the audience were often those, like
Crispan Mornu, who were most in favour of drumbles. Here
was an outsider offending their deepest religious principles,
yet encouraging their violent instincts. The first one to throw a
stone was attacked by his neighbour. Missiles were flying all
over the garden. Soon the first dagger bit into flesh. A man
ran among the flower beds, bleeding, and fell on his face.
Women screamed. Fighting became more general as tempers
and fears mounted. The awning collapsed.

As Alam Esomberr quietly left the scene, a miniature history of warfare was enacted on the palace lawn.

The chief cause of the commotion looked on aghast. It was beyond belief how people responded to scholarship. Holy idiots! A flying stone caught him in the mouth, and he collapsed.

Odi Jeseratabhar threw herself on SartoriIrvrash, crying and trying to ward off more stones.

She was dragged aside by a group of young monks, who punched her and then began to beat and kick the prostrate ex-chancellor. They at least refused to hear the name of Akhanaba defiled.

Crispan Mornu, in fear that matters were getting so out of hand, stepped forward and raised his arms, opening the black wings of his keedrant. It was slashed by a sword blade. Odi turned and ran; her garments were seized by a woman as she passed, and next moment she was struggling for her life amid a dozen angry women.

The clamour grew, a clamour that before the hour was out would spread into the city. Indeed the monks themselves spread the clamour. Before very long, they emerged blood-stained from the precincts of the palace, bearing above their heads the broken corpses of SartoriIrvrash and his Sibornalese companion, screaming as they went, "Blasphemy is dead! Long live Akhanaba!"

After the fighting in the gardens, there was a rush to the streets, and more scuffles there, while the dead bodies were paraded down Wozen Avenue before finally being thrown to the dogs. Then a terrible quiet fell. Even the First Phagorian in the park seemed to be waiting.

Sayren Stund's plan had terribly misfired.

SartoriIrvrash had intended merely to be revenged on his ex-master and to have the First Phagorian slain. That was his conscious aim. His love of knowledge for its own sake, his hatred of his fellowmen, had betrayed him. He had failed to understand his audience. As a result, religious belief was set at an intolerable crisis—and that on the day before the Emperor of Holy Pannoval, the great C'Sarr Kilander IX, was to arrive in Oldorando to bestow the unction of Akhanaba upon the faithful.

The most living words spring from dead martyrs. The

monks unwittingly propagated the heresies of SartoriIrvrash, which found ready soil on which to grow. Within a few days, it would be the monks themselves who were under attack.

What had goaded the crowd into such fury was the aspect of his disclosures to which SartoriIrvrash himself was blind. His listeners would make a connection through their faith of which, with his limited sympathies, SartoriIrvrash was incapable.

They perceived that the rumour long suppressed by the Church now confronted them nakedly. All the world's wisdom had always existed. Akhanaba was—and they themselves, and their fathers before them, had spent their lives in the worship of—a phagor. They prayed to the very beast they persecuted. "Ask not therefore if I am man or animal or stone," said the scriptures. Now the comfortable enigma fell before the banal fact. The nature of their vaunted god, the god that held the political system together, was ancipital.

Which should the people now deny in order to make their lives tolerable? The intolerable truth? Or their intolerable religion?

Even the servants of the palace neglected their duties, asking each other, "Are we slaves of slaves?" Over their masters, a spiritual crisis prevailed. Those masters had taken it for granted that they were masters of their world. Suddenly the planet had become another place—a place where they were comparative newcomers, and lowly newcomers at that.

Heated debates took place. Many of the faithful threw out SartoriIrvrash's hypothesis entirely, affecting to dismiss it as a tissue of lies. But, as ever in such situations, there were others who subscribed to it and added to it, and even claimed they had known the truth all along. The torment mounted.

Sayren Stund took only a practical interest in his faith. It was not to him the living thing it was to JandolAnganol. He cared for it only as oil which smoothed his rule. Suddenly, everything was in question.

The hapless Oldorandan king spent the rest of the afternoon shut in his wife's compartments, with preets twittering round his head. Every so often, he sent Bathkaarnet-she out to attempt to discover where Milua Tal might be, or received messengers who spoke of shops being broken into and a pitched fight being held in one of the oldest monasteries.

"We've no soldiers," wept Sayren Stund.

"And no faith," said his wife, with some complacency. "You need both to keep order in this terrible city."

"And I suppose JandolAnganol has fled to escape being killed. He should have stayed for the execution of his son."

That thought cheered him until the arrival of Crispan Mornu in the evening. The advisor's aspect showed that he had unsuspected reserves of gauntness in him. He bowed to his sovereign and said, "If I diagnose the confused situation correctly, Your Majesty, the central issue has shifted away from JandolAnganol. It now focusses on our faith itself. We must hope that this afternoon's intemperate speech will soon be forgotten. Men cannot long endure to think of themselves as lower than phagor brutes.

"This might be a convenient time to see that JandolAnganol is removed altogether from our attention. In canon law, he remains undivorced, and this morning we exposed his pretentions for what they are. He is a spent force.

"Therefore, we should remove him from the city before he can speak to the Holy C'Sarr—perhaps through Envoy Esomberr or Ulbobeg. The C'Sarr is going to have to face a larger issue, the problem of a spiritual crisis. The question of your daughter's marriage is also one we can settle, with suitable parties."

"Oh, I know what you're hinting at, Crispan," chirped Bathkaarnet-she. Mornu, in his oblique way, had been reminding his majesty that Milua Tal should be speedily married to Prince Taynth Indredd of Pannoval; in that way, a tighter religious grip over Oldorando could be established.

Crispan Mornu gave no sign that he had heard the queen's remark.

"What will you do, Your Majesty?"

"Oh, really, I think I'll take a bath. . . ."

Crispan Mornu brought an envelope from the recesses of his dark gown.

"This week's report from Matrassyl suggests that various problems there may come shortly to a head. Unndreid the Hammer, the Scourge of Mordriat, has died in a fall from his hoxney during a skirmish. While he threatened Borlien, some unity was preserved within the capital. Now with Unndreid dead and JandolAnganol away . . ." He let the sentence

dangle and smiled with a cutting edge. "Offer JandolAnganol a fast ship, Your Majesty—two if necessary—to get himself and his Phagorian Guard back down the Valvoral as speedily as possible. He may accept. Urge on him that we have here a situation we cannot control, and that his precious beasts must be removed or massacred. He prides himself on going with circumstances. We will see that he does go."

Sayren Stund mopped his forehead and pondered the matter.

"JandolAnganol will never take such good advice from me. Let his friends put it to him."

"His friends?"

"Yes, yes, his Pannovalan friends, Alam Esomberr and that contemptible Guaddl Ulbobeg. Have them summoned while I have myself voluptuously bathed." Addressing his wife, he asked, "Do you wish to come and enjoy the voluptuous sight, my dear?"

The mob was in action. Its gathering could be traced from the Avernus. Oldorando was full of idle hands. Mischief was always welcome. They came out of taverns, where they had been harmlessly occupied. They locked up shops and picked up sticks. They rose from outside churches, where they had been begging. They wandered along from hostels and billets and holy places. Just to have a share in whatever was going on.

Some hrattock had said they were inferior to fuggies. Those were fighting words. Where was this hrattock? Maybe it was that slanje standing talking over there . . .

Many Avernian watchers regarded the brawling, and the pretext for brawling, with contempt. Others who reflected more deeply saw another aspect of it. However preposterous, however primitive the issue that SartoriIrvrash had raised, it had its parallels aboard the Earth Observation Station—and there no rioting would solve it.

"Belief: an impermanence." So it said in the treatise "On the Prolongation of One Helliconian Season Beyond One Human Lifetime." The belief in technological progress which had inspired the building of the Avernus had, over the generations, become a trap for those aboard it, just as the accretion

of beliefs called Akhanabaism had become a trap.

Settled into an introspective quietism, those who ran the *Avernus* saw no escape from their trap. They feared the change they most needed. Patronising though their attitude was to the unwashed who ran through Goose Street and Wozen Avenue, the unwashed had a hope denied those far above them. Hot with fight and drink, a man in Goose Street could use his fists or shout before the cathedral. He might be confused, but he did not endure the emptiness the advisors among the six families endured. Belief: an impermanence. It was true. Belief had largely died on the *Avernus*, leaving despair in its place.

Individuals despair, but not peoples. Even as the elders looked down on, and transmitted wearily back to Earth, scenes of confusion which seemed to reflect their own futility, another faction was taking bold shape on the station.

That faction had already named itself the Aganippers. Its members were young and reckless. They knew there was no chance for them to return to Earth or—as the recent example of Billy Xiao Pin had effectively demonstrated—to live on Helliconia. But on Aganip there was a change for them. Avoiding the ever watching lenses, they accumulated their stores and marked out a shuttle they could appropriate which would transport them to the empty planet. In their hearts was a hope as bright as any to be found in Goose Street.

The evening grew slightly cooler. There was another earth tremor, but it passed almost unnoticed among the general excitements.

Calmed and refreshed by his bath, well fed, King Sayren Stund was in fit mood to receive Alam Esomberr and the elderly Guaddl Ulbobeg. He seated himself comfortably on a couch and assembled his wife behind him to make an attractive composition before summoning the two men to his presence.

All due courtesies were made, and a slave woman poured wine into glasses already freighted with Lordryardry ice.

Guaddl Ulbobeg wore an ecclesiastical sash over a light charful. He entered reluctantly and appeared no more comfortable to see Crispan Mornu present. He felt his position to

be dangerous, and showed it in his nervous manner.

Alam Esomberr, by contrast, was excessively cheerful. Immaculately dressed as usual, he approached the king's couch and kissed the hands of both majesties with the air of one immune to bacteria.

"Well, indeed, sire, you did present us with a spectacle this afternoon, just as you promised. My congratulations. How ably your old rogue of an atheist spoke! Of course, our faith is merely deepened by doubt. Nevertheless, what an amusing turn of fate it is that the abhorred King JandolAnganol, lover of phagors, who only this morning stood trial for his life, should this evening stand revealed as heroic protector of the children of God."

He laughed pleasantly and turned to Advisor Mornu to judge his amusement.

"That is blasphemy," said Crispan Mornu, in his blackest voice.

Esomberr nodded, smiling. "Now that God has a new definition, surely blasphemy has one too? The heresy of yesterday, sir, is now perceived as today's true path, which we must tread as nimbly as we can. . . ."

"I don't know why you are so merry," Sayren Stund complained. "But I hope to take a small advantage of your good humour. I wish to ask you both a favour. Woman, serve the wine again."

"We will do whatever your majesty commands," said Guaddl Ulbobeg, looking anxious and clutching his glass.

The king rose up from a reclining position, smoothed his stomach, and said, with a touch of royal pomp, "We shall give you the wherewithal with which to persuade King JandolAnganol to leave our Kingdom immediately, before he can delude my poor infant daughter Milua Tal into matrimony."

Esomberr looked at Guaddl Ulbobeg. Guaddl Ulbobeg looked at Esomberr.

"Well?" said the king.

"Sire," said Esomberr, and fell to tugging a lock of hair at the back of his neck, which necessitated his looking down at the floor.

Guaddl Ulbobeg cleared his throat and then, more or less as an afterthought, cleared it again. "May I venture to ask your majesty if you have seen your daughter just of late?"

"As for me, sire, I am almost totally within the power of the King of Borlien, sir," added Esomberr, still attending to his neck. "Owing to a past indiscretion on my part, sir. An indiscretion concerning—most unforgiveably—the queen of queens. So when the King of Borlien came to us this afternoon, seeking our assistance, we felt bound . . ."

Since he allowed the sentence to dangle while he scrutinised the countenance of Sayren Stund, Ulbobeg continued the discourse.

"I being a bishop of the Household of the Holy C'Sarr of Pannoval, sire, and therefore," said Guaddl Ulbobeg, "empowered to act in his Holiness's stead in certain offices of the Church . . ."

"And I," said Esomberr, "still remissly holding in my charge a bill of divorcement signed by the ex-queen Myrdem-Inggala which should have been rendered to the C'Sarr, or to one of his representatives of the Household, tenners ago— with apologies for using that now opprobrious word—"

"And we both having care," said Guaddl Ulbobeg, now with rather more relish in his voice, "not to overburden His Holiness with too many functions on this visit of pleasure between sister nations—"

"When there will be more contentious matters—"

"Or, indeed, to incommode your majesty with—"

"Enough!" shouted Sayren Stund. "Come to the point, the pair of you! Enough procrastination!"

"Precisely what we both said to ourselves a few hours ago," agreed Esomberr, bestowing his choicest smile on the gathering. "Enough procrastination—perfectly put, Your Majesty. . . . Therefore, with the powers entrusted in us by those above us all, we solemnised a state of matrimony between Jandol-Anganol and your beautiful daughter, Milua Tal. It was a simple but touching service, and we wished that your majesties could have been present."

His majesty fell off the couch, scrambled up, and roared.

"They were married?"

"No, Your Majesty, they *are* married," said Guaddl Ulbobeg. "I took the ceremony and heard their vows for His Holiness in absentia."

"And I was witness and held the ring," said Esomberr. "Some of the King of Borlien's captains were also present.

But no phagors. That I promise.''

"They are married?'' repeated Sayren Stund, looking about wildly. He fell back into his wife's arms.

"We'd both like to congratulate your majesties,'' said Esomberr suavely. "We are sure the lucky couple will be very happy.''

It was the evening of the following day. The haze had cleared toward sunset and stars shone in the east. Stains of a magnificent Freyr-set still lingered in the western sky. There was no wind. Earth tremors were frequent.

His Holiness the C'Sarr Kilander IX had arrived in Oldorando at midday. Kilander was an ancient man with long white hair, and he retired straight to a bed in the palace to recover from his journey. While he lay prostrate, sundry officials, and lastly King Sayren Stund, in a fever of apology, came to tell the old man of the religious disarray in which he would find the kingdom of Oldorando.

To all this, His Holiness listened. In his wisdom, he declared that he would hold a special service at Freyr-set—not in the Dom but in the chapel of the palace—during which he would address the congregation and resolve all their doubts. The degrading rumour that ancipitals were an ancient, superior race would be exposed as complete falsehood. The voice of atheists should never prevail while strength was left in his ageing body.

This service had now begun. The old C'Sarr spoke out in a noble voice. There was scarcely an absentee.

But two absentees were together in the white pavilion in Whistler Park.

King JandolAnganol, in penitence and gratitude, had just prayed and scourged himself, and was washing the blood from his back with jugs of hot spring water poured by a slave.

"How could you do such cruelty, my husband?'' exclaimed Milua Tal, entering briskly. She was shoeless, and wore a filmy white gown of satara. "What are we made of but flesh? What else would you desire to be made of?''

"There is a division between flesh and spirit, of which both must be reminded. I shall not ask you to undergo the same rituals, though you must bear with my religious inclinations.''

"But your flesh is dear to me. Now it is my flesh, and if you hurt it more, I will kill you. When you sleep, I will sit on your face with my bottom and sufflicate you!" She embraced him, clinging to him until her dress was soaked. He sent the slave away, and kissed and petted her.

"Your young flesh is dear to me, but I am determined that I will not know you carnally until your tenth birthday."

"Oh, no, Jan! That's five whole tenners away! I'm not such a feeble little thing—I can easily receive you, you'll see." She pressed her flower face to his.

"Five tenners is not long, and it will do us no harm to wait."

She flung herself on him and bore him down onto the bed, fighting and wriggling in his arms, laughing wildly as she did so.

"I'm not going to wait, I'm not going to wait! I know all about what wives should be and what wives should do, and I am going to be your wife in every single particle."

They began to kiss furiously. Then he pushed her away, laughing.

"You little spitfire, you jewel, you posy. We'll wait till circumstances are more propitious and I have made some sort of peace with your parents."

"But now is always a popiters time," she wailed.

To distract her, he said, "Listen, I have a little wedding present for you. It's almost all I possess here. I shall heap gifts upn you when we are back home in Matrassyl."

He took from his tunic the timepiece with the three faces and held it out to her.

The dials read:

07:31:15   18:21:90   19:24:40

Milua Tal took it and looked rather disappointed. She tried it on her brow, but the ends would not meet at the back of her head.

"Where am I supposed to wear it?"

"As a bracelet?"

"Maybe so. Well, thanks, Jan. I'll wear it later." She threw the watch down and then, with a sudden movement, pulled off her damp dress.

"Now you can inspect me and see if you are going to get good value."

He began to pray but his eyes would not close as she danced about the room. She smiled lasciviously, seeing in his eyes the awakening of his khmir. He ran to her, seized her, and carried her to the bed.

"Very well, my delicious Milua Tal. Here beginneth our married life."

Over an hour later, they were roused from their raptures by a violent quake. The timbers about them groaned, their little lamp was pitched to the floor. The bed rattled. They jumped up, naked, and felt how the floor rocked.

"Shall we go out?" she asked. "The park jumps about a little, doesn't it?"

"Wait a minute."

The tremors were long sustained. Dogs howled in town. Then it was over, and a dead silence prevailed.

In that silence, thought worked like maggots in the king's head. He thought of the vows he had made—all broken. Of the people he loved—all betrayed. Of the hopes he had entertained—all dead. He could not find, in the prevailing stillness, consolation anywhere, not even in the perspiring human body lying against his.

His eyes with their leaden stare fixed on an object which had dropped onto the rush mat on the floor. It was the timepiece once owned by BillishOwpin, the article of an unknown science which had woven its way through the tenners of his decline.

With a sudden shout of rage, he jumped up and hurled the timepiece away, out through the north-facing window. He stood there naked, glaring, as if daring the thing to return to his hand.

After a moment of fright, Milua Tal joined him, resting her hand on his shoulder. Without words, they leaned out of the window to breathe cooler air.

An eerie white light shone to the north, outlining horizon and trees. Lightning danced noiselessly in the middle of it.

"By the beholder, what's happening?" JandolAnganol asked, clutching the slender shoulders of his bride.

"Don't be alarmed, Jan. It's the earthquake lights—they soon die. We often see them after a particularly bad quake.

It's a kind of night-rainbow.''

"Isn't it quiet?" He realised that there was no sound of the
First Phagorian moving about nearby, and was suddenly
alarmed.

"I can hear something." Suddenly she ran to the opposite
window, and screamed. "Jandol! Look! The palace!"

He ran to her and looked out. On the far side of Loylbryden
Square, the palace was alight. The entire wooden facade was
ablaze, with clouds of smoke rolling up towards the stars.

"The quake must have caused a fire. Let's go and see if we
can help—fast, fast, my poor moth!" Her pigeon voice
shrilled.

Aghast, the two dressed and ran out. There were no phagors
in the park but, as they crossed the square, they saw them.

The First Phagorian stood armed, staring at the blazing
palace, guarding it. They watched without movement as the
flames took ever firmer hold. Townspeople stood at a distance, gazing helplessly, kept at bay by the phagors.

JandolAnganol went to break through the phagorian ranks,
but a spear was thrust out and his way barred. Phagor-Major
Ghht Mlark Chzarn saluted her leader and spoke.

"You may not make a coming to more nearness, sir,
because danger. We have made a bringing of flames to all
Sons of Freyr in that church-place below the ground. Knowledge reaches our harneys that the evil king and the church-
king would bring killing to your all servants of this Guard."

"You had no orders." He could scarcely speak. "You've
slain Akhanaba—the god made in your image."

The creature before him with its deep scarlet eyes brought a
three-fingered hand to its skull. "Orders have formed in our
harneys. Make arrival from long time. Once, this place izz ancient Hrrm-Bhhrd Ydohk. . . . Further sayance . . ."

"You've slain the C'Sarr, Akhanaba . . . everything . . .
everything . . ." He could scarcely hear what the ancipital was
saying, for Milua Tal was holding his hand and screaming at
the top of her voice, "My moth, my moth, my poor mother!"

"Hrrm-Bhhrd Ydohk once ancient place of ancipital kind.
Not give to Sons of Freyr."

He failed to understand. He pushed against her spear, then
drew his own sword. "Let me through, Major Chzarn, or I
shall kill you."

He knew how useless threats were. Chzarn merely said, without emotion, "Not go through, sir."

"You're the fire god, Jan—command it die!" As she parrot-screamed, she raked his flesh, but he did not move. Chzarn was intent on explaining something and wrestled with words before managing to say, "Ancient Hrrm-Bhhrd Ydohk good place, sir. Air-octaves make a song. Before Sons of Freyr any on Hrl-Ichor Yhar. In ancient time of T'Sehn-Hrr."

"It's the present, the present! We live and die in present time, gillot!" He tried to wind himself up to strike but was unable to do so, despite the screaming girl at his side. His will failed. The flames burned in the pupils of his narrowed eyes.

The phagor obstinately continued her explanation, as if she were an automaton.

"Ancipitals here, sir, before Sons of Freyr. Before Freyr make bad light. Before T'Sehn-Hrr goance, sir. Old sins, sir."

Or perhaps she just said "old things." In the fury of the blaze, it was impossible to hear. With a roar, part of the palace roof collapsed and a column of fire rolled up into the night sky. Pillars crashed forward into the square.

The crowd cried in unison and stumbled back. Among the watchers was AbathVasidol; she clung to the arm of a gentleman from the Sibornalese embassy as everyone shrank from the heat.

"The Holy C'Sarr . . . all destroyed," cried JandolAnganol in pain. Milua Tal hid her face in JandolAnganol's side and wept. "All destroyed . . . all destroyed."

He made no attempt to comfort the girl or to push her away. She was nothing to him. The flames devoured his spirit. In that holocaust were consumed his ambitions—the very ambitions the fire would fulfil. He could be master of Oldorando as well as Borlien, but in that ceaseless changing of things into their opposites, that chastising enantiodromia which made a god into a phagor, he no longer wished for that mastery.

His phagors had brought him a triumph, in which he saw clearly his defeat. His thoughts flew to MyrdemInggala: but his and her summer was over, and this great bonfire of his enemies was his autumn beacon.

"All destroyed," he said aloud.

But a figure approached them, moving elegantly through

the ranks of the First Phagorian, arriving almost at a saunter in time to remark, "Not quite all, I'm glad to say."

Despite his attempt at customary nonchalance, Esomberr's face was pale and he trembled visibly.

"Since I've never worshipped the All-Powerful with any great degree of fervour, whether he's man or phagor, I thought I would excuse myself from the C'Sarr's lecture on the subject. Terribly fortunate as it proved. Let this be a lesson to you, Your Majesty, to go to church less frequently in future."

Milua Tal looked up angrily to say, "Why don't you run away? Both my parents are in there."

Esomberr wagged a finger at her. "You must learn to ride with circumstances as your new husband claims to do. If your parents are perished—and there I suspect you have hit upon a profound truth—then may I be the first to congratulate you on becoming Queen of both Borlien and Oldorando.

"I hope for some advancement from you, as the chief instrument in your clandestine marriage. I may never make C'Sarr, but you both know my council is good. I'm cheerful, even in times of adversity like the present."

JandolAnganol shook his head. He took Milua Tal by the shoulders and began to coax her away from the conflagration.

"We can do nothing. Slaying a phagor or two will solve nothing. We will wait for morning. In Esomberr's cynicism there is some truth."

"Cynicism?" asked Esomberr quietly. "Are not your brutes merely imitating what you did to the Myrdolators? Is there no cynicism in your taking advantage of that? Your brutes have crowned you King of Oldorando."

Written in the king's face was something Esomberr could not bear to see. "If the entire court is wiped out, then what is there for me but to stay, to do my duty, to see that the succession is legally continued in Milua Tal's name? Will I find joy in that task, Esomberr?"

"You will go with the circumstances, I expect. As I would. What's joy?"

They walked on, the princess shambling and needing support.

At length the king said, "Otherwise there will be anarchy —or Pannoval will step in. Whether it calls for rejoicing or

weeping, it seems that we do indeed have a chance to make our two kingdoms one, strong against enemies."

"Always enemies!" wailed Milua Tal to her failed god.

JandolAnganol turned to Esomberr, his expression one of blank disbelief. "The C'Sarr himself will have perished. The C'Sarr . . ."

"Failing divine intervention, yes. But one piece of better news for you. King Sayren Stund may not go down in history as its wisest monarch, but he experienced a generous impulse before he perished. He was probably prompted by your new queen's mother. His majesty could not quite stomach hanging his new son-in-law's son, and had him released an hour or so ago. Perhaps as a sort of wedding gift . . ."

"He released Robayday?" His frown left him momentarily.

Another section of the palace collapsed. The tall wooden columns burned like candles. More and more of the inhabitants of Oldorando crept forth silently to stare at the blaze, knowing they would never look on such a night again. Many, in their superstitious hearts, saw this as the long-prophesied end of the world.

"I saw the lad go free. Wild as ever. Wilder. An arrow from a bow would be a fair comparison."

A groan escaped JandolAnganol's lips. "Poor boy, why did he not come to me? I hoped that at last he had lost his hatred of me . . ."

"By now he's probably in the queue to kiss the wounds of the dead SartoriIrvrash—an unhygienic form of amusement if ever I saw one."

"Why did Rob not come to me . . . ?"

There was no answer, but JandolAnganol could guess it: he had been hidden in the pavilion with Milua Tal. It would take many a tenner before the consequences of this day's work were fully borne out, and he would have to live them through.

As if echoing his thoughts, Alam Esomberr said, "And may I enquire what you intend to do with your famous Phagorian Guard, who have committed this atrocity?"

The king threw him a hard glance and continued to walk away from the blaze.

"Perhaps you will tell me how mankind is ever to solve its phagor problem," he said.

ENVOI

The soldiery from the *Good Hope* and the *Union* landed on the Borlienese coast and marched westwards on Gravabaga-linien under the leadership of Io Pasharatid.

As the force progressed, Pasharatid gleaned news of the tur-moil about to overwhelm Matrassyl. The conscience of the people had been slowly roused as they digested the news of the massacre of the Myrdolators; the king would be unwelcome when he returned.

In Pasharatid's harneys a scheme burned with such convic-tion that it already seemed actual. He would take the queen of queens; Gravabagalinien would fall to him, and she also. Matrassyl would willingly accept her as queen. He would rule as consort; politically he was not ambitious, not greatly. His past, its evasions, disappointments, disgraces, would be over. One minor military engagement, and all he desired would be his.

His advance scouts reported breastworks about the wooden palace. He attacked at Batalix-dawn, when haze stretched

across the land. His gunners advanced two-by-two, wheel
locks at the ready, protected by pikemen.

A white flag waved from behind the defences. A stocky
figure cautiously emerged into the open. Pasharatid signalled
to his soldiery to halt, and walked forward alone. He was conscious of how brave he was, how upright. He felt every inch
the conqueror.

The stocky man approached. They halted when no more
than a pike's length apart.

Bardol CaraBansity spoke. He asked why soldiers were advancing on an almost undefended palace.

To which Io Pasharatid responded haughtily that he was an
honourable man. He required only the surrender of Queen
MyrdemInggala, after which he would leave the palace in
peace.

CaraBansity made the sacred circle on his forehead and
sniffed a resounding sniff. Alas, he said, the queen of queens
was dead, slain by an arrow fired by an agent of her ex-husband, King JandolAnganol.

Pasharatid responded with angry disbelief.

"Look for yourself," said CaraBansity.

He gestured towards the sea, lacklustre in the dawn light.
Men were launching a funeral barque upon the waters.

In truth, Pasharatid could see it for himself. He left his
force and ran to the beach. Four men with heads bowed were
carrying a bier on which a body lay beneath layers of white
muslin. The hem of the muslin fluttered in a growing breeze.
A wreath of flowers lay on top of the body. An old woman
with hair growing from a mole in her cheek stood weeping at
the water's edge.

The four men carried the bier reverently aboard the white
caravel, the *Vajabhar Prayer;* the ship's battered sides had
been repaired well enough for a voyage which did not involve
the living. They laid the bier under the mast and retired.

ScufBar, the queen's old majordomo dressed in black,
stepped aboard the ship carrying a lighted torch. He bowed
deeply to the shrouded body. Then he set light to the
brushwood piled high on the deck.

As fire took the ship, it began with the favouring wind to
sail slowly out from the bay. The smoke billowed out across
the water like lank hair.

Pasharatid cast down his helmet into the sand, crying wildly to his men.

"On your knees, you hrattocks! Down and pray to the Azoiaxic for this beautiful lady's soul. The queen is dead, oh, the queen of queens is dead!"

CaraBansity smiled occasionally as he rode a brown hoxney back to his wife in Ottassol. He was a clever fellow and his ruse had succeeded; Pasharatid's pursuit had been deflected. On the little finger of his right hand, he wore the queen's gift to him, a ring with a sea-blue stone.

The queen had left Gravabagalinien only a few hours before Pasharatid's arrival. With her went her general, his sister, the princess Tatro, and a handful of followers. They made their way northeastwards, across the fertile loess lands of Borlien, towards Matrassyl.

Wherever they went, peasants came from their huts, men, women, and children, and called blessing upon MyrdemIng-gala. The poorest of people ran to feed her party and help her in any way possible.

The queen's heart was full. But it was not the heart it had been; the heat had gone from her affections. Perhaps she would accept TolramKetinet in time. That remained to be seen. She needed to find her son first and solace him. Then the future could be determined.

Pasharatid remained on the shore for a long while. A herd of deer came down onto the beach and foraged at the high-tide line, ignoring his presence.

The funeral ship drifted out to sea, bearing the corpse of the servant who had died following injuries from a falling gunpowder keg. Flames rose straight up, smoke sank across the waves. A crackle of timber came to Pasharatid's ears.

He wept and tore his tunic and thought of all that would never happen. He fell to his knees on the sand, weeping for a death that had yet to occur.

The animals of the sea circled about the blazing hulk before leaving. They abandoned coastal waters and headed far out towards the deeps. Moving in well-organised legions, they swam where no man yet had sailed, to merge with the liquid wildernesses of Helliconia.

*   *   *

The years passed. That tumultuous generation faded one by one. . . . Long after the queen was lost to mortal sight, much that was immortal of her travelled across the immeasurable gulfs of space and was received on Earth. There, those lineaments and that face lived again. Her sufferings, joys, failings, virtues—all were called up once more for the peoples of Earth.

On Helliconia itself, all memories of the queen were soon lost, as waves are lost on the beach.

T'Sehn-Hrr shone overhead. The moonlight was blue. Even by day, when Batalix shone through the cool mists, the daylight was blue.

Everything perfectly suited the ancipital kind. Temperatures were low. They held horns high and saw no need to hurry. They lived among the tropical mountains and forests of the Pegovin Peninsula of Hespagorat. They were at peace with one another.

As the runts grew slowly to creighthood and then full adulthood, their coats became dense and black. Under that shapeless pelage, they were immensely strong. They threw roughly shaped spears which could kill at a hundred yards. With those weapons they slayed members of other components who infringed their territory.

They had other arts. Fire was their chained and domesticated pet. They travelled with their hearths on their shoulders, and groups of them were to be seen, climbing down to the coast on occasions, where they would trap fish, with flames borne on stone slabs upon their broad shoulders.

Bronze accoutrements were not beyond their understanding. With that metal they decorated themselves; the warm gleam of bronze might be caught about the smoking firesides of their mountain caves. They mastered pottery sufficiently to make coil pots, often of intricate design, shaped to resemble the pods of the fruits they ate. Coarse body coverings were woven from reeds and creepers. They had the gift of language. Stalluns and gillots went out to hunt together, or cultivated their scanty vegetables together in cleared patches. There was no quarrel between male and female.

The ancipital components kept animals as pets. Asokins lived commensally with them, and served as hunting dogs when they went out to hunt. Their Others were of less practical use; the naughty thieving tricks of Others were tolerated for the amusement their antics gave.

When Batalix set and light drained from the cool world, the ancipitals sank indifferently to sleep. They slept humbly as cattle, lying where they had stood. They switched off. No dreams haunted their long skulls during the silent hours of night.

Only when the moon T'Sehn-Hrr was full, they mated and hunted instead of sleeping. That was their great time. They killed any animal they came across, any bird, any other ancipital. There was no reason in the killing; they killed because it was their way.

By daylight, some of the components, those who lived to the south, hunted flambreg. That vast continent, the southern polar continent of Hespagorat, was populated by millions of head of flambreg. With the flambreg went clouds of flies. With the clouds of flies went the yellow fly. So the phagors killed the flambreg, massacred them separately or by the scores, killed the heads of herds, killed does, gravid or otherwise, killed the young, tried to fill the world with their carcasses.

The flambreg were never deterred from charging northwards across the lowlands of the Pegovin Peninsula. The ancipitals never wearied of killing them. The years came and went, and the centuries, and still the great herds plunged towards the untiring spears. There was no history among the components, except the history of this constant killing.

Mating took place at full moon: a year later, parturition occurred at full moon. The runts slowly became adult. Everything was slow, as if heartbeats themselves took their time, and the leisurely pace at which a tree grew was a standard for all things. When the great white disc of moon sank into the mists of the horizon, all was much as it had been when it rose from those same mists. Being one with this sluggish peace, the phagors were governed by its tempo; time did not enter into their pale harneys.

Their pets died. When an Other died, its body was casually cast aside, or thrown outside the area of the camp for vultures

to eat. The great black phagors did not know death: death was no more to them than time. As they grew older, their movements slowed. Though they remained within the shelter of their vaguely demarcated families, they became apart. Year by year, their abilities grew more circumscribed. Language was early lost. Eventually movement itself was lost.

Then the tribe showed a sense of caring. They cared not for individuals. They ministered to their infants, but otherwise only to those who succumbed to age. These superannuated phagors were stored safely away, revered, brought out on any ceremonial occasion, as for instance when an attack was intended on a nearby component.

Like embodiments of sluggish time, the elderly phagors passed without perceptible change beyond the shadowy division which distinguished life from other conditions. Time congealed in their eddre. They shrank to become over many years nothing more than small keratinous images of their former selves. Even then, the flickerings of existence were not entirely spent. They were consulted. They still played a part in the life of the component. Only when they disintegrated could it be said that they were visited with finality: and many were so gently handled that they survived for centuries.

This crepuscular life-style continued long. Summer and winter spelt little change in the club-shaped peninsula, extending almost to the equator. Elsewhere, in the winters, the seas might freeze; in the peninsula, up in the mountains, down in the afforested valleys, a lethargic paradise was maintained unaltered over many, many moons, many moons and many eons.

The ancipital kind was not readily responsive to change. The unknown star—the unheralded and unprecedented star— was a brilliant point long before it entered the calculations of the components.

The first white-coated phagors which appeared were treated with indifference. More of them grew to maturity. They produced white offspring. Only then were they driven out. The outcasts lived along the doleful shores of the Kowass Sea, feeding on iguana. Their tame Others rode on their backs, occasionally throwing twigs of dried seaweed into the portable hearths.

In the gloaming, phagors and Others could be seen, strung

out along the shore, flame and smoke at their shoulder, moving disconsolately towards the east. As year succeeded year, white phagors became more numerous, the exodus to the east more steady. They marked their way with stone pillars, perhaps in the hope that some day they could return home. That return was never to be.

Instead, the cancerous star in the skies grew brighter, eclipsing all other stars until, like T'Sehn-Hrr, it cast a shadow by night. Then the ancipital kind, after much consultation with the elders in tether, bestowed on the new star a name: *Frehyr,* meaning fear.

From one generation to another, there appeared no difference in the magnitude of the fear-star. But it grew. And from generation to generation the mutated white phagors spread along the coastlines of Hespagorat. To the west of the Pegovin Peninsula, they were halted by the dreary marshes of a land later to be known as Dimariam. To the east, they slowly covered the alpine lands of Throssa, to come, after two thousand miles, to the Cadmer land-bridge. All this was achieved with the spiritless determination characteristic of the ancipital kind.

Across the land-bridge, spreading over Radado, they entered lands where the climate more nearly resembled that of Pegovin. Some settled there; others, arriving later, foraged further. Always as they went they erected their stone pillars, to mark healthful air-octaves which led back to their ancestral home.

The time of catastrophe arrived. The ageing star, Batalix, with its freight of planets, was captured by the fear-star, young, furious, filling the space around it with radiation. The fear-star possessed a fainter companion. In the cosmic upheaval which followed, as new orbits were established, the fainter companion was lost. It sped away on a new course, taking with it one of Batalix's planets and the moon of Helliconia, T'Sehn-Hrr. Batalix itself moved into a captive position about the fear-star. This was the Catastrophe, never to be forgotten in the harneys of the ancipital kind.

In the subsequent upheavals which afflicted the planet, the ancient land-bridge across the Cadmer Straits was demolished by savage winds and tides. The link between Hespagorat and Campannlat was severed.

During this time of change, the Others changed. The Others were more puny than their mentors, but more nimble and more flexible of mind. Their exodus from Pegovin had transformed their role vis-à-vis the phagors: they were no longer regarded merely as pets of an idle day, but were required to forage for food in order to keep the component fed.

The revolution happened by accident.

A party of Others was foraging in a bay along the Radado coast when the incoming tide cut them off. They were marooned temporarily on an island where a lagoon provided a glut of oil fish. The oil fish were one of the manifestations of a changing ecology; they spawned in the seas in their millions. The Others stayed and feasted.

Later, having lost their mentors, they struck out on their own, moving northwestwards into an almost deserted land they called Ponpt. Here were founded the Ten Tribes, or Olle Onets. Eventually, their greatly modified version of Ancipital, which became known as Olonets, spread throughout Campannlat. But that was not until many a century has passed its hand over the developing wildernesses.

The Others themselves developed. The Ten Tribes broke up and became many. They were quick to adapt to the new circumstances in which they found themselves. Some tribes never settled, and took to wandering the face of the new continent. Their great enemies were the phagors, whom they nevertheless regarded as godlike. Such delusions—such aspirations—were part and parcel of their lively response to the world in which they discovered themselves. They rejoiced, hunted, multiplied, and the new sun shone on them.

When the first Great Winter set in, when that first turbulent summer faded into cold, and the snows fell for months at a time, it must have seemed to the eotemporal minds of the phagors that normality was returning. This was the period during which the Ten Tribes were put to the test: genetically malleable, they were to have their future existences shaped by the degree of success with which they weathered the centuries of apastron, when Batalix crawled through the slowest sectors of its new orbit. Those tribes who adapted best emerged the next spring with new confidence. They had become humanity.

Male and female, they rejoiced in their new skills. They felt the world and the future to be theirs. Yet there were times—

sitting about campfires at night with the star-shingle blazing overhead—when mysterious gaps opened in their lives and they seemed to look into a gulf there was no bridging. Back came folk memories of a period when larger creatures had looked after them and had administered a rough justice. They crept to sleep in silence, and words without sound formed on their lips.

The need to worship and be ruled—and to rebel against rule—never left them, even when Freyr again proclaimed its strength.

The new climate, with its higher energy levels, did not suit the white-coated phagors. Freyr, above them, was the symbol of all ills which befell. They took to carving an apotropaic symbol on their air-octave stones: one circle inside another, with rays like spokes connecting the inner with the outer. To the phagorian eye, this was first of all a picture of T'Sehn-Hrr moving away from Hrl-Ichor Yhar. It later came to be regarded as something different, as a picture of Freyr with its rays flattening Hrl-Ichor Yhar beneath it as it drew nearer.

While some of the Olonets-speakers were transformed, generation by generation, into the hated Sons of Freyr, the phagors slowly lost their culture. They remained stalwart and held horns high. For the new climate was not entirely on the side of the Sons.

Though Freyr never departed, there were long periods when it moved to such a distance that it hid its spiderous shape among the star-shingle. Then once again the ancipital kind were able to master the Sons of Freyr. At the next Time of Cold they would obliterate their ancient enemy entirely.

That time was not yet. But it would come.

END OF VOLUME TWO

In a career spanning a quarter of a century, Brian W. Aldiss has written more than two dozen books, many of which have come to be recognized as classics of science fiction. His novel *The Long Afternoon of Earth* won a Hugo Award in 1962, *The Saliva Tree* a Nebula Award in 1965, *Starship* the Prix Jules Verne in 1977. In 1969 he was voted Britain's most popular science fiction writer and the following year he received the Ditmar Award as the World's Best Contemporary SF Author. One of his most influential books is *The Billion-Year Spree,* a history of science fiction. *Helliconia Spring* and *Helliconia Summer* are the first two volumes of a prize-winning trilogy, his most ambitious undertaking. Mr. Aldiss lives in Oxford, England.